KASTURBA GANDHI

A bio-fiction

Giriraj Kishore

Translated from Hindi by

Manisha Chaudhry

THORNBIRD
NIYOGI BOOKS

Kasturba Gandhi: A bio-fiction: English translation of Giriraj Kishore's Hindi bio-fiction *Ba*, originally published by Rajkamal Prakashan in 2016.

Published by
NIYOGI BOOKS
Block D, Building No. 77,
Okhla Industrial Area, Phase-I,
New Delhi-110 020, INDIA
Tel: 91-11-26816301, 26818960
Email: niyogibooks@gmail.com
Website: www.niyogibooksindia.com

Editor: Gita Rajan
Design: Shraboni Roy

ISBN: 978-93-86906-48-9
Publication: 2018

Printed at: Niyogi Offset Pvt. Ltd., New Delhi, India

To
Women
who are committed to empowerment and who
preserve empathy in society and the family

&

To
Sarvshree Narayan Bhai and
Chandrashekhar Dharmadhikari who were
fortunate to experience Ba's guardianship

Writing Ba and the Writer

Why am I writing this novel was a question that raised its head repeatedly. Even more so, when it was hard to gather material for it. I had faced this problem when I had written *Pehla Girmitiya*' also. But Gandhi had a wide canvas and his personality was well known. There was also a wealth of published material on his philosophy and his struggles. At the time, I had made a list of about two thousand books in Hindi and English written by Indian and foreign authors. Making a list is easy but getting the books is another matter.

But there is not so much material available on Kasturba and there are no surviving contemporaries or people who knew her. But her personality has a vastness all of its own, in spite of staying largely limited within the home and the various Ashrams where she lived. Mohandas Karamchand Gandhi forms his own axis. All of Kasturba's life after her marriage seems to be steeped in Gandhi's life, and barely finds its own trajectory. While her life ran parallel to his, it is also completely embedded in it. To pick out Kasturba's life, independent of Gandhi's, is akin to picking out the grains of rice in a mixture of rice and sugar. I sensed this from Gandhi's own revelations as well as from the available literature. The maximum material on Kasturba is contained in Gandhi's autobiography *My Experiments with Truth.* I admit, however, that this question I put to myself, is meaningless.

I realised this gradually. A writer should never ask: *why am I writing this;* what the writer ought to ask is: *how do I write this?*

When I mentioned my desire to write about Ba to my friends, they were dumbstruck. My dear friend and 'enemy', the late Rajendra Yadav said in his inimitable way, 'You claimed Gandhi, now lay claim over the whole family.' Unsolicited advice and abuse are available freely in our country. Many friends said, what is the use of writing on Kasturba, write on the Indian Gandhi, you will sell in millions. My brethren seemed intent upon putting me up for sale. I had attempted to write on the Indian Gandhi in *Pehla Girmitiya.* I had even written two hundred odd pages when God knows, he vanished somewhere ... Anyhow, in connection with writing on Ba, I first went to Mani Bhavan in Mumbai. I thought I might get some material there. In institutions connected to Gandhi, there is not much to be found in terms of old literature. There is more material in South Africa and there are museums too. I saw Hasim Seedat's private library; perhaps no private collection here would have as much material on Gandhi.

But there was one bright spot. I met Ramdas Gandhi's daughter, Usha Gokani ji. She is very personable and is very active even at her age. Her father was the third son of Gandhi ji. He was a great favourite of Ba's. Because he was economically not well off, after Harilal, Ba used to worry the most about him. In her last moments, when Devdas told Ba that Ramdas was about to come, her reaction was, what is the point of his coming? The trains are so crowded and travel is so expensive ... When I told Usha ji about my plans, she grew emotional. She said, nobody thought of writing about Ba. She just remained a part of Bapu's life and no more. In a sense, Ba was independent of Bapu and she could be found in him. When the need arose, she became his follower, but she also took independent decisions. She shared an incident about her mother, Nirmala Ramdas. Cots were not used in the Ashram at the time. Ba arranged for a cot when she fell ill and looked after her like a close relative would, most unlike a mother-in-law!

Her brother, Kanu Ramdas, was staying at the Gandhi Peace Foundation in Delhi. The Foundation had given him a room. He looked unwell. I wanted to know his experiences related to Ba. He got upset. 'Why should I tell you? It is between Ba and me.' I tried explaining why I was asking him. He pushed that famous picture towards me where a child is holding Bapu's lathi and walking ahead on the seashore. 'This is me,' he said and no more. I felt that people tried to stay out of his way. It pained me that one of Bapu's grandsons seemed to be going through some kind of mental struggle.

I had gone to Porbandar, Bapu's birthplace, before writing *Pehla Girmitiya*. Govind Mishr was Chief Commissioner (IT) of Ahmedabad. I took help from him. Salaries were very low then. Now, even pensions are many times as much. He had a reputation of being a very honest officer. He arranged for my stay in a Bank's guest house. You could stay there but you had to make arrangements for food. He also arranged for a car to go to Porbandar. The journey from Ahmedabad to Porbandar was very interesting. When I got back, I asked the driver of the car, 'How much?' He called up somebody.

Perhaps they told him to take nothing and he left, although I had arranged for his food and stay, like I should have.

As I looked at Gandhi ji's three-four storied traditional house in Porbandar, a tourist asked me, 'Have you seen Kasturba's house?' I said, 'No, where is it?' He said it was right behind and gave me directions. I had two friends who had accompanied me, Suraj Prakash the writer and Additional Director of All India Radio also a writer. They had gone off somewhere close by. I set out alone. I kept stopping to ask people for directions and finally reached Ba's birthplace. There was no thought in my head at that time that I had to write about Ba. I met an old gentleman outside her house. I asked him, 'Is this Kasturba's house?'

He looked at me strangely. 'Do you know Kasturba?' he asked.

'No, I have read about her.'

'Nobody knows Kasturba anymore. Everybody knows M. K. Gandhi. Only some stray person lands up here.' His eyes held a hint of complaint. I could see a touch of irony and sadness too. I had no reply to his question and did not have the courage to ask him anything else. Not even who he was.

His query settled somewhere deep in my subconscious. Perhaps that was why, after a long gap, I thought that I should learn more about Kasturba. I began looking around for information. She was Gandhi's strength in many ways and an indispensable part of his life. I first looked for her in Gandhi's autobiography. I looked for references in books on Gandhi ji, written by Indian and foreign authors. Most of them dealt with their own content and point of view. The references were not too helpful in finding out more about Ba's personality. It was not possible to establish Ba's official role in Gandhi's epic scale of work and the struggle for independence, through these books. This situation would take me right back to the old gentleman whom I had met at her doorstep and his sadness. This was neither Gandhi's fault nor anyone else's. Everybody's eyes seek out the source of light. Because Kasturba was in penumbra, she was not visible, even if she had contributed to the source of light. My curiosity grew stronger. I first met Justice Chandrashekhar Dharmaḍhikari, in this connection. His father Dada Dharmadhikari, was an Acharya who was devoted to the service of the nation, the same as Bapu. In his later days, his wife had become psychologically disturbed. Judge Sahib had lived under Ba's guardianship for some time. He sent me the Hindi translation of Sushila Nayyar and Vanmala Parikh's Gujarati book, *Hamari Ba.* This book afforded the first glimpse of Ba's later life. I was astonished that Ba was such a fighter, both in life and in politics.

Vanmala Parikh wrote, 'Even though Bapu was a haughty husband, whenever she felt the need, Ba did not hesitate to warn or caution him.' (Pp 6, *Hamari Ba*) This apparently ordinary statement gave an initial introduction to her inner resources and her strength. If a simple wife such as Ba, could warn her arrogant husband about his responsibilities and rights, she certainly understood her own. This is what removes the veil of confusion from the mind and also establishes individual rights. There are many instances in Ba's life where she made use of her rights forthrightly. She also observed her wifely duties with complete dedication and composure. In Ba's heart, there was no conflict between her own freedom and family responsibilities and neither were they all mixed up as is often the case among women today.

The second book, *The Forgotten Woman*, was written by Manilal Gandhi's son, Arun Gandhi and his wife Sunanda Gandhi. The title of the book further opens up the pain that was evident on the face of the gentleman at Katsurba's doorstep in Porbandar. The book has been published by Ozark Mountain Publishing, Huntsville, Alabama, USA. The writer duo said that many times they heard people say that a book about their grandfather would be of greater interest. This also underlines the words of the old gentleman. I was told *The Forgotten Woman* would be available in Mumbai, but it turned out to be a false trail. I asked my son-in-law, Captain Salil Gupta, whose close friend Stephen lived in America, for help. I am grateful that he made the book available to me. As I read it, I felt that Arun Bhai and Sunanda ji had immersed themselves in all aspects of their grandmother's life and written this book. They also felt perhaps, that their grandmother had been ignored. These two books gave me perspective and a chance to internalise Ba's life. The credit goes to the two books and their writers for my writing a novel on Ba.

The biggest challenge was to make the material in the books and sundry other material my own, and then connect it to my own voice. As mentioned already, Bapu was the source of light and he is visible first. Only after understanding the dynamics between Ba and Bapu, can

Ba be understood and expressed. In *Pehla Girmitiya* Bapu is complete in himself and everybody else is found, around him. There was also the facility of being able to see all those places in South Africa and London that were his arena for action. Those places were like silent characters that made their own creative contribution. All the other characters also found their place in connection with Bapu. The situation was a little different here. Ba's character develops in the shadow of Bapu's character. Second, when you put Ba in the shadow and bring in other characters and grant them independence, it presents a challenge that an ordinary talent like me found hard to carry. All the characters had to be allowed in or out, according to Ba's needs and suitability. Bapu was still the axis. The biggest problem was that, throughout, Ba and the children were displaced from one place to another, after short periods. Initially, within the country, then in a foreign land, in the jails there, and finally in jails in India. By then, the children had gradually moved away from her. A woman's identity was defined by her husband and children. Ba's responsibilities were divided. The Ashrams, children, the Ashram dwellers, a husband such as Bapu and his own decisions and finally, her husband's political legacy, divided and pulled Ba in different directions. The biggest canker was her son Harilal's volatile nature and the yawning and ever-widening distance from his illustrious parents. It was a thorn in her side that pricked her grievously, until the very last. All this broke Ba, but her fighting spirit never dimmed. She fought for the country as for the family and for her own identity. There were such occasions where, for the country, she put her husband's life second. This, even as she had to go against herself ...

Lately, I got a chance to listen to reminiscences about Ba from Narayan Bhai Desai over his two day stay at Gandhi Peace Foundation. I have used those in the novel. He was called Babla at home. Ba had learnt the Ramayan from Babla. Ba's simplicity and a great desire to learn were her biggest strengths. Ba's life had so many questions that it would be a rare ordinary, uneducated woman who would be able to deal with them all on her own. And that, in a time when a woman's lack of education and poor awareness were considered a boon.

As I wrote this novel, I was constantly surprised that a woman who had been brought up in such an atmosphere and whose limits were defined by the threshold of the house, how did she participate in the freedom struggle so actively and fearlessly? And with no sense of inferiority. Ba was the first woman who went to jail with her associates for the 'crime' of satyagraha, on foreign soil in South Africa. Upon her return to India, jail became her second home. She died in Agha Khan Palace serving out her sentence. A woman can face such huge challenges only if her faith and her concerns are bigger than personal and she is ready to come out of herself and be a part of larger society. She was like the skylark soaring freely in the sky but who stays connected to the earth. Ba's biggest achievement was maintaining balance between all aspects of her life.

I express heartfelt gratitude to her grandson Arun Bhai and his wife Sunanda for writing *The Forgotten Woman* and presenting Ba to the world as a source of inspiration and a pillar of indomitable strength. I express my appreciation towards Parikh ji and Sushila ji for their book *Hamari Ba* which gave me a glimpse of the most difficult moments of Ba's life. It is these two books that gave me heart and basis for writing this novel. Dr Alok Vajpayee also helped me by sending me some links of other books. My gratitude goes out to him also.

Dr Shivkumar Dikshit is not just a scholar of Hindi but is also deeply immersed in literature. He read the first draft, word by word. His suggestions, given with care and empathy, became the basis for the second draft. I also took my wife Mira ji's opinions on board, on the initial section, and wrote a second draft. She is my first reader. Although I could have incorporated the suggestions in the first draft itself … I had made three drafts for *Pehla Girmitiya* also. It was only then that I felt confident that the final draft would satisfy the discerning reader. Dikshit ji also paid special attention to spelling and the like and I am grateful for that. My grandson, Tanmay Singh, who is an engineering student, felt that the first draft was a complete novel. This response, from a young reader, encouraged me a great deal.

The Managing Director of Rajkamal, Ashok Maheshwari, had wanted to publish *Pehla Girmitiya.* He had come to me in Kanpur with a mutual friend. I wanted the price of that novel to be kept as low as possible and things did not work out. I spoke to Bhartiya Gyanpeeth's then Life Trustee and present Trustee, father of Akhilesh ji, the late Sahu Rameshchandra Jain, who asked me what I price

I had in mind. I said I wanted it to be Rs. 300 for an almost 900 page novel. He conferred with the Director of Gyanpeeth, Mishr ji and said it could be Rs 325. I wanted the price not to be a constraint for the reader. I have no hesitation in saying that it was the golden period for *Pehla Girmitiya* with Gyanpeeth. But later, some people made their way into Gyanpeeth who either did not know its rich tradition and philosophy or did not see it as important. Even one of their Trustees. A time came where, in an organisation founded by Ms Rama Jain, the Director/Editor along with a former I.G of Police and Vice Chancellor, grossly insulted women in the magazine *Naya Gyanodaya* that was published from that house. Standing in opposition to that, I was forced to withdraw all my books from an excellent organisation. The Director put all sorts of obstacles in my way. He stubbornly insisted that he would return the books only at 50 per cent price. A long correspondence ensued but he continued to create problems. Because of the intervention of Gyanpeeth's present chair, T. N. Chaturvedi and Trustee Sahu Akhilesh Jain, it was decided that the books would be returned at the original price. The Managing Director of Rajpal and Sons, Mira ji, paid Rs 40,000 and picked up the rest of the stock. At that time, many literary friends had announced that they would also withdraw their books, in support. I know there is no other institution such as Gyanpeeth. The organisation may be shaky but there is utmost honesty. I pray that, in view of its traditions and beliefs regarding Hindi literature and litterateurs, it re-establishes itself with due respect and cooperation towards them. So be it.

When Ashok ji had come for *Pehla Girmitiya*, I had promised that when I write the next novel connected to Gandhi, I will give it to him. When the first draft of *Ba* was nearing completion, I asked Ashok ji if Rajkamal would be interested in publishing Ba. He was most enthusiastic. On August 15, 2014, he came to Kanpur via Lucknow and met me. I said the same thing to him again to keep the price low. He was agreeable. I am pleased that Rajkamal is publishing this novel. I thank Ashok ji for his cooperation.

15 March, 2015 **Giriraj Kishore**

Agha Khan Palace

Before starting the novel I wish to mention Agha Khan Palace. It is the star-crossed but holy place, where Ba and Mahadev Bhai, who was like a son to her, both breathed their last. I call it star crossed because, in spite of being a palace, it lay deserted. Its owners hardly ever visited. It lived with the pride of being a palace and waited for its Gods to come. Its grandeur must have been unparalleled. Whether beauty or grandeur, if there is nobody to appreciate it, it erodes into ugliness.

It is possible that in this palace of brick and mortar, some feelings or voices lingered. When people ask, who is this Agha Khan who built such a big palace, only to leave it to crumble, it must feel angry. It cannot speak and these words must hover, like a murmur … it is a crime to even speak like this about my lord and master. Why don't people understand that somebody who owns such a big palace, is no ordinary man. Take note of the generosity of his heart, he left me, but as a palace, an unfortunate ignoramus like me …

***

Agha Khan is not the name of a person. Agha Khan is the seat of the Supreme teacher of the Bohra Muslim sect. Whoever sits on that seat is called the Agha Khan- His Holiness Agha Khan. All his followers revere him next only to God. There is no king or Nawab in the world whose followers consider him next to God and kiss his feet. Even the Queen or King of the Empire where the sun never set, does not enjoy this status. His followers are spread across the world and are not confined to the boundaries of any kingdom.

Agha Khan lives in Switzerland. The country is famed for its neutrality. The whole of Europe was entangled in war but this nation stayed aloof. He is peace loving, therefore he decided to stay there. When there was unrest and resistance to the British government in India, Agha Khan gave his property to the Britannia government to keep some special prisoners as captives. This building, called a palace, must have rued this decision. One could call this the cruel blow of fate. The palace, of a religious leader, turned into a jail. The expensive flooring soon looked worse than the floors of a barrack. What could the palace say, but whenever anybody referred to it as a palace, it would shrink in embarrassment, as a wasteland would, if it was called the land of the evergreens. Forget the past, look to the future.

One day, the loneliness broke. There was a flurry of activity and the English Guard began stomping all over its grounds. British officials, jailers, superintendent and doctors, they all came. In the end came the jail warders. The palace must surely have felt that this was neither the arrival of the Agha Khan nor a high government official ... Is the government offended with the Agha Khan that the palace is being treated like an outlaw? It was bound to feel disappointed. It was a palace; once the government got ownership, it should at least have been granted the prestige of remaining a palace. Why did they turn it into a jail? It could not speak out nor could it file a complaint about its disaffection. All that remained was to lie quietly in the grave, awaiting the Day of Judgment.

***

Time passed and the situation became worse. Where there used to be peace and quiet, today it resounded with the clicking of heels. The incessant, incomprehensible chatter of the white-skinned British could be heard. One day, it was said, a man called a Mahatma was about to come. Was Mahatma the name of the prisoner or was it his title? I found out later that he was a dervish fighting for the independence of the nation. I had neither seen a mahatma nor a dervish, but it was said that he had shaken up the British Empire. Such a man should have a jail befitting his status. It should be secure too. It should not feel like jail and yet be one. The palace must have said to itself that at least it was not some hooligan who had come to stay. If the name of the Mahatma goes into the annals of history, the palace too would find a place. But the relationship with the Agha Khan would be broken forever. Even if he never comes, it is not good to lose hope. The death of hope is like foeticide.

That day dawned when the royal palace became a full-fledged jail. A half naked faqir, a middle aged man and a white woman entered the palace. He was walking slowly, holding on to her shoulder for support. There were no chains or handcuffs, just two official looking men with them. Later it was reported that he had gone to meet the King of England also, in his half naked state. The King broke protocol regarding dress for him. It is said that when asked, 'Why did you go half naked to meet His Majesty?' he remarked, 'He was wearing enough for the two of us.'

***

The heat had lessened but it was muggy. There was some relief only when there was a breeze. The Mahatma had come as a prisoner into the palace in May. Everybody called him Bapu. The big gates of the palace were opened for him. The big gates were thrown open only if some very special person was coming. Otherwise everybody used the small door.

It was August 1942 when the gates opened suddenly. Everybody was startled. They all knew the big gates were opened only for someone very special. A car came and stopped in the porch. An old and ailing woman got off with the support of a girl. A prisoner was sweeping the grounds. The girl asked, 'Where is Bapu's room?'

'The last one.'

Both of them reached the last room. The Mahatma's first question was, 'Did you file an application to come here, or did you get arrested?'

'Is it enough to file an application to get arrested?'

The girl said, 'No Bapu ji, we have been arrested and sent here.'

***

When the girl said that Ba was ill, Bapu's face showed signs of worry. Mahadev Bhai, the man who had come with Bapu, ran around and arranged for a cot. It may have been a palace but there was not even a bed available for a patient. The palace must have hung its head in shame upon hearing this. Ba's room or barrack was separate. She went to her room and lay down.

The girl who had accompanied Ba was called Sushila Nayyar. She had a small green potted plant in her hand. A tulsi plant …

——***——

THE EARLY YEARS

Children at play

There was a small courtyard outside Diwan Sahib Karamchand's house. All the children of the neighbourhood would gather there to play. Boys and girls. The game of 'I SPY' was their favourite. The 'den' would be a boy named Moniya. He was the youngest son of Diwan Sahib. He was always angling to make Kastur the 'den.' Kastur was the daughter of the Makan family. She lived right behind the house and the two families were close.

Kastur was clever and always managed to evade Moniya. He felt she was making him look small and grudged her these little victories. He grumbled, 'Who do you think you are! You cannot defeat me by making me run ...'

'It is you who is making me run. I will keep running. Go chase the others ...' Kastur would say, unyielding, not breaking her run.

'It is my choice. I can chase whoever I want.'

'I will not give up.'

'I am older than you.'

'No, I am older.'

'I have a *janm patri*.'

'You are always showing off about your *janm patri.*'

'I *am* older.'

'My ba told me that you came into this world six months after me.'

'You are a liar.'

Kastur would burst into tears. Hearing the commotion, Moniya's mother would come out of the house. 'You are troubling Kastur again,' she would scold Moniya.

'He called me a liar, Moti Ba! Ask the others. I am not a liar!'

'She says I am six months younger than her.'

'So, why should that upset you? If she says that you are six months older, would you become six months older?'

'Ba, you are taking her side!' Moniya was tearful now.

'Oh! You silly boy! As if six months this way or that makes one bigger or smaller...'

'Then why doesn't she believe that I am older and she is younger?'

'Just look at him Ba!... I will not believe it. Will not ...'

'Keep fighting, both of you. Nobody becomes smaller or bigger by fighting,' said Ba and went back into the house. She had to finish the cooking. Moniya's eyes flashed and he leapt across and touched her. Now the fight was about Moniya's cheating.

The children sided with Moniya. There were more boys than girls. The girls were with Kastur. Kastur said, 'We will go to Diwan Sahib's court.' That made Moniya nervous. 'If you go there, I will go to Chhote Kaka!' Chhote Kaka was Kastur's father.

'Bapu will agree with whatever Mota Bapu says.'

'Alright, I will be the "den" again. After this, you will be the "den,"' said Moniya.

'I will not! Why should I .... play the game like it is meant to be played.'

After many heated exchanges, it was decided that if Kastur went to Diwan Sahib's court, since nobody could lie in front of him, Kastur would win and Moniya would lose. That would not be a good thing, so the game was called off.

'We won't let the girls play from tomorrow,' said Moniya huffily.

'We will call Moti Ba,' retorted Kastur.

It was dusk. Even the birds and their mates were making a huge ruckus as they returned to their nests. The children made their way back home, making faces at each other.

——***——

Kastur

Kastur's mother was Brajkunwari. Her father was Gokuldas Makanji. Born in Porbandar, Kathiawad. Year 1868, date unknown. She was an only and much loved daughter. There were three brothers and two sisters. One brother and sister died early. Her elder brother Khushaldas left them in the prime of his youth. Only Kastur and her brother Madhavdas remained.

Gokuldas exported cotton and grain to Africa. Her grandfather Makanji Kapadia had done the same. He must have also have been in the textile business hence the name Kapadia. Gokuldasji had started using Makanji instead of Kapadia. May be he did not like writing Kapadia. The word Makanji had softer connotations. It is believed that Makanji had branches in Bombay and Calcutta.

The house where Kastur was born was an old building, bungalow style. They did not have a showy lifestyle but the house was well appointed. Kastur was born in one small room and since there was a very close relationship with the Diwan Karamchand family, her birth was celebrated in both houses. Diwan Sahib had three sons and one daughter. The *Diwanni*, the Diwan Sahib's wife, loved girls. When Kastur grew a little older, she would often go to their house. Diwan Sahib was also known by the name of Kaba Gandhi. Kastur used to call him Mota Bapu and the *Diwanni* Moti Ba. When she would play among the gaggle of children, Moti Ba would always look out for her. Two or three other girls from the neighbourhood would also turn up to play with Kastur.

The boys would run around the whole neighbourhood, but the girls would be mostly at home. As Kastur grew a little older, her house was her informal school. No books or slate in this school. She was taught things in a myriad different ways. The first lesson was through stories. The story of Sati Anusuya whose purity was tested by the Gods themselves but who succeeded by using her intelligence was recounted. The legend of Savitri-Satyavan. How Savitri defeated Lord Yama through logic and saved Satyavan from death. Taramati stood by her husband Raja Harishchandra and went against the devatas and sage Vishwamitra. Her only son Rohitashv was bitten by a serpent, but she did not budge. In the end, defeated by the staunch husband and wife, the devatas had to give him the gift of life, and return their kingdom. When she grew a little older, Kastur was amazed to hear the tales of sacrifice and forbearance of other brave women. She would wish that her mother and sisters would also be equally brave.

The other lessons were to do with housework and serving others in the household. Being the youngest daughter, she was expected to serve everybody. Her mother would teach her to cook a variety of things. She would explain to Kastur the close relationship between the heart and the stomach and would teach how good food kept everybody healthy. There was a tradition of singing bhajans in the mornings and evenings and she really liked to sing.

***

She liked Moniya but abhorred his propensity to quarrel and show his superiority by claiming to be older. If somebody called her a liar, Kastur would be incensed. She knew that Moniya was also not a liar. He would be scolded by Moti Ba. He was Moti Ba's favourite child and he returned the favour. He was deeply devoted to her. On a day of fasting, (during the monsoons), Moti Ba would not eat until she had seen the sun. If the sun did not show up, Ba would say she would eat the next day. He would run up to the terrace repeatedly and pray with folded hands beseeching the sun to come up because his ba was hungry.

Moti Ba was loved by all her children. Moniya did not like it when Ba would tell him not to play with the sweeper boy. Moniya would invariably end up playing with him. When he would get back, summer or winter, Ba would empty a bucket of cold water over him at the doorstep, and only then allow him to enter. It had become a part of his routine to play with that boy and then suffer a cold water dunk by Ba. Moti Ba maintained that it was not that child's fault – he was a good child. But it was to do with dharma. Moniya would keep quiet most of the times but would occasionally argue that nobody had any control on where they were born. What was Kastur's view is not known but she felt that Ba was right. Why would Moti Ba say something that was not right? Moniya was scared of Diwan Sahib, though he was his favourite child too. Kastur would sometimes compare her own family with that of Diwan Sahib but could not decide which was better. All the children were scared of Diwan Sahib but Moti Ba was universally liked. Makanji loved Kastur dearly and she was not at all scared of him. If Kastur's mother scolded her, her father would take her side. So she decided that her father was nice but on the other side, Moti Ba was very nice. She even scolded Moniya if he troubled Kastur. The two sides of the balance were evenly poised. She would feel quite pleased when she reached that conclusion.

***

As Kastur entered the third stage of instruction in the home school, Moniya and she had long stopped playing together. As the cooking classes picked up, it was time for the girls to tuck their wings in. Eyes were to be kept lowered. Moniya was busy with his studies now. Bapu would ask him what he studied in school each day and he would rattle off a series of things. Bapu had been tutoring him until classes four and five. A Diwan was not expected to be very polished. It was enough if he understood the politics of the kingdom and was trustworthy. Kaba Gandhi's father, Ota Gandhi, had not been very educated, but was a master of statecraft. It was said that he was so courageous that even after the Queen of Porbandar, Roopaliba, had cannons installed around his house, he left Porbandar only after he had buried his Muslim bodyguard, killed in the exchange of fire. Kaba Gandhi knew his scriptures and he was considered quite knowledgeable.

Maulvis, pandits, Parsi high priests and padres would gather at his house. Jain sadhus would pay regular visits. If there was a disagreement, it was usually resolved with Kaba Gandhi's intervention. Preparing his medicine or giving him an oil massage, young Moniya would listen intently and try and make sense of what he heard. He would not speak because he was painfully shy.

He was so shy that he would hesitate to step out before Kastur. There was no question of going to her house. Sometimes Kastur would visit with her mother, but there was practically no conversation between Moniya and her. The women would step out in the afternoons after finishing their kitchen chores. Moniya would be in school at the time. Even if he was at home, he would sit outside and read. Kastur would remember how he would fight with her for no reason and get scolded by Moti Ba. She would smile at the memory.

***

For quite some time, there were whispered conversations in Kastur's house. Kastur was perplexed because usually all matters were discussed quite openly. Nothing was kept hidden, whether it was about business or borrowing and lending. For the first time, Ba and Bapu were talking only to each other. She was very curious. Even so, she tried to divert her attention. Maybe it was about something that they did not want to tell the children. But it had never been like this. Should she be worried? Had Bapu suffered a loss? But he was not one to be affected by such things. One day it became clear that it was about somebody's marriage. Whose marriage?

She didn't know. All that Kastur understood about marriage was that it was a community celebration where a boy and a girl wore new clothes. There was much song and dance as if in a *swaang*. The girl usually was gifted new ornaments. The *halwai* made all kinds of sweet dishes and savouries and instruments were played. The boy was dressed up and put on a horse. The most fun part was the dancing by the women. Family and friends got together. Thinking about all this was exciting and she was eager to take part in the celebrations. She had seen the wedding of a tulsi plant. All the ceremonies had been observed. Lord Vishnu from a temple had come to wed Tulsi Mata. He had not come on a horse but as an idol in a palanquin. Kastur had thought of it as a game. When she mentioned this to Ba, she had rebuked her saying that she was not to speak so irreverently. Mother Tulsi and Bhagwan would take offence. She remembered a line from the aarti, *Tulsi Rani Namo namah, Hari ki patrani namo namah, …* Queen Tulsi, I bow to you, Bride of Hari, I bow to you.

Kastur was seven years old. She was told that she was engaged to Diwan Karamchand's youngest son. She did not understand what it meant to be engaged. But she knew that this was Moniya, in whose courtyard they played *chor-sipahi*. She remembered that he was very proud of being older than Kastur. Kastur's mother maintained that he was born six months later. Kastur felt a lick of irritation, but then she thought it did not matter because she was hardly going to play with him again. She was fine in her house and surely so was the case with him. If she had said this out loud, somebody would surely have laughed and told her that even if she were older, now she would have to play the game according to his rules. She also noticed that everybody in the house looked elated as if they had landed a rare treasure. Kastur found out later that Ba and Bapu had really wished for Kastur to be married into Diwan Sahib's house. She would still be around for them.

***

The propitious day of the engagement dawned. The Pandits had chosen this date after much deliberation. There were elaborate preparations. After all, it was an alliance with Diwanji's family. The adornments and festivity all around matched the joy and enthusiasm of the people gathered. The men were congratulating Gokuldas Makanji on his good fortune that his daughter was marrying Diwanji's youngest son. Ba Brajkunwari was receiving similar felicitations. The families were well matched but Diwanji had an edge. He was the Diwan of Porbandar and enjoyed the trust of the king. He was highly respected in the durbar. His wife, the *Diwanni,* was close to the *Rajmata.* Porbandar was home to much affluence and everybody praised Makanji's daughter's good fortune.

Kastur sat all folded up, like a little doll, in the midst of all the women. She was only a little girl so she would doze off and then right her neck with a start. She would look around to see if anybody had noticed. The sounds of the *dholak* were heard. Auspicious songs were sung. Kastur craned her neck to see Diwan Karamchand Gandhi and her bapu Makanji embrace each other ceremonially. The purohit brought a big *thal* with fruits and gold ornaments. The members of the Gandhi family touched the *thal.* Then

Kastur was taken inside. The purohit put the *thal* on her head and blessed her. The auspicious songs continued. The women embraced and congratulated each other. Kastur was somewhat overwhelmed. She did not understand what was going on. Why was such a big *thal* put on her head? Ba picked up a heavy necklace from the *thal* and put it around Kastur's neck. She immediately began to finger it and all the women laughed. Kastur's face grew red.

——***——

Diwanji's Arrival

Soon after the engagement, preparations for the wedding began in earnest in both the families. There was an atmosphere of celebration, eager anticipation and joy. Kastur was restless as she tried to understand what was going on. Everybody would only laugh and say it is for your marriage. You have to go to your *sasural*. Her face would fall. She wanted to say that she was not going anywhere leaving her ba, bapu and bhai behind but knew better than to say this. Everybody had laughed when she had actually blurted it out once.

Moniya's state was not very different from Kastur's. Since he was not present at the engagement, he found out about it only much later. He reacted the same way as Kastur had done. He thought of it as a game. He could not understand why Bapu did not take him along. He found out that the groom does not go to the girl's house before the marriage. He couldn't ask what was the difference between an engagement and a wedding. Who could he ask? If he asked Bhabhi, she would make fun of him. What is the big hurry, Dewar ji? When he came to know that he was to be married to Makanji's younger daughter, he was worried.

He knew he prided himself on being older than her but also knew it was not true. If he said this, Ba took her side. It was a worry but like children's worries, it did not linger. She ran really fast and she was not afraid of anything. Now that was something that bothered him.

***

In the house, everybody was worried about something else. A short while ago, Diwanji had been appointed Diwan of Rajkot and had left to go there. He was getting on in years. Rajkot was the headquarters of the regional offices of the British empire. The ruler of Rajkot had summoned him so that he could manage the kingdom properly. Diwanji wanted to arrange Moniya and his middle son Karsan's marriage from Porbandar, at the same time. Karsan was Moniya's senior by three years. Diwanji had lived all his life in Porbandar. He knew that Rajkot was a big kingdom and he would have more work. He would have to work hard and at a whole new level. This was also Moniya's third chance at an alliance. The first two did not work out because the girls did not survive. Child mortality was very common. Everybody was alert and concerned that this time things should work out. There was a huge age difference between Putlibai and Karamchand. Putlibai was his fourth wife. His third wife had insisted that he take a fourth, so that there would be children. Putlibai kept her own counsel and so did Karamchand.

Being the head of the family, Karamchand wrote to his brother Tulsidas, saying that his son Motilal's wedding could also take place in the same mandap, along with the two boys. Tulsidas was very happy to comply as Karamchand was his respected elder brother. Karamchand felt that if three brothers could be married off together, it would put less financial pressure on the girls' families and the guests would not have to travel repeatedly.

Traditionally, the wedding expenses have to be borne by the girl's family. The Modh Banias observed another tradition. The Vaish Sabha of Porbandar was the one to decide the standard of the weddings. Dowry, the gifts, the hospitality was to be in keeping with the status of Diwan Sahib. This matter was debated at length. Karamchand wanted the expenses to be divided equally between the three. Nobody should feel that they are higher or lower than the others.

Moniya was to be married to Kastur, Karsan to Ganga and Motilal to Harkunwar. Karsan was the most excited about the marriage. In the company of his friend Sheikh Mahtab, he knew what it meant to be married. Moniya was comparatively backward in such matters, so for him the wedding was just a celebration. Karamchand had arranged for leave from school and sent the boys to Porbandar, a month in advance. He knew he had been given a new responsibility so was not sure when he would get leave. At least the boys could go there and begin preparations. Thakur Sahib wanted Karamchand to complete all the important work before he went. He sent the people remaining in Rajkot, five days in advance, with a message that he would reach as soon as he could. He wanted all the members of the family to be present at the time of this grand joint wedding. There were some of Tulsidas's relatives, some of Kaba Gandhi's and many others from both the sides.

As he struggled to finish the tasks that were given to him, time was flying and he began to feel that he would be hard put to reach Porbandar in time for the wedding. His nerves were frayed as he tried his best to finish off all the work. When only three days remained, Thakur Sahib summoned him and said he should take the royal buggy. The horses were so swift that he would reach Porbandar in three days. Diwan Sahib was hesitant. Noticing his hesitation, Thakur Sahib reassured him saying that I kept you back because of the work, now it is my duty to see that you reach in time for your sons' wedding. Karamchand bowed his head in gratitude.

***

The day of the wedding was upon them but there was no sign of Karamchand. Or any news. All the family members had long faces. Was the wedding going to take place without the blessings of the head of the household? Tulsi Kaka was pacing up and down the outer courtyard grappling with the unwelcome idea that in the absence of his elder brother, he would have to shoulder the entire responsibility. Diwanji had called him to complete Moti's wedding and now he was saddled with Diwanji's two boys as well. Putlibai was worried sick about managing such a huge affair all by herself. The *nai* from the brides' side was coming again and again with anxious enquiry about Diwan Sahib's arrival. Three sets of people from the families of the brides were deeply uneasy. Everybody's eyes were riveted to the front door. The wedding celebrations could progress only if Diwan Sahib came.

When hopelessness descended and they were forced to contend with the idea that it was impossible for Diwan Sahib to reach, the coach of the Thakur of Rajkot was spotted in the distance, shimmering like a drop of hope. Everybody was shocked. Thakur Sahib's coach? There was no advance information about his coming nor were there any arrangements made to receive him. If Diwan Sahib had been there he would have managed. Thakur Sahib was coming but where was Diwan Sahib? Everybody's brains went into overdrive. If it were Thakur Sahib, his flag would precede him as would his horsemen and there would be a ceremonial band. Suddenly Diwan Sahib could be seen alighting from the buggy and everybody's faces looked like a dry field of paddy that had suddenly received rainfall. But why did he need assistance to get down? He had bandages all over his body. There was shocked silence.

***

All along the way, Diwan Sahib had asked the *syces*, 'Can't the horses go a little faster?'

'Huzoor, they are going full clip. They are dripping with sweat. If one of them missteps, we will not be able to control the buggy.'

No sooner was this said that the wheel hit a stone and the coach listed to the left and then overturned. Horses have the amazing capacity to halt even running at full speed. They take all the weight on their forelegs. The sun had not set fully. People gathered when they saw the royal buggy in this state. They hesitated to touch it but after getting a signal from the *syces*, they turned it right side up. Diwan Sahib was injured. The *syces* had scratches. The horses must have been hurt too but they immediately stood upright. Their ears indicated danger. A dhoti was extracted from Diwan Sahib's box and strips of bandage torn from it. A local healer applied medicine and bandages. The horses were released and watered. Then they were put in harness again. Porbandar was a few hours away. The horses began to gallop. Diwan Sahib was getting tossed around. He was forced to say that their pace should be a steady trot – they would make it to Porbandar by nightfall. This pace was fine and their hooves drummed a comforting rhythm ...

As he reached home, Diwan Sahib declared with his usual elan, 'Let the wedding ceremonies begin.' He did not show any signs of discomfort. He kept a tight hold over himself as he went in. He emerged shortly, spruced up and with all the paraphernalia of the *Diwani*. But his gait was slower and he leaned on a cane.

***

According to tradition, the *barat* has to reach the girl's doorstep. Since three boys from the same family were getting married at the same time, the three brides' families had rented one mandap. It was decorated beautifully. Lengths of flowers adorned every corner. There was no electricity but there were excellent arrangements for lighting. There were torches and petromax lights burning with their usual hissing sound. There were three small wedding mandaps. Each one had four flower bedecked poles. In front of them was a big ceremonial pot, on which were balanced five auspicious pots made of brass. Three duly decked up brides had been asked to sit in the mandaps by the pandits. They kept up chants for some time but then they fell silent. The brides were mere girls. The barat had started late because of the delay in Diwan Sahib's arrival. The brides could not be taken back into the house from the mandap. The girls grew drowsy and began drooping, this way and that. It was a very odd scene. The women of the house had to look after the brides until the barat came. Others were singing *mangal geet.* The songs had messages for the *baratis* and the prospective in-laws. The *baratis* were garlanded by all the families of all the three brides. All the guests wore fine clothes. Some of them wore *pagris.* Karamchand was in a horse drawn carriage. The grooms were on horseback. Karamchand was having difficulty with every movement. But his royal bearing was intact. He was attired in royal finery. He alighted with assistance. Escorted indoors, he was led to a high chair placed at an elevation. Six chairs had come from the Porbandar durbar. Two for the in-laws, and three for the grooms. The highest chair was for the Durbar Sahib whether he was present or not. Such a grand *barat* was seen in Porbandar for the first time ever. Guests from the brides' side were making loud comments about the three grooms – on their height, their complexion and the like. Similar remarks were being made about the brides. Kastur got the lion's share of compliments. For her appearance as well as for her good fortune. People were indicating with signs which groom was the son of our Diwan Sahib and which one was the son of the senior Diwan Sahib of Rajkot. Marks were being freely allotted on appearances.

Mohandas, also known as Moniya, was the youngest. He was taken to the middle *mandap* that was the best decorated and asked to sit on a low stool that faced east. On another low stool, Kastur was made to sit facing west. Kastur's face was covered with a *ghoonghat* but she managed a slanting glance at the face of her groom. She was seeing him after some years. It felt good. A white sheet was stretched out vertically between them. Kastur saw her ba-bapu sitting beside her, facing northwards and she was elated. Finally somebody familiar in the sea of strangers. Then her father Gokuldas stood up and declared the time, eon, era, place, country, year, season, day, town, the planetary positions and the place of the wedding. Calling upon all the devatas, he said, 'I place the hand of my healthy daughter Kastur in the hands of Sriman Mohandas, the younger son of honourable Karamchand and leaving aside filial affection, give up the rights that my wife and I had as her parents.' A low sob was heard. Along with a blade of *doob* grass, he placed the hand of Kastur in the hand of Mohandas. The groom's side made sounds of joyous celebration. The hearts of the people from the bride's side grew heavy. The same thing happened in the other two mandaps.

Kastur's small, soft hand in Moniya's looked like a white lotus bud. Moniya also stole a look at Kastur. She was older and very pretty. After this was the *saptpadi*, at every step, Panditji would pronounce a promise and Moniya would repeat it. Kastur would repeat it too. Moniya, walking alongside, was the only one who could hear her as if she was saying it only to him. The same ceremony was being conducted in all three mandaps. The conch was blown thereafter. The purohits then recited their respective patron's *virudavali,* which listed the names and other details of the members of that clan, their lineage, as well as achievements and qualifications of various clan members.

A festive atmosphere prevailed with showers of flowers all around and joyous voices resounding from all sides. Guests from both sides congratulated Diwan Sahib and Tulsidas. There was a crowd of in-laws and family friends. It is a rare occasion in a Hindu household where three sons of a family are wedded in a common mandap, at an auspicious time. All three were in their teens, but Karsan and Motilal were almost the same age. Motilal was a year older than Karsan which made him seventeen. Moniya was the youngest. The sounds of the conch and the band were exhilarating. Moniya was enjoying the gifts, the fine clothes and the sound of music. He was also thinking that he would get a long lost friend to play with. But both of them had big questions to grapple with. How would they face each other and how would they address each other?

Of the two, Moniya was more worried. If I speak, will she reply? He was only thirteen. He did not know anything about married life. His bhabhi had given him a few leads. There is a saying that if you don't know the lesson, it is difficult to cheat. How much could Bhabhi tell him anyway? How much would Kastur know? His cherished belief that he was older had been shattered by Kastur's father's declaration. That was a shock.

Much later did Mohan understand that such relationships open out gradually. Leads from the outside are only a beginning.

***

Kastur's background was one where girls are schooled into patience and forbearance. It is possible that such thoughts were also roiling inside her, as the ones that were troubling Moniya. She felt torn. Her home, her ba-bapu and brother and other family members was one part. Will I have to leave all of them? Why? Why can't I stay here? Why are Ba-Bapu sending me away? What have I done? She had asked Ba tearfully. Ba had broken down. When she leaves, every daughter has the same question in her heart. No mother ever has a satisfactory answer. Ba had come to this house with the same question. After that she learnt to be patient. Such patience, so early in the life of a young girl, robs her of her childhood. Until the *vidai*, she nursed the hurt.

——***——

Kastur's New Home

Like all children, Kastur was excited at the prospect of a journey. In those days, journeys could only be undertaken by road. Men and women used different vehicles. Horse carriages or camel carts. Ganga and Kastur were together. Ganga was younger, but as she was Moniya's elder brother Karsan's wife, her rank was higher. She was Kastur's *jethani.* But she would not stop crying. Kastur also felt like crying but she checked herself. She tried pacifying Ganga. Kastur had always been fearless since her childhood. She was not intimidated by the new place, like most brides of her age.

The two grooms and elder brother, Lakshmidas, sat with their injured father, in the carriage. The royal coach had been repaired and sent back, the syces duly rewarded. The rations for the horses had also been given. Both the brides were sitting in the bigger carriage with elder sister-in-law Nandkunwarben and mother-in-law Putliba. They were huddled in a corner. This was the longest ride of their lives. Putliba enquired about their comfort throughout. They would take a break at a dharamshala or at an acquaintance's house. Since they were back from a wedding, they had ample food supplies.

Everybody was apprehensive about another accident. Diwan Sahib had not fully recovered. Nobody spoke openly, but in everybody's heart was a prayer for a safe end to this journey. As soon as the coachman increased the speed, Karamchand would tell him to go slow, the horses will tire. Kastur wanted the coach to race ahead. If Bapu had been there, she would have insisted that the coach go faster. Now she had to sit quietly. Ganga was fast asleep. Ba had put her head in her lap. She asked Kastur to sleep too, but since the elders were awake, she did not sleep. She was older than Ganga. She would just catch a brief nap now and then.

When the coaches finally reached the house of the Gandhis, the women breathed a sigh of relief. The men echoed this with the ironical aphorism – safe and sound the fools return. Well, wrong to call them fools, they were the wise men who returned with two new daughters-in-law. Moniya's elder sister, Raliyatben, welcomed them ceremonially with an *arta.* All the other formalities were duly observed. After this was the ceremonial *dwar rukai,* the barring of entry unless a gift tax was paid by the grooms. Moniya and Karsan being under age and without an income, Ba gave the girls the gift amount levied, so that the grooms and brides could enter the house. The old adage of two rotis and ghee smeared too, proved true in the case of Putliba. Two daughters in law at the same time. Putliba was fatigued, but elated. The women from the neighbourhood who had gathered even before the formal occasion of *munh dikhai,* the viewing of the bride's face lifting the *ghoonghat*, were freely voicing their opinions about Moniya's bride being pretty. Ganga lowered her head. Maybe she even shed tears. She may have wondered about whether it was her fault. Ba held the *munh dikhai* for both on two separate days after an auspicious time was declared. All the talk of keeping things the same had not happened in front of the brides. People did not exchange presents those days. Sweets, copra or a few auspicious coins were given as gifts. Ornaments could be given by close relatives but there was neither expectation nor compulsion.

***

After all the celebrations, Moniya went back to school. Because of the presence of guests, Moniya and Kastur could only look at each other. Moniya was restless. It felt good even to look at her. Kastur would stay among the womenfolk, but her eyes also roved. If they accidentally came face to face, they pretended not to see each other. Putlibai was a kind mother-in-law. She did not ignore anybody. She would try to have the daughters-in-law sit by her, at least once in the day. She would stroke their heads and even hug them. She would tell them that she had been in the same state as them. I know how you must be feeling. I can't become your mother, but at least I can be someone like her. Both the brides would remain quiet, but they felt better. She would divide up the chores amongst the daughters-in-law and Raliyat equally. She knew that both of them were very young. Once Ganga sat down to pound the chillies. When the chilli dust stung her eyes, Ba washed them, applied ghee and comforted her in her lap for a long time. She told Kastur also that neither of them should undertake such tasks, without asking her first. She would not let them go near the fire. Kastur would do all the other chores. At the end of the day, after the kitchen had been closed, she would be the last of the daughters-in-law to go to her room. Karsan would take Ganga away on some pretext or the other. Moniya, on the other hand, would keep waiting.

Even after the wedding, many minor ceremonies went on for days. Worshipping the well, the river, etc. After all this was over, Kastur's normal life commenced. She missed her home. She would travel to her parents' place mentally whenever possible, and shed a few tears. Nobody knew when Ba-Bapu would come or when she would be with them. This was a secret pact. There had been one more change. Kastur's name was suffixed with Bai which indicated that she was a married woman. Kasturbai.

——***——

Husband and wife

Kastur was everybody's favourite in her own house. Makanji, her father, had been the mayor of Porbandar. She was not used to doing heavy chores or a lot of them … Although her mother would call her, whenever she was making something special. She knew how to cook food for daily meals. It was not usual to have meals cooked by unmarried daughters. It was believed that after their marriage they would have to do the cooking and grinding anyway. At least they should enjoy their time in their parents' home, without being saddled with a lot of work. But they were all well trained. Although her father-in-law was the Diwan of the kingdom, everybody did their own chores. So much so, that whenever he got time, her father-in-law would sit under a tree and slice vegetables. He would chat with visitors who came for official business and keep up with his chores at the same time. When Kasturbai saw this for the first time, she was quite taken aback. But she could see that this was the way to get work done. Diwan Sahib completes the work of the house and the outside, at the same time. We can do the same, she thought. She had not seen this way of working in her own house.

Putliba was good natured and soft spoken. She was not enamoured of fine clothes and ornaments. She was totally devoted to her dharma and her household. She would not eat a morsel before her bath and her puja. She believed that fasts and other such observances by the lady of the house, were necessary for the welfare of the family. It was believed that fasting was necessary for cleansing and self discipline. If she took a certain vow on a festival, she would observe it to the letter. She would eat only once a day, during the period of *Chaturmas* (the monsoon season from July-October). Once she decided to eat only on alternate days, in the *Chaturmas* period. On the third day also, she would break her fast only after seeing the sun. It would rain continuously for days sometimes. Once it rained incessantly for two or three days. When the children saw the slightest ray of light, they would rush to call Ba, but by then the sun would be covered by clouds again. The children grew quite worried. Moniya would be the most upset. She would just laugh and say, 'As God wills ... tomorrow it is then ...' She would not break her own rule. Kasturbai was greatly impressed by her firmness. Although Kastur's mother was also very religious, Putliba did all this with a minimum of fuss.

***

After she had become used to her new routine, and after seeing Moniya at close quarters, she felt that he had changed. Both of them liked each other. But Moniya was increasingly getting more possessive. Possessiveness gives rise to jealousy. There was no obvious reason. When he was at home, he would read short four-leaved storybooks, other than his text books. If you mentioned this, he would get irritable. Kastur was upset by this behaviour. Since she was unlettered herself, she interfered as little as possible. She felt she had no right. Later she found out that Moniya read cheap tawdry tracts about marital relations between men and women. She heard his Muslim friend saying this. He was the one who got him these books. She did not like this. But whom could she tell? Kastur knew that Moniya loved her. He had no other motives. But what was the meaning of this? This was complicated. The best course was to keep quiet, to wait and watch.

But the matter did not rest there. Kastur had no idea or experience of such male behaviour. He would say she should take a pledge to be faithful. During the wedding *pheras*, both of them had taken this pledge. It was impossible for her to fathom who else could she be faithful to. Who was teaching Moniya that she was not faithful to her husband? What worried her even more was that Moniya had begun to believe, that to ensure faithfulness, a husband had to use his rights over his wife. Wasn't this right inherent in their relationship? It is imbibed from the time of birth. Kastur may have been unlettered and young in years, but her *sanskars* were deeply ingrained. She respected the permanence of relationships. They could not be broken. She would silently listen to the hurtful things that he would say. Interpreting her silence as contempt, he declared one night that she should tell him, before she went anywhere. And to tell him whom she met and why, upon her return. Kastur was livid. Tears sprang to her eyes but she did not let them flow. She thought she would not show any weakness. Her answer would be her conduct. This was an astonishing resolve. She thought about whether her mother-in-law sought permission from her husband or did the elder sisters-in-law ask their husbands when they went anywhere. She already saw that not just the elder ones, even Ganga who had entered the house with her, did not go looking for her husband, if she wanted to visit someone or go somewhere in the neighbourhood. Kastur was hurt and humiliated.

One day, when Putliba was going to the temple, she asked Kastur to accompany her. The heart finds peace by visiting the temple she said. Kastur immediately went with her. Moniya was at home. The next day, she went to the temple and then she went to meet some friends, with the elder sisters-in-law.

Moniya was in a temper because she had been going out for many days without asking him. 'I had told you not to go anywhere without asking me and to tell me when you return. You just go off wherever you like ...' he said irascibly.

Kastur was fed up of Moniya's orders. She spoke up for the first time, 'Do you want me obey your orders over Ba's?' He had no answer.

'If the elders in the house ask me to accompany them, should I tell them that I cannot go anywhere without your permission?' was her next query.

Moniya could see that without convincing her, it was not easy to make Kastur accede to his wishes. He was disturbed. This affected his studies also.

***

Amidst all this, there was a call for Kastur from her parents' home. After marriage, the bride is supposed to go to her parents' place for sometime for *pad pher*. She had been at her in-laws since the marriage. Kastur was in two minds. She did not want to go just then, because of the state of mind of her husband. But how could she refuse? If she asked Moniya, he might refuse to let her go. Her dilemma would be resolved but it would break the heart of her family. When she did ask Moniya, he promptly said, 'Go by all means. They must be waiting for you.'

It had been so long since she had met her father, mother and brothers that she really wanted to go. But she was hurt by Moniya's terse words. Every woman craves to hear that she holds a special place in the heart of her lover that cannot be taken by anybody else. She went to her parents' home feeling divided. She had lived there heart-whole, thinking that this was her home and always will be.

For few days after reaching Porbandar, she continued to feel torn about whether she had done the right thing, by leaving Moniya behind. He might have agreed to let her go, but he must not have approved. After a few days however, she fell into her old routine. There were no strictures on her here. Whenever anybody asked her about her in-laws' place, she would praise everybody by name. About Moniya, she would say that either he is busy with his studies or serves her father-in-law, Diwan Sahib. Her friends would rib her about what happened at night. Did he wake her up for a chat or...? She would blush furiously. She met her friends and family freely. Every day felt new and full of excitement.

There was much talk, laughter and song. She loved singing. When a daughter comes back, it is as if times past are reborn. Kastur's original marital home was in Porbandar. The difference was that now that her father-in-law was the Diwan of Rajkot, he had his brother Tulsidas appointed as the Diwan of Porbandar. So this was her second marital home. His son, Motilal, had married Harkunwar at the same time as Kastur. So the marital home was never too far away from her mind. She often visited that home too. The best part was that Harkunwar was like a friend. After paying her respects and talking to her *chachiya saas,* she would go off to chat with Harkunwar. Having been married at the same time, there was a natural bond between them. She could speak to Harkunwar about all that she hesitated to share with her other friends. She could talk about her worries and the difficulties with her husband. She narrated how she would finish all the tasks in the kitchen and be the last to go to her room. He would come even later, as he would be doing all chores for her father-in-law. He would wake her up if she fell asleep. If he was there before her, he would be pacing up and down or reading a book. Harkunwar was intrigued. 'Devar ji, reads books?' Harkunwar was astonished and admiring. As if to suggest that her partner was .... Harkunwar was reticent but her reactions revealed what she felt. Then Kastur told her that her husband would play pranks. He would pinch her or draw up the covers and pretend to be asleep when he saw her coming. He kept the lights burning at bedtime whereas she did not like to sleep with the lights on. But Kastur would not object because she did not want to trouble him. She knew Moniya was scared of the dark.

Kastur very hesitantly and putting the entire blame on herself, recounted how she had started going against his wishes soon after the marriage, not once, but repeatedly. She seemed to be talking to herself as she spoke. So Mohandas had changed. Hadn't she changed? She used to be somebody else but she had changed so much. He had become so demanding that it was not possible to agree with him on everything. She knew that as a good wife, this was not how it should be. But what could she do? How could she explain that a wife has a life of her own too? Everybody has their own way of navigating. She said that she wanted to be a good wife but also had to be true to herself. Her husband did not understand this. After all, he was a man.

Harkunwar sighed, 'The man's end of the balance is heavier.' She said no more. Harkunwar's face was expressionless. There was neither surprise nor approbation on it. 'Don't you think so too?'

Kastur did not say anything. Neither a word of assent or disagreement. She merely smiled deeply.

***

Moniya could only think of Kastur after she went to Porbandar. Arguing fiercely with himself, he would say, if she does not care about me, why should I? At other times he wondered how she was keeping. What would she be doing now? I am sure she does not remember me. As if she cared for me even when she was here ... The others in the house were more important. He would work himself into a state and then quieten down. She would understand his love for her ... as if he had understood it. The mental state of a newly married wife and husband is akin to that of lovers. You know how you feel but what do you know of the love of the other person? Sometimes he tortured himself, what if she does not come back and that would agitate him even further. He did not know whom to ask. Then he would comfort himself with the thought that a wife has to return to her husband's house. That would bring relief.

***

Another strain of thought was disturbing him. How was he to make up for all the time lost because of the wedding? If there is any glitch in the exam, not only would he earn a bad name but Kastur would also be subject to innuendos. He could take it but how would she hold up? Moniya was different from both his brothers Karsan and Motilal. Their studies were practically at a standstill, after their marriages. For Moniya, his studies gave him a sense of purpose. As things turned out, he cleared his exams with good marks. He was happy that Kastur would not be subjected to taunts. He waited for her arrival. He wanted to share the news of his success. He also wanted to feel less lonely. In the meanwhile, he hatched up a plan to make her happy. He would teach her to study. This would surely bring them closer. He dreamt of making her an ideal wife. She would be like him. She would not depend on anybody but be totally self-reliant. Self-reliance is true independence, although she was so already.

The problem of being unlettered was a big one for Kastur. Moniya could not share his happiness with her, through a letter. She is sure to be delighted by his plan of educating her. She must feel that her husband really cares. If she could read he could have indicated that he expects her to return soon. Such thoughts galloped around like wild horses in his head only to collapse. He had to suppress his desolation. He had no option but to wait for her to come back.

——***——

Her new home

After her stint at her parents', when Kastur returned, her eyes skittered like restless fish. Where was he? Her *sasu ma* had welcomed her warmly. But her worry was whether Moniya was still upset with her. Her younger *jethani* Ganga's eyes followed her wandering gaze. Where would her eyes pause and rest? Her mischievous smile waxed and waned as she followed Kastur's gaze.

Kastur remembered that during the day, husbands and wives did not even look at each other, to say nothing of meeting. She was too embarrassed to ask where her husband was. When her younger sister-in-law took a dig, the elder one admonished her saying do you cosy up to your husband all day? Kastur will also meet her husband when the time comes. Her dig was a serious one and touched a raw nerve in both. Kastur waited for the night. When she was done with all her chores, she found Moniya was already pacing up and down in the room. Kastur just stared at him in silence. He looked thinner, but his colour was healthy. She thought he must have been studying hard. Although she had entered on tip toe, her *payal* had betrayed her. Moniya spun around and gazed at her in relief. 'You found the time to tear yourself away from everybody else! You did not think of me even today…?' he launched into a complaint.

Kastur thought that there had been a change. She paused for a second and then these words popped out of her mouth. 'I was looking for you since morning. Ganga Bhabhi was making fun of me. Badi Bhabhi scolded her saying do you stick to your husband all day long.' Moniya's face relaxed. 'You were looking … for me?… Amazing!'

'Didn't you miss me?'

Moniya came closer and laughed as he said, 'It seems you were very well looked after at home.'

'Nobody needs to look after you at home. The plants growing in their own soil always flourish.'

Moniya held her hand and made her sit next to him, on the bed. She did not know whether she was floating in the sky or walking on the ground. Her stiff husband was a changed man. Very enthusiastically he said, 'I have a plan for you. You will be delighted to hear it.' In his excitement over his plan, he had forgotten to tell her about his success in the exam.

'Plan?'

'Yes, my plan …' said he. He told her he would get books for her and teach her to read and write everyday. He would make her smarter than everybody else. He babbled on about his plan late into the night. It had been a long day for Kastur and sleep threatened to overcome her. It was with great difficulty that she could keep her eyes open. She did not want to dampen his enthusiasm. When she tried to say something, he put a finger on her lips.

'It will be difficult in the day, but at night, before going to sleep, we will study. You will learn and I will teach. I will make you an ideal wife. Whatever I have learnt, I will make sure you learn that too. You will become just like me.'

Kastur did not understand. She laughed to herself. How will he make an unlettered girl like himself? How will a girl learn what men are supposed to do? Why will he turn her into a sinner? This thought chased the sleep away from her eyes. Questions and doubts rained down on her head. She wanted to be an obedient daughter-in-law and wife. He says he wants me to be a free thinking wife. Free of old beliefs. This was a contradiction. More than Moniya, she was grappling with herself. She did not know whether women were meant to carry out household duties and serve others or talk freely after getting educated. A husband wanting to educate his wife and make her free? When the other women find out that Diwan Sahib's daughter-in-law and Makanji's daughter was studying and would become a lettered madam, a *sahabni*, wouldn't she lose face? Because Moniya was talking to her so lovingly after so long, she did not contradict him. But there were many argumentative voices within her head.

***

All postponements and excuses notwithstanding, Moniya's grand plan was initiated. Moniya wanted his wife to be free of old beliefs and wanted to educate her for this purpose. But he himself was afraid to break the beliefs in his household. When Kastur would be dead beat after doing the household chores all day, she would see that her husband was waiting with books and slates. She would immediately feel doubly tired. She was supposed to be on the path to her liberation, but she was increasingly hemmed in by her husband's designs. She felt like a cow on a long rope. Household chores by day and studies at midnight ... she had neither the stamina nor the desire for this. There was also the danger of whispers starting in the house. There was much scope for misunderstandings. As it is, studies were not considered a respectable activity for women. What she had learnt from Pultiba, her own mother and her elder sister-in-law was that even a small spark in a joint family could result in a vast all-consuming conflagration. It is better to be humble. Kastur had another fear: that her elder sisters-in-law would feel that she is ploughing a separate furrow. What would Putliba think of her? She wanted to be an ordinary woman, like the others. She wanted to be one of the birds on the bough where all the birds sat.

Kastur did not oppose Moniya to his face ever. Nor did she express disagreement. She had borne the rough edge of his temper once. She resolved not to memorise her lesson. She would be half asleep when Moniya was teaching her. When he made her repeat things, she did so. When he would ask her the next day, she would be blank. Moniya would sit with his head held in his hands. Kastur would feel bad but she would excuse herself saying that she got no time from her chores. Moniya had no answer to that. But he did not want to concede defeat. This teaching experiment went on for weeks. But the results were zero. Many times at the point of high excitement, they would throw the books aside and get into bed. That distraction could rise up at any time.

——***——

Moniya's Friend

This fact troubled Moniya always.

If he had not given way to his baser instincts, Kastur would be the ideal woman. He always held himself culpable for not being able to construct Kastur into the woman of his dreams. He had the urge to share his marital complications with somebody. Sometimes they cast such a stranglehold over him that he wanted to talk to somebody to lighten the load. A deep attachment to Kastur on the one hand and the pain of not being able to mould her according to his wishes ... He struck up a friendship with a boy called Sheikh Mehtab in Class Ten. Mehtab was a friend of his older brother, Karsan. Mehtab's father was an official in the police force of the kingdom. It was a matter of honour for him to be friends with the Diwan's son. Karsan had handed over Moniya to him when he was leaving school. Moniya was physically a weakling, so in a way, Sheikh Mehtab was his protector. Moniya knew his shortcomings but felt that he was a loyal friend. Kastur, Putliba, elder brother Lakshmidas and others were not too pleased with this friendship. When his mother and wife objected, they were silenced by the declaration that he was trying to reform Sheikh Mehtab. Ba knew of his helpful nature. She thought it would be a good thing if Sheikh Mehtab improved in the company of Moniya. She told Kastur the same thing.

Mehtab was a tall, well built, athletic young man. He was high in the pecking order of the school. Because he lived across the road, Kastur knew a lot about him. He was spoilt, a braggart, lazy, etc. When Mohandas said he was going to reform Mehtab, everybody had accepted without demur. But Kastur did not like Moniya to spend so much time with Mehtab. She would restrain her urge to say something about this to him. One day when it became too much to bear, she expressed her reservations to Moniya. He was impervious. He kept up with Mehtab as before. Kastur thought to herself, after all that he made her do to turn her into 'an ideal woman'... she had not complained. But now she had mentioned just the one thing to him and he ignored her completely. She was upset. What was going to happen?

Sheikh Mehtab and Moniya were inseparable. Kastur was apprehensive of their extreme closeness. Instead of changing Mehtab, Moniya was changing. He had begun to tell Mehtab everything. He went so far as to tell him that he was scared of the dark whereas his wife was not. He exposed his weaknesses to Mehtab. He also told Mehtab that he was scared of snakes, ghosts and thieves and could not sleep for imaginary fears but his wife slept deeply, unaffected by all this.

Mehtab got a chance to say, 'You should eat meat ... look at me, I am not afraid of anything.'

Moniya stared at him dumbstruck. How could he suggest meat eating to a boy from a Vaishnav family? Mehtab did not give him a chance to object. He kept on, 'You all are scared because you eat only leaves and vegetables. I can grab a snake with my bare hands. I don't believe in ghosts. I owe my height, my strength and my prowess at sports to my being a non-vegetarian. The British have been ruling over our country because they are meat-eaters.' He repeated a popular saying among Gujarati youth:

'Look at these brave Whites
They rule over Bharat
They are meat eaters
And are six feet tall'

Mehtab did not stop here. He whispered in Moniya's ear, 'Many Hindu school teachers eat meat secretly.' After a pause, 'Even your brother Karsan.' Moniya was shocked but did not say anything.

After much discussion, Sheikh Mehtab convinced Moniya that eating meat was something of a moral fraud, but not a grave misdemeanour. Moniya's lynchpin of morality stood loosened. Mehtab reassured him that all this would be secret and his father and mother would never come to know. Even Karsan would not find out. If meat-eating could make him strong and fearless, then what was the harm? He would no longer need to be ashamed in front of his wife. He would turn into a fearless patriot also. To kill two birds with one stone was an irresistible prospect.

Sheikh Mehtab got a dish of tasty meat cooked for him and spirited him away to a secret hideout near the river bank. Moniya had swung between yes and no all day long. But he was so much in awe of Sheikh Mehtab that he could not refuse. As Kastur had feared – heaven knows what was going to happen now. Moniya ate mutton and bread. He tossed and turned throughout the night. As if the lamb was alive and protesting in his stomach. But when he thought of not losing face before Kastur and how he would send the British packing from his country now that he was so strong, his repentance would evaporate. What had started as an experiment became a part of habit. He would test the limits of his body sometimes, to see the difference it had made. Sheikh would fan his vanity by saying that your face has a certain glow now. If you keep this up your frame will fill out. They began frequenting restaurants after emerging from the secret hideout. Moniya would be very alert while going into a restaurant. He did not wish to be spotted. He would skulk in a corner where nobody could see him.

——***——

Kastur's Turmoil

Kastur could sense that her husband was changing again. His will to study was getting steadily eroded. He could not remember when he had even taken such a vow. Earlier Moniya would keep her awake for long. Now there was no chance to talk. He would get into bed as soon as he got into the room. He would put out the light. In the morning, he would get up and quickly get ready for school. Kastur noticed that Mehtab would be waiting for Moniya outside. He would return late in the evening. Putliba had admonished him many times saying that he never used to be this late. He would not lie but would say he got late with Mehtab. Ba would not be pleased with this answer. He would eat just a little bit and then get up saying that his stomach was upset. Ba would scold him saying that if his stomach has been upset for so long then why doesn't he get some medicine? He would make light of it saying that it was probably just seasonal. But Kastur was not fooled. His parents might believe him, but she felt that something was not right somewhere. She smelt a certain odour on his breath and she would turn her face away. She was caught in a dilemma where it was a sin to say that he had become a meat eater on mere suspicion. She had not felt such an odour emanating from anybody else in the house. The body odour of vegetarians is different. She was forced to accept, with a heavy heart, that her husband had begun to eat forbidden foods, in the company of Mehtab. She could not rid herself of this feeling even during moments of intimacy. She would feel impure until she was able to bathe the next morning. It was only water that could purify her heart and her body. She believed in the mystique of tulsi leaves right from her childhood.

She was faced with the galling question of how to save Moniya from this sin. She did not want to make a big scene by telling the others in the household. When the elder brother had gone abroad, he had to undergo difficult penance to wash off the sin. This was far worse. Did Moniya realise this? If he would not stop, what was to be done? Prayer was the only recourse. Prayer has always been the buttress and strength of the weak. Kastur's prayer was effective.

***

Moniya's meat eating experiments went on for nearly a year. It did not add so much as an inch to his height or the dimensions of his frame. Instead his self disgust had increased. He sensed that whether anybody else knew, Kastur certainly did. May be he even shared this with Mehtab. He must have said that women do not understand and she will accept whatever you tell her. Moniya's state of mind grew unbearable and he declared, 'Although the youth in Hindustan need to turn meat eaters to improve their condition, I think it is better

I stop lying to Ba-Bapu. While they are alive, it is impossible for me to continue lying every evening and consuming meat. I will not eat meat until they are there.' Moniya felt better for deciding this. But the fact that he had hidden this from them continued to prick his conscience. Until they were alive, this question chased him. Should he tell them? It would break their hearts. They never came to know that two of their sons had become meat eaters. He tried to make up for his lapse by admitting to this before Kastur. Kastur had maintained silence. She had atoned for this by staying away from him for some length of time.

***

One day while talking to Mehtab, Moniya wondered whether it was only Kastur who was passive during sex or were all women like that? His lack of experience provided no answers. Sheikh Mehtab set himself up as rather an expert in such matters, so Moniya had no other recourse to improve his knowledge. But his answer did not help. Instead it led to major complications.

'Don't worry, women are usually scared. They are restrained, not very active.' said Mehtab. 'It is also possible that she may desire somebody more than you,' he added.

In an inexperienced mind, such thoughts firm up quickly and lethally. That night Kastur was in real trouble. There was a flood of questions.

'Who is it who you desire more than me?'

'You care for somebody else. You don't love me and therefore are cold.'

He hurled a relentless flurry of accusations. Such theatrics went on every night. A storm of humiliation and agitation raged in Kastur's heart. She was forced to bear it in silence. Kastur knew who was behind all this ugliness. She knew who had sparked this off. His eyes betrayed his intentions but Moniya was unable to see this. She could not confide in anybody. Mehtab had scattered the seeds of suspicion. They had fallen on fertile ground and doubts sprouted like weeds.

***

Kastur found out only much later. It was not even as if she found out. Once Moniya had become Gandhi, he told Kastur about the whole incident. What could be worse for a wife to learn that Mehtab told Moniya to learn more about the real nature of females from a woman who understood what goes on between men and women. He suggested that Moniya visit a brothel. Not only that, just as he had arranged the meat party, he also arranged the visit to the brothel. He made all the payments. After demurring initially, Moniya agreed to go. He might have gone out of curiosity but the consequences were disastrous. To be humiliated by a prostitute is not an ordinary insult. Moreover, how could he face himself after he had betrayed the promise that he had made to be faithful to his wife? All because he was plagued by baseless suspicions. For someone who hated to lie, such an incident was bound to lead to extreme self disgust. Kastur had been so wounded by this that she could not speak. Much later, her husband Mohandas, had written this verbatim in his autobiography. A prostitute had not only insulted his masculinity, but also Kastur's wifehood. Even though it was not her fault, she felt guilty about it for days.

Mohandas says that after being turned down by the prostitute, when he stood on the road, he felt relieved that the promise made to Kastur at the time of the *pheras,* had not been broken. The insult had saved him from committing a grave sin. Before he admitted to it so much later, he had feared that he would have to listen to her recriminations. The kind of allegations that Moniya had made that night, on Mehtab's behest, Kastur would have been justified in making some, seeing his reprehensible conduct. But she kept quiet. When she heard the shameful account, she felt, after her marriage, this was her trial by fire. What was needed was restraint and understanding. She had overcome her trauma with love, trust and generosity. Mohandas had hardly expected this from a fifteen year old girl. Kastur remembered her mother's words that if you meet fire with fire, it only flares up. She had not said a hurtful word to Mohan. There was nothing to feed the fire.

——***——

An Aging Diwan

The injuries that Karamchand had suffered, on the way to Porbandar from Rajkot, for his sons' wedding, had not healed fully. The position of the Diwan in Rajkot was safe however. A British surgeon in Bombay had told him that he needed an operation. But the Family Doctor was not in favour of this, given his age and physical condition. His general health was failing too. Earlier he could move about with assistance, but now he was bedridden. Only his voice still had the same authoritative ring. He managed the affairs of the kingdom sitting at home. The expense of medicines had gone up. The responsibilities of the household had increased. Until he worked, he got his salary from the treasury. Later it turned into a pension. The household expenses were getting higher.

It was Mohan's first chance to nurse and care for his father. Both his parents needed care. From his childhood, Mohan had been very caring and compassionate towards the sick and the suffering. His elder sister Raliyat would narrate an incident from his childhood, where he had climbed up a guava tree with bandages. He wanted to bandage the fruits that had been pecked by the birds. She would narrate this often, just to rile him.

***

There was no change in Diwan Sahib's Durbar. Despite his illness, every evening, Jain, Hindu, Parsi and Christian preachers would gather. There would be discussions and debates on matters of faith. Moniya would be all ears, while preparing medicines, as he heard the chanting of mantras, learned analysis and the tenets of other religions. Ayurvedic medicines were used. Pounding and powdering with a mortar and pestle was essential in their preparation. Whenever there was an argument, Diwan ji would intervene as his judgment was acceptable to everybody. Once when he heard the Gujarati translation of the Ramayana, Mohan felt that truth was the basis of all other good qualities. That seemed to be the pivotal message. He got a new perspective on different religions. More so, on Hindusim. When everybody departed, Moniya would wash his father's feet. He would then massage it until Bapu fell asleep. Kastur observed purdah, so she could not assist her husband in all these chores. She would feel upset about how little time was left for his studies. But Kasturbai was very gratified that all the nauseating food experiments and other despicable acts that had been done under Sheikh's influence, had come to an end. Moniya had not ended his friendship with him despite all the machinations. It is just that he had less time where he could be in his company. He still maintained that he would bring about a change of heart in Sheikh. From Kastur's point of view, this was a distant mirage. Kastur was carrying. She felt that there should be an end to the association with Sheikh. But it was relief enough that Moniya could not meet him, because he was busy.

The new dawn in her life had ousted most of her doubts and fears. She did not find much time to think about her father-in-law's illness. She liked to daydream about the life growing inside her. Mohan was caught in conflicting emotions. Father, wife, the child who was going to come and the growing distance from his friend. Sometimes his attraction for his wife would overcome him and his father's ill health would recede. He would behave strangely when the urge to be with his wife was overpowering. As the evening darkened, even as he was at his father's service, he would keep coming in to his small bedroom. Kastur would have changed her attire and combed her heavy swathe of hair. She would be waiting in bed. He would wait for his father's formal command of release, 'Go beta. Go to sleep now. It is very late.' Bapu would say most often.

As Diwan Karamchand's condition worsened, relatives began arriving to enquire after his health. His younger brother, Tulsidas, had come from Porbandar that day. Mohan could hardly wait to sprint to his own room. Seeing that he had been tending to his father since many hours, he said, 'Moniya, you go now. I am sitting with Mota Bhai. Bahu must be alone.' Tulsi Kaka's words were like a drop of water to a thirsting man. He bowed to his father and uncle and bounded towards his room. Kastur had dozed off. He woke her up and got into bed after changing. It was a moment of ecstasy for both of them.

Shortly after, there was a knock on the door. The servant was calling out, 'Come at once. Diwanji is sinking.'

Moniya leapt out of bed. He scrambled into some clothes and ran towards Bapu's room. Everybody else was there already. Mohan was the youngest. He had been serving Bapu all this while. It was as if a mountain of grief broke over him. One thought pierced him like the sharp point of a trident. When Bapu was leaving us, he was in the arms of his pregnant wife. He was slave to his desire, so he had left with such alacrity at the first opportunity that presented itself in Chacha's words. Why? All his care came to nothing. Desire slices through sacrifice in an instant. Kastur could not go to Bapu's room nor was there anybody she could ask about Bapu or what had happened. She was assailed by doubts – what if the unspeakable had happened? If it had, she would not be able to show her face anywhere. Never mind if nobody else knew about this. She knew it. She had no basis to exonerate herself. When she found out that Bapu had departed before Moniya could reach him, she felt that her face had been forever blackened. She felt utterly helpless but she could not share her agony with anybody. She had never felt so alone. Even more than a child whose father had left her forever ...

***

Four days after Diwan Karamchand's death, Kasturbai gave birth to a premature baby. The baby survived for a very short time. Between the observance of the *sootak* and that of the *paatak*, there were but few days. Before Kastur's desperate eyes swung the images of Bapu or her beloved child, who did not even open his eyes. The Gandhi family was plunged into gloom. The revered elder and the newest arrival had both departed within the space of a few days. Fathers are like a tree that shades you and your son is like a step towards the giant umbrella of time. Kastur could hardly decide which was the bigger sorrow. Moniya was in a similar state. Kastur was assailed by the thought of her child's presence followed by immediate absence. Husband and wife were crushed under their grief. They say that when a child goes, a mother's perennial breast dries up slowly. When sorrow is mixed with guilt, it is like a fire that refuses to die. Moniya's grief was augmented by something else that made it unbearable. The child who was awaited by the entire family had gone because of Moniya's unbridled sexual desire. Kastur's unfulfilled body that ran with milk, reminded her incessantly of her dead baby. He came and he went. She remained in the same state. She could not be a mother nor did the child stay to carry her to motherhood. They never got to know each other. There were no auspicious songs sung and no gifts for the newborn. He was sent away wrapped in a white shroud. The grief of this loss was like a stake in the heart of both his parents.

The financial crisis in the house deepened after her father-in-law departed. Such is the fate of honest people when they are alive, and after them, that of the others around them. For two generations, the position of Diwan had been held by this household. First Ota Gandhi, Kaba's father had been appointed the Diwan of Porbandar, on the strength of his competence. But he had fallen prey to Queen Rupaliba's excesses. On the allegations made by a maidservant, a storekeeper was sentenced to hang. A bid to save him had resulted in cannons being trained on his house. He had to escape to his village Kutiana with his family in the dead of night. Kutiana was a part of the kingdom of the Nawab of Junagadh. Ota Gandhi died in the exchange of cannon fire, but not before burying his Muslim bodyguard, according to Islamic rites. After that Kaba Gandhi or Karamchand Gandhi was the Diwan of Porbandar, who spent his final days as the Diwan of Rajkot. Putlibai wanted the position to remain with the family. Due to the interference of the British, this did not happen. Her elder son, Lakshmidas, was a minor lawyer. Karsan, the middle brother, was a sub-inspector in the royal police of Rajkot. The English language enjoyed a prime position, even in those times. These two brothers did not succeed because their English was not considered good enough. Pultilbai's attention was now fixed on Mohandas Gandhi, her younger son. She wanted him to complete high school soon and then go on to college for a degree. He would be the first degree holder in the family and the hopes for the *Diwani* would brighten.

Mohan had quietly accepted his mother's wishes. When Kastur had returned to the house from her natal home, Mohan's rank in the class had risen. His scholarship had increased from Rs four to ten. He used to hand over that amount to his elder brother, Lakshmidas. Silver rupee coins were in use. They were also called *kaldar*. Kastur had nothing to do with all this. What was important for her was that her husband was changing. He was brimming with energy. His confidence was growing. A certain momentum was evident in all that he did. His speech reflected a sharp agility, rather than shyness. Mohan was growing in every way. What was significant was that there was no difference in his attitude towards Kasturbai. He loved her just as much. He was always eager to meet her. However, she knew that she was not the beginning and end for him, because there was a lot more. But she was content.

——***——

Mohan travels to London

Both of them were happy. Mohan stood before Kastur in his new avatar. The greatest source of joy was that before he left for college, Mohan knew that his likeness was growing in Kastur's womb, bringing new hope. The grief of losing the first one was dimming. Occasionally, remembering the previous time, Kastur was assailed with doubts but she would soon check herself. Hopes grow like tendrils on a newly sprouted creeper. She did not want to cloud the coming of a new life, with the memories of the past ... She would accompany Ba to the temple for reassurance and pray for the safe birth of a healthy, beautiful baby.

Mohandas went to college to study but came back with no wish to return. He fought a losing battle with loneliness, all the while that he was away. The medium of instruction was English. All his time was spent in struggling with the language. The thought of the growing life within Kastur made him restless and afraid. When the college closed in May, he came back home. Kastur was glad that the father of the child would be present at the time of birth. There was no question of her going to Porbandar. Everyone was going out of their way to be solicitous, as the last episode trembled like a low flame of fear, in everybody's hearts. Not that they spoke about it. Mohan's unilateral decision, not to go back to college, had shattered Ba's dreams. The question of what he would do if he did not go to Samaldas College loomed large. Kastur was confused as to why this was such a major issue. There were two months to the college reopening. Anything could happen in that time.

Putliba did not want the possibility of retaining the *Diwani* to be lost. Mawji Dave had been a friend of the late Diwan and was now a trusted adviser to the Gandhi family. He was admired as a learned and experienced Brahmin. Ba sought his views on the problem. His advice was a blow to Kastur and the others in the family. He was of the opinion that Mohandas should go to London to study Law to be able to take his father's place. Sending him to college in Bhavnagar, barely a hundred miles away, had been so tough for the family. London? For law? Even if the question of money was put aside, how could he be sent way across the seven seas? A traditional Hindu family was to send their son there willingly when they believed that London society was the hotbed of impurity! Mawji Dave told Ba that until Mohandas studied British Law in London, there was little hope of his getting the post. In British India, this was the only way ...

For Kastur, this suggestion was most worrying. What changes would London bring in Mohandas? For him, the idea held promise. It was emerging as the one solution to all the problems in the family. Before Mawji's words, this had not figured in anybody's calculations. Other than Kastur, this altered everybody else's perspective. London and English became firmly established as talismans. Until now they had been worrying about what he would do here if he did not go to college. Now their imagination soared to transport him straight to London. Kastur wanted to pull him back. The others gave their reactions carefully. Kastur was beset with fears and doubts. Didn't people become lawyers by studying in their own country? Don't they earn a living? Her brother-in-law was supporting the whole family with his law practice. Lakshmidas and Karsan were concerned about the money. How should they raise the four thousand rupees that Mawji said would be needed for his three year course? Pultiba was grappling with another dilemma. She had heard that London ruined young men from India with alcohol, meat and women. This fear was wreaking havoc on her beliefs. How could she willingly send her son across the seven seas?

***

As Kastur went into labour, Mohandas' future plans continued to be unresolved. She prayed privately that the birth of the child should change his mind about going to London. The rest of the family was apprehensive because of what happened the last time. Everybody waited silently for the secrets of the future to be revealed. As soon as the *dai* beat upon the *thal* to announce the birth of a son, the atmosphere became festive. Dismay was banished and it was as if London had never been mentioned. Everybody got busy informing relatives and sweets were distributed. It was the time for feasts. The sixth day ceremony was held. It is believed that Goddess Bemata writes the destiny of the child on this day. After this, the naming ceremony was held. The grandfather holds the child and whispers his name into his ear. In the absence of the grandfather, Lakshmidas picked him up and the grandmother whispered his name. He was named Harilal. Mohandas was ecstatic. The birth of a child is indescribable for the parents. Kastur was thankful that this day came soon after the last accident or she might have been the butt of taunts. Even if the immediate family said nothing, outsiders pretended to an intimacy to make cutting remarks.

Until there was the festivity of childbirth, everybody seemed to have forgotten about other matters. As the tide receded, the ground of reality began to emerge. Worries began to assume their positions. Happiness dethrones worry for a while but can never unseat it fully. Ba's religious concerns and other worries about her son's London sojourn began to tighten their grip. Both the brothers set about arranging the money in full earnest. Kastur was stricken with sadness. The first child was taken away by God and now that he had sent Harilal, his father was going off to London. Won't he feel that he grew up without the touch of his father? It is a father's touch that is needed to bring to life the capabilities needed for the outside world even as a mother's touch awakens compassion. Mohandas looked elated and bereft by turns. Kastur desperately wanted to talk to him but she was still in her confinement period, so could only watch him from afar. Her words were trapped like a bumble bee's buzz, deep within her.

***

The general counsel given to Mohandas was that since his father was the Diwan of Porbandar and now Tulsi Chacha held that post, he should ask Chacha to put in a word to Mr Laily, the political agent. Mohandas covered the distance to Porbandar on foot and by camel cart. Chacha was setting off for a pilgrimage. He flatly refused Mohan's request saying that since he was going on a trip of self-purification, he would not put in a word for something that was not right. He said that Mohandas could go by himself as Mr Laily knew the family. After Chacha's refusal, Mohandas gathered courage and went by himself fully prepared with what he had to say. But alas, he got no chance to put his case forward. Mr Laily had come from abroad and this was Mohandas's first encounter with the white bureaucracy. Before he could complete his plea, Mr Laily interrupted him by saying that he could not expect any financial aid. 'First get your college degree,' saying this he turned around and walked away indoors. Nobody had anticipated that Laily, who knew the family well, would show such curt behaviour. Mohandas returned to Porbandar dragging his feet. When Kastur found out the whole story, she wondered why Mohandas wanted to go to London, in spite of such humiliation. She knew that if she said this out loud, she would hurt him even more. A wife's assessment of a husband's respect or humiliation can break his confidence. Silence reigned over the house that day. After all, how could they fault Laily when his own uncle had snubbed him so badly?

Mohandas may have been disappointed, but he was not in despair. Kastur was dumbfounded. Women were not supposed to interfere in such matters. They were supposed to keep quiet. Mohan and the two elder brothers had accelerated their efforts towards gathering funds. But all those who made promises to help, went back on them.

The political agent in Rajkot, Mr Wilson, had given a letter of introduction to someone in London and washed his hands off. Thakur Sahib, who had trusted Diwan Karamchand's advice implicitly, signed his photograph and handed it to Mohandas as if he was the King of England, known to the whole world! As if it was a talisman to ward off evil spirits or the royal ring of a Mughal emperor ... When Mohandas told Kasturba that Sheikh Mehtab was also a member of the money scrounging team, she could hardly speak. She felt acutely helpless. Apparently he was writing to his relatives for a loan but fortunately, nothing came of it. Kastur sent up a silent prayer of thanks that her husband had been spared the need to be beholden to him.

When a person is disappointed by the outside world, he turns towards his own. Everyone's eyes turned towards Kastur's jewels. It is said that nobody else has any rights over a woman's *stridhan*. But when a wife is faced with the question of her husband's self respect and future, she sacrifices her right for him. When Mohandas put the proposition before Kastur, she was rendered speechless. She could not take a stand. The important question for her: were the jewels more important than her husband's desire to go to London to study? It was a rhetorical question and of course, she knew the answer. There was also apprehension. The jewels would go but would her husband too be lost, to the bright lights of London? Putliba was worried about this. Kastur's major concern was about her son. Oblivious of everything right now, how would he get to know his father? But Kastur was aware that her husband's priority was to go abroad to study. His wife, son, mother, brothers and their families came much later. Kastur's last hope was Ba's Vaishnav upbringing and *sanskar* that might put a stop to the whole thing. But her maternal love prevailed over everything else. She called Jain monk Becharji for counsel. He suggested a way out. Mohandas took a vow that he would not touch wine, woman and meat. Putliba put all her faith in her son's vow. Kastur handed over her jewellery to Mohandas in Ba's presence. Her face displayed neither sorrow nor joy. It was schooled into silence.

***

On 10th August 1888, all friends and relatives gathered at Gandhi Bhawan, Rajkot to bid farewell to Mohan as he left for Bombay. Motabhai Lakshmidas was going to Bombay along with the money. Putliba was deeply distressed. Her eyes kept welling up at the thought of whether they would ever meet again. But she would not let her tears flow. Mohandas was among his friends. Kastur stood behind the door holding on to her son. Her heart was wracked with grief. Mohandas knew that she stood there with the child. Society did not approve of a wife bidding a public farewell to her husband as he left to cross the seven seas. Mohandas entered the room on the pretext of fetching something where Kastur stood sobbing as he hugged the child. The two stood facing each other as if turned to stone. 'Don't go,' she cried. Much as she tried, she could not conceal her tears. Hari looked from his father to his mother. Mohandas did not speak but kissed both Kastur and Hari. He was struck dumb. He stood there for two minutes till he got a hold over himself. He kissed Kastur again and then he left. Kastur felt abandoned. Anguish rose like a wave. It was not just hard to conceal it, it was impossible.

——***——

The Seashore

Lakshmidas had thought that he would see his brother off safely to the ship headed for England. But the seas were stormy. Mohan was caught between two storms. He carried one from Rajkot within him, where all the faces rose and fell in the waves before his eyes. The other storm stood in the way ahead. Both the storms met at one single point.

Both the brothers were staying at Raliyat's house in Bombay. Her husband Vrindavandas had also heard that the sea was turbulent. He said that it was not safe to travel in such conditions. The other travellers they met also suggested that Mohandas should postpone his travel for some time. Lakshmidas was in a bind as he could not neglect his work for long to stay on in Bombay. The adage of digging a well every day to quench his thirst applied to him fully. So he handed over Mohandas to Raliyat and Vrindavandas and returned to Rajkot. He handed the money over to Vrindavandas.

As soon as Lakshmidas left, there was an unexpected turn of events. The Modh Vaishya Sabha of Bombay issued a decree that Mohandas should cancel his travel to England. The President of the Sabha was related to the Gandhi family.

The fact of the matter was that no Modh had ever crossed the seven seas until now. They believed that to go abroad was an insult to the community and against their religion. It did not end there. Mohandas was ordered to present himself before the Sabha and clear the matter. He did not hesitate and declared the truth. 'I am going abroad to study to be a barrister, with my mother's permission. There has been no barrister among the Modh Vaishyas. I have made a promise to my mother that I will avoid all the things that you fear will pollute me. My vow will protect me.'

Mohandas' assurance was not enough to pacify the Sabha but he was also not one to yield. The Sabha could not conceive of this young boy daring to go against their decree. The Sabha ordered that he be expelled from the community. No Modh was to see him off to the ship. If anybody tried to help him, he would be punished too. Although Mohandas was isolated he was not to be deterred. The punishment was applicable to his entire family. Raliyat and Vrindavandas would be affected immediately. The first dilemma was whether to allow Mohandas to stay with them. The second decision was a real trial. The money from selling Kastur's jewellery for the expenses of the journey and the stay in London was with Vrindavandas, left in good faith by Lakshmidas. Lakshmidas had left a note. Vrindavandas could not give it directly to Mohandas after the decree. This was a catastrophic bolt from the blue. He circumvented this by taking a loan from a *Patwari* family friend. Vrindavandas gave the money in safekeeping with him, to that family. Although this was tantamount to helping Mohandas, it prevented

Vrindavandas and Raliyat from being in the direct line of fire from the *biradari*. Mohandas held his peace but he felt that this was akin to twisting your arm round your head to hold your nose, rather than simply holding it from the front.

Mohandas set off to England on the ship *SS Clyde* on 4 September 1888. Kasturbai and Harilal were left behind to wait for three years. Kasturbai did not know all that he had to endure. She prayed silently for his safe passage.

——***——

Battling loneliness

Being directly related to Mohan, Kasturbai and Hari were equal recipients of the punishment meted out to him. Hari was a child. What did he know of banishment from the community? But Kastur would go to her natal home to fill the emptiness of Mohan's departure. She knew that the emptiness of the absence of a partner was not one of a place or a thing, but the absence of love. She would be seized by an acute feeling of being a sinner while she was living in her natal home. Having been expelled by the Modh Vaishya Sabha meant that because of her, both her natal or marital home could plunge into a crisis. The Kapadias were also Modh Vaishyas. Until her husband returned, these were the two places where she could live with her son. When her tension would reach unbearable proportions, she would stay afloat thinking of all that he had endured, so she had to bear up too. In both the homes, the family was careful not to make any reference to the expulsion. When Kastur would go to her own family with Hari, the other relatives would almost stop visiting. It was the same situation in her marital home. No sooner did Mohandas board the ship than people began to avoid the route to the Diwan family's home. After Karamchand, there was nobody else who commanded that measure of respect.

Kasturbai's nights were lonely and not restful. If the Modh Jati Sabha issued another decree, she would have to take action. She had heard Mota Bhaiya, her elder brother-in-law say that Moniya's wife and her son were their responsibility. She had taken heart from his words. But she was acutely conscious of the sword that hung by a mere thread over both the families. In spite of having money to go to London, Mohandas had to take a loan from somebody else. What if he hadn't managed to get it? What sort of *biradari* was this that pushed one's own out into the swift current and believed it was safeguarding religion? Your close relatives turn into aliens. Hari's father did not even have enough money to come back to Rajkot. What would he have done? Thank God for the friend who gave the loan. Our own people forced us to beg for help. The loan was repaid but what about the loss of self respect? It will always be said that if the *Patwari* family had not helped Mohandas Gandhi, could he have become a barrister? A man can emerge unscathed if buried under mud, but is that true of an obligation? As she tossed and turned, tears would seep from the corners of her eyes. They helped cool the heat inside. In the morning, after Hari woke up, it would all change. The night felt strange and now the day was her own through Hari. She could forget everything else, when she looked at him. A child lives for everybody, whether they are sad or happy. He breathes life into the others. For him, even a snake turns into a rope. Kasturbai would look out at the world through Hari's eyes. A toy ...

London was mentioned often, in both households. Everybody knew the city through Mohandas. Listening to imaginary stories about London, it became a magical place for Kastur. Somebody said that the women in London were enchantresses. They turned men from India into talismans and wore them around their necks. These symbolic speculations were not designed for comfort. Although Kastur did not fully believe all this, the dust of doubt did come and settle on her heart. But she would be reminded of the conviction that shone on Mohandas's face when he was taking his vow before Putliba and her doubts would recede. However, doubts are like evergreen weeds – the more you cut, the faster they multiply. An enchanted world took shape inside Kastur as she listened to all the speculations. Here she looked for the Mohan she knew. Where would he be found on this map? Was he alone or with somebody? What would he be doing? Her imagination sparked further speculations. The glimpse of Mohan in her imaginary world evanesced as quickly as it appeared. Her heart was always questing for him. He was visible to her in the house, rather than in London. He was right here. Now where was he? She would wonder what had come over her. She would haul herself out of this enchanted well with the help of Hari. She would hug him tight and sit quietly.

Kastur knew she and Hari were totally dependent on her elder brother-in-law. He had said that Mohan's family was his responsibility. Responsibility implies dependence. She gradually began cutting down on her expenses. She set aside all her little habits from her girlhood. She could have asked her sisters-in-law for clothes if she liked. Without ornaments, dressing up in fine clothes felt a bit odd anyway. She cut down on her food also, just like her mother-in-law. She would eat only after everybody else had eaten. Every now and then, she would fast. If somebody caught her out, she would say she ate late or that she was not hungry. Her effort was directed towards Hari getting sufficient food of his choice. She nursed the desire to cook golpapri or any other sweet that did not spoil and send it for Mohan. Mohan was fond of golpapri. Her heart would well up at the thought.

A lack of dialogue continued between Mohandas and Kasturbai. There were no phones. Husbands and wives did not correspond with each other. For Kastur, it was impossible. But often, as she lay down, she carried on a one-sided conversation with him believing that her voice was heard by him. But this was not possible. Imagine that you are a branch of a tree and I am a restless bird. Hari would be sleeping next to her. He was the medium of the conversation. 'Do you know that Hari understands few words now? But how would you know? After some days, he will ask, where is my bapu? What does he look like? When will he come? What will I say to him? I cannot give away the Mohan who lives inside of me or else what will I be left with? I know that he has greater right over you than me. You had tried hard to convince me to study but I followed my own whims. It was my fault, but both of us were lax … If I had listened to you, I would have been able to read and write letters at least. I could have waved one in front of Hari and said, here is a letter from your father. Children need a basis for surmise. Many a times a letter can make a person appear, even if they are abroad. I am innocent of that pleasure. A letter going out, brings another in. Who is going to send a letter to an illiterate like me? A wall. You can't see through it or tip toe to take a peek above it. A wall that is human or a human who is a wall. Ba is illiterate like me. She knows all about dharma and karma. She can rattle off shlokas for everything. She has tested out whatever she has heard. Mohan writes to his elder brother only. There was one time he sent a letter in my name to his friend Sheikh's address. Ba told her elder son, tell Moniya that he should not send letters for *Bahu* to his address. After that there were no letters. My elder sister-in-law would inform me if a letter came. Sometimes she would even give me the letter. I used to say, I cannot read and write. What should I do with this? What is it worth for me? She would say this is not about measuring worth. Just keep it. I would put it away carefully. Once it fell out of my blouse and I was the butt of jokes for days in the house.'

***

During the second year, Mohandas sent his photograph to the family. Ba personally came to Kastur with the picture. Kastur was abashed. She did not lift her gaze to look at the photograph. 'Why are you feeling so shy? It is your husband's picture who is across the seven seas. Take a look and tell me if you like it,' admonished Ba. Kastur stole a quick glance.

'Why are you taking such a stealthy look? It is your husband, not some stranger.' Ba's voice was louder this time.

She was forced to raise her eyes and she was astonished. Without a *pagri*, is this my husband? Black foreign attire, white stiff fan-like shirt collar and a floral bow tied at the neck somewhat like a moustache. It was all strange. This is Hari's father, she thought, this serious face, shining deep eyes and well combed and parted hair. She had never seen a man dressed in foreign attire before this. As her eyes found his right ear, she was reassured. This photo could only be her Moniya because the ear was larger than normal. She used to wonder, will we ever meet again? Will I recognise him? There was no question of Hari recognising him.

——***——

Mohan's Return

In 1891, Mohandas was returning to his own country. Kastur was all aflutter. What would she do when they came face to face? That photograph of Mohandas was the main reason for her disquiet. Recalling how he looked in the photograph, she was convinced that he had turned from an Indian husband into a foreigner. When he returned, he was a youthful barrister of 22 years. People came to take a look at him. He wore shining clothes of a foreign cut and his face and eyes had the sheen of a foreign education. Mohan had the degree now for which Laily had taunted him in Porbandar when he had sought financial help and had turned his back on him. His uncle had called it a sin. Now he had achieved this through his own efforts, or, Kastur's help had borne fruit. The lustre of her jewellery, now sold, could be seen in Mohandas's face. Laily's humiliating snub had festered inside, all the while when he was in London. He would also remember how Kastur had given up her ornaments without saying a word. But for her, he would have been deprived of such an important experience in his life.

He caught sight of her behind the same door where she had stood with Hari when he had come to say goodbye. Don't go, the words had escaped her like a groan. Mohandas had turned from a Gujarati into a foreign gentleman, in nearly three years of being away. He had turned into somebody else while she remained the same, she thought to herself. But she was not put out. Instead, she was happy that her husband had turned into a Sahib. It was like two people on a race track. One of them raced far ahead while the other one was waiting at the starting point. Why does this happen with women that they remain at the same spot while the man sprints ahead? Mohandas looked so changed on the outside that she could not get a glimpse of the Mohan that she knew. Occasionally she would be touched by a shadow of doubt that people expressed under their breath ... foreign women were enchantresses ... Kastur had wanted to ask Mohandas, did he save anything from what he had taken or had everything turned to leaves like the moneylender's boat in the *Satynarayan Katha.* She said nothing. Instead, one sentence popped out, 'From a Gujju, you've become an Englishman.' 'It is difficult for anybody to change themselves and become somebody else,' was all that he said in return.

Although she knew her husband did not lie, she wondered about the truth of this statement. However, later she understood that her husband had not turned into a foreigner. Not in his speech nor in his lifestyle. Even after such a long sojourn in London, his fabric remained the same. His words revealed that a London education had not erased his religion or his memories of home. Kastur would delight in his accounts of London, narrated to his brothers. Mohandas had honoured his vows to Ba. If she was here, she would have been overjoyed. He had to search high and low for vegetarian food when he reached London. He had survived on fruit, vegetables, milk and porridge and this brought a sob to Kastur's throat. While she was gorging here, her husband had been running from pillar to post, hungry and thirsty. She heard him tell Bade Bhaiya that after five months of missing home, he had found himself on the doorstep of a vegetarian hotel. This warmed her heart. That was the day that he ate to his heart's content after a long time. Kastur was hungry for such stories. She was reminded of what her mother used to say. A *grahani* is satiated only when her husband and children are well fed.

Mohandas had made many white people a part of his life and turned them vegetarian, like Jains and Vaishnavs. After that he never had to go hungry.

***

It was at the start of the year that Mohandas had to return to India when that terrible tragedy occurred. The whole family was in shock and even outsiders were plunged into grief. Pultiba suddenly took ill. She was the fulcrum of the family. Even while Diwan Sahib was alive, it was she who managed the house. A leaf could not stir without her approval. Nobody could have imagined that she would be gone so suddenly. Everybody believed that she would be fully recovered, by the time Mohandas returned. While they all waited for Mohandas to come back, she left. Kastur felt darkness gathering in front of her eyes. It was she who held Kastur so dear, before and after Mohandas' departure to London. Ba could not leave without setting eyes on Moniya was what everybody believed. She loved all of them, but Moniya was the apple of her eye. Scarcely a day passed when Ba would not mention him. Sometimes it would be for his devotion to Diwanji, at others, for his many fears. Remember when Rambha gave him the *Ramnam* Mantra … He would chant that mantra for all situations, especially at night. She swore by his truthfulness. When she would ache to see her Moniya, Kastur would put Hari in her lap. He would become Moniya for her. When Moniya had been unable to keep the secret of having sold some gold from a bangle, he wrote to his bapu to confess. Ba was narrating this when Karsan checked her. She rounded on him saying he had not sold the gold for himself, it was to save Karsan from a debtor …

Putliba had been patiently waiting for her younger son to come back. The last incident she narrated was from his school where he had spelt some words in the English dictation wrong. The teacher had made signs for him to copy the correct spellings from the child sitting in the next row. Moniya had not copied the words, even though he could see that child's notebook. When the teacher mentioned this to Diwanji, he had said, 'Masterji, you should consider yourself fortunate to have a student like this.'

After Putliba departed, the family had to decide whether Mohandas should be informed about this in London. Opinion was divided. Mohan was taking his exams. His elder brother felt that if he did not inform him, he would not be able to look him in the eye. Ba loved Mohandas the most. Karsan maintained that he was due to return shortly, so the news could be held off until then. The women believed that Mohandas would be the worst affected by the news of Ba's death. When Kastur was asked, she said, 'When you all know that Hari's father would be heartbroken, if he decides to forego his exams, all the hard work of three years will have been for nothing.' Everybody concurred with her. Even though it was a sin to conceal this from him, it would save three years of hard work.

***

Ba perhaps loved Kasturbai as much as she loved Mohandas. She was Kastur's greatest support. Kastur felt isolated after she went. She knew that she would miss her affection and loving guidance. She was deeply grieved. It was Ba's wish to see Hari sit in his father's lap. Hari will also get to know his father. But what will become of Mohandas when he finds out that just few days before his return, Ba had gone? Will he turn away from his son? What did his first child think, in the few days that he lived? Kastur's heart would quail at these thoughts. The only option she had was to live with all these doubts and fears, and quietly wait for Mohandas.

***

It was the month of August and the weather was changing. *SS Assam* brought Mohan via sea to Bombay where Lakshmidas waited for him at the port. He had purposely gone alone to receive Mohan. He wanted to spare any other family member from the wrath of the caste assembly. Until Mohan alighted, he paced about furiously. He could not imagine how he would face Mohan's queries about Ba. The other big concern was that his brother was arriving all westernised. The photo sent to Ba was ingrained in his mind. What would be his attitude towards his wife and child? How will the other family members take to him? All this was still manageable, but if he did not accede to the wishes of the caste assembly, the entire family would be expelled. However, when he saw Mohan alight in his new garb, Lakshmidas could scarcely contain his pride. His younger brother was arriving as a barrister. The first among Modh Baniyas! Then the familiar apprehension – would he be able to adjust to Indian ways? This was also Kastur's concern. As soon as he got down, he bent down to touch his elder brother's feet. Both pairs of eyes were wet with tears. Lakshmidas was relieved. He was as he had been. There were some superficial changes but inside was the same *khaddar* that Ba used to weave.

In the kitchen, there was a tradition of sitting on a low stool and eating in a *thali* with *katoris*. Perhaps he would want to change that. Lakshmidas had told his wife Nandkunwarben that she should buy china dishes and a table and chair for his convenience. Kastur had protested saying that he had eaten sitting on the floor all his life, so what could have changed in three years?

The first question that Mohandas asked was, 'How is Ba?'

Lakshmidas had dreaded this moment. He fell silent. Mohandas waited for a whole day to get an answer and then repeated the question. Lakshmidas could see that he could no longer put off giving an answer. He could not speak as his throat closed up. He said slowly, 'Ba knew that you would come back to India after your exams. Ever since she got your photograph, she could hardly wait to see you. She had begun to keep poor health in the winter.'

Mohandas looked stricken. He asked urgently, 'How is she now?'

Lakshmidas tried to control himself but ultimately could not hold back his sobs. There was nothing more for Mohandas to hear. He put a hand on his elder brother's shoulder and said, 'Let's go.' He walked ahead. Mohandas maintained his composure as if nothing had happened. This was the greatest punishment for Lakshmidas. Why wouldn't he say anything or ask any more questions? If only he would. Perhaps this blow was worse than the death of his father. There was no outward manifestation of his grief but what was happening inside? Until a volcano erupts, you have no idea of what has been fractured deep within.

The next day, at an opportune moment, Lakshmidas said, 'Ba's last wish was that you should return to the *biradari.* For three years, the family has been treated like untouchables. Kastur has been moving between Porbandar and Rajkot furtively. We were faced with some real shocks when we lost Ba. We had to give up many formalities after her cremation. Many family friends who loved Ba and she fully returned their affection, did not even attend the cremation. If something like this could happen to Ba … who was so pure, heaven knows what may happen to the rest of us. The entire family is worried that if this caste boycott continues, it will affect your future as a lawyer.' Mohandas heard his elder brother out in silence.

Lakshmidas had met the elders in the community to find out what could be done to atone for the sin of crossing the seven seas and end the caste expulsion.

Mohandas agreed to honour Ba's last wish and to give respect to the wishes of the elders in the caste, 'It does not matter to me whether I remain within the caste or not. It is not likely to be of any importance in the future either. I lived alone in London. I lived in the midst of people and they were my family and society. But because this was Ba's final wish, I will do what is needed, even against my own wishes. I also don't want my other family members to be harassed on my account.'

He had to go through three stages of purification. Both the brothers went straight to Nasik from Bombay. Mohandas entered the holy waters of the Godavari and took a full dip to atone for his sins. He did not feel that the dip in the Godavari was *karmakaand*. In Rajkot, both the brothers, Lakshmidas and Karsan, had to host an atonement meal. All the elders of the Modh caste took part. The third stage was difficult. Mohandas and his wife, much against his wishes, had to carry out the leftovers of the guests. He felt as if he were standing before Ba and they were both carrying out her orders. Kastur neither cried nor did she shy away from that chore. She liked standing by her husband. She had her ceremonial veil but she was standing by her husband who had returned after three years. They had not been able to meet until now. It was an anxious wait.

***

How are you?

Kastur had got news of Mohandas reaching Bombay. But she did not know that both the brothers had gone directly to Nasik from there. She waited for Mohan eagerly. Until he arrived, she counted every day, hour and minute. Every moment felt like the one when he would arrive. She grew weary and hopeless as time passed. She would only say to Hari, he still hasn't come, he must be about to come … these words helped to bolster her patience. Hari may not have seen Bapu, but he knew the word alright. His chanting Bapu-Bapu made her restless. Why had the two of them gone to Nasik? Nobody at home could give an answer.

Kastur felt that if they lived together, they would get to know and understand each other. Until now, they had stayed together in name alone. Diwan Sahib went and then when his son came, Mohan went like he was a bird of passage who had stopped by only for a momentary rest. Ba had shown her that photograph and she had felt this was Mohan's new avatar. Since his appearance had changed, he must be changed too. Maybe her memory was stuck in his heart somewhat like some leftover milk stuck to the side of a *kadhai*. When she would think of Hari, her eyes would well up. She would ask herself, is it possible for a father to not remember his son? Maybe just this much that his son was more than three years old and, he must be walking by now. Whom did he resemble? Everybody seeks to find a resemblance. Does he look more like his mother or his father? In the photograph, Hari's father's face looked quite changed. His speech must also have changed. Three years is a long time. The world can transform, in this much time.

Kastur and Mohandas had both turned twenty two. They had been married nine years. They had stayed together for four. Those four years were also broken up. Of these four, one year had been spent in her parents' home. What remained had been sacrificed at the altar of her husband's arrogance and anger because of Sheikh. We women just bear up; we don't talk, we listen and absorb. She had seen Putliba also just bear up.

***

After Mohan's atonement, they felt that they were normal human beings again. A normal human being is one who remains normal in abnormal circumstances. The sword hanging over the heads of her in-laws and natal family was finally gone. The fear of its dropping at any time was gone. Although she could see its deadly steely glint all the time, her courage did not desert her nor did she lose hope. Being ousted from the *biradari* was like suffering imprisonment without a lock and key. A lone woman and child. Whenever Ba was upset, she would say that caste expulsion did not exempt you from caste allegiance; it just felt like being on death row.

Her longing was finally over now that Mohandas was back. Loneliness had plagued her through long nights. She was diverted only by Hari's stirring in his sleep. Something fell Plop! In still waters. Some ripples and then silence. Mohandas's return was a huge and joyful event. His presence sometimes threw into relief, all the loneliness that she had felt. Kastur began to feel that he had not changed. She was also happy that the loss of the first child had receded and he was fully drawn to Hari. He would play with him all the time. He had won the hearts of Hari and all the other children.

But this halcyon period was not to last. The same old restlessness began to surface. Kastur was worried. Was it the memories of his London stint? Later she learnt, it was because of the changes that were imminent. Mohandas was approving of the table-chair and china that Lakshmidas had arranged. He wanted to go a step further. He initiated a change in the menu. Porridge, oatmeal and cocoa made an appearance at breakfast. He wanted Hari and the other children to have an English upbringing. They should also grow up as strong and fearless as the English. He bought shoes for all the children and instructed them not to go barefoot. Although Kastur had grown up believing that children grow well, playing in the mud. He would take the children to villages nearby after they got ready, so that they got to know their own surroundings better. There was a proper class in the morning where they had to exercise. The mothers were pleased; at least they got some respite from the kids.

***

Orders began to figure in Kastur's life also. The studies that had been started after marriage were resumed. Kastur was surprised. She could not understand the point of all the rote memorising at this age. Mohandas was insistent, Kastur indifferent. Their friction had resurfaced. Mohandas's baseless jealousy and doubts and needless allegations had begun again. She refused to accept them. Tension and arguments were back. In such a situation, husbands behave like the police, either toe the line or else face the music. Kastur would wonder to herself, has he not changed at all? He was a schoolboy then, but now he has returned as a barrister from London ... Does a barrister have only two jobs, to forcibly educate his wife and to keep a watch over her movements? His accusations grew wilder and it was difficult to give credence to them, now or any time in the future.

Everybody in the household was worried about Mohandas. Kastur understood her elder sisters-in-law's concerns. Lakshmidas and Karsan had been fully responsible for her until he was studying. Now he had gone as far as London to study and returned a barrister. How much money had been spent? All of Kastur's ornaments had been sold. Both the brothers had pitched in, according to their means. It was assumed that after a London education, you knew English and you could do anything. Everybody wanted him to use his education and put an end to all their collective troubles. Kastur knew that Lakshmidas' condition was quite precarious. She also wanted Mohan to start sharing his burden. But Mohandas remained blithely unaware of all this. He seemed to have little sense of his responsibilities. He was not even trying to acquire any professional position. All his attention was focused on Kastur. Either in attachment or criticism. Both of these were self contradictory. One night when he was in a loving mood, she took courage to ask, 'Do you know the extent of debt on Bade Bhaiya because of your foreign education? And all the money spent to keep up appearances during your stay in London? The changes in the house have also led to expenses. Now he needs your help.' Kastur had never spoken so openly before this. Mohandas was furious. Not just furious, he was shaken to the core. The consequence of this was that the next day, without saying a word, he put Kastur with Hari, on a train to Porbandar. All through the journey she wondered whether she had made a mistake by drawing his attention towards the financial condition of the family. A voice inside her said, no, not at all. This was her duty. She felt ill used but she stayed quiet and equable. Was it a sin to draw attention to the right thing that she and her child had been shown the door?

On his return from London, Mohandas had been amazed to see Kasturbai. Their eyes met for the first time in three years. She had become a woman of rare beauty at the age of twenty-two. For the first time he felt a pang at staying away from her for so long. She was really lovely. She had always been attractive but now she had blossomed like never before. Her soft and peachy skin, big eyes framed by dark lashes, her attractive frame wrapped in a dark sari, her long and well coiffured dark hair made her a treat for sore eyes. All her mannerisms were dignified and stately. There was music in the sound of her anklets. Mohandas felt that anybody would be proud to receive her love and surrender. He, who had battled loneliness abroad for so long, before he tackled his responsibilities, he had a right to take pleasure in her company. He wanted to forget everything for a while to enjoy his wife.

When Mohandas evicted Kastur and Hari unceremoniously, shortly after his return from London,

Kastur left without uttering any protest. She had learnt to take his anger in her stride. This was also a way of protesting. The family was also aghast at his behaviour of sending away his wife and child, after three years of separation. Nobody had the courage to ask the London returned barrister any uncomfortable questions. But Kastur turned this incident into a welcome chance to meet her parents and brothers. She turned her husband's anger into a God-given opportunity for Hari to meet his maternal grandparents. Travel was much faster and convenient too, compared to the last time. There was a railway line between Rajkot and Porbandar. Travellers had been freed from the need to travel by camel cart. Kastur understood very well that the problem was not with her, but with Mohandas. She took this break at her maternal home, not as a punishment, but as a holiday. She would have time to think about her child and also about her husband's low tolerance. Knowing Mohandas's attachment to her and the child, she knew he would call her soon. And that is exactly what happened. Within a month, she had been called back. Kastur did not complain or cavil and went back to Rajkot with Hari.

Things seemed to have changed when she returned. Perhaps her exile had been for the better. No class at night, no suspicion and no arguments. There was a bridge of gravitas between them. Mohan opened up his heart to Kasturba for the first time. Kastur felt that his words were as much for himself, as for her. What Kastur had said had touched him somewhere. He was seriously considering options for the future. He was considering starting his practice at Rajkot. But there was also the dilemma of becoming a laughing stock – studied in London and landed at Rajkot. He also believed that the Law he studied in London was useless in Indian courts. Kastur found this odd. How could somebody who studied in London for so many years not know the Law? 'What are you saying? Someone who has studied in London knows everything; that is what everybody believes.'

Mohandas glanced at his wife. She had said this out of curiosity. If she had said it earlier, Mohandas would have lost his temper. He said seriously, 'I don't even know as much as a legal clerk. The Law, as applied here, is partly from statute and the rest is at will, in an arbitrary way.'

Mohandas had done deep study of Common Law, Roman Law, etc. He believed that the Mukhtar or village head, or his elder brother Lakshmidas knew far more about Hindu and Muslim Law than he did. If he practised, it would be nothing short of betraying his clients.

Kastur may have been illiterate, but she understood her husband's dilemma. She tried to encourage him by saying he was lucky because Bade Bhaiya was with him. Share your problems with him. Take his counsel. Her words struck home. He shared with Lakshmidas all that he had told Kastur. He also shared his plans for the future. Between the brothers, a consensus emerged that Mohandas should go to Bombay to practice. It was also decided that Kastur would stay on in Rajkot with the child. She would join him when he found a house. Kastur was going to be separated from her husband again. But she understood his difficulties. She also understood that she would have to give up as much, if his dreams were to be fulfilled. He had to become a successful lawyer. He was sent to Bombay to make his fortune. This time Kastur's good wishes were with him. But she had concealed some personal news from him for two reasons. The first was that she did not want his attention to be diverted. He should settle down well, in a new place. She also wanted to be sure that she was pregnant.

Mohandas rented a room in Bombay. He employed a cook. But the cook was so inexperienced that he had to cook himself. First the cooking, then walking miles to get to the High Court ... the expenses were borne by both the brothers. The debts were mounting. Therefore he cut down his expenses. Just then, he found out about Kastur's pregnancy, through a letter from Lakshmidas. Although this was happy news in itself, the effect it had on Mohandas was that since there was going to be an addition to the family, he must earn more. Right now, it was difficult to support himself. Weeks would pass and he would go empty handed and that is how he would return. He took on a part time job in a boy's school to teach English. It paid him seventy five rupees monthly. It was better than nothing.

Although nobody said anything to Kastur, sometimes inadvertently somebody would make a remark ... Mohandas went as far as London to study but luck did not favour him. Kastur wanted to contradict them saying, you never know when luck can turn, but she would keep quiet instead. She knew both the brothers loved Mohan dearly, but now his idle status and no earnings was disturbing. When he was studying in London, it was a matter of pride, and even then, she was dependent on the brothers-in-law. Now her husband was in the country, but it felt as if he had not returned. Many a times she would wonder, could you feel your husband's return, only through his income?

Then one day the message came from his elder brother that he could not bear the expense of his staying in Bombay. Come back. A horse is controlled by reins made of leather but a man is held fast with the reins of money. Come and practice in Rajkot, he wrote. It may be that you may have to make do with writing petitions for some time. Lakshmidas was a lawyer with a small practice but he had good contacts. He could get him jobs relating to documentation. Mohandas returned to Rajkot under the shadow of defeat. Kastur was subdued, compared to the enthusiasm at the time of his going. She took heart thinking that he would be there for the second child's birth.

***

The second child of Kastur and Mohan was born in October 1892. He was healthy and bonny. It is said that the birth of a healthy baby brings joy and peace. The family celebrated and sweets were distributed. Ceremonies associated with birth were held. Presents were exchanged. The worries that Kastur had about Mohandas were temporarily suspended with the arrival of the little one. Hari was happy and busy with the new arrival but Kastur had to be careful. Mohandas was also more relaxed, staying in Rajkot. His office was ready. He started getting a lot of work of writing memoranda and petitions. Lakshmidas's friends and others began sending work his way. Making briefs for other barristers was also something that Mohandas was doing. He earned about ₹300. Kastur was happy that she was not dependent on anybody but could finally do something for them instead. Hari's mischievous ways and the charm of the little baby kept everybody busy. Compared to Hari, he was a quiet baby. But Kastur's peace of mind was not to last long. One day there were words exchanged between Lakshmidas and Mohandas about a British bureaucrat. Kastur was very hurt. Bade Bhaiya was not familiar with the ways of the Whites and when Mohandas tried to explain, tempers ran high. Kastur could not side with her husband nor was she in a position to say anything to her elder brother-in-law.

When Mohandas was in London, Lakshmidas had been appointed the secretary to the prince of Porbandar, on the recommendation of his Uncle Tulsidas. Due to an increase in his salary, there was financial stability in the family. Everybody grew hopeful that when the prince would be crowned, their fortunes would look up. But the prince stealthily removed some diamonds from the royal treasury. Lakshmidas did not get to know. Just then a new political agent had arrived and people whispered canards in his ear. When questioned, the prince said that he had done this on the advice of his secretary. Lakshmidas's services were terminated. The financial stability turned out to be a ruinous mirage. Everybody in the house was in shock. Lakshmidas grew very quiet and his wife was stunned. Kastur had to handle all the work. She had to look after everybody and raise her children.

Lakshmidas knew that Mohandas had been meeting Charles Olvent, the new political agent, in London on social occasions. They were on friendly terms. He wanted Mohan to meet Olvent and get his job back for him. Mohandas tried to explain that they were acquainted but could hardly be called friends. White people don't react favourably to requests in such circumstances. Lakshmidas was offended and he spoke quite forcefully about it. He felt that Mohandas was avoiding helping him. Mohandas was in a dilemma – his elder brother was asking for a favour for the first time, how could he turn him down? He appeared before the British agent travelling from Rajkot to Porbandar. He had not forgotten the encounter with Laily. When he made reference to their meeting in London, the agent cut in, 'Well Gandhi, I hope that you have not come to misuse our acquaintance?'

As Mohandas mentioned Lakshmidas, he interjected, 'Your brother is a crook. He will get no work in Porbandar. He should put forth his case as per procedure. You may leave.' When Mohandas requested him for permission to put all the facts of the case before him, he called the *chaprasi* and asked him to throw Mohandas out. Who knew that the man he was throwing out would be the reason for all of them to be thrown out, one day.

When Mohandas recounted the whole incident to his elder brother in Rajkot, he was so upset that he could not speak a word. This was Mohandas' second experience of being humiliated by a White. He wanted to avenge the insult. He went so far as to meet Sir Firozeshah Mehta, a senior lawyer and leader to confer on a legal route. Firozeshah

Mehta told him that Indians had to put up with all kinds of injustice. Take this insult honourably. Mohandas felt restless for days. Olvent's words pricked him constantly like stubble that appears on a shaved face.

It was Kastur who said, 'Neither the court nor we can do anything. Hold on to it in your heart and bring it out when the time is right. When even Raja Ravan had to go, do you think the Whites won't?'

——***——

The Letter from South Africa

A letter suddenly arrived in 1893.

Nobody had expected it nor hoped for something like this. Everybody was sunk in despair. Despair is like holding darkness inside. Being dependent on others, Kastur's darkness seemed the pitch dark of a moonless night. Mohandas's idleness was pushing the entire household towards a deep well of economic insecurity. The letter seemed to be a ray of light that enters through a tiny crack. While Kastur found some reason to be happy, there was also the possibility of uncertainty in her life. But she knew that it was on the stability of the husband that the possibility of her stability as his wife rested.

A Muslim family friend was a shareholder in a large professional concern in South Africa called *Dada Abdullah & Company*. It worked as a ship freight company in Porbandar. The company's business flourished in South Africa. Dada Abdullah's elder brother looked after the work in Porbandar and he was a friend of Lakshmidas. He knew of Mohandas's unemployment as well as his capabilities. He wrote to Dada Abdullah. Dada Abdulllah felt that the company would benefit if he joined the business. The company was embroiled in a case of forty thousand pounds in South Africa and many of the documents concerning the case were in Gujarati. Their lawyer, Mr Baker, did not know the language. Dada felt that Mohandas could explain the contents of the Gujarati documents to Mr Baker. Being a barrister he would also understand the legal aspects. Dada Abdullah wrote in a letter that Mohandas would get £105 per annum. His passage to and fro, his board and lodge would be the company's responsibility. The company would send a first class ticket for his passage by ship. Other than the annual salary, most of the other conditions were similar to a *girmitiya* contract. The duration of the contract, instead of the customary five years, was for a year, which could be extended by mutual consent. The contract appeared like a welcome anchor in Mohandas's precarious condition and it also seemed a beacon of hope for the financially straitened circumstances of the Gandhi family. Because the company was bearing all of Mohandas's expenses, a major part of the salary would come to Lakshmidas. There would be financial relief for a whole year. For Mohandas, it was a chance to see another part of the world. There were Coloured subjects and a White government, both here and there. The experiences of the two countries were as dissimilar as they were similar. That desire to take on the English, for which he had secretly consumed meat on his friend Sheikh's suggestion, could be tested out there too. On his return to India, Mohandas had felt that he did not know Hindu Law and Muslim Law. He was as clueless about South African laws. The difference was that he was unemployed here whereas he would at least be employed there.

Kastur was once again faced with the challenge of living with the children, without her husband. When she found out about this letter, her mind was made up to be up for this challenge. This time, she would not feel like a dependent. She had learnt that an unemployed husband meant that the wife was forced to live the life of an interloper. Although her elder brother-in-law tried to ensure that she and the children did not feel this way, there were limits to his patience. Mohandas was also going through a curious experience. First he had to leave Kastur and Hari to go to London to study. This time he would have to leave the new baby whom he loved playing with. The hardest part was to leave Kastur again and again. He often wondered if Kastur must think that if he had to leave her repeatedly, why did he marry her in the first place? All the love he professed felt like a sham. Why couldn't he provide them with stability? Suddenly Kastur would appear before him as if she were standing on the far shore. Mohandas was astonished at her fortitude. How does she find balance between her expectations and disappointments? Whenever he put this question to her, she gave an odd reply. She would say that expectations could turn into disappointments, but they stay connected to hope. Yesterday she was upset that he would leave and she would be left behind, but today she accepted it as fate. Was it because Mohandas explained to her that £105 of his salary would come to Lakshmidas and she would not remain a dependant? Her two children would be supported by her husband's earnings. This gave her reason to live and hope. She knew that he was going only for a year. They would all be together after that. Kastur chafed at the thought of her husband being not just the most capable person in the family, but in all of Rajkot; all the hopes of his family being pinned on him; and he had not found his own niche in all these years. When would they find stability?

For all these many years, she had lived with her self-respect and notions of self-reliance intact, because she felt that the debt owed to his brothers on account of his studies would be paid up. She was still optimistic. There was a basis for her self-respect again. Mohandas was sure to succeed abroad and would repay the debt. The day came when Kastur and the two children went to see him off on the train to Bombay. The second child was as young and clueless as Hari had been at the time of the London sojourn. The Arabian Sea and the ship setting sail to South Africa … all of Kastur's hopes … were seen floating on the waves ahead.

——***——

The South African Sea Shore

A month later Mohandas alighted at the Eddington port in Durban to see a clean beach and bougainvillea blossoming in profusion. He was pleased. But just an hour later he heard the Whites throw taunts at Dada Abdullah and realised that everything was not as it seemed initially. The darkness of racism was everywhere. Dada Abdullah was among the prominent traders here. Mohandas knew that life would not be easy. This thought turned into bitter experience after a few days. He was evicted and thrown off the First Class compartment of a train because Blacks could not travel in that class. This experience was akin to a wake-up call to his destiny, to what his future had foreordained. He was not inclined to share this incident with his family and rob them of their peace of mind. Although, a little voice had whispered, Go Back! But there rose another, challenging and exhorting him to oppose racism. He felt Kastur marching in tandem. Kastur had turned up here too? Many successive experiences only sharpened this feeling. Kastur only found out much later. How she wished she had been there with him …

Mohandas wrote to Lakshmidas that he would surely return after a year. This only deepened the furrows on his forehead. After some time came a letter, the people here held him in such regard, they don't want to let him go. The first letter had worried the brother, the second worried Kastur. Why had he written this? She kept quiet. The third letter revealed that Dada Abdullah had fixed the date for his farewell. This news had opposing effects on Lakshmidas and Kastur. Wife and children were happy … But ultimately everything went topsy-turvy. The issue of voting rights loomed large before the *girmitiyas.* Some leading Indians, who had voting rights until now, were to be robbed of them. It was difficult to carry on this fight without Mohandas. He wanted Mohandas to stay for a month and guide the protest. His expenses would be borne by the traders jointly. Mohandas decided to forego payment for his expenses but agreed to do the work. Lakshmidas looked remarkably tension free because of this. He knew it was difficult for a lawyer to extricate himself from such matters. Kastur and the children, or rather Hari, felt that Mohandas was breaking his promise of coming back after a year. Kastur's parting began to look like a long one. She felt darkness gathering before her eyes. However, she pondered over it and decided that a person with an uncertain future could hardly be expected to keep his promise of coming home. His destiny is to face the present circumstances.

***

For weeks she assured her children that Bapu will come back soon. She had to see to them as much as she had to keep up her own spirits. When it became inevitable that Mohandas had to stay on in South Africa to get justice for the *girmitiyas*, Kastur found herself with two warring emotions. One was akin to Lakshmidas' state of relief that she would not have to be beholden to her *jeth-jethani's* benevolence. The other made her question what was it that was going to keep him away, from hearth and home, in an unknown land? On balance, she was happy that finally he was getting recognition and respect for his work that he had not got in this country. Respect may not be like money but family members also divide it up amongst themselves, in different ways. He was helping the exploited in a distant land. Bade Bhaiya's household would be taken care of, in much the same way as he looked after ours. There would be protection from the barbs of sympathy and sarcasm. Sometimes they are more painful than hunger.

All these things could give her satisfaction but not relief from worry ... They had stayed together for about four years. It was an incessant saga of meetings and partings. Even so, the story of his success after many failures was giving her the strength to bear up. The big worry was the effect on her children for being away from their father. Will they not grow up thinking that a person appears in the Gandhi household like a guest and then departs? A father earns his title by his presence, the same as a mother.

Hari understood that somebody would appear for some time, play with him, sing, take him out and by the time he could be a father, he would leave. All his happy memories turn to sadness. By the time of his next arrival, he is a stranger. Perhaps this was the reason Harilal was closer to his uncles, whom he called Bade Bapu and Chhote Bapu. This was a cause for concern for Kastur. She could see that it was not enough to be father and son, continuity of that feeling was essential. The younger son Manilal was in his second year. He was learning to walk and talk a little. He addressed Lakshmidas as Bapu. In Mohandas's absence, Kastur could hardly insist that he say Bade Bapu. In any case, such a small child could not easily say Bade Bapu. Young children change words to suit themselves. All this made Kastur grapple with a barrage of questions. Time lost, can it ever be found again or the occasions that have slipped by, ever be recovered? In the lives of these children, will their father ever return as a complete father? Kastur dealt with such thoughts night and day. She dreamt of a time when she would live with Mohandas and the children in her own house. On some days, this constant tension along with work, wore her out so completely that she even forgot to chant prayers for her husband's safe passage back from South Africa.

——***——

Kasturbai's Vigil

Mohandas's letters would come addressed to Bade Bhaiya. There was an extended absence of dialogue between husband and wife. An absence of communication is a very fertile ground for doubts and questions. Along with questions there are the weeds of suspicion. Some choice bits filtered through her *jethanis* would reach her. Through them she found out that Mohandas had opened his own law office in Durban. She was shocked. Had he decided to live there? Would he even come back? Her heart quailed. Who could she turn to? If she said anything to the *jethanis*, she would be the object of ridicule. They had not suffered the sorrow of parting. The pain of others is like flowing water. Dip your hand, agitate a little and move on. Kasturbai also found out that Mohandas was sending quite a lot of money to Lakshmidas which ensured that the debt incurred for his education would soon be repaid. At least he was shouldering his responsibilities well. There was hardly any talk of debt and scarce money in the household.

There was no mention of calling Kastur and the children. Nor any mention of Mohandas's return. The family was happy as there was a constant supply of money. Her children did not want for anything. Days, nights and months were passing. The day went by in household chores and with the children. Like the refrain of a rosary, thoughts of Mohandas never left her. He was so open and trustworthy ... perhaps a little too much so. Kastur had full faith in God and in him but the worry was constant. How did he live in a strange country, what were his peers like, who looked after him, with whom did he share his worries and disappointments? Was she there in his lonely moments? One day her *jethani* told her that Mohandas had left his crowded small quarters and taken a large well appointed bungalow in an exclusive area of Durban in keeping with his status as a barrister. He has also kept a cook. Since it is a large house, he had his office colleagues also staying there. Being familiar with his urge to be of service to others, this did not surprise her but she did feel a bit odd. Along with Kastur, Mohandas also had a secret desire to have his own house where he could live in the way he liked. Perhaps this is why he kept making houses and then leaving them. First he went to Bhavnagar, then made a home in London, rented a house in Bombay and now had switched houses in South Africa. He lived life on his own terms. Will Kastur be a part of his life? This was the question that nagged her constantly.

***

Suddenly there was news that he was taking leave of absence from work for six months to come to India. He would try to convince Indians to support the struggle of Indians in South

Africa for their freedom. He would also bring his family back with him. Kastur was pleased to hear that for the first time, he had thought to have his family with him. She had some apprehension about how he would take to living with them when he had become used to staying on his own. She was elated and depressed at the thought. At least her children would have their father in their lives. Her imagination beguiled her with images of the children being shy, then hesitantly touching their father and climbing onto his lap at the first signal. This made her smile. They might tease her about how it felt to be in their father's lap. Children find energy in a mother's lap and security in a father's. After three long years, the day dawned when Mohandas alighted on the docks in Bombay. In the months of June-July, when Rajkot burns, the thread of hope united Mohandas with his family.

***

It was the summer of 1899. The heat in Gujarat was at its peak. Kastur did not know how it would be to live with Mohandas after he had failed in India, but had tasted success in South Africa. The children had stood behind the door and peeked at their father. These were moments of eagerness mixed with uncertainty for them as well and it fell to Kasturba's lot to reassure them. It is not easy to stay separated from your husband but it is as difficult to stay with the husband who has been away for years. It is not immediately evident how much his head has turned and at what latitude. Repeated separations and then connecting again are like rising and falling waves in a gulf. The togetherness of few days was pleasurable but also complicated. Extra caution makes you tense. While she was pleased, there were high and low points. Getting past them was hard for both of them.

Happiness can be expressed but grief must be swallowed. It becomes intensely personal like your savings. Not to be opened before family and children. Kastur's happiness was so personal that she would express it only by making Mohandas's favourite foods. But she could not serve him nor watch while he ate. She could not have the pleasure of sitting and eating with him. After Pultiba's demise, the coveted duty of serving the men had passed on to the elder daughter-in-law Nandkunwar. Kastur had to be content with imagining that her message had been conveyed to her husband.

She had a whole world of news to share. All that had happened with her and the children was banked up. The welcome change that she could observe was that everybody addressed Mohandas with respect now. Kastur followed suit. Mohandas had much to say as well. He spoke about South Africa. For the first time, he said that he would take Kastur and the children along. Kasturba had waited a long time for these words. She could hardly decide whether she was excited or gripped by fear at the thought of going to a strange country. He described the new house to her in detail. It was like a dream come true. She was greedy for more but he hardly had any time. He was constantly busy in Rajkot. Either he was writing or meeting people. He would slip into deep sleep while talking to her. When he opened his eyes, he would continue from the point he had left off but by now, Kastur would be asleep. He woke her up less often now. Kastur could not gather courage to wake him up and there was no question of asking him anything. Until her eyes closed again, she would think that this person, lying next to her, was her new partner.

Kastur had seen him in every shade. A boy hell bent on establishing superiority on account of being older, a child scared of school, a serious but uninspired student, a son hurt by the absence of his father, a father deranged by the untimely death of his son, an infatuated lover, an unemployed English speaking young man grappling with a traditional family's needs ... Now he had grown into an intelligent and capable man after the experience of South Africa. It was as if he had found his idiom. Not just Kasturba, all the people around him remarked on this change. Both his sisters-in-law became great supporters. Mohandas would remain quiet, almost as if it was his right to get this regard. He did not say so explicitly but wanted his family members to understand that his work took top priority. Witnessing this, Kastur would be assailed by disquiet. How was she to take her partner who put his work above everything else? The success and prosperity that had earned everybody's respect and the pressure of her own needs made her feel very ambivalent. There loomed a question mark over the prospect of a new life for her children. What would it be like when they reached a new land? The very air, water and language would be changed. They would be dependent for everything on foreign soil.

***

As the clock ticked, the time for leaving for South Africa was getting close. Apprehensions and worries began to hem her in. She would constantly unravel the skeins of their complex web. Her biggest misgiving was that she, who had not stepped a hundred miles out of the radius of Rajkot, how was she to face the challenges of a new country, thousands of miles across the sea? She knew nobody there and there were no comforting circle of relatives to act as a safety net. Her partner was all she had. When you step out is when you realise that a man is free to soar in the sky and perch anywhere at will, whereas a woman is like a caged bird in the house. She looks at her own wings wondering if they will ever spread wide and how would it feel? She will be the household mynah there and would her children stray? When would she meet her father, mother and brothers? All these intensely personal thoughts swirled around her head like dried leaves in a storm. The one thing that kept her spirits up was that at the end of a long arduous journey, she would have her own house. She would be living with her own family. Raliyatben's son was going with them. He was a few months younger to her own first born. Mohandas had told Kastur that Parsis are well regarded in South Africa. She did not understand at the time why he was hell bent upon turning her and the children into Parsis. The Parsi style sari and clothes were a sign of high birth. 'We will have to pay such a high price to stay there! We will have to change our lifestyle.' She burst out but one look from Mohandas was enough for her to know that he was unmoved and implacable.

Kastur and the children were shocked to see how anglicised he was on the ship. He wanted Kastur and the children to wear shoes from the time they got up until bedtime. They were not to remove their shoes even for a minute. Nobody had ever done this in Rajkot. They went about barefoot and sat on the floor. Their feet developed sores and their socks stank. Mohandas walked about on the deck to encourage this habit and made Kastur and the children do the same. He also took note of their posture and style of walking. He constantly gave them orders – keep your neck and back straight, place your feet properly. In the initial days, Kastur felt she was about to fall because of the shoes and the quick pace. They would wait for nightfall to be rid of the shoes and socks. They missed the freedom of Rajkot. There were no such strictures and you could wear what you liked, so long as you observed veiled decorum before the men. You could lie down anywhere from the floor to the bed. You did not have to stick your neck up like a camel, nor were you forced to eat with a knife and fork. There were pewter *thalis* to eat in and you could eat with your fingers. Here even the children were not permitted to use their fingers. The china saucers were so small that not just the children, Kastur too had a tough time gathering all the food together. The eating of meals was such a drill that there was no question of tasting anything, to say nothing of the scolding that accompanied it. Close your mouth when you chew, hold the knife and fork properly, don't make any sounds. Both the children and Kastur were often reduced to tears. Mohandas was like a hawk waiting to pounce on their failings, rather than a partner or a father. To push food down the throat with the help of implements was a trial in itself. Compared to the food at home, this food was like a punishment. For the vegetarians, there was bread and boiled vegetables. The children had never eaten something like this before. Kastur also tired of its blandness. She wanted to reach Durban as soon as possible so that she could cook for everybody. Would that day ever arrive?

***

Durban was only five days away. All of a sudden, there was a terrific clap of thunder and a huge storm was upon them. The waves rolled somewhat like a passive crowd that had been lathi-charged unexpectedly and there was mayhem as if a revolution had struck. Everything on board tossed and turned. It was difficult to tell the ship from the sea. The two seemed to be at loggerheads with each other. The two ships that had sailed placidly one behind the other until now, they were suddenly being tossed about like tiny balls. It was as if the sea had decided to teach these two upstarts a lesson because they had dared to challenge her. The first time travellers were terrified and sought shelter first. They were not thinking about the danger to the whole ship. Everybody was sent down to the hold. People of all faiths prayed. Faced with a common danger, the Gods may have been different but the urgent pleas for help were the same. The travellers fell about, seemingly with no control. Kastur and the children were among the first timers. It was as if the ferocious gusts of wind were bursting in their bellies, as well all over the ship. Other than the sailors, Mohandas was the only passenger who remained unscathed. He sat the children down in the cabin and tried to pacify them. After this, he went to each passenger to bolster their spirits, on the request of the Captain.

***

Kastur held the two children close and pacified them. She was also worried about her partner who was going from person to person, as the ship heaved and pitched. It is only the fearless who can inspire others to live through tough times. She was reminded of a story heard in her childhood. He also peppered his conversations with stories. There was a caravan and a boy was travelling with it. Suddenly there was a thunderstorm. Everybody took shelter under a banyan tree. Lightning seemed to come down repeatedly on the tree and then retreat. Everybody was petrified. They conferred amongst themselves and decided that there was somebody among them, who was attracting the lightning. They decided that all of them would sprint to the nearest tree and run back. Lightning would strike the blighted one and the others would be safe. In the end, only the boy was left. They all said it is only because of him, that lightning was threatening to strike. He is being saved only because of us, they said. When it was his turn to run to the next tree, he refused saying that he was not afraid but he did not want to go. They pushed him out nevertheless. He sprinted away. As soon as he left, lightning struck the tree and they were all charred to death. You are all like that boy. You are all saving each other. Or wouldn't the ship have sunk by now? At times like this, stories that reassure you of divine protection in life are comforting.

Kastur kept telling the children that they would be in Durban very soon. They wanted to go to Bapu. Their hearts were in safekeeping with their mother but for a feeling of safety, they wanted their father. Mohandas had gone to meet the captain. Kastur suffered in isolation. Who was there with whom she could share her travails? Every hour seemed like a lifetime. Who knows when the end might come. The ship rolled uncontrollably. Every roll felt like the last one, before it sank. Kastur believed that they would all drown in the wild storm-tossed sea. If only Mohandas would come, they would be together when they met their end. She could hardly bring herself to think that these children who had barely begun their life would soon meet a watery grave. She suppressed a scream. How can I allow such thoughts? If I survive this time, I will never set foot on a ship again.

Finally, everybody's Gods heeded their prayers. The sky cleared and the sun shone. The shadow of death lifted and life's radiance shone from each face. Hunger, that had been cowering under the fear of death, now demanded the utmost attention. The travellers were overjoyed for having emerged unscathed from the jaws of death. Some seniors offered namaaz to show gratitude. Others bowed their heads to the ground to thank the maker. Some others looked skywards to lock eyes with God. Mohandas, who was called Mr Gandhi by the travellers, set out with the children to stroll around the deserted deck, washed clean by the foamy waves. The children had worn their socks and shoes happily. The other travellers who slowly made their way to the deck were respectfully greeting Mr Gandhi. He, who had left his family to give succour to others. Both the ships, *SS Courtland* and *SS Naderi*, would soon reach port.

The travellers danced spontaneously and it seemed like the dance of life itself. Everybody was feeling the ebb and flow of life within themselves. The waves of the sea seemed so slight in comparison to this. Then suddenly the sea stilled. Before the ships could cast anchor, black and white officials from the health department, swarmed around the ships in small boats. They had an order with official seal that said that no traveller could step off the ship for five days. Under the quarantine requirements in view of the plague in Bombay, the two ships had to be under surveillance of the government. The travellers were as shocked as they had been by the storm at sea. The plague in Bombay had spread two months ago. The hapless travellers on *Courtland* and *Naderi* had to pay for that on the shore of the Indian Ocean in South Africa, so many days later.

Mohandas, also known as Mr Gandhi, was busier than ever. He set about trying to reduce tensions among the travellers. Indoor games were organised. Gandhi took part along with his children. It was also Christmas Day. The Gandhi family and other cabin travellers were invited by the ship officials. Gandhi spoke in English and called Christianity one of the foremost religions of the world. Kasturbai could not understand anything. He held forth on the importance of peace and non-violence. He held that western civilisation put forth beliefs and practices contrarian to Christian faith and this civilisation was the regressor of Christian faith. Kastur, meanwhile, was grappling with a sense of foreboding of another storm.

***

After the Christmas day celebrations, the duration of the quarantine was extended. This information was the last straw for Kasturba and the children. Soon it became clear that it was neither the plague in Bombay nor any epidemic in Durban that was the cause. It was the anger of the Whites against Gandhi and this was very disturbing for Kastur. What did he do on board the ship to cause such a reaction? As it is, he had been in India since the past six months. She did not breathe a word to the children. But the whispered consultations with Mohandas only added to the tension. A report had come from Dada Abdullah's company and they were discussing it in English.

Kastur's worry was compounded by the fact that she could not understand the language. All that she had understood was that they were talking about some booklet. When Mohandas had a moment she asked. 'What is this about a booklet?' He tried to make light of her question. She was aghast. 'You are laughing! I am stuck on this ship with my children in the middle of the ocean. All of you are hiding something. I don't know the language and I don't know what is going on. There is nobody whom I can ask. Where should I go? Whom do I ask?'

Mohandas was silent for a moment. Then he spoke, 'You remember in Rajkot, the children had helped me in sticking stamps on a green booklet that I had mailed to many people. Somebody has spread false news that M. K. Gandhi had defamed Whites and the White government in the green booklet saying they ill-treat Indians. A rumour had been spread that the author of the green booklet,

Gandhi, was bringing in two shiploads of Indians to settle in South Africa. These Indians will steal their jobs. I don't even know how many Indians are there on these ships and why they are travelling to South Africa. But don't be afraid because Mr Laaton, the company lawyer is coming to pick us up at the port.'

'Why are these Whites so opposed to you? What did you write in that booklet?'

'I have not written anything new. I have only written what I have been saying in Natal about repealing the inhuman laws against Indian labourers. If they talk to me, I will explain.'

'If they are angry with you, why would they listen to you?' Mohandas was aware of this. He had but one answer ... to trust.

***

This situation continued for nineteen days.

The White agitators demanded that the ships be turned back. The second demand was that Indians should be thrown out of Natal. The government was siding with them. There was a conspiracy. If the ships would not turn back, the travellers could not alight until the Whites were not completely satisfied. Tensions rose with every passing day. Food and water shortages loomed large. Mohandas tried to keep up the spirits of the travellers. Kastur also wanted to help him, but language posed a problem. He spoke encouragingly that they should not be affected by threats. They have as much right over Natal as the Whites. They are also outsiders. Kastur was most apprehensive about her husband and children. There were meetings against Mohandas and slogans – Hang Gandhi from a sour apple tree! Hanging from a sour apple tree was the worst punishment.

Finally that day arrived when the restrictions on the ship were lifted. It had been forty four days since leaving Bombay and nobody had stepped on land. When permission to enter port came through, people danced for joy and relief. The decks of both ships were packed.

For Kastur this news was not as joyful as for the rest. She was fearful of how the Whites would treat her husband and children. They had no close relatives here.

When news broke that everybody was to get down at Eddington port, the children held on to Ba. They had not set eyes on land for nearly eight weeks. Fish live in water whereas human beings breathe on land. The children wore new clothes. Ba packed. They waited for Mohandas after making all preparations to disembark. The children's impatience grew as time passed. Kastur was plagued with untoward thoughts. A sailor had come and taken Mohandas away to the captain's cabin. Since then he was missing. All the others were going down the steps. Soon most of the ship had emptied out. The children were chafing and Kastur's misgivings were eating away at her insides. Five year old Manilal was irritable even in his sleep. Harilal and Gokuldas were edgy and fretful. For the tenth time, Harilal asked irascibly, 'How much longer do we have to wait here?'

Kastur had the same answer. 'What can I say, Bapu will come and tell us.'

After some time, Bapu entered the fast shrinking cabin to say something. The children were in no mood to listen to him. He was never irritable with them. 'No, until it is dark, we cannot get off the ship,' he said. The children were stunned. Manilal burst into tears. Mohandas ignored the tantrums of the children and began explaining the situation to Kasturbai. As soon as the news of the ships casting anchor spread across the town, angry Whites had gathered at the dock. There was nothing to worry about as now the crowd had thinned. But my friend Ascombe has sent word that the situation is not favourable towards us so it is not safe to alight in daylight. He is a very senior officer and understands such situations.

'Who are the people who live in Durban? Why have we come to live in such an awful place?' said Kasturba in anger.

Mohandas had kept this fact from Kasturba that the seashore is deserted at night and it is easier to hide from your enemies. It was not natural for him to leave in this surreptitious manner. But he did not want to jeopardise his family and fellow travellers. He knew that the Whites could go to any extent in the grip of their hatred.

Mohandas was pacifying the children and Kasturbai when the Captain called him again. Kastur was irritated, 'What is the matter with the Captain that he cannot stay away from Mr Gandhi.' By the time the words were out of her mouth, Gandhi had left the cabin. Kasturba's head was whirling with confused negative thoughts. What did fate have in store for them? But this time, he came back quickly. Shockingly, he said that things had changed and they must leave immediately.

The doors of the prison opened by themselves for the children. They hugged Bapu. But Kastur was frightened. Was this a plot? Hadn't his friend asked him to stay put until it was dark? Mohandas and Gokuldas were putting the luggage outside. Mohandas was explaining that Dada Abdullah's legal adviser, Mr Laaton, had come on board the ship with a message from the company. There was no need to heed Mr Ascombe's warning. Mr Laaton believes that to stay on would be foolish and there was no need to sneak into the town under cover of darkness.

'Right now, the crowd of agitators had thinned so there is no danger. I agree with Laaton. The Port Commander of Durban has arranged for a vehicle. All of you go to my friend, Jiwanji Rustomji's house in the vehicle. He is an affluent gentleman and you will be safe there.'

'And you?'

'I will walk on foot with Laaton. He says there is no problem and we will reach soon.'

Kasturbai said, 'The children will go by the vehicle. I will accompany you on foot.'

Mohandas opposed her forcefully, 'Not possible. How can the children go into a new house by themselves? You have to be with them.'

Kasturbai could see that things were not what they seemed. If her husband was in danger, she must be with him. It was also not right to send the children to a stranger's house. She knew that he did not want to put the children in danger. He wants to hoodwink the Whites and leave quietly with Laaton. She was also very scared of all the rumours she had heard. How appropriate was it to put the children in a stranger's vehicle to reach someone's house? Who would recognise her there? As it is, Rustomji was a Parsi and they were Hindus, so things were even more difficult. Mohandas must also have thought of this. He knew that Kastur would not go to a stranger's house. Kastur was shocked at herself. As a brave woman, how could she think of such things at this time? It was as if she had woken up from slumber. This was a moment of crisis. Mohandas must also be thinking similar thoughts. He had always done what he asked others to do so this was the time for her to step up too. She should listen to her husband to get past this situation. She should cast her doubts aside and do what was needed, fearlessly, for the safety of the children.

She decided to acquiesce without protest. She went to the deck with the children. Hurrying down the steps, they got into the waiting buggy. She looked across at the ship standing peacefully in the water where she and her family had spent forty-four days. Mohandas stood there at the railing looking out at his departing family. There was a White sahib with him. Probably Laaton. The buggy moved ahead as she thought about her husband. Perhaps this was the path she had to tread with him. She covered her face with the *pallu* of her sari.

***

Suddenly there were shouts of, Gandhi … Gandhi.

The crowd ran towards where Gandhi and Laaton were walking. Before they could gather their wits, some young toughs began pushing him around and raising slogans against him. After some time, older men joined in the bullying. Laaton left Gandhi in the midst of the violent mob. Gandhi was alone in that vast crowd. Maybe Laaton was helpless. He hailed a rickshaw and yelled, 'Gandhi get in and leave.'

The mob shouted at the rickshaw puller, 'Scram, or else you will be in the same condition as this traitor.'

The rickshaw puller ran away as fast as he could. Gandhi ji was at the mercy of the mob. They tore off his *pagri.* He was being pelted with rotten eggs. People were landing blows on him and slapping and kicking him. He fell over the railing. If Sara Alexander, the wife of R. C. Alexander, the Police Superintendent of Durban had not been passing by, the violent mob of Whites would have lynched him. When she saw that the mob was brutally beating up somebody, she tore through the crowd. When she saw that it was none other than M. K. Gandhi whom her husband and she greatly respected, she was stunned. Not losing a moment, she spread her umbrella over him. The mob paused momentarily. A lady stood before them. A passing Indian seeing the terrible condition of Gandhi, informed Mr Alexander. A posse of policeman reached the spot immediately. By then the mob had dispersed. One of them had realised that the woman who had saved Gandhi was none other than the Police Superintendent's wife.

***

The children and Kasturbai had reached Rustomji Parsi's home safely. Mohandas was nowhere to be seen. Kasturbai's misgivings grew with every passing minute. The children sat constricted in a stranger's house. After a long time, when

Mohandas was spotted, everybody breathed a sigh of relief. As he drew closer, they saw that he was accompanied by a policeman. Kasturba thought that given the disturbance in the city, he must have asked for a policeman for safety. But such a thing had never happened before. By then they had come closer. Mohandas was bleeding from several places. He had scratches everywhere and there were blue bruises all over his face. His clothes were in tatters. Kastur felt her heart leap into her throat. The thought that he was alive and standing before her was no less than God's grace, gave her some solace. The children stared at him fearfully. A voice told her to rush to his side. She wanted to clean his wounds and apply ointment. But everything was strange and new here. Her *sanskars* also stood in her way. Any show of feeling that brought the relationship between a husband and wife into public view was not appropriate. She grappled with contradictory impulses. A mountain of trouble had broken over them in a strange land. She could not just stare at him silently from a distance. She cast all her doubts to the wind and leapt towards him and her throat was heavy with tears as she said, 'How could those people do this to you?'

'It is nothing. Just a few bruises. They will be fine.' He tried to pacify his wife and children. The children also surged towards him along with Ba.

Ba was not to be deterred by her husband's words. She began cleaning his wounds with her handkerchief. In a short while, a doctor arrived. He examined Gandhi and found that some wounds needed bandages.

***

The anger of the Whites had not abated yet. People began gathering in front of Rustomji's house. Soon there was a sizeable crowd. The Police Superintendent also reached with a posse of policemen. Seeing the swelling crowd, he realised that the posse was not sufficient. Alexander began cracking jokes instead of using force. He tried to create an atmosphere of jokes and laughter to reduce the anger in the crowd. The crowd continued to swell. The danger of an attack was growing. They were threatening to break down the doors. They yelled that they wanted Gandhi. Rustomji sent both the families upstairs in view of the tense situation. The slogans could be heard upstairs as well. Kastur was at a total loss. If she had known the English language, she would have gone and asked them what did her husband do, for them to thirst for his blood? Is it a crime to help your countrymen? She was also upset that Rustomji's family was in danger because of them. Harilal and Manilal kept crying. It was difficult to pacify them. Gokuldas had lost his father a short while ago. In the midst of this violence and the threat of ruin, Kasturbai was trying to maintain her balance. The Police Superintendent sent a message to Mohandas, 'If you want to save the family of your friend and your own family, disguise yourself and leave immediately. You have to decide now.'

Mohandas had no option. He went upstairs to inform his family. After that he disguised himself as a policeman and left with two constables from the secret service. They were both White but had darkened their faces like Indian workers and left with Mohandas. Mohandas had reassured his family that he was being taken to a safe spot so there was no reason to worry. Kasturbai could not decide whether to believe him or not. Laaton had also given just such an assurance. What had happened subsequently was there for everybody to see. But there was no other recourse. Kastur was sick with worry at the speed of their departure. It was as if a goat was being led to sacrifice. It had been rumoured that Gandhi would be hanged. This news had travelled as far as to the Delhi Viceroy who had expressed concern. The colonial administrator, Chamberlain, had ordered action against the agitators. Mohandas was asked to identify his attackers. He had refused to take part in retributive action. He maintained that the rioters were young men who had been led astray by the false news spread by Reuters. The same statement had been submitted to the Attorney General. Although Kasturba was initially against submitting such an interpretation, she thought about it and changed her mind. Mohandas had done similar things in Natal before this.

***

When newspapers in Durban published the news that in spite of Chamberlain's orders, Gandhi wrote to the Attorney General against following the path of retribution, people were astonished. The situation turned when his statement, supported by facts, was printed in the newspapers. Even the extremists were converted. While an attack had been made on his life, it helped forge a new identity. Not just his friends, but his clients increased. Indians were regarded the better for it. Kastur thought to herself that if love begets love, forgiveness is the road to respect.

***

Mohandas lived for two days under the protection of Alexander, in the police station. The husband-wife duo took good care of him. When the atmosphere was calm, Alexander personally accompanied him to Rustomji's house. The alienation that Kastur had carried within herself melted away. The unstinting love that the Rustomji family had showered upon her filled her heart with respect and gratitude. She realised for the first time, through this encounter, the respect that her husband commanded. She also felt that tolerance and sacrifice increase respect manifold. Fame and acceptance come after facing stiff trials.

Living with the children in a Parsi household had its problems, but she consoled herself that it was just a matter of a few days. The tribulations that the family had undergone were strange and unusual. There was no comparison or similarity between what Kasturbai and the children were faced with, and the danger that Mohandas was facing outside. Kasturbai had never left the secure confines of the kitchen and women's quarters in Rajkot with her face uncovered. Here she had been thrust into an unfamiliar world where men and women sat together routinely and conversed. They went about their business without covering their faces. They even kept their heads uncovered. Added to this was the food that she had to eat, which was not to her liking. She had to make special efforts to feed the children so that the hosts would not know that they did not like the food. Every home carries the smell of the food that the inhabitants eat. It brings forth feelings ranging from attraction to repulsion. A guest has to be prepared for it. Kastur and the children had smelt it the moment they entered. The odour and nausea had been experienced at the same time. The nausea can be tamped down but the smell permeates you.

Fish was an intrinsic part of the Parsi family's daily diet. For a Vaishnav, meat and fish are taboo. The eagerness to get to her own house and cook what her family would relish, had even dampened the gratitude towards the Rustamji family. With Mohandas's return two days later, Kasturbai took leave with mixed feelings. Gratitude and relief. This was the first time that Kasturbai had understood how food plays such a key role in the relationship between host and guest. She had been so awkward when she came but that had been short-lived. The closeness between the two families had made them friends for life. The shared adversity had ensured that they would share a deep bond. Jal Rustamji, the son of Rustamji had experienced the travails of the children and Kasturbai deeply, when the crazed mob had surrounded their house.

Kasturbai's joy was incandescent when she left Rustomji's house to go to her own house with her partner. For the first time ever, she would not have to be subservient to anybody. Her new home would run under her word. She had become Kasturba from being Kasturbai. The children in Rustomji's family addressed her as Ba, just like Hari and Mani. This was a full acceptance of her status as Ba. Kastur took stock when they reached home. It was a double storeyed house of ample proportions with five rooms. There was an iron gate that gave her a feeling of security. There was a small garden and a sea-facing balcony. She had never seen such an open house before this. The balmy sea breeze reminded her of her childhood in Porbandar. The lower floor was done up in European style. This was odd for Kasturba but she held her peace. Mohandas revealed that a rich businessman client had been responsible for the decor. There was a carpeted sitting room and sofa, the likes of which had never been seen in Porbandar or Rajkot. There were two recliners. A bookshelf housed Mohandas's law books. A dining room had a square table with eight chairs arranged around it. There was a cornice. The rooms upstairs were simple with a wardrobe and a wooden bed each. What bothered her most was that there were no pictures of Gods and Goddesses where she could perform puja. There was no courtyard for bhajan and kirtan like in Rajkot. There was no tulsi plant that removes obstacles by its very presence. All this affluence but no sign of dharma? Such questions bounced around in her heart. Were there no Hindus here or had they given up all this? Was her husband party to this?

Kasturba gave her attention to the smallest of chores. It took her many days to make the house clean and comfortable with the help of the children and a few servants. She also kept trying to produce the family's favourite dishes from the inconvenient new style kitchen. The kitchen meant satisfying meals for the family and guests. In this strange and foreign kitchen, it was hard for her to put this belief into practice. The hardest part was to cook standing up, wearing shoes. Mohandas was a relentless supporter of cooking with one's shoes on, even if it meant aching feet. Kastur had always cooked on a *chulha*, sitting on the floor, in her *sasural.* Here she had to cook on a table as high as her chest and she was short statured. There was a six burner wood fired stove that Mohandas had taught Kasturba to light. She was always afraid of burns while she was firing up the stove.

She learnt to make a valiant peace with her ever-shifting destiny.

Kasturba missed Rajkot where she had company. Her sisters-in-law were her companions in the kitchen. Loneliness haunted her when she stood in her villa, cutting fruit or peeling vegetables. Managing the house, cooking and serving all by herself, was altogether too much for one person. Chores were divided in Rajkot. Cooking was a community activity and it never stopped. The *chulha* never grew cold. Childcare and laundry were all shared chores. What she missed even more was the conversation. Jokes, innuendo, gossip, news were all part of the daily exchanges that livened up their lives. She really missed all the women friends that she had left behind. Now she got news of her sisters-in-law and the children only through Lakshmidas' letters. Mohandas would quickly read them out to her. She often felt alone in a foreign land among strangers, when she had been among her own not so long ago.

***

Kasturba was the queen of her household, just like her mother-in-law, Putliba had been. Kasturba had felt totally under her control. Diwan Sahib consulted her on everything. It is believed that Putliba had a major role to play in the three weddings in the family. Now in Durban, when she had her own household, she understood the weight of responsibility.

It was a crown of thorns, this villa in Durban, just like the house in Porbandar had been. One day Gandhi bhai said to Kastur, 'The people working in my office are Indian and they don't have a place to stay. Our house is mostly lying empty so if they stay with us, their problems will be solved.'

Kasturba was agreeable. With only the two of them and the children, the house was big enough to accommodate more people. If these people move in, the house will not seem so empty and it will be good for Mohandas. Word got around that Mr Gandhi's house was a refuge. On another day, Mohandas showed Kasturba a man in the street, 'He is a leper. His master has thrown him out and he has no place to go. He can live in the shed downstairs and will not be a bother to anyone.'

Kasturba thought for a moment. Very hesitantly, she said, 'Fine, try it out. But ... it is a house with children ...'

Mohandas put him up in the basement. He would bandage his sores daily. Murmurs about him could be heard around the house and word reached Kastur's ears. The children held their breath when they crossed this area. Finally Kasturba was forced to bring this up with Mohandas. Everybody was upset and scared and the children complained of the stench. Mohandas refused to evict him and the pressure was mounting. Finally, he admitted him in hospital. Kasturbai thought long and hard about how the body was the biggest friend and the worst enemy of a person. Never mind what happens after death, even while alive, it could turn against you. Sorrow and helplessness had dripped from the eyes of the leper as he left. Kasturba felt the same in her eyes when she thought of him. The body was also the seedbed of disease was a nagging thought that troubled her.

After the leper had been put into hospital, Mohandas had remained quiet for days. Kastur felt that his experiment at serving others ended before it had begun. But she was in a dilemma too because the children would complain to her. Mohandas spent a considerable amount of time on putting his bandages. He had to alter his daily routine for it. Having been separated from the children for so long, he felt that he should spend more time with them. They needed him too. Kastur was worried about their education as schools were a problem. The good schools were for the Whites and the Blacks had to make do with schools of poor quality.

If Mohandas had wanted, he could have had the children admitted in the school for Europeans. But if a school was not open to Indians, he did not believe in making an exception for his own children. There were two reasons for this. The children would have developed a complex about their own language and the snobbishness of a European education would cut them off from other Indian children. Indian children studied in the Missionary school where there were some good teachers and some not so good ones, who did not pass muster with Mohandas. So the children were not admitted to any school. Kasturba wondered if her inauspicious shadow had been cast over her children with regard to education and was troubled by other such useless thoughts. Will they remain uneducated like me?

Not one of them will take after their father? Manilal was young, Harilal was sharp and Gokuldas was shy. They were growing up quite fast. Kastur was concerned about their future. She asked Mohandas directly. 'When will the children start school?'

'I have arranged for a White teacher who will come and tutor them at home,' he said.

When she started coming, the difficulties for the children grew apace. She gave lessons in English whereas the children were true Gujjus. She would speak slowly because it is impossible to teach without dialogue. She would deliver her piece and leave. Kasturba could see what was happening but she kept quiet. She could not talk to her. Finally she had to tell her partner. The arrangement was short-lived.

Mohandas decided to teach the children himself. Kastur was reminded of her own time. Was he going to take responsibility for their studies in the manner that he did with her? She could not help but laugh to herself, as she admitted her own culpability in what used to happen. She stayed silent. Mohandas was so busy that he returned late each night. By then the children would be dozing. If he woke up early then the children were only half awake. Kasturba watched and finally said, 'This can't carry on. Schools exist to teach children and that is where they should go. You have studied in schools yourself. I have learnt all this from others. When they see other children studying, they will be motivated too.'

Many times Kastur thought that if she had been educated herself, she would have gone by herself and got them admitted into school. Here nobody would understand her language and she would not be able to explain what she wanted. What was the use of regrets now ... it was ultimately her own fault...?

South Africa was like a thorny jungle of trials for her. It was natural that she miss Rajkot and Porbandar. Porbandar was her parental home and also where she had been married. Rajkot was her *sasural* and now the home of her sisters-in-law. Lakshmidas was like a caring father-in-law. Everybody had borne the punishment of her husband's banishment from the caste. Nobody had ever made her feel that it was her husband who was responsible. Banishment, while still at home, is harder than banishment to the forest. Everybody shared the travails and bore up. Putliba always said that sorrow came from *prarabdh* or accumulated karma but suffering was inevitable.

***

Kastur's first tough test had come in Beachgrove Villa. It could have gone either way. A traditional illiterate woman, completely helpless in a strange land. She would shiver at the memory. When Mohandas had asked his office staff to stay at the Villa, he had made a rule that the inmates had to empty out their own chamber pots in the morning and clean them. There was a sub-rule that if a chamber pot got left by oversight, then Mohandas would empty it out and Kasturba would help him. Because no occasion had arisen for the sub-rule to be applied, Kasturba had raised no objection to this unpleasant order. But she could not rid herself of the question: what was the need to have to have such a rule in the first place? And what was the need to include this awful task in it? Who gets his wife to clean other people's waste? Had he brought her to a foreign land to humiliate her in this fashion? Such thoughts skittered around her head. What angered her even more was that she had seen only those considered very lowly carry out such tasks. She fumed in silent resistance. How could a man be so insensitive towards his wife when he was so considerate of other people's beliefs and feelings! She prayed constantly that he should not bring things to such a pass that she would have to stand up to oppose him.

But that day did come. They had a new guest. He was a Christian from a caste that does cleaning chores. He did not know about the rules of the Villa. He left the chamber pot in the room. Kastur thought that the first responsibility was Mohandas' so he would do the needful. She felt equally bad for him to do it as she would for herself. But that day, he asked Kasturba to do the chore. She was livid. She wept as she carried the pot downstairs and emptied it out near the staircase. She felt as if she had been unveiled. Mohandas was watching her from upstairs. He wanted Kastur to carry out the task happily, in the spirit of service. Surely, even they, who had been doing this for as long as anybody could remember, could not have been doing it happily. Was it not enough to have asked a woman to carry the waste of another man? Mohandas shouted from the top, 'There is no place for such foolishness in my house.'

Kastur felt his words pierce her through. 'Keep your house to yourself. I will leave,' she said in a fury.

Mohandas lost his temper. It was as if Kastur's retort had blown away any remnants of compassion in him. He came down and dragged her by the arm to the door. He opened it to push her out, even as a deluge of tears flowed from her eyes. 'Have you no shame? Where will I go in this strange country? Has it even occurred to you that I have no parents or relatives who will give me shelter? Do you think you can insult me like this just because I am your wife? You want to show your real savage self to the people here?'

The children watched helplessly, their faces in silent entreaty. Mohandas dropped her arm and lowered his head. Perhaps he was reminded of the incident when he was thrown off the train in Pitermaritzburg. Kasturba was going through the same torture ... and perhaps the children too.

***

Kasturba and Mohandas put this incident behind them and turned their gaze to the future. Nobody spoke about it. Both of them tried to put it out of their minds and vowed never to let something like this happen again. There was the news of another life growing in Kasturba's womb. It was a tough pregnancy. She was tired and irritable. She missed Rajkot where her other two children had been born. Both her elder sisters-in-law treated her with utmost care. Things were vastly different here as she had to look after everything and put up with all kinds of bother. She bore it all with fortitude and without uttering a word. The house ran smoothly as she prepared for the new arrival. It was quite a solitary exercise. In a new country everything had to be done differently. Beachgrove did not even have a confinement room like the other houses and the rooms were all open. If Mohandas had been in Rajkot, he would have left these matters to the family and freed himself of further responsibility. But here he had to plan and anticipate every eventuality. He wanted his wife to get the best medical attention. They decided that the doctor would be summoned only when it was time for labour. Kastur was grimly opposed to the idea of a male doctor and that stumped Mohandas. He had to work very hard to convince her. Labour was a woman's business. A male doctor, even if he was an Indian, attending to Kastur, felt vaguely immoral. But in South Africa, it was mostly male doctors who attended to childbirth. The second problem was of finding a nurse. They had decided to employ a nurse to help with the care of mother and child. Kastur did not want a White nurse. She maintained that since Mohandas would be in office all day, how would she converse with her? It was difficult to find an Indian nurse in Durban. Mohandas believed that European nurses were comparatively smarter and cleaner. Finally, it was Kasturba who took on the responsibility of caring for the baby. She was mother to two and she would look after the new born. They would hardly have kept a nurse if they were in India and she had already brought up the two children. She used to look after the child, while the others did all the other chores. The children had grown up and were very keen to help. Mohandas also happily became a member of the helping committee. He believed that since a mother bears the pain of childbirth, the father should help in childcare. He read the Gujarati book titled 'Advice to Mothers' to prepare himself to look after the baby.

The third child was born in May 1898. The labour was a difficult one. Mohandas assisted the doctor with alacrity. Kasturba had become quite weak and had not been able to leave the bed for several weeks after the delivery. She even found it difficult to breastfeed. Mohandas left nothing to chance in looking after mother and child. He also helped the older children with their baths. They were happy with the new arrival and to get Bapu to help them with their tasks was even more fun.

***

It took several months for Kasturba to come back to her normal state of health. Mohandas had hardly any time to think of his own problems in this period. Ever since Kasturba had recovered somewhat, she could see that her partner was in turmoil. Could she help him? In India, her concern had been that her husband was capable but his earnings did not match his capabilities. This used to bother her. His earnings had gone up significantly ever since he came to South Africa. There were twelve people working in his office. The income from his practice was 75,000 pound sterling or 1.25 lac dollars. Even so, he was clearly worried about something. Kasturba could hardly ignore this. One day he said, 'I feel oppressed by life in the villa with all its comforts.'

Kasturba felt odd listening to him. But at least, now she knew what was bothering him.

'We will have to reduce our expenses. We must simplify our lifestyle. The only way is to reduce household expenses so that there is less pressure to earn more. By reducing our expenses, we will be able to spend a large part of our earnings on social service. Self reliance can only be achieved by incurring fewer expenses,' he said.

The servants bore the first brunt of this austerity drive. It was decided that everybody, including the children, would do household chores along with their own chores. The largest responsibility came upon Kasturba. The most taxing task was to cook for all the members and guests and serve them, along with looking after the children. Kasturba pondered over the problem and concluded that by doing this, the family would draw closer. Mohandas was an early riser. He first did his own laundry. He had to change his shirt and collar every day to go to court. He had bought a book to learn the fine art of washing clothes. He would read it aloud and carefully so that Kasturba could also listen. Actually she needed the book more than Mohandas.

Mohandas bore repeated humiliations, but each defeat helped him grow. In Pretoria, he had entered a White person's salon and he was thrown out. Mohandas felt terrible but then it occurred to him that if this White was seen cutting a Black person's hair, the Whites would stop patronising the salon. He remembered how in India people from a higher caste don't let their barber cut the hair of a lower caste. Instead of harbouring anger, he bought hair cutting implements. He set up two mirrors and gave himself a haircut. His colleagues in court asked him in jest if he had got mice to give him a haircut. They are my own hair not borrowed was his rejoinder. Slowly he got better and started giving haircuts to the children.

***

There was famine in India in 1899. Mohandas started a relief fund. By then, he was so popular that Africans and well heeled Indians gave generous contributions of charity. Even the *girmitiyas* gave as much as they could. Kasturba and Mohandas were very gratified by this.

There had been tension between the Boers and the British since many years over gold mines and finally there was war. The Indians did not want to be a part of this war. Mohandas sided with the Boers on this. But being a subject of the Empire, he could not support them. It would have redounded badly on the Indian *girmitiyas.* He found a non-violent way to assist them. He became a part of the war without bearing arms. He persuaded forty people to lead an ambulance unit. About 800 *girmitiyas* were permitted by their owners to take part as well. Three hundred ordinary citizens joined in. Mohandas was first refused permission to run the ambulance unit. The logic was that Indians are cowardly and unreliable. But when the Boers surrounded Lady Smith and inflicted losses on the White army, the officers were reminded of M.K. Gandhi's non-violent unit. They overturned their initial decision and promised vehicles and uniforms to the unit to serve the injured soldiers. Thirty-six people were honoured with war medals for their dedicated service. 'Ahimsa (non-violence) is what saves you from hinsa (violence),' is what Kasturba said.

When Mohandas was in the war zone, he learnt that Kasturba was pregnant again. The household was her sultanate and she was the queen and chief servant. She lived with the children in a well organised way. This was her first taste of independent ownership. However attractive and necessary independence may be, it brings the restraint of duty along with it. To be able to live in her own way, looking after the children as needed, and now to welcome another new life was satisfying, but also scary. Visiting new friends in Durban and returning their hospitality, trying not to worry too much about Mohandas …

The time for the birth of the child was getting closer. This time Kasturba felt even weaker but maintained silence as always. Mohandas felt that he had failed yet again to overcome his weakness. He had not forgotten Kasturba's words, 'I am satisfied with three children. Husband and wife should come together to have children. Human beings … and animals also cohabit at certain times.' Mohandas was forced to contend with his weaknesses … he felt them rise up before him like a *Bahubali* flying in the face of his ideals. They bested him at his own game. It is not Kastur's fault, he concluded.

He carried the weight of his own lack of self control and he was also worried seeing how weak Kasturba was becoming. As the date approached, Mohandas tried to stay home as much as he could, to look after Kastur, although there were doctors attending to her. Sometimes Kastur would say. 'This is a payment on your account.' He could only give a weak laugh in return. It was like a thorn pricking him deeply. When he was bathing her, he felt there was a Shravan Kumar inside him, nudging him towards serving others … from the time of his father to the leper, and now Kastur. There is perhaps a bit of Shravan Kumar in all of us. Dormant in some, active in others.

Kasturba moaned in pain. Mohandas was busy with work but he ran to her side as he heard her. Her pains were so intense that there was no possibility of summoning the doctor. Such intense pain happens only when labour is advanced. Mohandas could not think of what to do and he began to make preparations himself. He carried the guilt of knowing that this was the second time his uncontrollable sexual urge had brought things to such a pass that anything could happen. He did not lose courage. He had read many books about childbirth in the interim. He boiled a knife and warmed water and pulled out rubber gloves from his first aid box. He made all preparations for delivering the baby. When Kasturba saw this she resisted angrily, 'I'd sooner die than have you deliver the baby ...' Mohandas tried to reason with her, 'I can't leave you in this condition to get the doctor. Whether he is a man or woman, he is still an outsider. We are man and wife and have been together in everything. I had assisted the doctor during your first delivery. Please let go of your old ideas. The baby knows neither me nor the doctor. It will not wait. It will not understand your hesitation and my dilemma. Relax and think of the new arrival ... our real guest.'

The pains reached a crescendo. Kasturba was bathed in sweat as if she had taken a dip in water. Mohandas stroked her stomach. He was moving the baby downwards with gentle pressure. Kasturba was caught between pain and her wifely restraint. The touch of Mohandas's hand was not as assured as the doctor's, but it did make her feel better. And secure. Mohandas was concentrating fully on what he had to do. Because she had given birth to three children, she also balled her fists and began pressing down. As soon as the baby was out, Kastur felt as if a steep mountain had been scaled. Her sweat felt cold. Mohandas cut the umbilical cord. He held the baby in one hand and cleaned up with the other. He swathed the baby in a clean cloth and put it next to the mother. Only then did he wipe the sweat off his brow. Mohandas scrubbed and cleaned both mother and baby. Kasturba forgot all her complaints and looked at the baby and was entranced. Mohandas murmured, 'The greatest pain and such indescribable joy!'

When things normalised, Mohandas laughed and said, 'Did you approve of my midwife services?' Kasturba smiled.

Mother and child were both exhausted. Mohandas also took a breather and sat down on a chair. It was natural for Kasturba to be spent. The baby's eyes were closed. He seemed to be in the womb in spite of having come into the world outside. His skin was red and seemed as soft as cotton. It looked like it would come off if touched. Mohandas looked at him closely after a short rest. His first concern was to check if he had hurt the baby in his ignorance. The baby looked calm and unblemished. Mohandas settled down on the armchair again. He was alert for anything that the mother and child might need.

He felt the baby stir. Kasturba was in deep sleep. The baby's lips puckered as if he was sucking, even as he slept. Mohandas had played his part in bringing him safely into this world. He pondered over the twin roles he had played and how desire manifests itself in such different ways. Kastur had given up on the pleasures of sexual desire from the time that they had taken vows of celibacy. Mohandas found himself to be the weaker one. She never expressed a need nor did she oppose it. Kasturba had assumed the wifely mantle of neutrality, she embraced her pregnancies lovingly and carried them in optimism. Desire creates and leads to a new birth. Could these tender twins not lead to such creative desire for a world where there is no violence, no bloodshed, no hatred and no rule of death? There is no hunger for power for its own sake? Could something like this be done? Such questions agitated Mohandas.

Kasturbai had woken up and she softly asked for water. Mohandas warmed some water and propped her up as she took two sips and she had to rest again. Mohandas sprawled on the chair began thinking. He had witnessed her physical pain and mental stress during the delivery of their fourth child. He could not arrive at a positive definition of a man's role in procreation. Was it restricted only to satisfying his carnal desire? He could not accept this. There were two battles raging inside. The second was to do with the complicated perspective arising from the situation in South Africa. The anger at the exploitation of the Indians, the daily dance with law, the urge to free all human beings of pain and his defiance of traditions, all added to this potent mix. He was interrogating the inequality inherent in Indian culture. He also felt the need to shift the balance in the man-woman relationship. Why shouldn't a woman have the right to say no? Shouldn't this possibility be explored? For the first time, he understood that Kasturba believed he was as committed to the marriage as she was. Doesn't commitment demand that duties should be defined and observed?

——***——

Motherland Calling

She was uneasy. From the time of entering Durban, all the mishaps that had taken place would come to life before her, rising as a grim picture. Her heart would suddenly quail at the thought of what was to come next? Everybody from the kids to Mohandas would get drawn into the arc of the question. Although Mohandas was respected in Durban, Kastur had a host of questions with regard to the children's education. Manilal was almost nine. The elder three were much behind their contemporaries. This thought made Kasturba's heart beat faster with anxiety. What will become of these children? Mohandas had many invitations from his country. Come and see your own land, they said. What is it about Durban that you have forgotten about your own country?

Kasturba also missed her own people terribly. There was a child-like enthusiasm to show off her two children born in Durban. The education of the older ones was confined to Mohandas' own rather patchy efforts. She felt that they were inadequate. However attractive a foreign land may be, with all its conveniences, it does not call out to you like your homeland that says, come back ... your place has been kept safe, I'll do my best for you. You may ignore this plea or it grows weaker over time, but the murmur never really dies down. Mohandas had lived abroad for many years, but the voices from across the seven seas never grew so faint that he could not hear them. In the hum, a sea of faces also floated up. Rajkot and the country were playing a tug of war with Mohandas. Kasturba's invitation was both from Porbandar and Rajkot. In 1901, Mohandas suddenly decided that they all had to go to their country. Durban was not inclined to let him go. Dada Abdullah, his previous boss, was among the first to oppose the idea. This time Mohandas was not to be dissuaded. Kasturba's will power and the call of home was stronger. Mohandas did have to concede that whenever Durban called, he would come. Kasturba did not approve of any such reassurance. On the other side, Bade Bhaiya and all the other family members could hardly wait. Kasturba's highest priority was the children's education. She held her peace as this day had dawned after much difficulty. Dinners and farewells had begun. Presents were coming in. Gold and silver ornaments and diamonds and precious stones. Kasturba was gifted a gold necklace. That was the point where the disagreement between husband and wife began.

The presents had been arranged on a table. Ba and the children were proud of the spread. It was such an honour that her husband was held in such high regard in Durban. People had given such expensive gifts. They had never expected this. But Mohandas was broodingly silent. He paced up and down through the night. What was to be done with these expensive ornaments? It had not been possible to refuse at the time of receiving them. All their friends would have taken it amiss. But to keep them would be even worse. A quid pro quo is against morality. Anyway, his wife and children would have no use for these. Simplicity was the governing principle in their family. After brooding through the night, he decided that the gifts were an endorsement of the principles of the Congress. Therefore, through a Trust, they should be given over to the Natal Indian Congress for the welfare of the Indians. He was relieved when he worked that out. He got the Trust deeds ready through the night. He appointed his Parsi friend Rustomji as the President and some other friends as Trustees.

The next morning, he found a suitable opportunity and called Harilal and Manilal. It was not hard to explain things to them. They agreed to talk to Ba. Harilal said, if needed, we will arrange for these ourselves as self-reliance is the greatest joy. Mohandas was pleased. Both the kids went to Kasturba and brought her back. Mohandas said, 'We should return these gifts.' Kasturba maintained that if friends gave something with love and respect, it should be accepted in the same spirit. She took an opposing stand. 'What are you saying? It is immoral to return gifts given with such affection.'

'Isn't it immoral to accept costly gifts in return for social service?'

'I don't understand why they cannot be accepted.'

'What will you do with them?'

'I will keep them for my *bahus*,' said Kasturba in turn. It was perfectly justified, from the point of view of a mother.

'The children are young. There is a long time before they marry.' Mohandas had to ponder over this answer.

The children interjected. 'Ba, we don't want anything.'

'Who asked you?' Ba admonished them. Turning to Mohandas she said, 'You are turning my children into sadhus and mendicants. Let them become men first.'

'We will not choose such *bahus* for our children who covet expensive ornaments,' was Mohandas's strange rejoinder. 'We will give them diamonds. I will arrange them.'

Are you planning to turn your *bahus* into someone like me ... these words almost escaped Kasturba. Her normally calm tone hardened. 'You are giving up everything ... from where will you get diamonds?'

'I have made the papers for a Trust.'

'Who asked you to?' she said as tears rolled down her cheeks. 'What right do you have to give away my gold necklace? Just as you have got presents, this is my present.'

Mohandas maintained his cool, 'This gift has come to you as a consequence of my service.' This didn't seem like a boast but it hurt her through.

She lost her self control and wept bitter tears. 'Your service is evident. Whether you served or I did, are they separate? I slave for you all night and day, is that not counted as service?'

Kastur's argument silenced him for a moment.

Perhaps Kasturba mistook his silence for assent but when they left Durban, the necklace and all the other presents had been left in the Bank locker. This was not a victory for Mohandas. It was a victory for his obstinacy. Kasturba had embraced silence.

——***——

Home and the World

Mohandas reached Rajkot with the family. It was December and people are generally cheery in the winter. They were greeted by the family and their arrival was like a celebration. Kasturba wondered privately whether Mohandas had been actually missing Rajkot. She had not asked him and he had not volunteered any information. But she felt that this sudden turn was not driven by an innocent desire to come home. Nor was it for attending the 17th session in Calcutta to present a motion on the excesses on Indians in South Africa. It was more to revive the relationships with leaders that were initiated five years ago. A mere three days after arriving, Mohandas left the family in Rajkot and departed for Bombay where all the leaders thronged. He travelled on the same train as the one that all the prominent leaders were taking. He took the time to meet Sir Pherozeshah in his cabin. Dinshawvacha and Chimanlal Setalvad were with him. When Mohandas was ushered in, the three of them were discussing some important matters. When Sir Pherozeshah saw Gandhi standing in the doorway, he was polite, 'How are you Gandhi? When did you return from South Africa?'

Gandhi wanted to tell them about the sorry state of lakhs of labourers in South Africa. But Pherozeshah continued, 'Sorry Gandhi. We will not be able to do anything for you. We are slaves in our own country. We have practically no rights. Until we attain self-rule, what can we give to other colonies? At best, we can pass a motion expressing solidarity with their cause.'

Gandhi wanted to interject but Sir Pherozeshah raised his hand. Who could say anything after a signal of dismissal from the uncrowned king? The door to the saloon opened and Dinshawvacha stuck his neck out, 'Gandhi, let me take a look at the motion before presenting it.'

'Yes.'

The door closed and the train stopped. Mohandas got off to board his own compartment.

***

After the Congress session was over, Mohandas stayed back in Calcutta to apprise Gopal Krishna Gokhale of the problems in South Africa. Gokhale took him to the India Club to play billiards and meet influential Bengali families. He introduced Gandhi as an important person. There was a contradiction that emerged in their dialogue. Mohandas lectured Gokhale on self-reliance. Gokhale had an air of nobility. Nobility depends on the service that others give. Mohandas asked his Guru and protector to simplify his lifestyle. Instead of using his own vehicle, he advised him to use the tram or walk as that was good for health! Gokhale did not take this amiss and perhaps he did not pay much heed to it. Gokhale also gave some advice to Gandhi. The first was to know his own country better. The second suggestion was to work for the Congress, staying on in India. Burma was then a part of the country.

Gandhi was first attracted to the women's freedom movement going on in Burma and made his way there. But seeing the general indifference of men and the rats that overran the Golden Pagoda, he returned disappointed. On his return to Calcutta, he made an itinerary to visit all the places en route to Rajkot that he had not seen until now. He got off at Banaras, Agra, Jaipur and Palanpur and roamed around like an ordinary traveller. When he had announced that he would travel third class, Gokhale had made fun of him, although it was he who had advised him to be in touch with ordinary people. But Gokhale did not have that class in mind that Gandhi wanted to know better. Gandhi already knew that he had to connect with ordinary Indians at every level. When he reached the station to begin his journey, Gokhale was present, wearing a silken jacket and *pagri* and he had a tiffin carrier filled with laddoos and puris. Gandhi was decked out in a Gujarati coat, dhoti and canvas shoes like an ordinary third class passenger. Gokhale was startled, but withheld comment.

As Mohandas's journey progressed, his indignation at the state of the third class cabin grew. The people were treated like sheep. The coaches were dirty. There was no regulation of the crowds. He was even more upset by the indifference of the railway staff. Compared to other countries, the facilities were negligible. Pushing and shoving, blowing cigarette and bidi smoke and treating the coach like a spittoon after chewing paan and tobacco had all become general habits. He worried about how all this would improve. He thought about it throughout the journey. If educated people travel third class, counsel the other travellers against disorder, present a good example and make the officers accountable, it would be possible to bring about change. This was Mohandas' first lesson in a third class compartment.

***

As Kasturba set foot in her country, she was overwhelmed. She went through a lot of confusing emotions. At home or outside, there was no let up in welcoming celebrations. Even after Mohandas went to Calcutta, the invitations poured in. Kasturba wondered why she merited such a welcome. Earlier, when Mohandas returned from abroad, it was a different matter. She was the first among her friends and relatives who had returned from abroad with her children, after such a long stint. Kasturba had been constantly worried that the *biradari* should not excommunicate the entire family. Where would they go? Will the children also have to put up with all that Mohandas had been through? Because the entire family was united, there had not been much of a problem. Nothing had happened to Mohandas either. Ultimately, she would bolster her spirits saying that if they could bear it once, they could bear it again. How long can anyone live in dread? Mohandas had not brought this up and neither did Kasturba. In fact, she found that things had changed drastically. Instead of banishment, she and her children were being feted. Those days, everybody in her two homes, had been worried about being outcastes. They had persevered and today even her children were being showered with love and respect. People reached out and hugged them. Was this because Mohandas' social position had improved or because beliefs were changing?

In these five years, Kasturba's family had also seen many changes. Both her parents had passed on and she missed them sorely. They had not lived to see the better times. She had not received any news of their passing. The *biradari* had not done much upon her departure to South Africa, but a daughter had been separated from her parents. Only her brother remained. Kasturba's heart welled up as she remembered every nook and cranny of her home. There is a saying that when a daughter leaves, her mother's womb is empty but with her parents gone, a daughter can barely claim a roof over her head. She did not go to her parents' home and nobody asked her to come. She got news that her brother was well. There had been additions to her *sasural.* Nandkunwar Ben had given two sons to the Gandhi family in these two years. Ramdas and Devdas played all day long. Gangaben, her younger sister-in-law had also given birth to a daughter. Her older two, Hari and Mani were delighted at being promoted to the position of *Bade Bhaiyas.* Kasturba was very pleased to see that Harilal had an open and easy relationship with Mota Bapu and Chote Bapu. He told Mota Bapu that he wanted to stay in Rajkot and study as Bapu did not approve of the schools in Durban. Mota Bapu promised to keep him here so that he could continue his education.

The children's education was Kasturba's biggest worry. She wanted everybody to stay together in Rajkot. She also wanted the children's father to concur. But Mohandas had given assurances in Durban that he would return if needed. Who knows when there would be a call and he would pack up and leave?

***

When he returned from Calcutta, Kasturba broached the subject of settling in Rajkot only to be met with his silence. He neither gave his assent nor did he refuse. Kasturba was familiar with this behaviour. There was no point in asking him again. She felt that this time around, his experiences during his travels had changed him. He was no longer the clear-headed Mohandas of South Africa who would work tirelessly on his chosen priorities. He did not know where to place himself in the face of the innumerable complications of India. In this period of uncertainty, the old friend and well wisher of the family, Mawji Dave, had given him three cases and he had won all three. Kasturba wanted that he practice law in Rajkot. But she knew he was in a conflict. There was the pressure of settling down in Rajkot and the invitation of his Guru Gokhale to come to Bombay. He wanted him to practice in Bombay and also work for the Congress. Mohandas also wanted this but he hesitated. Not just him, even Kastur could remember how he had gone to the courts for months and returned empty-handed. Often on foot.

One fine day, Mawji Dave reappeared. He said to Mohandas, 'We will not let you rot here anymore. You should go to Bombay.'

Mohandas sat in absolute silence for some time. Then in a rasping voice he said, 'How will I survive in Bombay?' With an effort at self-control, he continued, 'Bombay is a big city. Living is expensive. I will need a house for the family. I will need an office.' Perhaps the memories of the bad days in Bombay surfaced when he could not earn a paisa.

Mawji Dave tried to instil confidence in him, 'Don't worry. I will send you cases from here and I will have you back for consultations from time to time.'

Mohandas was enormously relieved. This time he joked, 'So you want to get rid of me?'

'No, not at all. I believe that you are not making good use of your time and talent. Your inclination towards social service and politics will bring you to the service of the people. You will get many opportunities in Bombay.' Mohandas could only stare at Mawji open-mouthed.

It was as if Mawji Dave had voiced what was in his heart. Before you know it, your heart's desire becomes a reality. The decision to move to Bombay was taken. An office in Fort area and a small bungalow in Girgaum were rented. On Lakshmidas's advice, widowed sister Raliyat's son was admitted to school in Banaras and Harilal in Gondal. At both places, there was only one vacant seat so who went where was decided by the toss of a coin. In July, after finishing all these chores, Mohandas left for Bombay with Kasturba and the three children. Kasturba felt the sea breeze in a new city. The soil for them changed again. A new place, a new life and new interests. But Kasturba felt at home. This newness was quite different from the strangeness of Durban. The main reason was that Kastur's father had opened the biggest branch of his textile business in Bombay. His son and heir had his own house there. Many relatives and friends from Porbandar and Rajkot had also moved to Bombay. Kasturba was glad that the loneliness of Durban had vanished like a dream.

The bungalow in Girgaum was not fully ready when the Gandhi family moved in. They were plunged into a crisis immediately. Manilal had been struck by small pox two years ago. His eyesight had been weakened. Bapu and Ba were worried about him. Suddenly he contracted typhoid and pneumonia together. They took him to a Parsi doctor. Manilal was extremely weak. The doctor said that he was so weak that it would be hard for him to bear the onslaught of two diseases. He must be given eggs and chicken soup to become stronger. The family was already worried on account of his illness and the doctor's advice only added to their woes. How could Vaishnav tradition be broken on the advice of a Parsi Doctor? Mohandas called Kasturba aside. He said, 'It seems God is testing us. Testing our faith ...'

The doctor heard him and said, 'I knew this ...'

'But the point is how do we save Manilal?' was Kastur's question.

Mohandas said, 'I have studied hydrotherapy. I believe in its efficacy. I want to use it for Mani. Do you have any objection? Manilal is as much your son as he is mine.' Kastur was tormented. What if something went wrong? But unless there was a good reason, she should not repudiate anything. She gave her consent. Mohandas clarified, 'If Mani had been older, I would have left the decision to him. But now it has to be the mother's decision.' He turned to the doctor, 'I need your help. I think that the treatment of the German Doctor Ludwig will cure him. I request you to come and examine the child daily to see if he is getting better.'

The doctor agreed. As soon as he left, the treatment commenced. For three days, Ba and Bapu gave repeated hip baths for a minute or two. His diet consisted of water and orange juice. The doctor came daily and shook his head after examining the child. Both of them could see that Manilal's fever was not breaking. At night, he would be delirious. Their nervousness was growing. Doubts would rise in Ba's heart, but not disbelief. She could sense what was going on in Mohandas's mind. Was it possible to cure him with hydrotherapy? Does a father have a right to play with his son's life? If something were to happen to Mani, will Kastur be able to forgive him? She was patiently carrying out Mohandas's instructions for the treatment. She knew that when you set course, you do not return to the starting point for fear of it being too long. One evening, Mohandas was sitting by Mani's side. Suddenly he called out, 'Kastur ... Kastur.' He asked her to bring the thermometer. He had a temperature of 104 degrees. His body was on fire. Mani was much more restless than usual.

Mohandas turned to his wife. 'I want to conduct one more experiment and that is my final treatment. I don't know if the fever will break. But I will not stop trying. I need your help.'

For the first time Kasturbai felt her own face turn a fiery red. Her son's rush of blood was entering her own frame. But she patiently wet a white sheet according to her husband's directions. In the interim, he had stripped Mani down completely. Both of them wrapped him in the wet sheet and covered him up with two blankets. His face was left uncovered. Kasturba could sense that Mohandas was deeply distraught. She put her hand on his shoulder and pressed gently … He was relieved. 'I want to remove myself from here, for a little while. Let me take a walk outside. Please put a cold compress on his forehead.'

Since she knew how tense he was, she stayed calm, 'Yes, you go. I will stay here and do that.'

She took over, without raising any question. She did not even ask what she should do if Manilal took a turn for the worse. As soon as Mohandas exited, she sighed, 'It is God who gives life and it is God who takes it away. We have to keep trying and trust. It is His will that prevails in the end.'

Mohandas walked some furlongs down the deserted beach. He silently chanted … *Ram Ram*…. When he had been a child, he was scared to go up the stairs in the dark. His helper Rambha had given him this mantra of *Ram Ram* and it would carry him up the stairs. Today he was a grown man, but this mantra was still on his lips. His faith came limping back. His hopes were returning. He turned back. He returned to Kasturba watching in wonder at what unfolded. Mohandas could scarcely believe his eyes. Manilal was bathed in sweat. The fever had broken. The child who had been babbling in delirium had come back to himself. As Ba wiped his sweat, his pain was rolling down as tears from his eyes. For the first time in days, his heart was at peace.

As soon as Mohandas set foot in the room, Manilal, who had been quiet until now, yelled, 'Bapu, take this blanket off. I am soaked through.'

'Just a second ...' said Mohandas moving swiftly. He looked at Kasturba in gratitude. Kastur's face had a beatific smile as if she had witnessed a miracle.

Manilal was completely well. Kasturba always felt that the house was dark and suffocating. Even a healthy person would fall ill in a house such as this. She was uneasy with regard to the two other children. Mohandas agreed to changing houses. 'I felt the same,' he said.

The hunt for a new house began. They found a very good one but it was next to an abattoir. Kasturba could not bear to see animals being slaughtered. Rather than the animals, she felt that children were being slaughtered. After much effort, a bungalow was found near Santa Cruz in outer Bombay. It was open, airy and had a garden in the front. Everybody liked this house.

Mohandas had got a first class season ticket. He could travel anywhere in the city. Many times he was alone in the first class compartment. Then he would remember how he had to walk to court from home and back. All these journeys, just to earn a living ... Although he hardly got any cases, chamber practice enabled him to meet his expenses. The facility he enjoyed was of the Library in the High Court. He would sit by the window enjoying the sea breeze and listen to the court proceedings. Gokhale kept his promise to look out for him. Many times a week, he would come to the chambers. Often he would take him to meet prominent people to expand Mohandas's network. He would tell him what all he could do for the Congress. Life was comfortable. Kasturba was satisfied. For the first time she had felt settled and happy living in India. Living in a protected environment, she talked freely with everybody. She liked making new friends. She felt like she owned her household for the first time. It was easy for her to carry out her responsibilities here.

In South Africa, most of the families residing in their neighbourhood were English-speaking Christians or Muslims. It was difficult for Kasturba to converse with them. But she welcomed everyone happily. Often she thought about the number of caste and traditional taboos she had left behind. Her husband's insistence and her own understanding of practical necessities were the reasons for this change. She had understood afresh, many things to do with food, baths, cleanliness and bringing shoes into the house. All these were part of a new world. Until she had not returned to Rajkot from South Africa, she had not realised how troublesome these changes had been for her. There is a difference between habit and behaviour. She had never protested but faced difficulties in turning habits into behaviour. One day, talking to her elder sister-in-law, she spoke about her dilemma. Mohandas was serious about following his own changed beliefs and making sure that she did too. Although, initially Kastur did not accept all of them in her heart ... She used to think that the great sages of the past, the *rishi-munis* must have decided to have division of labour in society on a sound basis. Nobody had a right to raise any doubts about it. But society cannot remain straitjacketed either. Her sister-in-law gave her a reassuring response but it was also unsettling.

'In South Africa, you were a good wife. There is bound to be a difference between what was good there and what is so over here,' said Nandkunwarben. 'While you are in the role of a good wife, there is no harm in giving up traditional practices.'

From that day on, Kasturba had almost stopped blaming herself. She was very relieved to be living by her own rules in the bungalow in Santa Cruz. Whatever Mohandas had wanted in Durban, Kasturba was happy to do here. Everybody began to feel certain that they would stay on in India. But this was not to be. In November 1902, Mohandas got a telegram. It said, 'Chamberlain was going to come to Natal, come immediately.' Kasturba's dream of settling down in India stood shattered. The children also wanted to stay here and study. Kasturba protested. 'We cannot keep uprooting our lives because something is happening in South Africa. We have to think of the future of our children. Their studies are getting affected badly.'

'This means that I will have to go alone. I had made a promise,' said Mohandas. 'It will not take longer than a year for me to do what I am being called for. I will arrange for you all to stay on in Santa Cruz.' Kasturba remembered when Mohandas had gone for the first time, he had said it was for a year. But he is still there. He comes and then goes again. She did not say any more even though she wanted to protest....

Mohandas sent a cable the very next day that as soon he got the money for the ticket, he would leave. The people in Durban sent the money immediately. The insecurity of the family, in his absence, began to bother Mohandas. The house was on rent. The jewels had already been sold for his education in London. If something were to happen to him, Kasturba would have nothing to fall back on. He sought out an insurance agent whom he had refused to entertain earlier. Kasturba had reassured him that he should go without worrying about such things, since he had decided he must go. He should travel unencumbered. However, he got an insurance of ten thousand rupees with Kasturba as the beneficiary. When he handed her the insurance policy at night, she spoke angrily, 'In spite of my telling you, how could you think of doing something so inauspicious before going? An Indian woman can bear anything but inauspicious thoughts about her husband. She will want to go before her husband.'

Mohandas tried to reason with her, 'This is not about anything inauspicious. Anything can happen to anybody at any time. I would be a fool not to think of all eventualities.'

'It is the responsibility of a living being to find resources for survival. How long will somebody live on insurance money?' said Kasturba tartly and went inside.

Mohandas did not want to annoy her. He kept the policy papers aside and got busy with other arrangements. There were two families – the one in Rajkot and the one in Bombay. Harilal and Gokuldas had been sent to the local hostels of their respective schools. He had asked Lakshmidas to keep an eye on the children. He had even asked his barrister friend to allow them to play in his tennis court. Chhaganlal, a close relative, was a clerk in Bombay. He told him to shift into the

Santa Cruz bungalow. He and his family were to look after Kasturba and the children. Chhaganlal could teach Manilal. Chhaganlal had one son, younger than Ramdas and Devdas. His wife Kashiben and Kasturba got along very well. She was like a younger sister-in-law to Kasturba.

After making all these arrangements, Mohandas felt satisfied that he had done the best possible under the circumstances, and he left Bombay in the second week of November. After a year, he would resume life with his family just where he had left off.

***

I am with you...

In January of 1903, there was an unexpected event. Harilal was turning fourteen. He was very close to Mota Bapu. Mota Bapu Lakshmidas arranged his match with Gulab, the eleven year old daughter of close family friends, the Voras. Haridas Vora was a senior lawyer in Rajkot and a good friend of Mohandas. He was also a Modh Vaishya. Lakshmidas had not taken Mohandas and Kasturba's opposition to child marriage very seriously. When Mohandas found out, he opposed the match fiercely. When he was given assurances that the children would be married off several years later, he acquiesced with great reluctance.

Autumn had come. Dried leaves changing colour and blowing everywhere made Kasturba restless. She appeared calm outwardly. Her helplessness as a wife and mother was like an ember smoking constantly. The translucence of smoke enveloped her ...

***

At the end of the year, instead of returning, there was a message from Mohandas that as soon as she could, Kasturba should come with the children to South Africa. There was no mention of when they would return. With all her heart, Kasturba wanted to be a good wife but she was apprehensive about leaving Harilal in Rajkot. He did not want to go to Durban with his ba. Everybody in Rajkot praised Hari for his brilliance in studies. He was extremely intelligent, and the plaudits he received made Kasturba proud. She believed that his insistence on studying was a positive sign.

Kasturba was assailed by fears and doubts. Compared to the last time, the prospect of the sea voyage was alarming. She would have to go alone with the children. Thousands of miles ... the last experience ... what was her family's destiny, she wondered. Mohandas's letters seemed to indicate that South Africa was changing rapidly. What sort of change would it be? She felt as if she was going to a strange lonely place, for the first time. As it is, Mohandas had taken a house in Transvaal rather than Durban because he was practising there. Kasturba had only heard the name Transvaal until then. The whole family had to stay in Johannesburg. Creole was the spoken language there which was different from English. She would have to start afresh with regard to food, lifestyle, house, the children's studies and Mohandas' new ideas. Change had become a constant in her life. The thought that she could rise to the challenge gave her strength. After all, she had learnt to deal with changes. She would not be afraid. She had lived with changes in the past and she would live with them, going forward.

She was faced with another dilemma. She did not want to give up the freedom she had living in Santa Cruz. Women were perhaps not familiar with the hazards that come with unlimited freedom. Kashiben and Kasturba had made improvements to the house thinking Mohandas would approve when he comes back after a year. Kasturba trusted Kashiben completely. But as the time to leave came closer, Kasturba's joy in her independence diminished. The attachment to the bungalow in Santa Cruz began to weigh down on her. She would miss Kashiben. Who knows when they would meet again? Attachments cause grief, whether to people or places. Relationships you build cause pain when you have to scatter in different directions ...

***

From the time that Mohandas had returned to South Africa a second time, he was witness to many unexpected changes. After the defeat of the Boers, the Indian subjects had hoped the excesses would be stopped now that the British were victorious. But the era of humiliation and exploitation had not come to an end, the selfless service of the Indians to the British army notwithstanding. At the time of the Boer War, the British had declared one of the reasons was the treatment meted out to the Indians. By 1903, things had taken a sharply downward turn.

When Mohandas got to know of the state of the Indians, along with all the co-workers of the Natal Indian Congress, he went to meet the Colonial Secretary, Chamberlain, who was camping there. People believed that Chamberlain was sympathetic to the Indians. He received Mohandas with due respect. After listening to the arguments of the Indians who respected British law, he did not waste a moment in showing Mohandas and his friends the door claiming to be busy. He just said, 'Mr Gandhi, we do not interfere in colonies. I will do what I can. My personal advice to you is that you should try to win the trust of the Europeans if you have to live with them.' After this, he left to inspect war-torn Transvaal.

Chamberlain's attitude was a big blow to the morale of the Indians. They turned on Mohandas. 'You had said that if we side with the British in the Boer war, they will be sympathetic to our problems.' Gandhi had to concede that he was mistaken about the British administration.

——***——

Gandhi's Friendship

Mohandas met a German architect, Herman Kallenbach. He was a successful man with a free mind who had studied Buddhism and was interested in vegetarianism. Gradually, the two of them began discussing other such matters of common interest. Kallenbach introduced him to a British property agent called Louis W Rich. Rich was the convenor of the Theosophical Society of Johannesburg. With Rich's help, Mohandas got an office on lease on Risick Street which was a wonder in itself. Before this, no Indian had ever set up an office in Risick Street. Mohandas had been registered as an advocate in the Transvaal Supreme Court in spite of opposition and objections from the Bar Council. He was the first black to be registered in the Supreme Court. When he got there, he had the uncouth White officials of the Asiatic Office removed, in spite of the jury rejecting the evidence of Blacks against them. This seemingly insignificant incident had brought him on an equal footing with European lawyers. His practice was also growing. In Durban, his practice had never paid him so well. He dreamt of changing the world. Expanding his business based on his spiritual beliefs and his intellectual engagement, this was a creative and decisive period in his life. It was not as if he was unaware of his familial duties. Having become a public leader and being completely immersed in the problems of his immigrant countrymen in South Africa, he had almost given up the idea of returning to his country. This is why he did not do anything regarding getting Kasturba and the children to South Africa, for a long time. For months, he lived alone in the rear of the office. Although she was close to his heart, Kasturba was across the seven seas. Over there, a new Kasturba was emerging who was a match for her husband in endurance and responsibility.

In the meanwhile, when he went to Natal, a Gujarati businessman by the name of Madanjit Vyavharik got in touch with him. Vyavharik owned a printing press and he convinced Gandhi to bring out a weekly newspaper in South Africa, to connect with the Indian community. This would also arouse their interest in important issues. Mohandas concurred and also assured him of financial help. The new paper was called *Indian Opinion.* The publishing of the first edition was another sad story as all manner of difficulties cropped up. On 4 June, 1903, the first edition in English, Hindi, Tamil and Gujarati came out as scheduled. Later, due to financial constraints and seeing the percentages of the Indian population, the Hindi and Tamil newspapers were discontinued.

——***——

Kasturba's Distress

Mohandas's practice was much more successful in Transvaal, compared to Natal and Bombay. He lived in a big house. Whenever he was alone, he would be upset by the thought of all those who should have been living in this house being thousands of miles away. Why were they missing out? But right then, it was not possible for him to go and get them. Situations were changing rapidly in Transvaal every day. He knew that Kasturba was the children's mother, but to subject all of them to a voyage of a thousand miles, would be no less than a trial by fire. So he kept putting off their arrival. But the more he put it off, the more pressured he felt. Finally, he asked a friend, Revashankar Bhai to make his way to Kasturba and tell her to wind up the house in Santa Cruz and come to Transvaal with the children as soon as possible. His house seemed to echo with emptiness. He also informed his elder brother that Kasturba and the children were coming to Natal.

When she got his message, Kasturba was furious. 'I don't want to go anywhere. What does he think? First he dumped us in Durban. Now he sends a *hukmnama* to come with the children! Why should I have to listen? To a person who does not know his own mind? He could have taken us along when he went, but no, he wouldn't do that. Is it a joke to travel so far with such young children?'

Revashankar Bhai tried to reason with Kasturba, 'Don't say this. Mohanbhai has called you. He is alone there and he needs you. Once you board the ship, you will get off only at Durban. Mohanbhai has made suitable arrangements.'

Kasturba could not sleep that night. Heaven knows what was going to happen, will they sink or survive? Everything terrible that could have happened had happened the last time. The Police Captain's wife had turned up or else he would not have survived … who could say that to him? Help others by all means, but at least don't put your own life in danger. His arguments make no sense – don't women put their lives in danger when they want to become mothers. Could anybody reason with him?

Her biggest problem was that Hari was not ready to go. He wanted to stay with Mota Bapu in Rajkot and study.

Mohandas did not have to think of anything. Whatever popped out of his mouth was right. After all, he was a man. But I have to think of others. Lord Ram had crossed seven seas to find Sita Mata. Here it was all the reverse.

***

When Kasturba boarded the ship, her eyes were wet and her heart was heavy. Her heart was wrenched asunder because Hari was being left behind…. Even plants need the support of a fence to grow straight and upright. The perils that lurk for somebody of a tender age do not announce themselves. Hari should not get left behind ...

***

Kasturba sat on the deck and brooded about Hari. He had turned sixteen. How much time had he spent with his father in these sixteen years? Their contact had been akin to touching the entrance of a house. Now that the time had come to learn something from his father, he had chosen to stay with his uncle. He had been so scared of water when he had gone to South Africa, the last time. His father had taken him to the deck repeatedly to make him get over his fear. Now, even little Devdas was running about on the deck. Water is beautiful but also makes you fearful. Just then a man came running and said, 'Your child has been hurt.'

Kasturba panicked. 'Oh God! Do you have to test me all the time?' Ramdas was weeping inconsolably. Many sailors had gathered around and a White sailor was carrying him in his arms. Ramdas could not move his hand and the swelling was increasing by the minute. The sailor made him lie down in the cabin. He was the ship's doctor. He said, 'Mrs Gandy, no doctor can be called from outside since the ship is at sea. If you permit me, I can bandage his hand at least, so that he can make it to Durban.' There was no other option. Kasturba had to agree. He bound up the hand with two slats of wood and hung it from his neck. Ramdas felt a little better but he was still extremely restless. Kasturba felt Mohandas's absence in every breath. He is sitting pretty over there, while my child is writhing in pain. More than missing him, she felt angry. He wants to get accolades from everybody. He neither needs his wife nor his children. I must be crazy to be bringing a shipload of children and counting the waves in the ocean. Once a man, always a man ... all that is dear to him is his work ... She held Ramdas in her lap all night long. In her loneliness, the sounds of the ship felt as if *pralaya* was nigh and the shore was breaking up into pieces that were adrift.

They got off at Delagoa port. There was a fellow passenger by the name of Vasudev Bhai with them. He was a Gujarati and he knew Mohandas. They bought first class tickets and sat in the train. Manilal insisted on sitting next to the window. Kasturba and Vasudev Bhai tried their best to reason with him, but he was adamant. Suddenly the glass of the window came down and his thumb was injured. There was no Doctor at hand. Vasudev Bhai wet a cloth and tied it up. Kastur had borne up under Ramdas's injury but she was completely done in by now. Ramdas had not bled so she had been able to bear it. The blood flowing from Manilal's wound was as if her own blood could not be staunched. A mountain of pain broke over her but she could not weep openly. One child was left behind and two were injured.

***

When they got off at Johannesburg station, Kasturba's eyes desperately searched for Mohandas. There was no Mohandas nor anybody sent by him. Kasturba was deeply offended. A traitorous thought wormed its way into her mind – we are at a point where Mohandas thinks – if the children arrive it is good, and even if they don't, it is fine. There might be some rancour against her but what was the fault of the children? Devdas even asked, 'Ba, Bapu…?' It was hard to say anything to him and it was just as hard to know the meaning of this behaviour. How uncaring were those she thought of as her own? How could anybody else be expected to care? It was I who was foolish to care about others ... she thought bitterly.

When they finally reached home, Kastur noted the shock on Mohandas's face to see Ramdas's hand in a sling and the bandage on Manilal's thumb. 'What happened?' he exclaimed worriedly.

Kastur could not hold back her tears any longer. They were a mixture of sadness and helplessness and regret.

Mohandas tested Ramdas's hand. He moaned in pain. When Mohandas undid Manilal's bandage he could not restrain his sobs. Turning to Kasturba, Mohandas shouted, 'You could not even look after the children?'

Kastur paused for a second and then said, 'You are right. After all, you were sitting here. It is not easy for me to explain the state of a mother with three children to look after.' Vasudev Bhai maintained an embarrassed silence. He introduced himself and gave a full account of what had happened. 'I had heard about you and wanted to meet you. I did not want Kasturben to travel alone with two children who were injured.' Mohandas listened to him in silence. His face revealed that he knew how insensitive and boorish he had been. When Vasudev Bhai was gone, Kastur no longer held her temper in check. 'You could not even come to the station! Do you think it was easy to bring three young children across thousands of miles by ship? Were the children supposed to just sit and stare at their mother's face? You gave me a fine reward instead ...' Mohandas did not say a word. Perhaps he could not think of an answer.

He asked her, 'Should I put a mud pack on Ramdas's hand?' Kastur nodded. Then it was Manilal's turn. He washed his wound with potassium permanganate and applied a mud pack. After few days, Ramdas's bones began to knit. Mani's wound was also healing.

***

Mohandas's routine was fixed. He would leave early in the morning either on a bicycle or on foot. He would return by dinner time. Often, he was accompanied by his associates. Mohandas liked dining with them. Kasturba cooked keeping this in mind. He often worked late into the night. He had to write articles and editorials for *Indian Opinion.* He slept in his own room. Sometimes he would come into Kastur's bed. He came to satisfy himself and Kasturba knew this. She cooperated as best as she could. She understood that she was not a part of his life, and had not been in the past either. She held her peace.

He believed that it was important to increase the readership of *Indian Opinion.* To close it down would be humiliating for the Indians and it would shut down dialogue between the Indians and the government. This would be bad for the movement. Every month, he gave his contribution of £75 to keep it going. One day he sent a message that he would not be coming back at night. This had never happened before. However late, he had always come home until now. Kasturba had no clue why he had violated his own rule. There was nobody she could ask. She fed the children and went to bed. She was worried sick. As it is, the Whites did not like him. When Mohandas returned to rest and freshen up, he merely said that the Indians had been in a crisis.

After he had freshened up, Kasturba asked him again. He said, 'There is an outbreak of the Black Plague in the settlement of the workers. Twenty-three patients have been admitted. A storeroom had to be cleaned for a temporary arrangement to house the patients. It should not spread further.' He had kept this from Kastur lest she worried to hear about the Plague. But he was tense and disturbed himself. Pneumonic Plague had spread rapidly across the settlement. It had first appeared among the African workers working in the gold mines. It had spread to the settlement of the Indian workers. Madanjit had broken the lock of an unoccupied house and isolated the patients. After that he had informed Mohandas.

'Last night was horrific. Let us see how it goes today. I must leave immediately. Who knows what might have happened ...' he said.

Kasturba showed no fear, nor did she stop him. Unexpectedly she said, 'I will come along to help you.'

Manilal was listening and he immediately piped up, 'I will also come along to help.' Both of them ignored him. Mohandas stared at his wife in astonishment and just uttered one word. 'No.' Kasturba was crestfallen. Looking at her disappointed face, he suggested a less risky way to be of use,

'If you want to help, go to the Indian workers' settlement and talk to the women. Explain how to stay healthy, observe hygiene and how to recognise the symptoms of Plague. Tell them how to stay safe.'

Kasturba was uneasy at the thought of entering strange houses to give unsolicited advice. Then she was struck by the need for prevention from such a dangerous illness. She resolved to do what she could. She left the younger children in Manilal's care and went with Mohandas into the settlement. She sought out the women to give them all the information. Even the women who did not understand Gujarati welcomed Kasturba's spirit of service. She suggested to some of them that they go to the store where the sick had been isolated and clean and polish the floor. Kasturba and some other women went door to door and collected mattresses, sheets, pillows, dishes and bed pans. They did not go home until everything needed for the sick had been collected. She was nervous about the kids. She kept her faith in Manilal's capabilities. She knew he was clever and responsible. Patients were dying at an alarming rate. It was a real crisis. A White nurse sent by the municipal authorities soon succumbed to the Plague. It was like the dance of death.

The hardship of the Plague had barely ended when there was fresh adversity. The municipality of Johannesburg declared that since the Plague had originated from the Indian settlement, it had to be burnt down. This was when it had originated from the workers in the gold mines. The municipality had never done anything to clean up the settlement. It did not give any notice before deciding to destroy it. Mohandas was very disturbed by this unjust unilateral order. He had always and continuously raised his voice against the lack of hygiene that leads to the spread of disease and asked for sanitation measures. The inhabitants were forcibly removed from their homes and sent to camps and their settlement was set on fire. Mohandas filed a case against this atrocity with his own money and in 69 cases out of 70, he got the tribunal to give compensation to the workers. He took half the fees decided in court when compensation was awarded. Even this fee, he gave over to *Indian Opinion.*

In this period of crisis, Kasturba was also among the people who had impressed him. For the first time, he saw that even in such life threatening situations, Kasturba had amazing strength to work with women and inspire them. She showed empathy and displayed great capability. Not only was she conscientious, but also stayed steadfast and committed even in the face of unprecedented problems.

——***——

Mohandas and the Children

Mohandas and Kasturba had just emerged from the crisis that had hit the Indian community. Life in Johannesburg had just settled into a rhythm. Mohandas had managed to save two patients from the thirty hit by the Black Plague with his mud and hydro-therapy and this had made him feel better. He felt equable under the circumstances. His associate, Dr Godfrey, had not been able to save twenty one; everybody was astonished that Gandhi had saved two.

Now he turned his attention towards the education of the children. Even during the Durban sojourn, the kids' studies had been a constant bone of contention between husband and wife. Hari had chosen to stay with Mota Bapu in Rajkot only because he had not been able to study properly. Kasturba would be overcome every time she thought of Hari. She always considered him her brightest child. Mohandas still baulked at the thought of putting his children in a normal school as he thought that he could teach them better. Even though she was illiterate, Kasturba believed that education was better imparted in a school. Mohandas took Manilal and Ramdas for a five mile walk every morning. He taught them all the way. Intermittently, this sort of nomadic school had been conducted by him with Harilal and Gokuldas, in Durban also. Now it was fairly regular. He took Manilal and Gokuldas to office with him. He gave them writing and memorising tasks there. They were supposed to complete the tasks within a fixed time. During this time, he would talk to clients, deal with office work and give dictation to his assistant Ms Shlesin on drafts and letters. Ms Shlesin was Jewish and she enjoyed Mohandas's trust. She never tired of work but she also exercised her freedom. On one occasion, he called for something but she did not leave her seat and continued to smoke a cigarette. Mohandas would often get up and go to the seat of an associate. Even after he got there, she continued to smoke. 'What is this?' he asked.

She did not reply but blew smoke into his face. Mohandas, who normally did not lose his temper even under extreme provocation, was furious. All of a sudden, he slapped her. Almost immediately, he regretted it and sought her forgiveness. Shlesin laughed loudly. 'I wanted to see if Mr Gandhi ever got angry.' Gandhi did not say a word and left. He was troubled by the thought that anger was a kind of violence.

Kasturba noticed that he was perturbed. He told her what had happened with Shlesin. Kasturba burst into loud laughter. Mohandas could not understand the reason for her mirth.

'What is so funny?'

'You must not have laughed so I am laughing instead. Isn't it funny that she set up the whole thing to be slapped and then laughed? You should laugh now at least. She must have been disappointed that you did not laugh.'

***

One day Mohandas covered a long distance and reached the office with the children. He got busy and the children began doing their work. He noticed Manilal reading holding the book very close to his eyes. 'Why haven't you put on your glasses?' he asked.

'I forgot to get my glasses. They are at home.'

'Your glasses should have been with you. Go home and get them so that you never forget them in the future,' he said angrily.

Manilal reached home in the heat of mid-day, totally drained. Kasturba was shocked to see him there at this odd hour. 'What happened? Why are you here alone?'

'I forgot my glasses. Bapu sent me to get them, but I have to return immediately.' He was hot and fatigued.

Kasturba made no comment on Mohandas's orders, but hurriedly got a meal ready and fed him. As he ate, she dried off his sweat. How could she explain to her twelve year old son that her husband's immutable ideas seemed hard but they were based on important principles? They could be understood only if you are close to him. I am grappling with them myself. 'I can understand how you must feel about Bapu making you do this,' she said to him. She waited to observe his reaction. 'You remember, something similar had happened with me in Durban?'

Manilal was listening attentively but he kept quiet. Ba reminded him how Bapu had set tradition aside and made her empty out the chamber pot of a Christian guest. She had been deeply hurt. He did not intend to insult her. He wanted it to be taken in the spirit of service. He wanted the hidebound ideas of untouchability to be discarded. He also cleaned pots. He had almost thrown her out of the house when she cried. Later, she understood how important it was for him to clean pots. It was a way to quell arrogance that creeps in unbidden. She tried to understand his sentiments in whatever he asked her to do or did himself. Kastur, on her own had decided that she would not listen to her husband, until she understood his logic. She must understand, only then she would follow him willingly.

Finally she told Manilal, 'Your bapu may appear headstrong, on the face of it, but he is a good human being. He wants you to be a good son, so he asks you to do things that are hard. He believes that physical labour strengthens the mind and the body.' She ran her fingers through his dishevelled hair. 'Do as Bapu says, even if it is tough. Now you should leave, or he will wonder where you are.'

Mohandas got a letter from Bade Bhaiya from Rajkot that Harilal was seriously ill. When he told Kastur, she was distraught. How could she be with Hari since she was so far away? It was not easy, in fact, it was impossible to reach Rajkot from Johannesburg and then return. Lakshmidas had left Rajkot with his family and moved to their old house in Porbandar. Only his widowed sister Raliyat was in Rajkot. Lakshmidas had also written that Hari's father-in-law, Haridas Vora had taken Harilal to his house so there was nothing to worry about. There was no male in Raliyat's house who could run around, in a crisis. Harilal was being well looked after. Mohandas and Kasturba were not pleased to hear this but they were quite helpless. Kastur felt like a bird flapping its wings in vain. She desperately wanted to be with her child.

Something else was brewing there. Harilal was convalescing at Harilal Vora's house, who was also his prospective father-in-law, as he was betrothed to Gulab, his second daughter. The two had fallen in love. When Harilal shifted back to his own house as he got better, there was an ongoing exchange of love letters between them. Nobody was any the wiser until a long time.

***

This was a complicated period for Mohandas. *Indian Opinion* was in dire financial straits. The debts were mounting. Madanjit, the manager who looked after it, was returning to India. Mohandas was looking for a reliable replacement. He came upon Albert West, an Englishman. He had been a partner in a press in Johannesburg. He was willing to go to Durban and take charge of *Indian Opinion.* He invited Mohandas to come to Durban and present his plans for the future of the paper.

——***——

Friendship with Ruskin

When Mohandas was going to Durban, Henry Pollack had arrived recently from London. Mohandas was acquainted with him from before. He had come to Johannesburg station to see him off. Mohandas knew Pollack's father. Pollack had come there on Mohandas's behest. Pollack pressed a book upon him as he was leaving, asking him to read it. It was John Ruskin's *Unto the Last.* Mohandas could not put it down through the night. He forgot everything else as he immersed himself in the book. He could think of nothing else the next day. This book had been published in 1862, but even after several decades, it could shake up its readers. Ruskin had written that money was a powerful medium to enslave a human being. Ruskin wanted the wealthy to serve the poor rather than spend on their comforts. They should understand that the real wealth of a society lay in the welfare of all its members. By the time the train reached Durban, Mohandas had resolved to mould himself according to the principles laid down in the book. The picture of the village in Natal in Marianne Hill which he had seen a few years ago, flashed before his eyes. It was a fully self-reliant village of the

Trappists. They fulfilled all their needs by themselves. Their ideal was to work in cooperation and harmony.

The plans for *Indian Opinion* that he presented were not supported by anybody except Albert West and the machine-man Govindswami. They believed that shareholding meant taking responsibility whereas a salaried person remained free. It was after great difficulty that the others agreed to his plans on an experimental basis. The next day, he put an advertisement in local newspapers seeking land near the railroad station. A landlord in Phoenix, eighteen miles from Durban, sent a proposal. Mohandas went to see the land, along with Albert West. He bought the excellent stretch of twenty acres with orange, guava and mango trees for a thousand pounds. Mohandas began to dream of actualising Ruskin's ideas. First he established a press and invested in the construction of the settlement thereafter. Phoenix was the laboratory for his dreams.

He began planning a break from his practice and wanted to move to Phoenix with the family. But he had to spend most of his time in Johannesburg. Considerable financial resources were needed to run the newspaper and the settlement. Some people such as Louis Rich, Albert West, Henry Pollack who believed in free consciousness, were devoted to Mohandas's ideals. There were others in South Africa who supported him at a time when only few people were aware of his ideas. His work was without precedent. But he was not well known until then. Kastur and the children felt that Mohandas was capable of influencing others.

Pollack had gone to Johannesburg from Durban to practice law. Gandhi had invited him to be a part of the

Gandhi family. Kasturba had not been put out by this. She had Mohandas's office colleagues living in her house in Durban earlier. She had no problem with Pollack being British. There was only the problem of dialogue. Soon she and the children grew to like having Pollack in the house.

After some time, Pollack's fiancée Millie arrived. She did not believe in staying for an extended period as a guest in anybody's house. But Millie also became a part of Kasturba's household like her husband. Kasturba had experienced the benefit of living in a joint family in Rajkot. A joint family draws singles into its fold. It nurtures participation and forbearance. Kasturba and Millie got along famously. They planned out all the chores in the kitchen. When one cooked, the other cleaned the dishes. Mohandas worked as an interpreter between the two. The courses in the meals also kept changing. Millie knew that Mohandas, Kasturba and the children were entirely vegetarian and she cooked accordingly. Kasturba had no objection to their cooking meat separately, but Millie chose not to. They also found out ways to communicate with each other. Millie taught Kasturba the words for things and many verbs.

——***——

Millie and the Gandhi Family

Millie used to keep poor health in London. Pollack and Millie's marriage was imminent. When Pollack's father discovered that Millie was going to South Africa in spite of her ill health, he wrote to Gandhi that he should prevail upon Pollack and Millie to hold off the wedding until Millie was well. Millie's health is not so robust that she will be able to withstand the struggles of life in a colony. Gandhi wrote back to Pollack senior that if Millie was determined to come then she should be allowed to do that. If a girl does not keep well in London then she should do well in the moderate climate of South Africa. She will become stronger in the pleasant atmosphere and get better with loving care. He wrote a second letter addressed to Millie, saying that she was welcome to their house and they would look after her well. 'Your betrothed is already with us and you will improve in no time at all …'

Millie got off at Juppy station on 30 December, 1905. Gandhi and Pollack were ready to welcome her. When Pollack and Millie met each other, Gandhi went off for a bit. Both of them absorbed each other's warmth for a long time.

Millie liked Kasturba's spacious, eight roomed house. Gandhi, his three sons – Manilal, Ramdas and Devdas were there of course. There was an Englishman who worked in the telegraph department. There was Pollack and an Indian manservant. Outside was Kasturba's favourite small garden. The day after her arrival, Mohandas took Millie and Pollack to the magistrate's court for their wedding. He placed all the documents before the Marriage Registrar. He looked at them but quite suddenly, he excused himself and vanished. This was the first experience of racism for Millie and Pollack. When it was near closing time, Gandhi went to the Chief Magistrate whom he knew and he narrated the whole incident. The magistrate laughed uproariously. According to the Transvaal law, marriage between a White and a non-White was illegal. The officer who conducted such a marriage could be fined and punished. The Registrar could not say anything to Gandhi so he had quietly excused himself and made himself scarce. He thought that since Pollack and Gandhi were close, Pollack must be Brown too. Gandhi reminded the Magistrate that when Pollack's father had come the last time, he had introduced the two. The Magistrate remembered it well. Everybody laughed because of the confusion and comedy of errors. It was like a Shakespearean comedy. Because of the Magistrate and Gandhi, Millie and Pollack were finally married. When Mohandas came and narrated this story at home, it sounded like something out of a play and everybody had a hearty laugh. But as they remembered the racism inherent in the situation, their smiles faded.

In the evening, Gandhi, Millie and Pollack sat down together to consider the problems that may arise in the near future. The first problem was the education of the children. They did not go to school, instead, they were taught by their father. Millie did not entirely agree with his practice of taking them to the office and then checking their work in the evening. Kasturba maintained that just as a child learns discipline and traditions in the family, he would learn the rules and ways of the school. However, since the father of the children did not agree to send them to school, Millie assumed the responsibility of teaching them. She began to give them classes in English reading and writing, maths, drafting and basic grammar. Whenever he found time, Mohandas would teach them Gujarati. The children spoke to Ba-Bapu in Gujarati. In spite of being their mother, Kasturba could not take part in these discussions regarding their future because she did not know English.

Millie and Kasturba stayed as strangers on the first day. After Mohandas and Pollack left for office, there was no conversation between the two women. At that time, both of them felt that however fine your feelings may be, the absence of a common language creates a distance. Since both of them felt this acutely, they found a way to communicate. Eyes and hands were used freely. When they did not understand each other, they used to laugh a lot at themselves. If the children were around, they would join in the laughter. Kasturba's English was improving. Mohandas had not succeeded in teaching his wife to read Gujarati, in spite of being her husband but the pull of friendship and the tug of the need to have a dialogue, helped Kasturba to learn English. When

Kasturba was able to share things personal with Millie, they became close and they both began to socialise with Whites. Kasturba began taking part in conversations in her broken English.

Mohandas was a good host. He wanted to introduce Millie to all his friends and the Indian leaders there right away, especially the leaders whom Pollack had met before and who had begun to respect his views. Mohandas invited fifty people to his house. The thought flitted across Kasturba's mind that she had been here for so long but not once had he invited anybody over to meet her. But this was followed by a self deprecatory laugh. She thought of how she would have just sat there, mute, not able to understand or converse in a common language.

There was a muddle that took place in preparations for the party. There was a Hindu manservant by the name of Galal who was trustworthy, but rather simple minded. When Mohandas was leaving for office, he asked him something in Gujarati. Mohandas just said yes. Galal immediately set to work and whitewashed the wall paper. Since the head of the household had given him permission, who could have stopped him? When Mohandas returned in the evening, he was struck dumb to see the state of the room. He shrugged philosophically and called for the husband of his former secretary. He was a builder and decorator. Mohandas asked him to restore the room by noon the next day. The next day, when Millie was getting the furniture arranged, the first guest arrived. Mohandas had to explain the reason for Millie's absence. Slowly all the guests found out and it became a source of much merriment. A song for 'Galal the Great' was also sung.

***

Mohandas was changing.

From the day after the lunch, all the members of the house got down to their work according to the time-table. At 6:30 am sharp all the men were ready and they gathered at the grinding stone to grind flour. Mohandas and Pollack did the job. Sometimes Kasturba would hum a traditional song. Millie loved listening even if she did not understand the words. The *rotis* in the house were made of this flour. The grinding went on for half an hour in earnest and everybody enjoyed this chore. There was ribbing and jokes. This was the perfect combination of exercise and getting freshly ground flour.

One day, Pollack returned from office looking very agitated. Millie was worried. She wondered if she had done something wrong but could not think of anything. Pollack was not talking to Mr Gandhi. Dinner time was normally noisy and lively with laughter but that evening, people ate in silence. Pollack immediately retired to his room and Mohandas was quiet. Millie followed Pollack into his room.

'What happened?' she asked, 'Why are you so upset?'

Pollack told Millie that a well known journalist from South Africa had written an article in a prestigious magazine that was full of falsehoods and which could harm the migrant Indians and Indian business community in Transvaal. But Gandhi was silent. Not only that, he had refused to refute the false and very damaging facts presented. And he knew that these things will have a terrible effect on the government in London.

Millie was sympathetic to her husband. Perhaps Pollack was over-reacting. If Gandhi thinks that the article is not important enough to take notice, then why was Pollack so worried? Millie was quite a novice here and did not understand politics and how it played out so she could not be dismissive of Pollack's concerns.

Kasturba was perplexed and silent.

Four days passed in a similar state. Everybody was tense but nobody spoke. Pollack and Gandhi did not speak one word except for bare formalities or business talk. They cocooned themselves in their rooms in the evening or paced up and down the verandah.

The house seemed to be upside down. Finally Kasturba asked Millie in her broken English, 'What Mr Pollack? What for he cross with Bapu?'

Millie said, 'Yes, Pollack is cross with Bapu.'

'What Bapu done?'

'He has not done anything, that is why Pollack is cross.'

Millie had heard enough in those past four days. She slowly explained Henry's views to Kastur.

Millie figured that Kasturba was not particularly put out about Henry being upset with Bapu.

That night, after dinner Gandhi called Pollack, 'I want to speak to you'. They went into the room while the others waited outside.

Gandhi asked Pollack, 'What is the matter? Why are you so frustrated?'

'You know why …' said Pollack in return.

'I want to hear it from you.'

'Your attitude to the article in the N...K Review...'

'But why are you so worked up about it?' Gandhi's tone was calm.

'You know it is a pack of lies!'

'Yes, I know. But how does that matter?'

'It matters,' said Pollack forcefully. 'It matters a great deal. You can't just ignore such a misrepresentation of facts. The world does not know that it is all lies. Unless a reliable person calls it out, how will the readers know? Such articles add to the troubles of the Indians and makes life impossible for them. It is essential that the truth should reach the people. This will be in the interests of the Indian community.'

'What do you want from me?'

'You should write to counter the falsehoods. Put the facts before the people. Who knows them better than you? It is matter concerning your community,' said Pollack in a normal tone.

'You also know all this.'

'Yes, I do. If anybody investigates, they will come to know. It is easy to disprove Mr N.'

Conversation stopped for a moment. From Gandhi's tone it seemed that a solution had been found. 'If you feel so strongly, then you write about it. People will believe you.'

The matter was resolved. The article was written and published. It received praise. This was Pollack's first written dialogue with the people. The morning after it was published, everybody met at breakfast. Kastur asked Pollack, 'You crossed with Bapu?' and everybody laughed.

Nobody knew of the role that Kastur had played.

——***——

A Shiftless Life

In 1906, Mohandas was counted among the major lawyers in South Africa. His law practice flourished and he was the only Indian origin lawyer in Natal and Transvaal. A blemishless record and a reputation for honesty and capability were his biggest assets. The white lawyers' rates were exorbitant. Although he smarted at being called a coolie, Gandhi was satisfied with his work. But he also harboured a deep disquiet. He felt he was wasting his life on material achievements. He was betraying his family and himself. His life was meaningless if he measured himself against the teachings of the Gita which advocated renunciation and the message of dignity of labour in Ruskin. His biggest challenge was to teach Kasturba and the children to be self-reliant and to manage with less. His prime desire was that his family stays in Phoenix Ashram and is a part of his experiment in self-reliance. The burden of working the grindstone fell on the women and children in the absence of Pollack and him. Manilal, Ramdas and Devdas enjoyed the task. Kastur was excused on account of her health. She used to make tasty *rotis* from the un-sifted flour. Only Millie was left, who enjoyed doing things with the children anyway.

Kasturba did not approve of her husband and children doing chores that were considered women's work. She felt it was against tradition for men to do domestic chores. Gandhi was against such distinctions. He believed all the members of the household must be ready to handle any chore. Millie and Henry agreed with him. Gandhi had sent away all the domestic servants. Kasturba had more work now, but she knew she couldn't say that to him.

For Kasturba, the biggest worry continued to be the education of the children. What could she do? Women can manage with the help of men, even without an education, but men had to be self-supporting. The men who could not get an education were *girmitiyas* here and labourers back in India, with not much respect or financial security. Her heart would quail at the thought of her children being one of them. Mohandas was so involved in social causes that he got little time to teach the children. Without the discipline of being under the watch of a teacher, studies took a backseat. Whenever she brought this up, he would say that the children were living at home and were getting an education for leading an honourable life and good *sanskars.* Why did everybody in the world send their children to school was her question. Mohandas would say our children will end up as interpreters, they will not know their own language well nor will they know English … but is English the only subject taught in schools and nothing else? All these questions would raise their heads but remained unasked. When the time was right, she would bring them up with Barrister Sahib directly.

***

Although life was peaceful and stable at home, Kasturba felt something was amiss. There were some stray indications but nothing was clearly expressed. Mohandas seemed equable but he was internally disturbed and she did not know the reason. Kasturba was also restless.

In actual fact, Mohandas had attained success as a lawyer but he was not satisfied with his achievements as a social worker. His untiring hard work, editorials in the *Indian Opinion* and his speeches had little effect on the unjust and repressive laws of the land. The government was unwilling to do anything. He blamed himself for this. All that he had done was not enough and he should have worked harder ... He should have gone deeper with his analysis ... he should have taken harder decisions ...

When her husband had voluntarily chosen to embrace frugality as his life's ideal, Kasturba had not been taken by surprise. He asked himself: should I not separate myself from my wealth in the interests of social good? Was this a way to free myself of this dilemma? Kasturba had seen the signs of frugality and eliminating creature comforts and she had accepted this without protest. She had tried to resist it the last time, in the context of her presents. Sensing her unease, Mohandas had clarified, 'It is not as if I will stop earning. We are only giving up our personal ownership over wealth. We will not hoard money for luxuries. More money than what is needed, only violates the rights of others. The extra money will belong to society.' Kasturba was relieved to hear that he will earn as much as necessary. If he had turned into a full-fledged Baba, what could she have done? Such people hold their zeal dearer than money.

Another incident hurt her deeply. Mohandas had written to his elder brother. He had fulfilled all of Mohandas's needs in his limited income and had been like a father to him. Mohandas wrote him a letter saying he should not expect any financial assistance from South Africa. When Kasturba reminded him about the debt that he had incurred for Mohandas, she was told that it had been repaid. Kasturba knew Lakshmidas was responsible, calm and careful. After Diwan Sahib's death, he had always fulfilled his responsibilities towards everybody. When an elder brother looks after everybody like a father, should a capable and successful younger brother hold back from helping his senior in times of need? Mohandas was the younger brother.

——***——

Lakshmidas's Anguish

Lakshmidas sat in a daze when he got Mohandas's letter. Is this my brother Moniya's letter? How could he write this? This was not a shock, it was a blow beyond his imagination. He was deeply wounded. It was unthinkable that Mohandas had decided to renounce wealth. This was the brother for whom he sacrificed the little wants of his family; the entire family had stood as one to ensure his best education … incurred debt on his account, provided everything for his children … He is turning his face away from his responsibilities? Such ingratitude was unjust and an insult to the entire family. It was not about returning the money that the family had spent. Mohandas was successful and wealthy today. He was in a position to help anybody in the fa mily, if there was a need.

Karsan and Lakshmidas were deeply dismayed. They could not believe that Mohandas had become a sadhu. This vow of living a frugal life was just a cover for his covetousness. He has stopped sending money to his family in India because he wants to amass wealth for his family in South Africa. Doubts can sprout without roots and grow like Jack's beanstalk in the fairytale. They blamed Kasturba. She could have stopped him, if she really wanted. She must be the one to give him such ideas. Her parents were wealthy and now her brother was very prosperous. Kastur understood the importance of money since childhood. Her feelings towards us changed once she got there. She is responsible for this elaborate charade to cut off Mohandas from our family by pretending to take a false vow of poverty.

Lakshmidas wrote a stiff, cold reply to Mohandas reminding him of Diwan Karamchand who took responsibility for the entire family, all his life, and surely he would want his sons to carry forward the same tradition.

Mohandas wrote a two line reply. After all the formal salutations, he said:

'Respected Bhai Sahib,

I have done exactly what Bapu had done. The only difference is that I have increased the circle of my family to include the whole of humanity ...'

This reply put Lakshmidas in a quandary. Is Moniya's vow genuine? Is it his own decision? We were wrong to blame Kastur. This means that Moniya is now touched in the head! A man in his right mind thinks of his own children and his family first. He does not decide to turn into an ascetic, at such a young age. There are people in this land who have left their wealth, property and family at the age of fifty, to go and meditate in the forest. But Moniya is renouncing everything at thirty-seven and seems to have lost touch with reality. How could Kastur let this happen?

What will become of the children? He began pacing up and down.

Lakshmidas called Harilal who happened to be there. He looked him over for some time and then he said, 'I think I should marry you off while I am still around.'

'Bapu..?'

'If your bapu was concerned about you, he would not have sworn off the world.'

'Mota Bapu, I don't understand ...'

'He has taken a vow to distribute his wealth among others and live frugally. I will have to marry you off ... how will you carry the entire burden? Let me talk to Vora ji.'

'Will Ba and Bapu take part? They were not in favour of this match.'

Hari had not liked Ba and Bapu's disapproval of his relationship with Gulab. He could hardly forget how they had been in South Africa when he had fallen ill and Mota Bapu had gone to Porbandar from Rajkot. How could Phua have looked after him all alone? It was Gulab and her family who had nursed him back to health.

Lakshmidas conferred with Gulab's father and set a date for the wedding. Vora ji asked, 'Hari's ba and bapu...?'

'It will be difficult to call them from so far at such short notice.'

2 May, 1906 was fixed as the wedding date. With the help of Mota Bapu, Bichle Bapu, the girl's father, the wedding was celebrated with all due pomp and ceremony.

Exactly a month later, Mohandas was leaving for Durban when Lakshmidas's letter was received. His face creased into a deep frown and he muttered, 'This is a complete betrayal.'

Kastur was in the kitchen. She heard him muttering angrily. 'What happened? Why are you so upset?'

'Bade Bhaiya has married Harilal off ... is this some sort of revenge?' Kasturba was struck dumb. Mohandas went on, 'This is revenge ... his defence is that it is in Harilal's interest.

Is he the only one who thinks of Harilal's best interests ... Is this the age when he should have been married?'

Kasturba felt her husband's rage in her bones. She knew that his anger was not against his son but directed at his elder brother. He was more upset and helpless than angry. For a mother and father, there could be no greater celebratory occasion than their eldest son's marriage. A turbulent storm raged inside her. Not a word to the groom's parents about the wedding? Harilal's moment of joy and the biggest occasion in his life – they had been robbed of the chance to be a part of it. Harilal will always carry this hurt that his ba and bapu were absent for the most significant event in his life. Will this sow the seeds of a poison tree?

'When did it happen?' asked Kasturba.

'Last month. Everybody except us took part.' Mohandas read out the guest list attached to the letter.

'Harilal and Gulab are no more than children. Bhaiya had said himself that they will be married after a few years and Vora ji knew about this. He broke my trust and he has really hurt me. Both Harilal and Gulab had so much to learn before beginning their married life.' Mohandas's voice shook.

Questions swirled in Kasturba's heart. Wouldn't Bade Bhaiya have considered whether an early marriage was in the best interests of the children? How could Gulab's family agree? She is their daughter after all. They are in the same country and must know all the facts. We do not know what happened because we are so far away, in South Africa. Common sense seemed to indicate that the reason for the early marriage must have been Hari and Gulab's love for each other. Gulab's parents must have been aware of the perils of this situation. Indians consider pre-marital sexual relations sinful. They must have thought that it was better that they are married before such an eventuality arose. Mohandas thought it was his elder brother's anger towards him that was responsible for this turn of events.

Kasturba tried to reason with him. 'Perhaps Hari wanted an early marriage ...' She said softly, attempting to soothe his outrage.

'No, that is wrong.' Mohandas fumed, 'How could they not know that such an early marriage was inappropriate?'

'When did our families think so?' Kasturba looked at him and spoke softly. Mohandas did not look approving. Kasturba checked herself. He is our son. She knew Hari was sensitive, impatient and single minded. She thought about Mohandas and how he was impatient, stubborn and how hard it was to resist him when it came to a physical relationship. How hard it had been for him to control his desire … If his son and Gulab had deep feelings for each other then they could hardly be faulted. It was the wise thing to have done to get them married. Parents know their children best.

It is not possible to share everything in your heart, sometimes not even with your husband. Mohandas wrote to Lakshmidas, 'For me, Harilal's marriage is of no importance.' This was the last letter to Lakshmidas. Even though the letter was against Lakshmidas's decision, it was also a rejection of Harilal and Gulab's marriage. Perhaps this letter also fuelled the bitter relationship between father and son, later?

Kastur had the same feeling. If Hari ever read Bapu's letter, the seeds will grow into a tree very soon.

——***——

The Zulu Uprising and Gandhi's dilemma

Gandhi had begun to feel uneasy. This comfortable life with all its conveniences was beginning to make him uncomfortable. Just four months after arriving in Johannesburg, Millie was beginning to feel that he was not as relaxed as before. One day she asked Kasturba. Her response was, 'I am used to this. We have changed many cities and houses like nomads. There is always some excuse to be uprooted.' She laughed and continued, 'It is Bapu's nature to keep moving, to walk new paths.' There was neither anger nor sadness on Kasturba's face as she said this.

At the dinner table, conversation turned to the Zulu uprising. Mohandas expanded upon his concerns over the political impact and the military manoeuvres. Kasturba did not understand the full context but still said what she felt, 'I think that you should go and help them.' Mohandas was surprised that she gave her opinion so naturally. As if she knew what he was going to do ...

Mohandas looked at everybody seated at the dining table and said, 'I am thinking that we should have an ambulance squad like last time.' He looked at Kasturba. 'This means we have to lock up the house and go to Phoenix,' she said in return.

Mohandas knew she hated this daily nomadic existence. It was not her fault. Because of me she has been uprooted repeatedly and had to settle in new places. As he looked into her eyes, he could see that she knew what it would mean for her and the children.

Mohandas sent a proposal to the Governor the very next day. Kastur slowly gathered their things for departure. Some of the things were sold and some sent on to Phoenix.

Kastur knew that the Governor would accept the proposal. Even if he did not, Mohandas would find some way to be involved in the battle. She also knew he had a terrific zeal to tend to the sick and the wounded. Even if she wanted, she could not have stopped him. She and the children would have to go. She understood Mohandas's likes and his fixations. She had learnt to accept his beliefs. She had to live with his unique traits, good and bad, without complaint.

As expected, the Governor agreed.

The house was turned upside down. Mohandas gave a month's notice to the landlord. The house in Johannesburg was wound up without much ado. Pollack moved to a smaller house. Hearts grew heavy and there was much sadness. Manilal, Ramdas and Devdas were quite excited. They ran around helping in packing up things and asking Bapu questions about life in Phoenix and the children there.

On 2 June, 1906, the Gandhi family, along with Millie, left Johannesburg to go to Phoenix and start a new chapter of life. Kasturba's world was going to undergo a drastic change. She could never have dreamt of living this life. Phoenix was miles of sugarcane fields and a nest of snakes in the middle. Two miles had to be covered on foot. It was fortunate that Chhaganlal, Maganlal and some others from the settlement came to the station to help with the luggage. At least it did not rain that day, or else they would have had to wade through knee high slush and navigate through gushing waterfalls.

Millie was very disappointed when they reached Phoenix. What is this, she thought, dispirited. Imagine being dumped here after life in the city. All the domestic conveniences were of a primitive age and almost not fit for human beings. Kasturba and the children were feeling the same and everybody had long faces. Millie and Kasturba muttered under their breath in complaint.

Truth to tell, they were really fatigued. The train journey of two days and two nights had worn them all out. From the station, they had to take a tempo over a bumpy rutted track to reach the farm. There was the real fear of snakes. Snakes and jungles were synonymous with fear. Everybody had been working nonstop from the moment they arrived. They laid out beds after dinner and made arrangements for the night, but sleep was elusive. With great difficulty, the children drifted off.

Dawn broke as early as 4:00 am. Gandhi came down the staircase. He started pacing up and down in front of the room where Kasturba and Millie were sleeping. When he was reasonably sure that they were at least half awake, he entered and asked, 'What do you all want?' He sounded worried. He was disturbed by last night's behaviour. Kasturba said something in Gujarati. Millie did not understand. Gandhi begged them to be patient and assured them that they will make better use of locally available things and life will be easier. The essentials will be bought from the market. What he really meant to convey was that life in Phoenix will be an ordinary person's life, quite unlike Johannesburg.

***

On 22 June, 1906, Mohandas and his platoon kitted out in the uniform, heavy shoes and bandages given by the government, reached the battle ground by rail from Durban. Mohandas had been assigned the rank of Sergeant Major and under him were three sergeants. In his team were some Gujaratis and some coolies from south India. It was actually no battle but one sided killings. They cleaned the wounds of the Zulus and bandaged them because the Whites from the health department refused to touch them. The White people were mostly afflicted by malaria. The Zulu warriors' wounds were suppurating. They saw the people who were tending to them as having been sent from heaven. While the team was bandaging their wounds, the White soldiers were creating a disturbance and mocking them. They were also firing bullets. Mohandas knew that these were the soldiers who had carried out attacks on the unarmed Zulu warriors on orders from their ruthless officers. The social workers in the team remained focused on doing their job. The Zulu warriors' eyes were full of gratitude.

When the excesses of the Whites began to be reported outside, it was declared that the Zulu uprising had been contained so that the specious logic of this one-sided war would not have to be exposed. The soldiers were returned to their barracks and the ambulance team was sent back home.

Pollack had arrived in Phoenix in the meanwhile. By then the Indian community in Transvaal called Gandhi and he left. He instructed Millie and Pollack to follow within two weeks. Kasturba and the children were left behind in Phoenix.

***

In this period, Mohandas made another decision that directly affected him and Kasturba. He decided he would remain celibate for the rest of his life. He had been struggling with this for a long time, although he had not told Kasturba about it. In the quiet expanses, as he walked towards distant Zulu settlements, he witnessed scenes of carnage that led him to strange insights. There is a deep link between the violence of an armed militia and a man's sexual proclivities. Ericson points towards this in his book *Gandhi's Truth*. There were similarities between the violence that he had seen inflicted by the Whites on Black corpses that gave rise to sadistic sexual pleasure and that which he had seen as a child, perpetrated by men on women. Somewhere this led him to think about Kasturba. He had expected fulfilment of desire and physical satisfaction. Was she so weak and kept poor health because of his additional demands? When Harilal and Manilal had been in her womb, he had been in the grip of carnality and his desire was unbridled. The birth of Ramdas and Devdas had been extremely painful. At the time of Devdas's delivery, Kasturba had even said that I was responsible for her suffering. Will Harilal, who has married Gulab at such a young age, not repeat these mistakes of mine? For the past many years he had been grappling with the philosophical questions of his state of being and the meaning of life. His conflict was not so much between his responsibilities and higher commitments, but between his material and spiritual values.

If the purpose of life was an awakening of spirituality, then he must forfeit his right over physical pleasure. There was another aspect of his physical life that he had to give up. He had to liberate himself from the desire for physical pleasure, which according to Hindu texts, leads to the state of freedom from karma and ultimately to the hope of sublime pleasure in this lifetime. If I am caught up with the upbringing of the children, then in one word, I have to say that I cannot live a physical and spiritual life at the same time … It is only if I am resolute that I can open up myriad possibilities of service ...

Upon his return from the so-called battlefront, he was to tell his wife that he had taken a lifelong vow of celibacy. This decision had a direct impact only on Kasturba. It was hard for him to face her. He discussed this with Maganlal, Chhaganlal and Albert West.

Kasturba listened to him carefully. He had never brought this up in the past. She said only one sentence in reply, 'I have no objection.' She already knew the turmoil in his mind. After the birth of the third child, he had admitted in few words, 'It is not you. I lose the battle against my own self.'

***

Kasturba decided to invite the helper's team just returned from the Zulu uprising to a special meal of Mohandas's favourite puranpuri. When Mohandas saw Kasturba kneading the dough and prepare the filling for the dish, he called the children and said, 'Come, we will have a competition with your ba today. Will she win by feeding us all we can or will we defeat her by eating all the puranpuri she makes?'

Manilal was thirteen and he promptly agreed, 'Come on Bapu, we will defeat Ba. It will be so much fun.'

Kasturba heard this and she was amused. She said very affectionately, 'Come on, I challenge you all to keep up with me.'

The competition began. Kasturba began serving well fried puranpuri establishing her lead. Manilal, Ramdas and Devdas kept up for some time but soon gave up and ran away even though Manilal was quite the glutton. All the others ate and left. Bapu remained and was not in a mood to concede defeat. He kept eating until the dough was over. He said to Kasturba, 'You should give up now.'

He saw her kneading fresh dough. He took a deep breath, pulled a long face and got ready for battle. Kasturba looked at him. 'A woman can never let her husband go hungry. He can leave if he likes ...'

Mohandas had no way out. He conceded defeat, 'Right. You win and I lose.'

Kasturba laughed. 'Remember … I will never tire.' There was love and anguish in her eyes. Both of them laughed. She dabbed her eyes.

***

Leo Tolstoy had declared his intention to remain celibate. It had the opposite effect on the Countess. She had turned hysterical and had threatened to kill herself. She could not keep up with the ideals of sacrifice. Kasturba was from a different culture. Mutual trust was the basis of understanding. There was no discomfiture between Kastur and Mohandas with regard to sexual relations. Only they must know how each of them took Mohandas's decision that they will no longer live as husband and wife.

***

Mohandas stayed in Phoenix only for a few weeks after the charade of the Zulu uprising played out. He left for Johannesburg immediately after. The much debated 'Asiatic Law Amendment Ordinance' had been published in the official gazette. This Amendment was applicable to all Indians and the few Chinese in the country. But it was the Indians who were the real target. At first Mohandas thought it reflected nothing but hatred towards the Indians. But when he sat down to translate it into Gujarati for the *Indian Opinion* is when he understood how devastating it would be for them. According to the ordinance, registration of all men, women and children above eight was mandatory. This was humiliation for the entire Indian community. If they accepted it and allowed it to be passed, it would lead to ruin. The next day, he invited all the respectable people from the Indian community. They analysed and interpreted every word in the ordinance. Habib Sahib, a respected gentleman said agitatedly, 'If an official lands up at my house to fingerprint or register my Begum and children, I will shoot him down. Never mind the consequences.' Mohandas tried to maintain a tone of reason. 'I agree that it is better to die than suffer such humiliation. We have to be calm and oppose this bill. If this gets passed, wherever there are Indian labourers, in other countries also, there will be copycat legislations. It is our responsibility to put a stop to it right here.' He paused. 'It is not just a matter of the fifteen thousand Indians in Transvaal, but for the entire Indian community in South Africa.'

In Old Empire Theatre on 11 December, 1906 at 2:00 pm a public meeting was held. Three thousand people participated and there was not an inch of space. Speaker after speaker came and made impassioned speeches and there was real agitation among the people. A proposal was tabled. Habib Sahib had not changed his stance. 'As God is my witness, I will not bend before this black law.' He appealed to everybody to take an oath. The government was forced to take notice. It had committed many atrocities and never before had there been such united purpose in opposition. When the Legislative Assembly met in Pretoria on 21 March, 1906, the ordinance was passed on the lines of the one in England. The effect of the agitation was that women were kept exempt from registration.

Another consequence was that Mohandas had discovered a non-violent weapon against such arbitrary conduct. This weapon was named 'satyagraha'. He had called for suggestions via his newspaper for an appropriate name. Maganlal had suggested 'sadagraha'. Gandhi had changed that to 'satyagraha'. Thus 'satyagraha' was born in Transvaal. It was still to be tested.

In the beginning of 1907, Kasturba in Phoenix saw her husband engaged in continuous activity. He only ever stayed there for short periods. There was constant movement between Phoenix and Johannesburg. He was getting ready for a widespread satyagraha in Transvaal. Through *Indian Opinion*, published from Natal, he kept the Indian community up to date with every activity in the agitation. Kasturba may not have been part of those activities, but she understood the importance of his work and how essential it was. She was pleased that Harilal and Gulab had come when she invited them. This was the first time she was meeting Gulab. She was busy getting acquainted with her young and beautiful daughter-in-law. She was also renewing her relationship with Harilal. He had grown into a tall and handsome young man who looked quite confident. But as a mother, Kasturba felt that his restlessness had not abated. This was a cause of concern. She had hoped his restlessness would diminish with the maturity that comes with age.

In spite of their being together, Kasturba was worried about whether she would be able to see her son and daughter-in-law again. After repeated requests from Kasturba, just a few months ago, Bapu had finally bestowed his belated blessings on the couple. That had opened the doors to their arrival in South Africa. Mohandas admitted that he was not entirely dissatisfied with the marriage. He held the Vora family in high regard. Gulab was his favourite daughter-in-law. When she was a little girl, when he visited her father, she would sit in his lap and chatter away. His objection had been to their not being of marriageable age. This disapproval came after his own experience of an early marriage.

Gulab was apprehensive about coming to South Africa. She wanted to make a positive impression on her *sasu ma.* She had heard that a mother-in-law was like a forbidden fruit, and something of a necessary evil. Gulab was separated from her own family by thousands of miles. Sometimes she felt lonely but soon she knew that her mother-in-law was soft of heart and very affectionate. She was nothing like the dreaded mothers-in-law that she had heard about. Kasturba loved her like a daughter. She was attractive and her son loved her with the same intensity. Kasturba was a naturally caring mother. She had felt the absence of a daughter until now. Gulab was an intelligent and curious teenager. She also tried her best to keep Kasturba happy and Kasturba took her under her wing. Gulab felt welcomed in her marital home. The empty aching corner in Kasturba's heart for Hari was filled now with the presence of the son and daughter-in-law. She did not feel so lonely or distant from her children now.

***

1 July, 1907, the permit office had made preparations to fingerprint the Asians. In the major towns of Transvaal,

registration offices were functional. People had to apply for registration. It was time to test the strange new weapon of 'satyagraha'. His volunteers were ready. From the central command, which was Gandhi Bhai's own office, he and his associates were instructing people across the country to make sure there was no violence or impulsive behaviour. The registration law should be opposed fearlessly, with restraint, and peacefully. All the satyagrahis were repeating an oath to themselves. Our opposition is, in fact, not opposition, but a process of self inflicted pain for our self respect and the greater common good.

Public meetings were held at many places to train people to do satyagraha and to oppose the ordinance. Satyagrahis were wearing badges and sitting on dharna on the roadsides near the registration offices. The government had no intention of repealing the ordinance or arresting the satyagrahis. This cat and mouse game continued through the month. On 31 July, there was a public meeting in a big mosque in Pretoria where about 2000 unregistered Indians sat cross-legged on the floor, cheered each other on, and listened to speeches. It was being assumed that, by midnight, the satyagrahis and other Indians would be arrested. There was also the question of the capacity of jails. The satyagraha continued. The British Prime Minister General Botha and the Internal and Indian Affairs Minister, General Smuts were waiting it out until the economically deprived Indians would run out of steam. They extended the date for registration. The satyagrahis were greatly enthused by this and began putting up posters and more people began gathering for dharnas at the registration offices. Some Indians went to get registered … Gandhi Bhai's directions were that those who go for registrations should not be stopped. In this period, 511 people got registered. Botha and Smuts decided that the time was ripe to come down with a heavy hand.

On 28 December Mohandas K. Gandhi and twenty-six of his associates in the dharnas were summoned to the magistrate's court in Johannesburg. It was stated that if they did not get themselves registered within fifteen days, they would be punished. Nobody obeyed the order. After two weeks, on 10 January 1908, all of them presented themselves at the court under Gandhi's leadership. The court room was packed. Even the members of the Bar were present. They all stood in the box for the accused. The court gave time to Mohandas to speak on everybody's behalf. He said only one sentence, 'We should be given the strictest sentence.'

The magistrate was shocked to hear this extraordinary and unexpected request. It took him some time to normalise. He awarded a sentence of two months to all the accused.

When the crowd exited, people were heard saying, 'What sort of person *is* Gandhi?'

Somebody else joined in, 'Either seek pardon or present your case … instead of this, he is seeking punishment for everybody.'

'After all, he is a coolie.'

A satyagrahi heard this and laughed.

***

On 10 January, 1908, there was a celebration in Phoenix. It was afternoon and Gulab's seventh month of pregnancy was being celebrated. Among Hindus, the seventh month *sanskar* is observed for the well being of the child. It was a moment of great joy for Kasturba. She was celebrating the expected offspring of her son. She missed her husband. If only he could have been there too although, this occasion is celebrated by women only. All the close family was present. Chhaganlal's wife, Kashiben with whom she had lived in Bombay, was there too. Maganlal who was closely related, his wife Santokhben was present and the other women living in the settlement. Songs were being sung and all the women were enjoying themselves. They had all brought presents for Gulab. Kasturba could hardly believe her own good fortune. This was the first such occasion in her family. The happy sounds of a grandchild's imminent arrival could be heard all over the house. The other children were having fun too.

Kasturba had just served all the guests. Everybody was about to start eating when a young man brought a telegram from the railway station. Telegrams caused alarm bells to ring in those times. It was from Johannesburg and because Kasturba could not read, it was read out aloud. It said two months imprisonment for Mohandas and friends for the crime of not registering themselves. If it had not been read out publicly, Kasturba would have kept this under wraps. All kinds of things had happened but this seemed to be the last straw. This was the first jail term for Mohandas. To hear the word jail for the first time is a terrifying experience for the family and only they know how it feels.

Kasturba's world turned upside down. All the incidents of the past flashed before her eyes. When she had first set foot in Durban, the hatred and violence that she had seen in the eyes of people towards Mohandas had always kept her fearful regarding his safety. Like her husband, she had begun to believe that if you worked for the larger common good and truth was on your side, nobody could touch you. However, she had heard that prisoners in this country were clapped into cells and given thick and unwashed clothes of other prisoners to wear. You were given boiled potatoes, half-cooked rice and unsalted, tasteless corn porridge as food. Kasturba's eye fell on the feast in front of her and she turned her face away. Racing through her mind was the question: what will she be able to do in a strange country?

She addressed all the women and declared, 'I cannot share the hardship that my husband will undergo in jail, but I can at least eat the kind of food that he will get. I can sleep on the floor. From today, I will also eat only tasteless corn porridge without salt or sugar.'

Gulab got up and came to her *sasu ma*, but she did not know how to comfort her. Tears flowed from her eyes. Kasturba counselled her instead, 'You have to be even braver … you are the daughter-in-law of the Gandhi family. There will be many such situations, better get used to them.'

This was Kasturba's first satyagraha. Both of them stood for justice and against persecution of innocent people. The difference was that Mohandas was in jail while Kasturba was outside amongst the affected.

***

Kasturba had accepted Mohandas's frequent absence from home silently. But in these changed circumstances, he was neither an able lawyer nor had he been able to save himself and his associates. He was only an accused serving out a sentence. The government was convinced of the need to punish Mohandas for leading the agitation against the unjust ordinance of registration. Kastur had partially punished herself to be a part of that.

The only way to get news of Johannesburg in Phoenix, was to get the newspaper from the station. Kasturba would wait every evening for somebody to get the newspaper and translate it for her. Slowly, she found out that her husband was not alone. All his trusted associates were with him. Everybody repeated the words that Mohandas had spoken. They all had received the exact same punishment. The other satyagrahis had found new ways to go to jail. One hundred and fifty people had been arrested for buying and selling illegal goods. The newspaper reports gave no idea of how the satyagrahis were faring inside jail. This was the cause of Kasturba's greatest worry. She was agitated because of what she had seen immediately after coming to Durban. If somebody attacked him in jail, who would save him? The simple answer came from within – God. Just like he had sent Alexander's wife Sara, some other angel would turn up to protect him.

Bolstered by her faith, Kasturba slowly extinguished her doubts. Her basic predisposition was to be strong and courageous. She would never worry for herself. Whenever there was any adversity, she bravely accepted it. Her husband was in jail so her own responsibilities were clear. The entire Phoenix Ashram was now her household, just like in a joint family. She took the whole weight on her shoulders as if she were *matr shakti* so that nobody felt the pain of Bapu's absence. She would constantly update people with the actual situation in the movement. This was the only way to maintain faith in Bapu's principles and rules. Although Kasturba had not had a formal education, she naturally accepted people from different castes and religions living in Phoenix. Phoenix was, in fact, the first Gandhi Ashram. There were many among them with whom she could not hold a dialogue in their language but she would still manage to communicate with them. To a large extent, she managed to gain the respect of the residents of the Ashram. This was not because she was Gandhi Bhai's wife but because of her self confidence. She was determined to do the right thing with compassion.

Mohandas K. Gandhi kept accounts of every paisa. Kasturba did not know how to write so she would keep a mental account through the day and in the evening, get Albert West or Maganlal Gandhi to write it. In this way, she had a good sense of the finances of the Ashram. Phoenix Ashram had become Ba's centre for service.

***

This is an incident from 1908. Just after Mohandas went to jail, pineapple trees were planted over several acres of land. This was the first experiment in Phoenix Ashram with fruit production. The fruit had ripened. Big juicy pineapples adorned with a thorny crown were crying out to be harvested. All the people, young and old, were busy making neat packets of fruit to send to market. Kasturba kept reminding them how important these fruits were for the future of the Ashram. It was the sale of these fruits which would finance the publication of *Indian Opinion.*

After finishing off work in the kitchen, Ba sent her pregnant daughter-in-law to rest and stepped out in the scorching sun to walk to the pineapple orchard. Harilal was working in the press. All the others were harvesting the fruit. Kastur was looking for Manilal. Ramdas and Devdas had long since returned home, tired after a day's work. Manilal was tall and strong. Kasturba was proud of the fact that he never seemed to tire. He was intently cutting down pineapples without pausing for breath. As he saw Ba approaching, he straightened up and wiped his brow with his sleeve. 'Ba, I am really thirsty,' he said.

'*Are Bawle*, there are such juicy pineapples right in front of you and you are still thirsty?' she laughed, 'Who stopped you from eating some fruit?'

'All these are to be taken to the market to be sold ...' Manilal said open mouthed, 'May I have one of these?'

'Of course, they are meant to be eaten.' Kasturba was pleased with his hard work. She patted him on the shoulder and turned towards the house.

As soon as Ba left, Manilal sat down in front of the mound of pineapples. He cut the fruit with his sharp knife and ate to his heart's content. When Ba returned after half an hour, she was astonished to see a heap of peels.

'Are you still thirsty?'

Manilal was abashed, 'Ba, I was hungry also.' She smiled. He breathed a sigh of relief to see her smile. When he had to strain to stand up straight, Ba had to laugh. His stomach was so full that it was hard for him to bend down to continue working.

***

Kasturba might be lenient towards others but she was very strict with herself. It did not matter whether times were good or bad. The consequences of this were evident a few days later. Manilal had gone to cut the last stand of pineapples. Just then the post arrived. He stopped working and began to scan the newspaper. The next moment he gave a shout and ran towards the house.

Hearing him, Kasturba stepped out. Ramdas and Devdas followed her, 'What happened? Why are you shouting?'

'Bapu had been released!' Manilal's voice rang out with excitement.

A wave of joy rose inside Kasturba. But there was a niggling fear, what if this was false news? Five weeks were remaining, she thought to herself. She was as excited as her son and wanted to hear more but she kept her composure.

'That is very good.' she said softly, 'Now back to work all of you. Have you boys finished cutting the last stand?'

Kasturba paid no heed to the many stories swirling around until nightfall. None of them knew anything in the day, how is it they had all these details now? In any case, she needed to hear it straight from Bapu. But there was no such possibility in the near future.

***

The real story emerged later. One morning, Gandhi was taken to General Smuts under police escort. The General wanted to resolve the registration imbroglio through negotiation. He made a show of friendliness, 'I also studied to be a barrister in London. Many Indian boys used to study with me. They were my friends. How can I dislike you people?'

Mr Gandhi laughed and said, 'Ah! Friends!' Then he said, 'What does your government want from us?'

General Smuts was taken aback by the direct question. After a long hard discussion, both of them reached an agreement. The General gave an assurance that if most of the Indians in Transvaal got themselves registered on Gandhi's advice, the government would abolish the Black Law. All this was said verbally. Nothing was written down. Mohandas also did not insist on written documents. Gandhi believed that in a satyagrahi's life, there was no room for doubts. He is not afraid to trust. Smuts gave an order to release the satyagrahis. Smuts shook hands with Gandhi and said, 'Mr Gandhi, from this moment, you are free.'

They had been talking until seven in the evening. Mohandas was in a prisoner's garb. He did not have a penny on him. Gandhi said to the General, 'You have not done the right thing by setting me free, you will have to pay for it. I am sorry but I have no money for a ticket. You will have to give it to me.' Smuts' pocket was empty. He looked towards his secretary. He had a few pence, enough to buy a rail ticket. Gandhi laughed as he left, 'Your jails will get some respite now.' The General came to see him to the door. The secretary accompanied him outside.

***

When the news travelled to Phoenix, there was a celebratory outburst. The release of the satyagrahis in Transvaal was a victory. Everybody in Phoenix Ashram was overjoyed. Kasturba was happy that Mohandas would be able to come home, even for just a few days. She laughed and told everybody that his release meant that she was also free of her diet of salt free corn porridge. With Gulab's help, Kasturba organised dinner for the neighbours and all the family. But these celebrations were short-lived. About the tenth day, there was a telegram that said that Gandhi Bhai had been attacked in his own office, and he had fainted. The telegram said nothing more about the extent of the injury and who had carried out the attack and why. Kasturba was almost beside herself with anxiety. Somebody suggested that she should go to Johannesburg because she should be with her husband, at a time like this.

'No, no, I can't go,' she said immediately, 'Right now, Phoenix Ashram is in a financial crunch. The little money that is left, I can hardly spend it on myself. The Ashram's requirements are more important than my going to my husband.'

Albert tried to reason with her, 'We will manage ... You should go.'

Kasturba was firm, 'He has many friends there, they must be looking after him. My husband would not approve either, he has always wanted the people's money to be spent on them.'

After receiving a letter from Pollack, Kasturba and the children felt a sense of relief. Gandhi Bhai is in good health, he wrote. He has neither any broken bones nor a deep injury. He has some scratches, some superficial wounds and some internal pain and they are all getting better. Kasturba's biggest fear was that it should not be an attack like the one by the White hooligans in Durban. The letter went on to say, this had happened because of a misunderstanding about the agreement with Smuts by another Indian, Mir Alam. He thought that Gandhi had sold out to Smuts for monetary gain. Kasturba could not bear to listen to such an accusation. But she put her anger aside and concentrated on the fact that her husband was recuperating. In such times, the positive thoughts of loved ones, act like a remedy and a blessing. The letter further revealed that Gandhi was resting at Rev Joseph Doke's house. Kasturba sent them a silent prayer of gratitude. When the Police asked Gandhi to register a complaint, he refused to say a word against his attacker. He was stubbornly insistent that he should be the first to be registered. He called for the Asiatic Registration Officer and got himself registered. Millie and Pollack wanted to take him home but he was being well looked after by the Doke family. There was much murmuring among Rev Doke's followers that an impure Black person was being nursed in his house. Doke allowed people from all faiths to visit the patient. This also caused much discontent among his followers.

***

Mohandas had come to Durban. He was refusing to pay heed to rumours. He felt that it was his fault that he could not win the trust of his antagonists. He refused the proposal of his friends to stay in Durban. Mohandas had decided to stay in Phoenix and write a series of articles in *Indian Opinion* on the chain of events in Johannesburg. He wanted to bring the truth before everybody. After this decision, four people were willing to escort him. One of them was a Tamilian boxer. But Mohandas was adamant in refusing their services. He said that nobody can live in fear.

When Kasturba heard this, she said, 'I know you are ready for every consequence. Since you have come into public life, I have also prepared myself for every eventuality.' She paused as if to read her partner's face and continued, 'You don't worry about the children and me. That is all I want to say.' Kasturba really meant this. Mohandas looked relaxed. His eyes expressed gratitude and appreciation and Kasturba recognised that.

Nobody saw the tears that flowed when Kasturba was alone. On her face, you could only see struggle and resilience.

In the initial days of the satyagraha, there was a certain pattern to life. Social, political and personal events were moving so rapidly that there was no escaping the struggle that ensued. Kasturba felt as if they were caught in a whirlpool of conflicting feelings. Fear, excitement and release were all whirling on a wheel and came in quick unsettling succession.

***

10 April 1908 was a date to celebrate. Harilal's household welcomed a healthy, beautiful baby girl. Because there was no midwife, Kasturba and the other relatives conducted the delivery. In similar circumstances, the little baby's chacha,

Devdas, had been delivered by her dada Mohandas. Dadi had resisted it strongly, but there had been no choice then, just as it was now. Kasturba could not but be reminded of Devdas's birth. She was ecstatic and she had no words to express how she felt. The greatest joy was that Gulab's first born was a girl. Kasturba had four sons and this little one filled the place in her heart for a daughter. Gulab and Hari called her Rami. A week after her birth, Mohandas had come to Phoenix and on the day of the *Namkaran Sanskar*, the parents accepted formal congratulations from her dada. Dada said her name out loud into her ear.

But just as there was joy and celebration for Rami's birth, the wheel turned the other way and the whole scenario changed. A telegram arrived and sent everybody into shock. Mohandas's sister Raliyat's only son, Gokuldas, had been snatched cruelly by death. Gokuldas had come with Kasturba and Mohandas to Durban last time. He was like a son to them. Raliyat was all alone as she had also lost her husband. Her son was her solace and now he was gone. Gokuldas was planning to complete his studies and come to Phoenix with his wife. He had been married on 14 April and soon after, he had been hit by a ball at a tender spot, while playing cricket. This resulted in his death. It was an unbelievably cruel turn of events.

Mohandas had dreamt of a future for Gokuldas in social service. He was deeply affected by this accident. Kasturba was thinking of Harilal. The two of them had grown up together and Harilal was also in a state of shock. After a few weeks, Harilal decided to go to Johannesburg and take part in the satyagraha. Gulab and Rami would be under Kasturba's care. This was his first experience of such loss and grief and this was also his first independent decision. Kasturba did not interfere. Gulab did feel bad that he was leaving their very young child, but she kept quiet. Kasturba knew that just like Bapu, Hari was sensitive to the troubles of others but also quite stubborn. She also knew that his decision will be some consolation for Bapu and give him relief. He would make up for Gokul's absence for whom Bapu had many dreams.

***

Mohandas was pleased that Smuts would abolish the Black Law as promised and the Indians would breathe a sigh of relief. Mohandas had made good his promise on registrations. Most Indians had got themselves registered on his advice. But even after many days, there was no sign of reversing the order. Mohandas had written numerous letters asking that since he had kept his end of the bargain, what was the reason for the delay? There were evasive replies or silence from the other side. Smuts was trying to sidestep from his role. Instead, the Transvaal parliament was ready to rub salt into their wounds. There was a move to check the free passage of the Indians as per the agreement or *girmit*. Mohandas's associates were readying for a satyagraha to block this. They began flooding the jails with people. Harilal had given his name as a satyagrahi with permission from Bapu. As a consequence, he was arrested for selling fruit without a license.

On 27 July, when he was produced in court, Mohandas was present. Harilal boldly admitted to selling fruit without a license. The court fined him one pound and failing which, he was to be put in jail for seven days. Harilal refused to pay the fine. Bapu was the first to hug him and congratulate him on his decision. When he was released after seven days he was handed a document that decreed that he had to leave Transvaal within seven days. He did not comply. On 10 August he was arrested again. On that day's court hearing, Mohandas sat quietly in a corner. Harilal refused to say anything in his defence. He was given a one month sentence with hard labour. Everybody in the court room was surprised by Harilal's decision but Bapu was smiling. When Kastur found out, she said to Gulab that he was as stubborn as his bapu. This fight is bigger than a domestic dispute. It is our duty to stand with the decisions of our husbands.

Events were moving at the pace of dates changing on a calendar when you wake up after a night's rest. Mohandas found out that the Resident Law was going to be enacted on 16th August. There was no possibility of changing the Registration Law. Something had to be done to convey the mood of the people to the government. He sent a message to General Smuts that that if the Black Law is not abolished before 16th August, all the people who had registered would destroy their registrations in a public meeting. They will gladly bear the consequences of this act. Smuts rejected this as an insulting threat. The legislators ignored it as a presumptuous message to incite Indians.

This consequence of this casual disregard was that on 16 August, 1908, in the maidan of the Hamida Masjid, approximately three thousand Indians – Hindus, Muslims, Parsi and Christians, gathered. A stage was hastily erected on which was placed a huge four-legged coal stove, certificates that had been gathered from before and a container of kerosene oil. Mohandas had fixed 4:00 pm as the time for getting any response. At exactly 4:00 pm a cyclist was seen pedalling furiously towards the venue. Everybody awaited his arrival with bated breath, hoping against hope that the government may have sent a positive response. It was a telegram and it was read out aloud. Status quo. The Black Law smiled alongside the new repressive law. In went the kerosene into the stove. The flames leapt up. People began dipping the registration certificates into the oil and dunking them into the stove. There were shouts of Burn it, burn it all. As the fire caught, people's tempers ran high. The shouts grew louder. Those who had come in late and had held back their decision regarding the registration certificate also joined in.

One man emerged from the crowd and flung his certificate into the fire. People looked at him in astonishment. He raised his voice and said, 'Raising a finger against Gandhi Bhai was my biggest mistake. I beg for your forgiveness.' This was Mir Alam who had accused Gandhi Bhai of receiving money from Smuts and betraying the entire Indian community. He had made a life threatening assault on him labouring under this misconception. Gandhi Bhai stepped forward and hugged him, 'I have no complaint or any rancour towards you.' The applause was deafening.

It was later discovered that Mir Alam left Transvaal for good.

For Kastur, her monthly period had become very painful after the birth of the last two children. She would be greatly weakened due to the excessive blood flow. In addition, there was much emotional turmoil on account of her husband and son's constant clashes with the White government and their being in and out of prison. She was a living example of the sentiment in the lines '*hamari to aadat hai hum kucch nahin kehte*' 'It is my nature to remain silent.' She continued to do her routine work with efficiency and grace. You could hardly gauge her delicate health from her work routine. For Mohandas, nothing stood higher than satyagraha. When they came to Phoenix, it was not possible for him to notice the decline in her health. He believed that satyagraha was like walking a tightrope and you had to have single minded focus. Kasturba understood this well. As it is, satyagraha had been getting scattered lately. The burning of the certificates of registration had attracted attention but no great change had resulted.

When Mohandas came to Phoenix for two weeks, he was really busy. In the week of October, he went to Johannesburg thinking that his arrest might ignite the movement again. He sent a telegraphic message for *Indian Opinion* from there, 'Stay steadfast until the end, self inflicted pain is the only solution. Victory will be ours.' Kasturba was informed and she felt a great sense of relief. Women are the living image of this, she thought to herself and smiled.

Mohandas was allowed infrequent visitors in prison. It was the end of October. Mohandas was very happy to meet son Harilal and close friend Kallenbach. Just then he received a letter from Albert West. It said that Kasturba was bleeding heavily. He wanted her to be admitted to hospital.

He wanted Gandhi Bhai to pay the fine to get his sentence reduced and come to Phoenix. In return Mohandas wrote a letter to Kasturba:

Dear Kastur,

Mr West informed me of your difficult condition. Although I am concerned about your health, I am not in a position to come there and look after you. You know that I have given up everything for this struggle. If I come, I will have to own up to having broken the law to get released. Doing this will make our movement a laughing stock.

I feel if you stay strong and eat well, you will feel much better. Even so, if you die, it will be just as well for you to go before me. You know I love you very much. I will continue to love you the same way when you are gone. Even if you are not there, you will always be alive for me. Your spirit is immortal.

As for me, I want to assure you that I have no plans to remarry if you are gone. I have told you this innumerable times. Trust in God and let your spirit roam free. Your death will be the ultimate sacrifice for satyagraha.

My struggle is not just against the government but against nature itself. I hope that you will understand what I am saying and not be upset with me. That is what I expect of you.

Yours
Mohandas

Below there were some lines for Manilal and daughter-in-law Gulab—

Both of you may also read this letter and read it out to your ba ... I am worried but helpless. Please keep me informed about her health. Look after Ramdas and Devdas. I will pray that Ba gets well soon.

Ashirvaad from Bapu.

***

As soon as he was released from jail, he reached Phoenix. He was shocked to see Kasturba. She looked very thin, tired and lifeless. 'Harilal has been arrested again,' was the first thing she said.

Mohandas was very concerned to see the effect of this news on her. She had been so weakened that she could not carry out any personal routines. Only after many exhortations did she agree to a medical examination. He took Kasturba to his Parsi friend, Dr Nanji. He said she needed an immediate operation to stop the bleeding. Kasturba agreed and the operation was successful. She bore the pain of the cleaning very bravely. Nanji and his nurse wife took Mr Gandhi aside and said, 'It is not advisable to take the patient to Phoenix in this condition. Let her stay with us and we will look after her well. You can proceed to Johannesburg.'

Mohandas was concerned about the satyagraha that was underway in Johannesburg. After few days, he consulted with Kasturba and when she was agreeable, he left for Johannesburg. Kasturba's bleeding continued even while the medicines were being given. The Nanjis were non-vegetarians. Dr Nanji felt that vegetarian food will not help Kasturba's quick recovery. As soon as Mohandas reached office, the telephone rang. It was a strange sound for him.

Perhaps it was a new phone. It was Nanji. He said, 'Kasturbai is very weak. I think she should be given beef soup.'

Mohandas's first reaction was, 'Unthinkable!'

'I don't think it will be possible to save her in this condition.' The doctor was insistent, 'if you don't agree, you will lose her.'

'Did you ask Kasturba? I cannot answer for her.'

'Her condition is not such that I can ask her.'

'I am coming there. Until then, don't act on any of your decisions.' The next morning, when he reached Durban he found out that without informing Kasturba, a bowl of beef stock had been given to her. He held his head in his hands in despair. The doctor was a close friend. He knew that there was no ill intention behind giving her the soup. For those who eat meat as a matter of routine, they cannot understand the violence inherent in feeding a vegetarian meat by subterfuge, not just to the animal but also to the person's living faith. 'Doctor, you betrayed Kastur,' were the words that popped out of his mouth.

'I am a doctor and it is not necessary for me to treat patients after seeking their permission. Specially when it is a matter of life and death.'

'You will not understand. When she finds out that she has taken soup made with cow's meat, she will not be able to live. For some people, their beliefs are matters of life and death.' He did not want to utter these words and vitiate the atmosphere. Both husband and wife had put their hearts into looking after her.

Mohandas decided to keep this incident to himself. This was the second secret. The first had been keeping his own meat eating from his parents. He asked Kasturba, 'The doctor says that you have to get non-vegetarian soup to build up your strength...' As loudly as she could speak in her weakened state, she said,' Never! Take me home, I will recover.'

Mohandas was very relieved to hear her say this. She was determined and this is how a natural solution to a tough problem was found.

He told Dr Nanji that he was taking Kasturba to Phoenix. The doctor was taken aback and raised strong objection, 'You are such a brute! She is not even in a state to move and will not be able to bear the slightest movement.'

'Whatever it is, she wants to go from here.'

'Do what you want. Just remember that you are going against the considered opinion of a doctor,' the doctor warned Mohandas.

Kasturba sensed that something untoward had taken place. She thanked the doctor and his wife for their hospitality and care. She reassured Mohandas, 'You don't worry, nothing will happen to me. I will be fine.'

Mohandas was worried about how to take her to the station in this condition. She did not like rickshaws because a human being pulled another human being. Finally, a rickshaw had to be called. Dr Nanji was angry and indifferent by now. Doctors take it amiss if somebody takes a patient away, in the middle of treatment. When Mohandas assisted her to sit in the rickshaw he was shocked. She was no more than skin and bone. This brought home the seriousness of her illness and the trials of the journey. But Kasturba's face was strangely serene. Because of her weakness and ill health,

Kasturba had to sit in her husband's lap in the rickshaw and she was mortified. But she had no choice. At the station he had to take her to the edge of the platform in his arms. Luckily there were few passengers in the coach, so Kasturba was able to lie down until Phoenix. Mohandas had sent a telegram ahead to Mr West about his arrival with Kasturba by train. West had a hammock that required four people to carry. He had reached in advance with the hammock and four helpers and a flask of hot milk. Everybody waited as the train pulled in. First Mohandas gave her the milk. Then she lay down in the hammock and they made their way through the sugarcane fields to Phoenix. It was a tough walk of two miles through the fields. The leaves of the sugarcane are razor sharp and can cut the skin. It had rained in the morning so there was slippery slush. Everybody advanced with care. With every careful step they took, Kasturba's enthusiasm and faith grew. Finally they were home. Kasturba got a new lease of life meeting all the family and friends and she declared that she was feeling fine now. Mohandas smiled with relief.

Kasturba had no great faith in his curative experiments for her. But when Mohandas asked her to do mud therapy, she did not refuse. After a few days of mud therapy, the wounds of the operation began healing and she began to mend.

One day a sadhu appeared. Manilal and Ramdas were also present. Listening to the account of Kasturba's illness and soup, he said that our holy books prescribe no restrictions on meat eating. He quoted from Manu. Mohandas knew these were later additions and the two began to argue. Mohandas maintained that vegetarianism among the Hindus had been advocated in the holy books. From the point of view of morality and medically, vegetarianism is appropriate. Kasturba had to intervene to stem this pointless debate. 'Swamiji, whatever you might say, I don't want to be free of illness after partaking of beef tea. You are welcome to debate on the matter with my husband and children but don't bother me. This is my final decision.' Swamiji's arguments came to an end.

From the time after Kasturba's operation, the arrest and sentencing of the satyagrahis had begun. Kasturba got news about her husband and son eight times in twelve months. In the five years when satyagraha reached its pinnacle, Kasturba's family members had been to jail eighteen times. A few times, it so happened that father and son went to the same jail. On 25 February, 1909 Mohandas was arrested as soon as he reached Transvaal. He was sentenced to three months. He was sent to Volkert prison where Harilal was already serving out his sentence of six months. But father and son could not stay together for long. The government wanted to tighten the screws on Mohandas so he was transferred to Pretoria. It was much worse there and he had not been to such a jail until now.

Mohandas had the right to send and receive one letter in a month. You were not permitted to write a word about life inside prison. Manilal was also sixteen. Mohandas had many options in terms of addressing the letter. He decided to write to Manilal. He was worried about Kasturba, Ramdas and Devdas. He wrote, 'I know you feel that your education is being neglected. I have read a lot about this in jail. My belief has been validated that education is not just the knowledge of words. It means character building, knowing your duties ... what could be better than the opportunity you have to serve

Ba and look after Bhabhi Gulab. Take care that Gulab should not feel the absence of Harilal. You are also the guardian of Ramdas and Devdas.'

***

After being released from the Pretoria jail, Mohandas could stay in Phoenix only for a few days. He needed an extra boost of energy and strength after this jail term. But he was sent to London with Haji Habib. Kasturba's health was better but she was extremely weak. Even so, she took complete responsibility for the household chores. The satyagraha was weakening. Indian migrants had lost their way due to the punitive action and their own economic pressures. Internal dissensions had also surfaced. The enemies got a chance to launch a concerted attack. The governments of Natal, Transvaal and Orange Freestate wanted to form a union. The official representative, Prime Minister Botha and General Smuts were putting finishing touches to the proposal. The Indian community in South Africa was very small, in comparison. They were in a crisis in Transvaal and they had been boycotted in Orange Freestate. The coming together of these states was bad news for the Indians. The laws in these states were going to be extremely repressive. Therefore the community decided to send two representatives to London to put forth their point of view to the British government and parliamentarians. There was no option but to make Mohandas the leader of this two-member delegation. Kasturba knew that it would be difficult for her to stay with the children, in her present state of health. Even if her husband was not around, his protection was always there for the family. Neither she nor Mohandas could say much about his trip because the fate of so many countrymen was linked to his going.

Haji Habib and he left on 23rd June and reached London on 10th July.

***

Manilal also wanted to go to Johannesburg like his elder brother. He wanted to take part in the satyagraha and go to jail. But both Ba-Bapu were not in favour of this. Mohandas wrote to him comparing rural Phoenix and the atmosphere in Johannesburg, 'A person can seek out one's soul and one's truth there, unlike in the frantic atmosphere in Johannesburg. There is less chance of self development there because there are many dangerous attractions. It is difficult to stay honest and true to oneself in the midst of all this.'

Haji Habib and Mohandas returned empty-handed from London. Both Generals Botha and Smuts had beaten them to it and had succeeded in convincing the British government. The South African government was not willing to give any concessions and the British government was loath to speak up for the Indians. When the Union of South Africa Act was passed in October, there was no security for the rights of South African Indians. Mohandas was deeply affected by this failure. On the return journey, on the ship, he wrote a short but powerful text that exposes the shortcomings of British democracy and through the pain of the Indians in South Africa, is a revelation of the bondage of all Indians. The shadow of the bondage of all colonised nations can be found in it. It was called *Hind Swaraj*. After the Bible, it has been called the second text. It warns the entire population of the Third World to save itself from the diabolical nature of western civilisation. As he wrote this tract the major question in his mind was: are the Whites entirely without humanity and scruples? They were once so keen to get these Indian labourers that the White farmers of South Africa had passed a proposal 'A company should be established to bring Black (Indian) labourers. Until we take steps in this direction cotton, sugarcane and other such crops will not grow.' (*Pehla Girmitiya*, pg, 22, Giriraj Kishore). Those labourers who taught them how to grow these crops, now they are hell bent on evicting them from their homes and country. He connected this behaviour to the narrow mindedness and inhumanity of western civilisation. He infused every word in *Hind Swaraj* with raw energy. Before his eyes rose the villages of his own country and the ghettos of South Africa. He wanted our villages to be self reliant, unlike the dependent cities of the west. The basis of western civilisation is greed, materialism, hoarding of resources and unbridled sensual pleasure. When he was asked what he thought of western civilisation, his reply was, 'An interesting thought.' But when it came to his own country he said that India can find its original soul in the traditional forbearance of rural life. There is a glimpse of this in a letter to Ramdas: 'Don't be angry with me that I did not bring anything for you.' He clarified that he did not like anything there. 'I don't like European presents, I like things that are made in India. I don't like their lifestyle.'

——***——

Ba's Truth

Kasturba was once asked where she was in Bapu's *My Experiments with Truth*? She laughed and said, 'I have not read it and I could not have. I know that he has divided the responsibility of my illiteracy between both of us. I am present somewhat like a statue for decoration. Bapu has mentioned my beauty and used it too. I am the reason for Bade Diwan ji's passing. I have borne the experiments with truth that Bapu has conducted.' Sometimes she was forced to wonder whether she was a measure for Bapu's truth … or its medium?

When Bapu returned from the failed London trip to Phoenix in February 1910, Kasturba appeared weak. He heard that some bleeding had taken place in his absence. This was a matter of concern. Although Ba had gained strength after the operation, she continued to be underweight and thin. After he had gone to London she used to do all the housework. The remedy for a thin frame is adequate rest and a good diet. There is no congruity between work and rest. Whenever Bapu enquired, Ba would say I am not weak and I don't eat less. Mohandas wanted her to take the least responsibility for all the chores. She knew this was not possible but she did not contradict him. She expressed herself in a different way, 'You stay healthy if you work. In any case, your household's chores are your own and it is you who have taught us to do our own work.' He countered saying that health must come first and if you are healthy you will work well. Mohandas had a host of advice on what to eat and what foods should be avoided. He suggested giving up peas, beans, dals and vegetables in a pod. Although Kasturba and Mohandas liked good food, for the past few months, he was practising restraint on taste. He believed that food was only a physical necessity. Kasturba believed that eating well and with enjoyment, was good for building your body. Bapu asked her to give up dal. Kastur really liked dal so she got very upset. Not taking his words seriously she said, 'Why don't you give up urad dal?'

She did not know that a small statement, made in jest, would lead to such a big scene. Bapu always had urad dal and vegetables like beans in his meal. He replied calmly accepting her challenge, 'Fine, I give up dal for a year.'

Ba had been caught unawares, 'No, I was only joking! Why will you bear such punishment because of me? I will never be able to forgive myself.'

'This is not a joke. It is a serious matter. If I ask anybody to give up something that they like, I should also be prepared to do the same. That would only be fair.'

'I won't let you do this. You will have to take back this decision. I will do as you say.'

'You cannot take back words once uttered. Once they are out, they belong to the world. If something was said without ill intention, then there is nothing wrong. I know that you will be healthy with this kind of food and this will benefit me too.' Kasturba knew that even if the other person meant well, he would not turn back from what he said, however difficult. Their changed diet was enforced from that day itself. Some years later, one day Mohandas remembered this and he laughed uproariously, 'I am grateful that you made a quack like me look respectable.'

October of 1910 was a very tense period for Kasturba. There was her illness and the absence of her favourite foods. She grappled with the idea that just because he was her husband, it did not mean that he could rob her of the freedom to eat what she liked. Even if she disagreed in jest, must he trump her in a manner that she could not move either way. What is this if not the abuse of her personal freedom? If a husband gives up his favourite food in the name of his wife, how appropriate was it for her to reject his wishes because of her personal preferences? When she had first found out he had kept the beef tea story at Dr Nanji's from her, she had been upset with him for days. Her self-respect had been wounded. Mohandas explained that in her delicate state, he did not want to burden her with her unwitting act and risk losing her. She would not have been able to bear it, he said. I could not doubt the doctor couple because they did what they could, in a hopeless situation. I had also brought you to Phoenix against the doctor's advice, putting your life in danger since you were so brave. It was a moment of great challenge for me and you and our long-standing relationship with the doctor. There was nothing left for Kasturba to say after this. She saw how he had looked after her since. She knew that in a moment of crisis, Bapu was not one to turn away from the gravest danger. It was his nature to invite trouble. The heat of this was felt by the entire household. Only the intensity varied. But she often felt helpless. So much so that she had not even done justice to the children. Harilal has been here for one and a half years. He had been in Phoenix less than Bapu. Most of his time has been spent in the jails of Transvaal. He was serving a sentence since the last fourteen months. His wife used to look radiant but now looked pale and extinguished. Kasturba knew the pain of not having your husband close to you.

How could she explain to Gulab that when she was her age, her life was bleak without husband and children … How lonely she had felt in a household full of people ... Is this Gulab's destiny too? Aquatic animals stay in the water while forest dwellers roam free. We women live within ourselves. Hari had told her when he left Phoenix, but her heart quailed with each repeated arrest and sentencing. Why did she let him go? It hurt to even think of a quiet boy like Manilal also serving time since three months. When I look at Ramdas and Devdas, I am scared that they will have to take part in their father's satyagraha too. Like baby birds they will fly away from the nest leaving her alone. She dabbed the corner of her eye and got up. Your pain is yours alone.

——***——

Pad Yatra

The direction of the movement in South Africa had shifted. Upon Mr Gandhi's call, thousands of coal miners had left work. To provide for shelter and food for all of them was a huge problem. Mohandas felt that this was a very good occasion for a *pad yatra* against the entry and exit restrictions on Black people in Transvaal where children, women and all of these people could join in. If they get arrested, they will all have to go to jail and the government will have to provide food and shelter. If they don't get arrested, they will walk till Kallenbach's farm. The voice of resistance will reach the public. Kallenbach had given a part of his farm to Gandhi to establish Tolstoy Farm.

Kasturba was also to go and live in Tolstoy Farm. But owing to a delay in the construction of the living quarters, their going had been delayed by few weeks. For the last four years, she had been living in the small house with the family in Phoenix and that had begun to feel like home. But this had be left behind too. She was scared to call any place home. At least, there was a possibility of coming back. Her neighbours would remain and she would come and go.

Kasturba reached Tolstoy Farm on 9 October, 1910. When she went with Pollack and her two younger children, she was stopped at the border of Transvaal. They were asked obnoxious questions. When they were told that Kasturba was M. K. Gandhi's wife, she was allowed to go. When they reached, they were told that Harilal had been arrested again and he would be sentenced the following day. Kasturba did not know what to do. How much more pain was she going to bear? When would this drift ever end? She had really wanted to meet Harilal because she had heard that being arrested repeatedly and being punished had changed him.

***

In the first six months that Harilal had been in Phoenix, he learned that Chhaganlal was going to London on the scholarship offered by Bapu's friend Dr P. J. Mehta. When Bapu had gone to London to study, Dr Mehta had been his guide. In the beginning, Mohandas had stayed in his hotel. When Mohandas took his vow of austerity, Dr Mehta offered a scholarship, as he thought this would give one of his sons the opportunity to study in London. But Bapu thought it fit to give a chance to Chhaganlal so that nobody could charge him with partiality towards his son. Harilal had been deeply hurt by this decision. He had not shared his unhappiness with anybody other than Ba and his wife. He quietly went to Johannesburg to be arrested. This was a blow for Kastur also but she was quite helpless as Chhaganlal was also a close relative. She was upset by the fact that her elder son went to jail to assuage his unhappiness.

The second incident shook her up. Harilal's wife Gulab, along with her daughter Rami, left to go back to India while he was still in jail, to deliver her second child. After being released from jail, instead of going to Phoenix, Harilal went straight to Bapu to ask for permission and money to go to India. Bapu said that he did not have money and told him not to go to India but to stay on in South Africa. Until Gulab was in Phoenix, while in jail, he felt he could meet her and his daughter Rami at any time. But Bapu's refusal, in one heartless blow, decimated all hopes of meeting his wife and child. Instead of going to Tolstoy Farm, he chose to be arrested again. Kastur was hoping that when Hari would come, she would talk to him. But she understood how bad he would feel about Gulab and Rami's absence. Her biggest concern was that he should not see Bapu's decision as a mark of his wilfulness and lack of feeling. Harilal was not just angry but also turning against his objectives. Home or outside, it was all the same to him. Ba believed firmly that when he would return, she would be able to console him and lighten his heart's burden. But Harilal's choosing to go to jail without meeting her troubled her. There was a rift between father and son that was not easy to mend. Neither of them was going to back down. One of them had to yield or go. But what was she to do? She had no choice but to stay with Bapu. Was her son going to be estranged from her? A son leaving was like the future dissolving and a husband's departure was like both the past and the future vanishing. She was constantly and helplessly torn apart by these conflicts and her emotions.

Even against this backdrop, Ba felt Tolstoy Farm was different, although she was just as self reliant here, as she was in Phoenix. Harilal's going to jail after meeting Bapu hurt. She tried to gather herself and get involved in making a home in Tolstoy Farm and looking after the younger children. Hindu, Muslim, Parsi and Christian, all communities lived there. Most of the people had children and Ba was fond of all of them. Each person was given two blankets. When the weather was warm, the inhabitants used to sleep on the floor in the verandah and in the open. Including Mohandas, all of them wore shirts and pyjamas that labourers wore. There was a central kitchen where communal meals were cooked. Just like in Phoenix, Kasturba drew solace from prayer. Prayers were said twice a day. The morning prayer was the key to the day and the evening prayer, the lock for the night.

Kasturba's worries did not have an end, even in Tolstoy Farm. Her worry for the future of her sons continued unabated. Most of the children at the Farm were from poor families, whether literate or illiterate. Along with poverty, there was indiscipline. Because they were idle, they had become quarrelsome, dishonest, rude and ill tempered. They needed affection and guidance to make an improvement. Being a mother, Kasturba felt that her children were being influenced by the other children. She could not but remember how, in a bid to reform his friend Sheikh Mehtab, her husband had ignored his own mother's concerns. The entire household had been affected. She also knew that as always, her husband would pay no heed to her counsel. She shared her worries with Kallenbach. He was aware of the rowdy behaviour of the boys and was worried too.

After a few days, Kallenbach had a long talk with Bapu about the problem. He thought for a minute and lobbed the question right back at Kallenbach, 'What should I do, you tell me?'

'If you can't keep your children segregated, then let the other children go.'

'You mean, I tell my children that they are special which they are not …. I make them feel that those children have been asked to leave because they have to be kept away from them?'

'You could tell them that they are being sent away because they behave badly and do things that are wrong.'

'Won't my saying this make them angry and curious and encourage them towards more bad behaviour?'

Kallenbach words had no effect on Mohandas. He believed that his own children would gradually understand and see the error of the ways of the other children. If they would not listen, he would take them away from there. This is just what happened because they stayed on at the farm for a long time and no harm was done. Perhaps this was because Kasturba was worried and the children understood what they had to do themselves. But in the beginning of 1911, the smouldering tension between Mohandas and Harilal flared up, in spite of Kasturba's best efforts to cool things down. This time, there was no way that it could be suppressed. The tension became explosive when Chhaganlal fell ill as soon as he got to London and had to return to Phoenix, leaving his studies midway. All the leaders of Indian origin in South Africa knew that no one other than Mohandas Gandhi knew the law. The Indian National Congress could call him to India at any time, what would they do then? They began to exert pressure to send someone else to London to study Law. They had no objection to giving extra money. An essay competition was organised for this purpose. Mohandas was made the sole judge of the competition because he was the only one who knew the subject. After due diligence, a Parsi youth from Natal, Sorabji Adjania was chosen. He was among the first people to come to Transvaal and do satyagraha.

Sorabji would have studied and raised his voice against the laws that went against the interests of the Indians. Mohandas trusted him. But after just a few months, his lungs got infected and he died. Nobody could have foreseen something like this. It was the strangest coincidence that after the return of Chhaganlal, Sorabji departed before he could fulfil the expectations of the Indian community. There had been another young man who had secured higher marks than Sorabji. But he was the son of the judge of the competition. This was the second time that he had fallen victim to his father's idealism.

***

On 8 May, 1911, when Kasturba woke up, she found a letter next to her pillow. It was from Harilal addressed to Ba and Bapu. It said that he was breaking off relations with Bapu for the rest of his life. Ba was not surprised but she was wounded to the core. When respect becomes more important for parents than the well-being of a child, unknowingly, the child's ego becomes bigger too ... is what she thought. For days she lived in the hope of his return. Where had he gone? Where should they look for him? One day, a friend of

Hari said that he was waiting for a ship to go to India in the Delagoa gulf near Mozambique. Kallenbach told Bapu that he would go there and bring him back. He felt sure he could reason with him. Bapu gave no answer.

This sad chain of events reached a climax on 15 May, 1911 when Hari returned by himself. He looked tired and wan, after having meandered through fields and orchards through the night. Bapu asked, 'Where did you go without informing us?'

'Whom should I have told? You have put me out of your heart. There was no point in telling Ba and making her unhappy.'

'Who told you that I have put you out of my heart?'

'Will I have to tell you that? You were the decision maker. The one you sent to London last time was your nephew. This time you did not send the one who was at top position, but chose Sorabji. Is this not proof enough?'

'Do studies mean everything?'

'Ask yourself, could you have reached where you stand today without studying to be a barrister?'

'What do you mean?'

'Bapu, I also wanted to walk in your footsteps. But you did not consider me worthy.'

'I want you to join me in satyagraha.'

'I have done satyagraha at the youngest age and have been to prison the maximum number of times. Would I have sat at home after coming back from London?'

'Those who want to be in social service have to let go of their attachment to family and such attractions. That is their test.'

'I was taking that test.'

'Challenging the discretion of the examiner does not fall within the rights of the examinee.'

'Is it within the rights of the examiner to keep the examinee with the highest marks from getting his legitimate due?'

'I am also your father.'

'Is that always going to be my misfortune?'

'You think so.'

'I am being made to think so.'

The door opened. Kasturba's voice broke through, 'Why are you fighting, father and son? Please tell me what is the matter?' Both were silent. She continued, 'Hari returned after suffering heaven knows what troubles, and you ...'

'He is my son too.'

'This is what I have come to find out ... who is how much of a father and who a son ...?' Hari said sarcastically.

'Enough!' said Kasturba firmly, 'Is this how you speak to your father?'

'Ba, this is what I want to know, does any father trample over the dreams of his son for the sake of his own ideals?'

'It is such ideals that turn dreams into reality. You are free to think what you want. When you feel calmer, tell me what you really want.'

'As if there is anything left that I could want ...' said Harilal and went out. There was silence outside. Few people were seen near the waterfall. There was a touch of heat in the breeze.

Two days later, Kasturba saw that father and son were going out of the farm with Harilal's luggage. Neither of the two had told Kasturba anything at all. She grumbled, 'All men are the same. Husband or son.'

She found out later that Mohandas had gone to see Hari off to the Johannesburg railroad as he was on his way to India. He would live in India and study. It was like a great weary quiet descended in her. She had but one question, if he had met her before going, would she have stopped him? She consoled herself that when a child is disappointed, he seeks his own future. Perhaps Hari had gone to do that. She was looking for a way to forgive her husband for this incident. She was reminded of Harilal's words, 'Bapu … we are all for Bapu. Is he for nobody?' She knew this was his pain, his bapu must have some other … she stood moored between them. Holding their pain in her breast. Either she will have to forget all this to be able to live with them or she will have to live with it … all her pain.

***

There was a flurry of incidents in Kasturba's life. Hari had gone to seek his fortune all alone. The biggest canker in her soul was that he had broken all relations with his Bapu and there was bitterness in his heart. When relationships break, they scatter like a bundle of broken threads. She prayed that he would find peace and happiness in India. He should understand that his father does not want him to be dispirited but wants to electrify him into action. His methods might be different from his own ideas. Hari's departure in these circumstances was not just a blow for Ba, it had also stunned the other three children. Kasturba had borne the brunt of

Mohandas's temper at a time when young girls weave dreams for their future. He had thrown her out of the house and sent her to her parents' home for a long while, not once but twice.

——***——

THE LATER YEARS

Success of Satyagraha

In 1912, senior Congress leader and a prominent member of the Viceroy Council, Gopal Krishna Gokhale was coming to South Africa for a month. Mohandas considered him his political guru. Actually, it was on his insistence that Gokhale was coming to South Africa to see the conditions of the Indians there. He should see how the government was applying anti-*girmitiya* laws and making life very difficult for the Indians. Gandhi Bhai would update him regularly about whatever was happening in South Africa, so he knew quite a lot. Being a distinguished member of the Viceroy Council, he was given an official red carpet welcome in Cape Town. British and Indians, both were present in the welcome ceremony. The way the government had publicised his arrival, led to a surge of hope among the Indians that their demands would be approved. But Kasturba was not among the optimists. She knew that after Gokhale leaves, Indians would be victims of official neglect once again.

The government had put a railway car at his disposal. Mohandas and Kallenbach were on call for him. Gokhale had travelled extensively by railway car. Meeting almost all sections of society, he had taken detailed information and notes personally. He had two meetings with the highest officials of the South African government. After the meeting, he told Mohandas that all matters had been settled. The Black Law will be abolished, racial discrimination will end and the three pound tax will be removed. Mohandas was not reassured by the promises given by the government to Gokhale. He said, 'I know the government here very well. I understand the mindset of the ministers. Have they given anything in writing?'

Gokhale said with complete assurance, 'Whatever I have said will definitely happen. General Botha has promised me.' He gave Mohandas further personal assurance, 'Brother, you see after one year ... you will have seen everything go right and you will come to India, no excuses then ...'

Mohandas said with polite firmness, 'Forgive me, but I am not as hopeful as you are. Before I return, many Indians would have gone to jail.' It is hard to know whether Gokhale took Mohandas's words amiss or not, but he held his peace.

One day, very politely Gokhale ji criticised Mohandas's hard stance and domineering nature, 'You always do things your own way.' Based on his experience at Tolstoy Farm, he warned his disciple and friend that his personality, with its inexorable discipline and ruthless self sacrifice becomes autocratic for everybody else. He said this like a brother citing his own example. But upon his return to India, when he heard that the government of South Africa had gone back on its word, he saw light in Mohandas's strong convictions and his moral leadership. He accepted before the public of Bombay, that Gandhi had an amazing spiritual energy to make even his ordinary functionary a sacrificing leader.

***

In 1913, Mohandas announced that he was moving the centre of the Satyagraha movement from Tolstoy Ashram to Phoenix. This made Kasturba happier than she had been in months. She was not in the least bothered that it meant moving her household again. This was a return home.

One day, Mohandas said to Kasturba, 'Do you know that very soon I will not be your husband or you my wife?' This conversation was taking place in the kitchen and Kasturba was making preparations for dinner and Mohandas was cutting vegetables. She was taken aback. She thought that perhaps she had not heard him properly.

'What are you saying?'

'I was telling you that very soon you will not be my duly married spouse. You will be considered my mistress.'

Kasturba thought he was teasing her. 'What an inauspicious thing to say ... sometimes the things you say have no head or tail.'

'I am not saying this,' said Mohandas very calmly, 'General Smuts says that our marriage is not legal.'

'He is mad. He does not know what nonsense he is spouting. Where does he get his weird ideas from?' She was not willing to talk about the General's foolish pronouncements.

'Up to you ...' said Mohandas, 'But he and the government are quite serious about this.'

A Muslim woman had come from India to join her husband. She was stopped at the port. She had challenged this in court. The Supreme Court judge Mr Surley had given a judgment that a marriage that had not been conducted in the Christian tradition and if there was no certificate of marriage, it cannot be considered legal. In one fell swoop, ten thousand Muslims, Hindus and Parsi marriages had been declared illegal and the children illegitimate. The children could not be legal heirs to the property of their parents. Wives would be banished from the country. Any soldier can come and sleep with any woman in the household. Mohandas had written to General Smuts that the marriages in India, as per their religion, should be considered legal as they have all been conducted according to religious customs and tradition. South Africa is a colony of the British empire and the British officialdom recognises them. Therefore the court's judgment should be rejected. His request was not accepted.

Kasturba was deeply troubled by this whole episode. 'What will we do now?' she asked.

'Women will have to raise their voices against this humiliation. They will have to oppose it.' He paused, 'You should go to jail, like the men.'

Kasturba thought he was joking. The idea of women going to jail was laughable so she recovered her poise, 'You will send your wife to jail?'

'Shouldn't women be partners to the men in whatever happens? Sita took part in Ram's struggles. Taramati took equal part in Harishchandra's troubles. They bore incredible pain for their self respect and to protect what was good and true.'

'They were divine beings, we are ordinary mortals,' countered Kasturba.

'They are still worshipped today. Would that be so, if they hadn't sacrificed so much for the truth?' Mohandas was enjoying this discussion, 'We are the descendents of Ram and Sita. If we do the same, we will be known in the same way.'

'How will I live on jail food?'

'That is not a big problem,' said he in a neutral manner.' Ask for fruits and manage.'

'After all that I have heard from you about the officials in jail, how can I believe that they will make fruits available to me when I ask for them?'

'Perhaps not,' said Mohandas looking hopeless, 'There is only one way – hunger strike.'

'First you will send me to jail and then you want me to die in a hunger strike. What sort of husband are you?'

'If you die, I will worship you like a Goddess.'

'If that is the case, I will go to jail so that you get a chance to worship me.' Both of them laughed like friends do.

***

Mohandas had mentioned the possibility of her being called his mistress in jest, as the final judgment had not come until then. But now it was permeating the environment. There was wrath among the public. Kasturba was agitated. Mohandas had brought up childhood memories with the mention of Sita and Taramati. Even then, she used to wonder if girls could be like these heroic women? An image of Rani Laxmibai would come up. She remembered how her mother used to say that

Rani Laxmibai was a modern heroine born a little before our times. She had proved that all those who loved her, were under her protection. She was as brave as any man can be.

Kasturba had accepted that the battle that Mohandas was fighting was necessary. Her responsibility was equal to her husband's.

***

Mohandas knew satyagraha had reached a point of climax. This was the time for peaceful resistance to succeed. It was now or never. The Union government was going back on its word repeatedly. It had permanently forgotten the abolition of the three pound tax. After declaring marriages other than Christian as illegal, countless Indian families, rich and poor, were in a crisis, being subject to excessive fines and humiliation. There was renewed strength and energy visible in society at large. A non-violent movement of women had not been possible until now, but now the time had come. They were asking for a movement themselves. Just as in a total revolution, demanding imprisonment en masse as satyagraha was difficult, but it was necessary.

The movement had begun. The women living in Tolstoy Ashram had come out as volunteers and were selling fruit without a license. It was necessary to familiarise them with the methods of satyagraha. The police was also ready to deal with the opposition of the public. One woman was pregnant and some were carrying children in their arms. The police had ignored them. Mohandas held a meeting of the inhabitants of Phoenix. Everybody was invited except children below sixteen and Kastur.

Kastur knew that Mohandas had not consulted her when he decided to call a meeting. It was the month of September. The weather was neither hot nor cold. Mohandas was explaining his strategy of putting the government under siege to some Tamilian women. Kastur felt that she was being deliberately ignored. She remembered the conversation in the kitchen. Had his behaviour changed because of that? It did not seem possible ... Kastur called Mohandas aside and asked him directly, 'What do I lack that makes me unworthy of going to jail for satyagraha? The other day you were ready for me to go to jail and even die in a hunger strike ...'

Mohandas stayed silent for a minute, 'It is not a question of mistrust. If I had asked you to go to jail for satyagraha, you would have gone for sure, but only to honour my wishes. Because I am your husband. If you fell ill or could not bear the excesses there, I would never be able to forgive myself.'

Kasturba was not one to give up easily, 'If you can bear it and my children can bear it, then why not me?'

In two minds, Mohandas said, 'Think about the difficulties and hardships there ...'

'I don't have to think about anything, I will take part in this satyagraha.'

Mohandas could see determination and controlled rage reflected on her face. She was ready for the struggle.

***

It was 23 September, 1913. Sixteen people, twelve men and four women, were going towards Phoenix station with travelling bags. Behind them were some residents of Phoenix.

The sixteen took the north bound train to Johannesburg. The eyes of the people on the platform were moist. They had come to say farewell. Before she boarded the train, Kasturba kissed her younger son Devdas and said something to him. Kasturba was leading this satyagrahi group. There was Kashiben, her husband Chhaganlal, Santokhben and Ramdas Gandhi and others all from the Gandhi clan. Rustamji Parsi of Durban was also there in whose house the Gandhi family had found succour when they had come to Durban for the first time. He was Gandhi's friend and a staunch satyagrahi now. Before the train started, Mohandas had reached. He said to Kasturba, 'If your health fails, you can ...'

Kastur completed his sentence, 'You don't worry. Kastur knows that if jail is your home, it is my new *sasural.*'

She smiled and then the train pulled out. Mohandas bade farewell and returned to Phoenix and got busy with the people living there. He was worried about Kasturba. He said to Devdas, 'Your ba has gone in her enthusiasm. I hope she does not have to return on account of her health.'

Devdas said, 'No Bapu, Ba will never return. If there is a challenge, she gets up even if she is almost dead. Didn't you see her condition when she came from Parsi Doctor Kaka?'

Bapu looked at Devdas and as he got up to leave he said, 'It is good to see your faith in Ba.'

There had been no publicity of the Johannesburg trip of Kasturba and her associates. Not even an information piece in the *Indian Opinion.* No advance information had been given to the officials regarding the demonstration. It was possible that they may not be arrested at all.

Those non-violent attackers reached the borders of Johannesburg and did not speak, as had been decided. They did not show their permit nor did they disclose their identities and not even their names. So whatever had to happen did happen as expected and all the men and women were arrested. Until they were produced in court and charged as guilty, the police did not know anything about them. They were sentenced to three months of imprisonment with hard labour. Nobody had come to know their identities and where they had come from. Kasturba and the women with her were the first Indian women to go to jail on foreign soil for satyagraha. It is very difficult to understand the state of mind of Kasturba of those times. Fifteen year old son Ramdas was marching with the others associated with this satyagraha and going to the men's jail. She was going to the women's prison to protect the self respect of Indian women. Other than her youngest son, everybody in the family had served a sentence or was doing so now. She had become a part of them.

Her biggest anguish was that the male prisoners were transferred to Pietermaritzburg, fifteen year old Ramdas included. But Kasturba forced her mind away from that and told the other women to gather their courage and will to face the hard routine of the jail. She also asked them to finish all the chores of the jail and laundry daily so that they were not humiliated like the other women. She was assailed by the thought of Ramdas, many times in the day. How must he be facing up to the tough routine? She had told Chhaganlal Gandhi to look out for Ramdas. Rustamji Parsi was also a big support. When her heart would not stop clamouring, she would repeat Mohandas's words: you cannot do social service with a divided heart. You have to have a single point of focus. She would try her best to hang her heart on this peg.

In her broken English, Kasturba tried to tell the jail wardens in vain that they were all vegetarians so they would not be able to eat the food provided. They needed different food. The wardens would slip meals in, twice a day. The first day, they all nearly threw up when they caught sight of the food. Kasturba made a chequered calendar where she would cross out one square – one day less. It felt better to do this. Every evening, like in Phoenix Ashram, she would pray with all her associates. This was a source of solace. Powered by prayer, they declared a hunger strike. Non-violent and peaceful resistance by women under Kasturba's leadership was creating a wave of rage among the Indians in South Africa, particularly the women.

In support of the peaceful resistance of women, and on Mohandas's suggestion, eleven women who had unsuccessfully tried to enter Transvaal, attempted to enter Natal in mid-October. Mohandas called them the Tolstoy Sisters just like the arrested women were called the Phoenix Sisters. But the Tolstoy Sisters were not as lucky as the Phoenix ones. In spite of not showing a trade permit, they were not stopped nor were they arrested. This differential treatment under law was a conspiracy to create divisions amongst the agitators.

The condition of the four women in jail was deteriorating every day. They were threatened by the warders and the female warders made obscene gestures. Their ill health was ignored. The vegetarian food that was given to them was rotten and stale. The women prisoners said that they were willing to pay so that food could be brought from the outside. The reply from the authorities was that this was a jail and not a hotel. An infectious fever was raging in the prison. It caused great weakness. A young woman lost her life, a few days after her release because of the fever.

Kasturba looked more shattered and tired day by day. She would finish her work daily and do the evening prayers with complete faith. But the younger associates, Kashiben and Santokhben knew how much she was suffering. She was sick at heart. Who could have thought Ba's quiet and forbearing optimism would be put to such severe test after the arrest? From that day on, she was worried sick about Ramdas. In a letter from Phoenix came the news that Manilal had been jailed in Transvaal. Manilal was the quietest and nicest young man at this stage of his life. Then came news that Mohandas had also been arrested and jailed for nine months. He had been imprisoned in a place that nobody had heard of. She, both the sons, and Mohandas were all in different jails at the same time. If Harilal had been there, he would have been in another jail thought Kasturba. His tensions with his father troubled Ba greatly. The absence of dialogue between the two caused her enormous pain. The jail term and the strain between loved ones lacerated her in the same way. The loneliness of jail is imposed, but the rift between father and son was of their own creation, taking root through some external force.

***

The South African government was convinced that the focal point of unrest was located in Phoenix. It wanted to silence *Indian Opinion* anyhow so that things would quiet down. The police was sent to arrest Albert West. Maganlal Gandhi and Devdas were working twenty hour days to bring out *Indian Opinion.* The Indian question was becoming grave. The speech by Lord Hardinge, the Viceroy of India that no civilised nation would accept for a moment, the methods that the South African government was using to deal with the satyagraha movement had caused a stir. This was a clear warning to the government and cabinet. The British government had also expressed displeasure over the government's efforts to sort out the situation. On 18 October, 1913, Mohandas, Henry Pollack and Hermann Kalllenbach were released unconditionally on the pretext of their appearing before the Inquiry Commission.

Addressing a public meeting, Mohandas said, 'For those who were killed either inside or outside jail, instead of appearing before an Inquiry Commission, we will have to be ready to suffer more to purify ourselves.' On account of the killing of ten Indians, according to the Indian tradition, Mohandas had come to the meeting in a lungi till his knees (such as that Indian labourers wore), barefoot, with his hair and moustache shaved off, without a *pagdi,* in mourning. The next day, in the same attire, with Henry and Millie Pollack and Kallenbach, and many known and unknown faces, he was waiting at the gates of the Maritzburg jail for the prisoners. It was the day that the three months of Kasturba and the other women's sentence was ending. It was 22 December, 1913.

When the prisoners were released, a thin, small neglected figure of a woman stumbled towards them. People thought she was Mohandas's mother. They moved forward to greet her respectfully. It was actually Kasturba, the first Indian and probably the first woman in the world, to go to jail voluntarily for the cause of the self-respect of women.

There was a query from the crowd but no answer was given.

The struggle was reaching its climax. There was a sense of unreality about the meeting of Ba and Bapu. After reaching Phoenix, Kasturba cast a searching eye. 'When will Manilal and Ramdas come? If only they could have come before me ...' In the letter sent to General Smuts by Mohandas and his associates, a demand had been made to release all satyagrahis. The anti-Indian members of the Inquiry Commission should be replaced. If no Indian could be included, at least some just and fair minded Europeans should be included. Smuts reply said that the first demand had been met but the second could not be. Mohandas opposed this in a public announcement. On 1 January 1914, people would offer themselves to be arrested and a *Nyay Yatra* or a March for Justice would start from Durban to Pretoria.

***

There was an unexpected obstacle that appeared. The White labour of South Africa started a nationwide agitation for their own problems. The government imposed Martial Law. Mohandas halted the *Nyay Yatra*. When asked why he let slip this golden chance to pressurise the government into acceding to his demands, he said that his intention was not to decimate the other side but to win them over. Gandhi's tactics succeeded. General Botha and General Smuts agreed to solve the Indian problem through talks with Mohandas after dealing with the current crisis. In London, there was not much surprise at this benevolent attitude of the South African government. It was welcomed instead. To help Mohandas, Gokhale sent trusted friend, CF Andrews to South Africa. The Indians and Europeans felt that the non-violent agitation of the Indians was moving towards success, for the first time.

As talks progressed, there was another hitch. There was a call for Gandhi ji to come to Phoenix. Ba was seriously ill. Through some days of February and March, he had to stay in Phoenix. This was a time for aspirations and as well as deep remorse for him. Mohandas wrote to a friend, 'We were all mentally prepared for Kasturba's death.' Only when hope turns to despair, could a husband write this about his wife. In another letter, he had held himself responsible for her condition. Not just for Ba's sorrows but also for the sorrows of the others. In another, he said, 'I don't know what cruel parts of mine cause others to take on impossible tasks to please me.' But Ba's health improved and as her energy limped back, Bapu's heart revived. Ba also came back into her element. Mohandas was greatly relieved. Ba even demanded to go to Cape Town with him to continue the interrupted talks with Generals Botha and Smuts. Ba was as concerned about Bapu's health as he was about hers.

Gandhi and Smuts, who were suspicious of each other, now held each other in great respect and their hearts yielded somewhat. This would show in the General's jocular remarks. His secretary had once complained to Mohandas, 'Self flagellation by the satyagrahis, to win, makes us helpless and leaves us with few choices.' Satyagraha had managed to penetrate the armour of insensitivity.

Satyagraha and non-cooperation had succeeded to an extent. An agreement was taking shape by June. The parliament passed the agreement as a Relief Bill. The three pound per person annual tax on *girmitiyas*, approved by the Indian government was abolished, marriages other than those conducted in the Christian tradition were deemed legal, and further arrival of Indian labourers was banned after 1920. The Immigration law was made easier for educated Indians. One provision of the Black Act, regarding no rights to enter one state from another in the Union, continued unchanged. Other restrictions, such as most Indian labourers would stay in their own settlements, they will not have rights to buy land and in Transvaal, their rights to land will not be recognised, continued as well. In South Africa, this was the first victory of satyagraha over racism. Between two antagonists, the government and Indian labourers, talks were held at an equal level and they succeeded. It was for the first time that the world learned that non-violence and peace could bring equality between two unequal parties.

***

While in jail, Mohandas had made a pair of sandals by hand. In appreciation of his hard work and cooperation to get the Relief Bill passed in parliament, and in farewell, he had sent this pair of sandals as a present for the General, through his old secretary, Sozna Shlesin. Kasturba believed that goodwill cannot be expressed with shoes. Mohandas maintained that goodwill is inherent in labour and in a person's heart.

***

Kasturba's last days in South Africa were spent in victorious celebration. Those who had won a life of freedom garlanded her, businessmen felicitated her, mementos were presented, smiling photographs with officials and the gentry, tearful goodbyes from friends ... but Ba kept looking for Hari. If only he could have been there ... he had played an equal role in the independence of all these people. Bapu was contemplative. Ba would surreptitiously wipe her welling eyes, every now and then.

Crowds waving at them ... they reminded her of the crowd when they disembarked at Port Durban, which had mocked her husband, pelted him with rotten eggs and humiliated him in countless ways. They had bayed for his blood asking him to be hanged from a sour apple tree. She was astonished that it was now a mixed crowd of people from different castes and faiths. There was a vast distance between his farewell and that arrival. People were heard saying, Gandhi Bhai had wrought real change in South Africa. A little thief stole into Ba's heart asking if she did nothing? She laughed to herself. A familiar single line appeared before her, unbidden, '*Jis bidh rakhe Ram Ja Bidh Rahiye.*' 'Be, as the Lord keeps you....'

——***——

Home Again

Mohandas remembered the promise he had made to Gokhale ji that he would come to India, now that he was free of his responsibilities. Coincidentally, Gokhale was coming to London. He wanted to meet Mohandas to discuss plans for the future. Mohandas booked tickets to go to London with Kasturba. Herman Kallenbach was to accompany them. All the other India-bound Phoenix dwellers went straight to India. The three children went to India with them. Kasturba wanted them to go to London too but Mohandas insisted it was better for them to go to India.

They endured the nineteen day voyage in a small third class cabin according to Mohandas's wishes. Many things had happened in rapid succession in the recent past and he was quite worn out. Both of them kept themselves confined to the cabin. They even had their meals there. The shipping company had arranged for dry fruits. Mohandas kept busy sorting out his papers or he wrote letters. Each day he taught Kallenbach Gujarati for an hour. Many times Kasturba would laugh at the Germanic pronunciation of Gujarati. Kallenbach also laughed along with her. He planned to go to India from

London along with Mohandas. After this, Mohandas and Kasturba would sing *shlokas* from the Bhagwad Gita and *padas* from the Ramayan.

Kasturba's ever-busy hands would pause sometimes but her thoughts never stemmed. She was going to an unknown country for the first time. Because her husband had studied there, she was familiar with it peripherally. She had one unpleasant association with London in that Hari had not been able to study here. This fact had tightened into a knot between father and son. Her heart would meander around Hari and Gulab. She used to thrill at the very thought of holding Rami who looked like a little doll. Her eyes would shine at the thought of seeing Kanti and Rasik, Harilal's two sons, for the first time. Many loved ones would have gone forever in this interim. Mohandas was the only one left from among the progeny of Karamchand and Putliba. In 1913, Karsandas had passed away. This news had unbanked a flood of memories. Karsan was a friend along with being an elder brother. It was an age since Karsan, Tulsi Chacha's son Motilal and Mohandas's marriage was solemnised in the same mandap. In 1914, there came information via cable that Mota Bhai Lakshmidas was no more. As one storm abated, another storm rose to upset everything. Lakshmidas was like a father to Mohandas. Kasturba had spent nearly half her life under his protection. Kasturba got the saddest news of all that her elder brother Khushaldas Kapadia, his wife and daughter had all died of a fever, one after another. Only her younger brother Madhavdas was left. She was calm outwardly but there was much that was cracking inside.

On 18 July, 1914, when they left Cape Town for London on *R.M. Kinfauns Castle*, General Smuts said, 'A saint has left our shores, possibly forever.'

Mohandas's departure to London was not a secret. Reporters were waiting for the new leader from India. Many newspapers mentioned Kasturba also noting that she had suffered for the cause of Indian labourers and had gone to jail as part of satyagraha.

***

In London, a reception was held in Cecil Hotel to honour Mohandas and Kasturba. Indian friends and English friends attended in good number. But Gokhale, who had called Mohandas to London, was not there. His absence was noticeable. He suffered from diabetes and had gone to France for treatment. And since he was stuck there Mohandas and Kasturba had no option but to wait for him in London. Mohandas had also found out that his associate could not go to India because he was German. Relations between the two countries were tense because of the War. Kallenbach had no option but to take up architecture in Germany.

Mohandas took a cheap house on rent in Kensington with Kasturba's concurrence. He was in a quandary because of the World War. He felt a responsibility towards the British government. In South Africa, at a time of crisis, he had put together an ambulance team. He issued an appeal to the expatriate Indians in London, signed: MK Gandhi and Mrs MK Gandhi. Many doctors, lawyers and students came forward and gave their names. The names were sent to the Additional Secretary of the British government who was handling war matters. Mohandas spent his time in training and encouraging the relief team. Kasturba and Mohandas enrolled in the nursing assistance course of the hospital. However, owing to his physical weakness and the humid weather in London, Mohandas contracted pleurisy. He was confined to his room. Kasturba was suddenly faced with many challenges. A foreign language, his illness and the ambulance team. Mohandas's health was a cause for concern. The enthusiasm to work in the ambulance team was considerably dampened. The members who had been sent for training to the hospital refused to take orders from anybody but M. K. Gandhi. Kastur did not want to mention this problem in front of Mohandas. She did not know enough English that she could take over. This back and forth came to an end when the first injured patient from France came for treatment.

Mohandas's health was not improving. Kasturba was following the doctor's instructions faithfully. His diet had been modified. She had consulted a vegetarian expert also. He suggested repeated massages, consumption of raw vegetables, baths in lukewarm water and keeping all windows open. Kasturba did just that. But these experiments did not help and Kasturba also caught a severe cold. She called a doctor of Indian origin. He made it clear that if the patient stayed on in London, the upcoming winter would be even harder. The pleurisy would not be cured. Finally, it was time to go home.

***

On 9th January, 1915, when the ship cast anchor at Apollo Bunder, Mohandas and Kasturba were surprised to see a big crowd under the hot sun. When they got off the ship, their surprise only grew. They had all come to welcome them. While they had thought that a few acquaintances might turn up, they had not expected to see such a crowd. The tales of their service and sacrifice had preceded them to India. There had been a time when an English bureaucrat had him thrown out of his room. But now the Governor of Bombay, Lord Willingdon, had invited Gandhi and Kasturba with the greatest respect. Kastur had dressed in a plain sari and glass bangles that she had been gifted years ago, in her wedding. Mohandas wore a Kathiawadi outfit – a *pagdi,* a dhoti and a *choga.* Kasturba was relieved that Mohandas had discarded foreign and Parsi attire and he did not force anybody else to wear such clothes too. The Governor introduced Kasturba as the heroine of South Africa. Mohandas was introduced as the leader of the freedom of India. Mohandas contradicted him saying that he and his wife felt more at home with the contracted labourers in Natal, rather than the westernised gentry of Bombay. They were rural folk, he said.

From Bombay they went straight to Porbandar and Rajkot to meet the mourning families of Mota Bhai Lakshmidas and Karsan. Kasturba was shocked and grieved. Her *jethanis,* who had been full of life, looked like pale shadows without their husbands. They were cursed to live a life of widowhood. Kastur was overwhelmed with grief and she could not speak a word. The garlanded photographs of her brothers-in-law had been hung along with Diwan

Karamchand and Putliba's pictures. Life had changed for the two households. The crowds that they saw when they got off the ship and who appeared to be impressed with non-violence, the choice of a life of frugality, service and working for the common good, were nowhere to be seen. There seemed to be a strange air of innocence and helplessness all around. All the scenes of her as the youngest daughter-in-law, flashed before her eyes. From her mother-in-law to sisters-in-law, they all exercised their privileges over her, because she was the youngest. Today they scanned her face as if she were the elder one. One question chafed at her repeatedly. Does a woman have no identity of her own? Is she nothing without a husband? Her *jethanis* seemed to have lost all spirit and self confidence.

***

All the Phoenix dwellers had been staying in Shantiniketan. Albert West and Henry Pollack had not come with them but had reached Bombay two weeks prior to Mohandas and Kasturba's arrival. Ba and Bapu had reached Shantiniketan from Gujarat. Gurudev was travelling at the time but Charlie Andrews, who taught at Shantiniketan, welcomed them. Ba was happy to meet her children after so long.

Two weeks had not passed before they received a telegram. Their Guru Gokhale was no more. Ba and Bapu had met him recently, so his death was a real jolt. They immediately left for Poona with Maganlal. Kasturba had been in a third class compartment for the first time in South Africa when Bapu had made it a part of satyagraha. He followed the same tradition in India. But the third class here was different from the third class in South Africa, where there was a greater western influence. He had to stand in a long line to get tickets for Poona. The real face of an Indian Railways' third class compartment was revealed to Ba and Bapu. The staff was dishonest, selfish, greedy and filthy and the travellers badly behaved. Somehow they pushed themselves aboard the Inter class. They had to bear the discourteous behaviour of the railway guard there. The only difference was that unlike Pietermaritzburg, Mohandas was not thrown off. It was imperative for them to reach before Gokhale's cremation. So they had to pay extra money and put up with uncivilised behaviour. Travelling in Interclass rather than the third was like a burden for Ba and Bapu's spirit. Bapu was troubled by Ba's apparent normalcy and equable manner.

During the Poona journey there was an incident that was proof of some dishonesty but also their intimacy as a couple. They were sorely tired by the time they reached Kalyan. He got off with Maganlal at the station and bathed in the open, under the pipe. They were just casting about to see how Kasturba could also bathe when they met an associate of Gokhale called Kaul. He knew Mohandas so he asked, 'Where are you staying? Is there a problem?' Kaul said that Ba could use the bathroom in the second class waiting room. He knew that Ba was not entitled to use the bathroom in the second class waiting room. But under the circumstances, he chose to ignore this rule. Ba was not very keen, but for the first time her husband had not given rules greater primacy than his wife.

***

Mohandas Karamchand Gandhi was forty six in 1915. Of these forty six years, he must have spent half in India. Gokhale was his only guide in the field of social service. But he died just as the time came for Mohandas to be in his country. In their last meeting, he had said to Mohandas that if you want to give direction to the nation, you must silently observe and understand politics and you must know your country better. 'Travel and see and learn,' was his advice.

Mohandas took these words to heart like a devoted follower. He maintained silence throughout that year. It was like a vow of purity. He left the Phoenix dwellers and went on travels around the country with Kasturba. This was his year of probation. For certain periods, keeping Kasturba's feelings in mind, he would take Manilal and Ramdas along. Once when Harilal had come to visit Shantiniketan, he also came along for a short trip. Ba was overjoyed. She nursed a hope that this would bridge the distance between them. But it was not to be. He made it amply clear that he would do as he pleased.

***

Whenever Kasturba found time, she would become Mohandas's travelling companion. She was not very fond of travelling. She wanted to choose a permanent appropriate place for a home. The more they travelled, the more convinced she was that there was no place better than their birthplace, Gujarat. After her peregrinations at home and abroad, she wanted to name one corner her own. Mohandas was not in favour of acquiring property but every woman wants a home of her own. After such a long nomadic existence, Kasturba wanted her own place too. Mohandas also had roots in his place of birth. They chose Ahmedabad for two reasons. One was its beauty and the other, the ruins of old mosques and medieval structures. Ahmedabad had been the city of weavers in olden times. Mohandas wanted to revive these traditions of spinning and weaving. Now it had become a town of cloth mills. He believed that the mill owners would give financial help for setting up an Ashram. Living there, Mohandas and Kasturba would also ask their friends to settle there. A lawyer proposed setting up the Ashram in his bungalow in Kocharab. Husband and wife inspected it and agreed. In the interests of transparency, they declared that their Ashram would be open to all castes. Also to 'untouchables.' People laughed at first. Which untouchable would go and live there? 'Why don't you get a family of "untouchables" who will live in your Ashram first,' they said sarcastically. The privileged were sure that the untouchables knew that if they broke the ancient tradition, they would face ruin in society.

On 25 May, 1915, a group of twenty five came to live in the Ashram. Old and new families, children, women were all a part of the group. Kasturba was happy that they were back home. They would live here without a care and there will be the comfort of family. It will be a new beginning. Nine principles were laid down – truth, non-violence, control over the tongue, renunciation and honesty (no tolerance of theft). The additional three were – boycott of foreign clothes, fearlessness and most importantly, opposing untouchability. Bapu insisted on a vow to abide by all the rules.

***

For some time, the Ashram ran well. In September, as the weather was changing, Bapu received a letter. All the inhabitants of the Ashram and others had started addressing Mohandas as Bapu and Kasturba as Ba. Bapu read out the letter to everybody in the Ashram. One of Gokhale ji's associates had written to say that an honest and respected Dalit family wanted to come and live in the Ashram. The family has a husband, wife and a young daughter. The husband was a teacher in a school. There stood a challenge before the inhabitants of the Ashram. When they had all signed the charter of rules, they had not thought that they would be confronted with abiding by them so soon. They were all in shock. There was no basis to oppose it because they had all signed the charter. The people who were giving financial aid had also not thought that such a situation would arise. Knowing all this, Bapu wanted everybody to confront this without any delay. The day arrived when the Dalit family reached the Ashram. There were heated discussions everywhere. What will happen now? How were they to be dealt with? The people did not even receive them politely but directed them towards Bapu's *kutiya.* An ordinary looking man wrapped in a dhoti sat there writing. Dudha Bhai, who had come, thought he must be an assistant to the great Gandhi.

He asked, 'We want to meet Gandhi ji, where can we meet him?'

'Right here,' he smiled, 'You are Dudha Bhai and Deena Ben from Bombay?'

Both of them were uneasy. Bapu asked the couple to sit. He patted the little girl saying she was very sweet. He asked them few questions. Then he told them about himself and the Ashram. Finally, he said, 'Today, you are our guest and you will eat with us.' Dudha Bhai and Deena Ben were hesitant. They were worried about how the others would react. Bapu insisted that they eat with the others.

After the meal, Dudha Bhai asked, 'Where should we wash the dishes?'

Bapu called out, 'Rama, please wash his dishes.'

Dudha Bhai refused forcefully. Rama was Ramdas. Kasturba looked at Bapu. Bapu kept quiet but he shook his head. Perhaps he was giving a signal to remain quiet.

***

Even more than the Ashram, there was a real battle outside. The staunch traditionalists were not ready to accept the Dalit family. The first threat was made of stopping the water supply to the Ashram. The well of Kocharab belonged to the Zamindar. The caretaker of the well abused the Ashram inhabitants roundly and they did not counter him. Things appeared to have cooled down. The biggest clamour came from the people of Ahmedabad which brought the very existence of the Ashram under threat. A wealthy supporter took back his financial assistance saying that the Ashram could not be supported for besmirching religion. The day came when the accountant Maganlal Gandhi declared that financially, it was not possible to run the Ashram. There was not a paisa left for the expenses of the next month. Maganlal was told that the neighbours had declared the Ashram to be *Achhoot* Ashram or the Ashram of Untouchables. The use of civic facilities was banned for it so that the inhabitants would have no choice but to leave. Amazingly, Ba-Bapu were not in the least worried. Being used to opposition, they had deep faith in God. They believed they were doing God's work and God would show the way. Bapu said, 'If that happens, we will go and live in the *basti* of the untouchables. We will earn together and manage with what we make.'

Two days later, a child came running to Bapu and said that somebody was calling him outside. When he went out, a grand looking person emerged from a car and said, 'Bapu, I want to do something for the Ashram.' He handed over an envelope and left without further word. He wished to remain anonymous. It was discovered that he was Ambalal Sarabhai, the biggest mill owner of Ahmedabad. The envelope contained twenty five thousand rupees, enough for a whole year.

***

Bapu knew that the Dalit family's staying in the Ashram would cause an uproar. But he certainly did not think that even those he loved dearly will resist. He saw that Deena Ben was not allowed inside the kitchen, Dudha Bhai was stopped outside. If the little girl Lakshmi touched a vessel in the kitchen, it was washed post-haste and the kitchen scoured as well. Maganlal's wife was the cause of all this, and so was Kasturba. Kasturba had stayed abroad for so many years and met many kinds of people, so he assumed that her views would have changed. During the evening prayer, it was announced that Dalits had been accepted as per the rules of the Ashram. Those who did accept the Dalit family were free to leave. Ba was not an exception. At night, many Ashram dwellers came to Bapu to say that they would change their attitude. Some of them went to Deena Ben and Dudha Bhai to make amends. Maganlal Gandhi, who was very close to him, said he wanted to go to Madras and learn weaving to get over his own biases.

For many days after this, Kasturba quietly went about her work. Dialogue with Bapu had almost stopped and she would avoid his eye. There was a tumult of thoughts, all to do with Bapu. Will we be in a crisis because of having the Dalit family in the Ashram? Will the public reject his reforms completely? But she knew he was stubborn, and would not be moved once he decided. He was completely against untouchability practised against Dalits for centuries. He believed it was the opposite of the precepts of the Gita. He believed they were 'Harijans'. Just as parents love their weak child the most, God must love the Dalits. It was only the social structure that kept them powerless. The word harijan upset her. It reminded her of Harilal. He was the elder son but he was getting increasingly distant. He was not a harijan but Bapu was hell bent on treating him as one. Can any child of God be ignored in this fashion? Stray wisps of disconnected thoughts blew about in her mind. Bapu wants Dudha Bhai and Deena Ben to be treated as the children of God. How can something that has not happened for millennia happen so soon? Finally, she left the answer to God.

One day, Kasturba was sitting in the verandah. Little Lakshmi was playing all by herself. Kasturba watched her for a long time. She was surprised that until now she had not observed how Lakshmi was an exceptionally self-contained, good natured and attractive child. She remembered the children in Tolstoy Farm whose parents had gone to jail in satyagraha. She would look after them with love and no distinctions about whether they were her own or somebody else's. She was Ba to all of them. Many of the children were 'untouchable'. The Ba of Tolstoy Ashram, how had she become so narrow minded for this young child? Kasturba took her in her lap lovingly. They are all God's own. I was wrong and Bapu was right. Why can't we all love each other? If I am God's child then why not Dudha Bhai and Deena Ben? The answers to her questions were coming unbidden.

***

For Mohandas, the year of voluntary probation, inspired by Gokhale, had come to an end. But his role in politics was still not clear. The political situation was changing very rapidly since Gokhale's departure. There was an air of uncertainty. Tilak was already gone. Mohandas's entire early youth had been spent in another world. There they lived cut off from the Indian way of life. Everybody was oppressed and neglected there. When he was there, he would feel his responsibility towards his own country. But all the time had gone in trying to get a grip on the issues of the Indians there. Back in the country, he realised that things are challenging.

A vast population of oppressed Indians ruled over by Raja-Maharajas, their feudal lords and bureaucracy lived here and the country ran on the diktats of a handful of White officials.

In 1915, Mohandas had come to look for a role as a supervisor in the Bombay Annual Session of the Indian National Congress. He was surprised to observe that the Indian leaders seemed to be growing as an ad hoc bunch. All of them, whether Hindu or Muslim, were debating England's involvement in Europe's war.

Kasturba had often thought that the year of silence of her husband would soon turn into outspokenness. That is just what happened as he delivered an incisive speech at Banaras Hindu Vishwavidyalay in Kashi. Many kings, Pandit Madanmohan Malviya and Annie Besant were present, among others. It was said that he had insulted Indian rulers and launched an attack on the British government. His speech had put the nobility in the Congress in a crisis. The general view was that Gandhi's political career had ended before it had even begun. All the kings had staged a walk out. The Raja of Darbhanga had to remain because he was the President. Annie Besant had tried to check him two or three times. But the student body applauded wildly. When excerpts of the speech were published in newspapers, he started getting invitations from all over the country. The youth of the country were excited and agitated by the speech. Mohandas had touched a raw nerve. Since last year, he had not left Kocharab to speak anywhere. In his first speech, he had created a crisis for the British. The government did not want to take action against him and challenge the entire youth of the nation. At a loss, the only thing the government did was to refuse permission to the newspaper, *Leader*, to publish the full text of the speech.

Ba and Bapu could not talk much because they were both busy. Whenever she went travelling with Bapu, she could talk about the family and about the Ashram. There was news from Calcutta that Gulab was about to bear her fifth child. Maganlal and Santokhben were coming back from Madras and would adhere to their vow. All these conversations happened during their travels. Little Lakshmi's parents were taking her to Bombay. Ba had never thought that the little one would cause her so much heartbreak when she would leave. Her parents had to give an assurance that when she was a little older, she would stay in the Ashram for a longer time.

Ba-Bapu went on long trips across the country like ordinary people. Nobody recognised them. Once, a group of students came to meet them at Madras station. They kept looking for them in the first and second class coaches. Ba and Bapu were sitting all dusty and tired after a four day journey, in the third class compartment. The students were so impressed by their humility and forbearance that they chanted slogans of *Mr Gandhi Zindabad, Mrs Gandhi Zindabad.* Kasturba was astonished. They took them outside towards a horse carriage. The excited students let the horses loose and began pulling the carriage themselves. For Ba and Bapu, this was a bother because they did not want the students to be pulling the carriage, but it was heartening to see such enthusiasm and love for the country. This was the first time that Kasturba had seen anything like this.

***

A farmer from Bihar, Rajkumar Shukla, had been chasing Mohandas for quite a while. He would turn up wherever he went. He had heard that Mohandas had fought for the rights of labourers in South Africa for twenty years and succeeded. Whenever he got a chance, he would tell Bapu about the plight of the farmers of Champaran. Champaran was a place of indigo farms and most of the farm owners were White. He was also an indigo farmer. Mohandas knew nothing about Champaran or about indigo farming so he did not quite know what to say to Shukla. Because he was shadowing him, sometimes he wondered if he was making up stories towards some selfish end. Finally, he said, until I see it all for myself, I cannot give you any advice. He thought that would put an end to the matter.

One day Kasturba saw him hanging around near Kocharab Ashram in 1917. She felt that his persistence indicated that there was a major problem. He asked for a date when Bapu would come to Champaran. This time Mohandas yielded to his pressure. Perhaps Kasturba might have also said something seeing Rajkumar's persistence. In April, Mohandas had to go for a conference to Calcutta. Kasturba also wanted to be there for her daughter-in-law's delivery. He told Shukla that he could come to Champaran for a few days, on his way back from Calcutta.

Ba and Bapu reached Calcutta in the fourth month. Rakjkumar was waiting for them. Ba recognised him but she did not pay heed. She wanted to reach Harilal's place as soon as possible. After being in Calcutta for a few days, Bapu said he was going to Champaran with Rajkumar. Ba was immersed in her grandchildren she was seeing for the first time. The birth of the child was also imminent. After the child was born, she forgot everything and got involved with looking after Gulab and the children. A baby girl had been born and she was called Manu. Ba was totally caught up in childcare, cooking and the family. For the first time, she had a chance to be a part of her eldest son's household. In spite of all this, she was concerned about her son. Being a mother, she could see that he was in dire financial straits. Dealing with all this, Ba scarcely registered that Mohandas had initiated his first massive public protest in India, in Champaran.

It may be that Bapu needed to be politically active in 1917 but the indigo farmers of Champaran certainly needed a combative leader. Rajkumar Shukla gave fertile ground to Gandhi to launch an agitation and the farmers got a fearless, dedicated and upright leader.

Indigo farming in Champaran was enormously profitable for the Whites. It was also a means of terrible exploitation of the farmers. In 1860, the new Governor of the White government had toured the area by boat to find out how the farmers were being persecuted. Tens of thousands of men, women and children left their indigo fields and lined the banks of the river for miles to register their protest. The flotilla of boats passed by. This was the first non-violent protest. The Governor had been sensitive and recommended ways to ease the burden on the farmers. But shortly after that he was recalled to London.

On 16 November, Bapu was going from village to village, to assess the situation. He was arrested forthwith. The road was deeply rutted and sometimes he had to ride an elephant. In some places, there was a train and at others he had to go on foot. He was produced before the magistrate of Champaran. He ordered Gandhi to leave town on the first available train. With full respect, Mohandas said that given his responsibility towards the people, he was unable to obey the order. The case was adjourned until the next day. The next day, thousands of farmers began to gather in the court premises from the morning. They had come to support their leader. The magistrate asked him to post bail. He thought it better to go to jail than pay money to the government. The court released him on its own responsibility. This was unprecedented. Never had a White man's court released a Black convict on its own responsibility. Mohandas had written to the Viceroy apprising him of the facts on the first night itself. After a few days, on the Viceroy's advice, the Governor ordered the district administration to cooperate in Mohandas Gandhi's investigation. The farmers were overjoyed, the lawyers were in shock but Bapu was calm.

After the case, Bapu took a house on rent in Motihari. People began feeling that this agitation would be long drawn out. The house was crowded with lawyers, farmers and villagers. Bapu knew that education was necessary for his countrymen. The women should be made aware of this as they looked after the children. Only a woman could reach out to other women. There was nobody more suited for this than Kasturba. Her temperament and experience was what was needed. Bapu wrote a letter on the Ashram's address.

Ba had reached the Ashram from Calcutta before Bapu's letter came, asking the Ashram inhabitants to join him in the Champaran agitation. He wrote, teachers were needed to educate the villagers. Those Ashram dwellers as could be spared from their duties should come here and help. The most important thing is to educate the wives and daughters of farmers. Kasturba and Devdas should both come. Devdas could teach the children. He was seventeen at the time. This was Bapu's call for 'Arise and Act'. For a devoted wife, Kasturba, a proud son, Devdas, and all the devoted friends in the country, it was hard to ignore Bapu's call to action.

Throughout the summer, Bapu, the lawyers and other social workers grappled with the legal issues in Champaran. Kasturba and Devdas joined hands with the social workers to deal with health and social problems. Ba liked connecting with friends from Phoenix. Chhaganlal's son, Prabhudas and Henry Pollack were among them. They spent several weeks in India. Pollack had come to show a report to Bapu about the changes taking place in South Africa. How could he possibly stay away from the first public movement in India? There were language problems initially but ways were found to work around them. A dispensary was started under the supervision of a doctor from Poona. With the help of the villagers and the social workers, a thatched hut was made available to start a school. Devdas, Prabhudas and others began teaching the children. Changes were visible quite soon. Older people who used to put their thumb impressions earlier began to take pride in signing their names.

Kasturba was monitoring hygiene at the district level. The simple villagers were used to spitting and urinating anywhere and they dirtied the place without a thought. They were not aware of the danger to their health due to the spread of garbage. Kasturba went from village to village with a group, to instruct them. After working for few days, she felt that she could teach people quite naturally and easily. She would make teams of local women to clean up villages. First they were taught to make a broom and each woman was handed one. First she would clean out her house. Then all the women and children would clean out the open spaces and lanes. The remaining men and women, learned how to clean the well and how to drain out the dirty water from the village. Separate classes for men and women were held on hygiene and cleanliness.

***

As the movement gathered steam, the White landlords began to cast a jaundiced eye. Local newspapers began writing editorials and news items about how the agitators were spreading unrest. They viewed cleanliness and educating children and adults as ways to spread unrest. The farmers who were giving written testimonies to the lawyers in the movement began to receive threats. The bamboo and thatch structure of the school where Kasturba stayed was burnt down and she was saved by the skin of her teeth. But the farmers, with the help of social workers, erected a brick and mud structure at the same place.

One day Bapu was speaking about personal hygiene. He said everybody should bathe and wear clean and washed clothes daily. He had seen the village women dressed in dirty clothes. In that village, just like in the others, there was no arrangement for bathing and defecation in individual houses or in the community. Bapu's comments did not go down well. The women caught hold of Ba, 'Mahatma ji has suggested that we bathe and wear washed clothes every day. How can we do that? The clothes we are wearing are the only clothes we have.' One woman insisted on taking Ba to her hut so that she could see the actual circumstances. Ba was amazed to see that the mother-in-law and daughter-in-law had only one dhoti between them. Whoever went out would wear it. This was a bitter truth for Ba to swallow. Ba also kept three sets of clothes. She would wash one, wear the other and keep a third set for visiting. But this inhuman situation was very troubling. They had been working with these people for several weeks by now but had no idea that they lived in such shocking poverty. Ba had nothing with her that she could give them. Her voice broke as she told them, 'Give us a little time to think. We will find a way out of this embarrassing situation.'

Ba told Bapu and he felt that the truth was truly bitter. We may say things without knowing and be fooling ourselves. There is no limit to abject poverty and its constraints, in our country. This challenge for Ba and Bapu was linked to the self respect of those women. Ba also had to give them an answer. She came up with a plan. She took all the women and children to the river. It was enervatingly warm. Most of the people in the village had not gone to town on work but were working in the fields nearby. Ba saw that the women were simple and trusting. Let us play a game, she said. The women found that a bit odd but the children were delighted. Ba told the women to disrobe their children. The women were divided into two teams. One team was asked to take the children's clothes to the river for washing. The other team was asked to take the children to the shallow part of the river and bathe them. The children loved the game and happily splashed water on each other. The women held the hands of the younger children and bathed them. By the time they came out, the hot sun had dried their clothes. The children wore them and ran off to play. The village looked like it was lit up. As they ran off, Ba said to them affectionately, 'Your mothers have worked hard to clean your clothes. Don't get them dirty again.'

Now it was the turn of the women. They were divided into two groups. Under Ba's guidance one team entered the water. It came up to their neck. They took off their clothes and carefully washed them. They wrapped themselves in the wet clothes and came out where the second team shielded them with their hands. They dried their clothes in the sun and also shielded the women still in the water. When all the women were bathed and ready, they were all relaxed and happy. Their faces and hair were shining. Ba had never seen them so happy ever since she had come and she was delighted. There was a gleam of hope in her eye.

***

After returning from South Africa, Ba had travelled from one end of the country to the other. For the first time, she experienced the vastness of her land. She had witnessed its crosswinds and had been sobered by this experience. There were people surviving without the basic needs – food and clothes. There were others who were blissfully unaware of poverty and deprivation. Most of the people had been flattened out like dried leaves due to poverty. Just like Bapu she too wanted to help to lessen the burden of suffering. She wanted them to come out of poverty but what could she do? The country was huge and there was a mountain of problems. The toiling population was large and just a handful of people were working to help them. Champaran taught her that there was hope. Possibility is the lifeline of hope. A district, a village, a morning and an evening and a night are all units of pleasure and pain, and we all could play a part.

***

Harilal was facing great financial difficulties in Calcutta. He wrote to Manilal for help asking him to send the maximum amount that he could. Manilal was in a bind. Relations between Harilal and Bapu were strained. In the Ashram, all the people had been expressly told not to give financial help to Harilal. Manilal sent a money order of some money saved from South Africa. He forgot that Harilal's signature would be there on the receipt. If Bapu saw it, there would be hell to pay. When the post came, it was sorted and the receipt reached Bapu. He summoned Manilal. He said you violated my orders and sent Harilal money from the Ashram's funds. Manilal accepted his culpability. If he said that the money was from his own earnings, it would still have been against the rules of the Ashram. Life in the Ashram was a life of frugality. No member was allowed to keep personal funds.

Bapu said, 'You will have to atone for this.'

He said, 'I thought of Bhai's family going hungry.'

'Do you think their hunger will be satisfied forever with the ten rupees that you sent? Hard work is needed to deal with hunger. Hunger makes no distinction between the one who does not work or his family.'

Bapu announced his decision, 'I will fast for seven days because of your disobedience.' Manilal pleaded with him throughout the night saying that he, who had committed the crime, should be punished. The decision was changed in the morning.

'Yes, the one who has done wrong must atone for it.' A ticket to Madras was handed over to Manilal.

'You will have to go to Madras and stay there keeping your identity a secret. You will have to get by on what you earn. You will not take a paisa from here.'

Manilal left without a word of protest. Many times he had to sleep on the sands of Marina beach and live on peanuts. He told nobody that he was the son of Mohandas Karamchand Gandhi.

Kasturba knew, in his quest for wholeness and perfection, her husband inflicts pain on the object of his attentions. He also suffers but he can bear it. However, it can break the spirit of the other person. In South Africa, she had undergone such anguish when she had refused to clean the chamber pot. She knew it was hard to use logic to explain that the punishment was out of proportion with the wrongdoing. Ba found out that Manilal had been banished into staying incognito in Madras for a year for the offence of helping his brother's starving family. 'You are sending Manilal away to Madras for a year without any money?'

Without looking at Ba he said, 'He broke the rules of the Ashram.'

'You have also reached your position with the help of your brothers. Is it a sin for a brother to help his brother?'

'Hari can come here, who has stopped him? He should repent. He will also eat what the others eat.'

'For you rules are not as important as is the need to repent and say sorry.'

'The mindset needs to change, whether through repentance or punishment.'

'You have left one son and his family to starve in Calcutta, another in Madras ... he has been sent away with no money. I have to stay with you. All I have to say is don't make rules into chains so that one is forced to bear them as punishment or forced to break them.'

'You are a mother ...'

'You cannot shy away from your responsibility as a father.' Kasturba got up and walked away. Bapu sat there for a long time with his eyes closed.

***

After a few days, Bapu wrote to his publisher in Madras to give Manilal some work. He looked for Manilal and gave him a job in his printing press. Mr West was to return to London shortly. Bapu sent Manilal to Phoenix to take over his responsibilities, to continue the publication of *Indian Opinion* and to organise non-violent resistance to racism. When Ba found out, her first thought was heaven knows when she would get to see Mani again. The only saving grace was that at least Bapu trusted Manilal with *Indian Opinion.*

***

Kasturba bade farewell to Champaran around the spring of 1918. The women in the villages were sad to see her go. They felt bereft after having been with Ba for so long. They would often go to Ba with their domestic problems. She could bring about a resolution with a well timed scolding. Kasturba was proud of the fact that the women had joined her to bring about such a transformation. Would they be able to sustain it after she left? The streets in the villages were clean and the stench was almost gone. The mosquitoes were also not so virulent. The minimal clothing of children women and men were quite clean now. The men hesitated to urinate and spit anywhere. Ba exhorted them to keep the chain of transformation unbroken.

When she reached Sabarmati, she saw people building the ashram on the banks of the river. But there was little accountability. She became a little sceptical of the success of this objective and her self confidence also took a beating. Roads were being laid and trees were being planted alongside. Pavements were appearing and a cluster of whitewashed houses was growing, many of them under construction. The ones that were ready had schools, spinning-weaving centres and homes. Stone steps went down to the Sabarmati. There was a green grassy field nearby. Prayers were held here at sunrise and sunset. Kasturba felt like a traveller who had come to a strange place. One day this strange place was going to be more of a home to Ba than any other.

Women threw themselves into weaving with a passion. It was Bapu's dream that that this ancient cottage industry through the example of the khadi spun in the Ashram, becomes a medium for village development. But the art of hand spinning khadi from cotton was lost. Therefore in the Kocharab Ashram, cotton from local mills was bought and used. The *charkha* had come to the Ashram. Maganlal had made a few modifications and made a new model. Ba had begun to spin cotton on the new *charkha.* All the Ashram dwellers, including Bapu, would spin cotton on the newly developed model, for an hour daily. Ba would also do this and was soon the most accomplished expert in the Ashram. As Bapu's fame spread, more and more people joined the Ashram. Some of them became pupils here. The Ashram was always filled with guests. For Bapu, the world was his family. Ba had also accepted this and saw it as her dharma and one of the fundamental truths of her life.

Ba was hearing all kinds of things about Hari. She was very worried to learn that he kept changing jobs. He had also suffered financial losses. He had incurred considerable debt to start something new. He had written an insulting missive to a service provider. Ba was concerned about Gulab and the five children. In June 1918, Gulab arrived in the Ashram with the children, with no prior information. Kasturba was overjoyed and also astonished. She insisted on keeping them all in her living quarters. She wanted to talk to Gulab in private. It was heartrending for her to see the change in her delicate daughter-in-law. All her girlishness had vanished. The sixteen year old whom Kasturba had welcomed in South Africa was today twenty six and drained of energy. There was no trace of the old Gulab left.

Gulab felt Kasturba's concern and she bared her soul. Whatever Ba had heard was all true, even though, being his mother, she did not want to believe the worst. Harilal had lost faith in himself and in life. His heart was full of bitterness because of the injustice of his father. Controlling her tears, Gulab said that her husband had fallen into bad company and had picked up unhealthy habits. His present employer had also thrown him out of the job. As she narrated all this, she sobbed uncontrollably. Ba's heart broke. Some friends in Calcutta saw the dire situation in the household and put Gulab and the children on the train to Sabarmati. From the Ashram, Gulab was going to live in her parents' house with the children. Initially, Ba was angry when she heard about Harilal's habits. Since anger was alien to her nature, it soon turned to sadness. Her tears were as much for Gulab and the children as they were for Harilal. They all needed Ba's love and protection.

Ba spent weeks in the company of her grandchildren. She would bathe them herself, tell them stories and teach them songs. She would wash the elder daughter Rami's hair, comb it and just gaze at her lovingly. Her face had a glimpse of Hari as a child. It was Rami who had first given her the pleasure of being a Dadi. She would make sweets for all the grandchildren and also take them out. Late into the night, she would talk to Gulab. Nothing gave her greater pleasure than the smiles on their faces. It was their laughter that made the *kutiya* home. Gulab's nimble ways and her confidence were returning. Ba was happy that those who were dear to her were making others in the Ashram happy too.

Finally the moment of saying farewell to her beloved guests arrived. Gulab's health had improved but she was still underweight. Her eyes held the spark of hope now which indicated that after staying with her widowed mother for some time, she would return to Harilal in Calcutta. Kasturba went personally to see her off at the station. Ba maintained her smile until the train pulled out. She returned to the daily routine of the Ashram but found it tough to do so. She was restless. Loneliness grew like darkness in the evening. Bapu was travelling. Ba sent a message that she would like to join him.

Bapu wrote her a letter from Nadiad, district Kheda:

Dear Kastur,

I know that you would like to be with me. We must continue to do our work, so it is better if you stay where you are. If you think of the children in the Ashram as your own, you will not miss your own so much. When you will learn to love and serve the others in the same way, you will find your cup of joy will run over...

Two days later came another letter with another weak attempt at sympathy:

Dear Kastur,

Your sadness makes me unhappy. If it was possible to bring women along, I would surely take you ... have we not learnt to find pleasure in separation? We will meet soon, God willing ...

This was merely stroking a hurt.

The two letters hold another meaning and can be understood from a different perspective. To be addressed as 'dear' by her husband and who then goes on to say

'I know that you would like to be with me' somewhere carries his hidden desire to be with her too. Bapu had cautioned Kasturba, 'When you will learn to love and serve the others in the same way, you will find your cup of joy will run over …' She knew he was saying it as much to himself. 'Have we not learnt to find pleasure in separation?' This question was to himself too. 'We will meet soon, God willing.' This shows that the bond of love had not frayed. In that summer, he was gripped by a melancholy similar to hers. Many a times you cannot say what is in your heart … Bapu also needed Ba.

Bapu reached Sabarmati Ashram in August. Ba was stricken to see him in poor health. She was concerned as she had a premonition of his troubles. He looked half starved and skeletal. This was the first time that he looked so weak. In South Africa, he had not looked so bad, even after months in jail. Upon Ba's enquiries he said that he had fasted because of a bout of dysentery. Ba cooked some of his favourite foods: a bowl of moong dal and wheat porridge. Bapu ate it with relish and took a second helping. Ba was relieved. She pressed upon him to stay in the Ashram for some time. But because he had to reach Nadiad for recruitments, he left that night itself. Kasturba was upset and disturbed. Bapu took ill once he got there. This was the longest and most difficult illness of his life. His dysentery had become serious. He was delirious and could not walk. It was hard for him to talk. He felt that his end was near.

The news about Bapu filtering in from Nadiad was very worrying for Ba. What should she do? Bapu had refused all medicines. He was taking practically nothing for his nutrition. There was nobody in Kheda who could look after him properly. Ba wanted to bring him to the Ashram but his condition was not such that he could be brought by rail. Ambalal Sarabhai again stepped in to help. He went to Nadiad in his Safari car and brought Bapu to Ahmedabad so that he could be nursed back to health. The Ashram was a busy place and the general feeling was that Bapu should not stay there. The Sarabhai family had made arrangements for his best care. Ba would go everyday to see him and encourage him to take his medicines and eat well. Bapu's health improved slowly. When he asked to go back to the Ashram, everybody was hopeful that he would recover, but his statement, 'I would like to die in my Ashram,' plunged everybody into hopelessness. Ba's eyes welled up but she did not let anybody see her pain.

***

In 1918, Influenza had spread worldwide like an epidemic. Lakhs of people had perished. For ten months, death had danced at every door. In America alone, five lakh people had died of this disease and worldwide twenty crore people had lost their lives. India had one of the highest mortality rates. When the world was grappling with this crisis, the Gandhi family could hardly remain untouched. It was the month of October and there was a mild chill setting in. Kasturba received a telegram that Gulab's fourth son Shantilal was no more. Gulab wanted his last rites to be conducted in Ba's presence. Harilal was coming to Rajkot from Calcutta. Ba left the next day. When she reached

Rajkot, there was another patient of influenza in the house. Ba's most beloved daughter-in-law Gulab had been infected. Ba controlled herself and kept trying to bolster Gulab's spirits. But years of poor nutrition and repeated pregnancies laid Gulab low. On 18th October, the rose that had bloomed in the courtyard of the Gandhi family withered away. Ba and Rami were with Gulab when she went. Rami held her mother's hand as if she would not let her go. Gulab looked from Ba to Rami as if asking Ba to take over. And then all was quiet.

Harilal was half crazed. The hapless children, Gulab's widowed mother and Ba tried to deny the ultimate truth, as is often the case with death, but how long can you deny it?

***

When Harilal was trying to gather his senses in a world that had come apart, there came a letter from Bapu in Mahadev Bhai's handwriting. Harilal read it out to Ba. She could not speak. It said:

'Only one thing gives me joy. You have to keep yourself engaged in work that is pure. Real joy can be experienced only by those who understand this and live by it. If this tragedy takes you towards that mindset, then you will experience that joy and it could be welcomed.'

Harilal could not hold back his tears as he read. Ba was looking the other way.

Another letter arrived. It held the suggestion of a compromise;

'Prayer has no meaning for an arrogant mind. But I am bedridden, helpless and I am ashamed of the antics of my mind. When I sink into hopelessness, I wish for my body to be destroyed.

I will give you the full benefit of my experience. I am your true friend. How does it matter if we have differences over some of your plans? We can talk about them calmly and peacefully.'

Ba heard Bapu's cry for help in the letter.

***

Ba said to Hari, 'After the *tehrevin,* the thirteenth day rites, I want to help take some hard decisions about the future of the children. I will bring up your children and it will be their house until they are with me.' Ba knew that Hari would not be able to look after them alone. Gulab's widowed mother and sisters would also be overburdened if they were to do this. She could not stay on in Rajkot herself. In Sabaramati Ashram, Bapu was ill and he needed Ba.

***

The apprehensions that Ba nursed after receiving Bapu's letters, were not unfounded. In the Ashram, she had never seen Bapu so low. He was completely bedridden and had no appetite. Ba was told that due to the prolonged dysentery, he has a wound in his anus and it was unbearably painful. He had even agreed to be ministered by a doctor. One doctor said to cover his body with ice. Another said to give him arsenic and strychnine injections. Bapu was not ready for that. He said that these doctors are *jholachhap* like me and I will take no treatment. He gave up hope of living. He summoned all the inhabitants of the Ashram and recited all his shortcomings. 'I initiated plans only to leave them half way. Now the time has come for me to go. If that is God's will, then so be it.'

One week after Kastur had reached the Ashram, Vallabh Bhai Patel brought news that Germany had surrendered to the Allied forces. The World War was over so the British government announced that there was no further need for Indian recruits. Kasturba was very pleased to get this news. The reason for Bapu's worry and sadness was over. His health would improve. This news should have been of great interest for Bapu but he took it neutrally. The Ashram dwellers and friends believed that Ba's care would extenuate Bapu's pain and he will be free of thoughts of death. But Bapu made little of Ba's concerns in her presence. Ba was perturbed about his condition. He would express himself only in front of Mahadev Bhai. Mahadev Bhai listened carefully and took notes. One day Bapu made a shocking statement, 'I can't bear to see Ba's face.' He compared Ba's guiltless face to that of a cow. There was such selflessness in her pain. He also admitted that her simplicity and normalcy affected him deeply and stumped him and made him vulnerable under all circumstances.

Did he even remember this statement made in a moment of depression? Even if Ba had come to know, could she have changed herself? Ba was losing her fortitude. Bapu's refusal to eat, not taking his chosen medicine, a second time, the doctors refusing to endorse his belief that he was going to die ... all this was nothing but an exercise in self flagellation. The person who could transform others to believe in non-violence was committing violence on his own heart and mind. Kasturba was also suffering this violence, in her own way. He was choosing death. That had to be stopped. Ba had returned from a house where she had witnessed the deaths of two of her own. She knew that if she were faced with such a situation, she would choose life. Nothing but life. Savitri had defeated death and taken on life. She had to save her husband from himself anyhow. It is harder to save a person from themselves than from another.

Bapu's pain increased and this came to Ba's rescue. In December, he agreed to accompany Ba to Bombay. Dr Dalal was an old school experienced doctor. Only an operation could give relief from pain and the disease was his considered opinion. But the surgery was not possible until the body was strong enough to bear it. The doctor suggested that he be given frequent sips of milk right way. Ba was present and was listening intently to her husband. He flatly refused to drink milk.

Doctor Dalal wanted to know the reason for his refusal. Due to cruelty towards milch cows by the people in the dairy trade, he had taken a vow not to drink milk years ago. Nobody had been able to break his vow. As Bapu spoke, Ba's mind raced. After a pause, she said calmly, 'Fine, you will not have any objection to drinking goat's milk?'

Doctor Dalal caught on, 'Yes, goat's milk will be fine.'

For a moment, Bapu was nonplussed. He dug deep. Once more, he felt that his life partner had stumped him with her normalcy. When he had vowed not to drink milk, goat's milk had not figured in his calculations. He had only been thinking of cow's milk. So he could consume goat's milk keeping his vow intact. He would be able to start the satyagraha movement. Just the thought of that brought a surge of energy.

That evening Bapu had his first glass of goat's milk.

***

After the operation, Bapu took several weeks to recover. He was operated upon in Mani Bhavan under Ba's watch. Mani Bhavan had been gifted to him by his friend and relative Dr P. J. Mehta. Thirty years ago when Bapu had gone to London to study Law, he had been his guest. Mehta had been his guide there. Whenever he came to Bombay, he stayed in Mani Bhavan.

When a goat who gave 16 ounces of milk was brought for Bapu he named her Mothergoat. The one who feeds you milk is mother. The goat soon became everybody's favourite. Bapu's Mothergoat became everybody's Mothergoat. Bapu's weakness had not gone completely and Ba had her hands full in keeping him confined to the bed. When she would take a hard line, Bapu would laugh and say, 'You are coming back into the old dominating mode.'

'If it is to do with your health, I will not listen. I will show you I mean business,' Ba was quick to retort. She added, 'I will not let you run wild.'

'You are more hard-hearted than the British,' was Bapu's rejoinder. For Ba this meant that he was recovering his health, in body and mind.

In January, Harilal left his children at Mani Bhavan with their grandmother, on his way to Calcutta. The house had four scared and timid children now. They moved about cautiously afraid of giving offence. Whatever they wanted to say, they would whisper to elder sister Rami. Rami would tell

Ba. They had barely recovered from the heartrending loss of their mother. It was a sorrow so huge that it was difficult for young children to comprehend. Their mother had gone and also their brother who had been a playmate. There was a great emptiness in their hearts. Only Rami could understand the gravity of losing her mother and her brother Shantilal. She also knew that grandmother needed rest. Bapu would also help look after the children. That was a great source of comfort to Ba. When Mahadev Bhai came to Bombay after a week, Bapu got a letter written to his angry son Harilal. Mahadev read it out to Ba on Bapu's behest. In that long letter he had taken special care to refer to the children, 'Manu's sparkle is increasing, Kanti and Rasik play near my cot. They remind me of you.' Listening to this Ba felt that at least this tragedy has brought the family closer.

Bapu used to enjoy talking to Harilal's second son, six year old Rasiklal. He wrote a limerick for him:

Rasiklal Harilal Mohandas Karamchand Gandhi
Ke paas hai ek bakra
Bakra doodh nahin deta
Aur Gandhi rona band nahin karta.
(Rasiklal Harilal Mohandas Karamchand Gandhi
Has a Billy Goat
He does not give milk
And Gandhi doesn't stop crying)

***

Bapu had not recovered fully. On 18th March there was news that in spite of opposition from Indian members, the Rowlatt Act had been passed. He was in Madras at the time.

He had already sent a telegram to the Viceroy and declared this Law as unjust and anti-freedom. He spent the whole day at Chakravarti Rajagopalachari's house in a meeting to work out a plan for the future, but there was no way around the anti-people clauses. He retired to bed. He sat up in his sleep, all of a sudden because he had received a message in his dream. This was the voice of his conscience. The next day at breakfast, he declared that the Rowlatt Act would be opposed by a nation-wide strike. People from all religions and castes would fast for twenty four hours for self-purification. He had no idea whether the country would respond positively. If there was no compliance, it would send the wrong message to the government.

His message spread like wildfire across the country. The refrain that could be heard everywhere was that Bapu has asked us to oppose the black law by striking work and fasting. Bapu need not have worried about the country's response. On 6 April, 1919, the country stopped as if the heart had stopped beating in the body. People fasted in their homes and prayed. Bapu was leading the strike personally in Bombay. The brotherhood in the country was so powerful that Hindu holy men were invited to speak in mosques. Sarojini Naidu's speeches were heard widely. The British government was taken aback by this united show. A spectacular procession was taken out in Delhi. The Police panicked and there was firing where five Hindus and four Muslims were killed. General Dyer shot 386 men and women in Jallianwalla Bagh. Not just that, he did not let them receive medical aid for seventy two hours.

Kasturba was deeply hurt by this carnage. She could sense now that Bapu's sole aim was an independent nation. He had thrown himself into it heart and soul. He was travelling extensively without a thought for his health. In the time left over, he would write editorials for *Young India* and *Navjivan*. He could not give time to Sabarmati Ashram. Ba decided to run Sabarmati Ashram with Maganlal Gandhi. From the summer of 1920, she began this in earnest. She began taking note of the needs of the visitors to the Ashram and managing problems. She would wake up the resident pupils for the morning prayer. She would also resolve any misunderstandings between them. She was an old hand at sorting out domestic discord. She had enough family responsibilities of her own. At the age of fifty, she was bringing up four of Harilal's children. Bapu had written to his widowed sister Raliyat that she would find many brothers, children and their mothers here. At that time, Bapu would not have thought about Raliyat's extremely rigid beliefs about caste. Her presence would pose real problems for Kasturba and become a challenge to Bapu's immeasurably assimilative bent of mind. This time signalled the end of long term changes in Ba's life. Wonder, variation, resistance, acceptance, and victory, she went through this gamut of emotions with regard to her husband's views. She knew that Bapu wanted to teach the country that satyagraha was the only powerful means in the hands of the powerless. Ba was increasingly influenced by Bapu's objectives as the days passed. In 1920-21, lakhs of people shared this experience of Ba's. This was a delicate phase when people began to sense that the dream of an independent India could come true. This in itself was a great source of inspiration.

Because of her commitments at the Ashram, Ba could not accompany Bapu on his extended travels. She would sometimes go to places that were close by. When she was at the Ashram, she would spin on the *charkha* for an hour daily. Spinning made her concentrate. It also created an interest in the women from the villages nearby. Kasturba firmly believed that if the women in the country learned to spin on the *charkha*, and weave, they can play an important role in the economic progress of their families, villages and the nation. They can contribute to making a self-reliant society. Ba believed that the making of a family and the making of a society were similar, the only difference was in the scale. The images of Champaran would rise before her eyes. All that the women did there unitedly ... the other women could spin-weave and work for the country similarly. The women from affluent homes can continue worrying about trinkets and beauty tips but we should be thinking of adorning the society and the country. Ba had no vanity regarding her new role. She was fulfilling her dharma towards her husband as a wife, and her dharma of service to society. She felt that active participation in the khadi movement was in itself noble and also a part of duty towards the country. Whenever she went with Bapu, he would give a speech and Ba would be spinning the charkha. When Bapu gave a call to burn foreign clothes, Ba gave up her favourite silk sari that Bapu also liked. Gokhale had given it as a gift. Bapu had gazed at it sadly before the flames consumed it. After that many women had put their expensive foreign saris into the fire. Ba was slowly coming out of the glowing halo around Bapu. Service and creativity were building an ecosystem around her.

Once Ba went with Bapu to a harijan basti bear Baroda. She met each person there, went into their homes, listened to the problems of the workers, found solutions and gave direction. Bapu also took part in the meeting. The meeting on local issues carried on from morning until the afternoon. The weather was really hot and fans were not so common. The evening prayer was organised in a playing field nearby. Ba saw that Bapu was tired so she asked him to go inside and rest.

Bapu said, 'It is even hotter inside.'

Kasturba rolled out a mat under the tree and told him to lie down there and talk to his associates. She got a thin sheet for a cover. She sat next to him spinning cotton. She would not interrupt the conversations of others. If Bapu looked towards her, she would give her opinion. Gradually the day came to a close and it was dusk.

'Don't worry or be afraid.' Bapu was speaking softly to two men seated beside him. Without moving he said to them, 'Something is crawling next to me. Hold the sheet from both ends and shake it out on the other side of the bush.' They returned to tell him that they had dropped a six foot long poisonous cobra on the other side. When Kasturba heard this, she shut her eyes and prayed. She said that they should all go inside. Bapu laughed, 'Has he said that he will come again?' Everybody laughed.

Kasturba said, 'Who knows when an uninvited guest may turn up.' Bapu also laughed this time.

***

On March 18, 1922, something unexpected happened. A Police van came to a halt outside Gandhi Kuti. The Police Captain got off and and politely said to Gandhi ji, 'You are under arrest.' Bapu asked him to wait for five minutes while he got ready. He went outside to wait. By then his dhoti, two blankets and seven books had been gathered. Kasturba prayed along with ten or twelve students. As Bapu got into the van, he chanted verses for universal well being. The next morning, Kasturba prayed and sent goat's milk, grapes and clean clothes for him.

***

Gandhi ji presented his own defence. This case was named as the Great Trial by his biographers. The arguments he presented were so forceful that eminent lawyers and journalists from India and abroad were amazed. He took on the entire responsibility of having opposed the Rowlatt Act. He fearlessly acknowledged that he knew that he had been playing with fire. Justice Broomfield acknowledged that Mr Gandhi was a great man with high ideals. His work is one of Herculean struggle. After these introductory remarks, he sentenced him to six years. Kasturba was present in court throughout. People shouted '*Gandhi ji ki Jai.*' Some hands held flowers and some eyes were tearful. Ba gazed at Bapu being taken away, hollow-eyed. The entire country was aroused by Bapu's arguments in court. Never before had a convict given such an eloquent testimony and taken the risk of taking the entire responsibility upon himself. Few people know that at night, Ba had an appeal written to the people in the country that was published in *Young India* on 23 March, 1922:

> *My dear brothers and sisters,*
>
> *My husband has been sentenced to six years in prison today. I cannot deny that I have been affected by the long sentence. I could have reassured myself that it is not hard for us to pressurise the government to reduce the sentence much before it would end. I also have no doubt that if the nation awakes and takes the constructive program of the Congress seriously, it will not only result in Bapu being freed, but also find an acceptable solution to the issues for which we have fought and suffered hardships. The solution is in our hands. The men and women who feel for me and respect my husband and I, should throw themselves into the constructive program of the Congress and make it a success. Our success will not just solve the economic woes of the populace but also free us of our political slavery. India's first response to Gandhi ji's faith in us should be :-*
>
> - *All men and women give up foreign clothes, use khadi and encourage others to do so.*
> - *All women spin cotton as their dharma. They should inspire others too.*
> - *All traders stop buying and selling foreign goods.*

——***——

Kasturba

In 1924, on 13th January, there was a telegram in the name of Mrs M. K. Gandhi. Telegrams always brought worrying news in those times. It was from Colonel Madoka, Surgeon General of Sasoon Hospital in Poona. 'Last night Mr. Gandhi had an appendicitis operation. The night was uneventful and in the morning his condition is satisfactory.'

Ba sensed that the Colonel and other officers were scared because of Bapu's unexpected illness. If something were to happen to him in jail, the country would be up in arms. That was why he was taken to the nearest hospital. Bapu knew that his life was in danger. He set aside his bias against western medicine and gave permission for surgery and foreign medication. Ba's heart ached. She should have been with Bapu. But it was not possible to leave the Ashram at such short notice. It was a question of responsibility. She sent Devdas in her stead. Telegrams, messages and gifts arrived from across the country. The patient's recovery was slow. The British officials were worried. On 5th February, the government suddenly declared that Mr Gandhi was being released unconditionally with immediate effect. Ba could hardly be joyous but at least she was free of worry. She knew that he should go to a quiet place to recuperate. When she discovered that a Parsi friend had taken him to his quiet Juhu bungalow for some time, she was relieved. But Bapu's admirers turned that quiet time into commotion. They were celebrating his release.

As soon as his body regained strength, Bapu returned to Sabarmati Ashram. He got involved with the chores there. Ba was reminded of the times in Phoenix Ashram when he had been just as busy.

***

Although Ba had no writing or other contribution, but reports about her work were present in Bapu's newspapers. Sometimes it became a matter of discussion amongst the readers also. Most of it centred around Ba's role in finding solutions to the crises of those living in the Ashram. Once, a male calf in the Ashram became seriously ill. It was suggested that he be given a lethal injection to put him out of his misery. Ba rejected the idea of letting the innocent creature be freed of pain in this manner. She tried to treat him under her supervision. But when she saw how he suffered, she agreed to put him down. According to the tenets of Hinduism, it is the duty of every Hindu to protect the lineage of the cow. Reactions from the readers were inevitable. But Ba had felt right about ending the suffering of the dumb animal. When asked, Ba said that it is violent to merely observe mortal pain and it is non-violent to release someone from suffering. Bapu maintained silence when the question was put to him.

***

Manilal fell in love in 1926. The families knew each other. The girl was a Muslim. Manilal sent a letter through Ramdas seeking permission to marry. Since the two families were close, the girl's letter also reached Bapu. Her name was Fatima. Bapu wrote the following letter to Manilal:

Dear Manilal,

I read your letter sent through Ramdas. I also read Fatima's letter. You follow the Hindu faith and Fatima Islam … your wish to marry is against your religion. This will be like placing two swords in a scabbard. Which religion will your children follow? Which faith will they be influenced by? If Fatima leaves her faith she will be committing an injustice to it … have both of you stopped believing in your respective faiths?

Your marriage will be a shock to both religions. This problem cannot be solved by an inter-caste marriage. It is difficult for you to forget that you are my son. If the two of you marry, will you be able to serve your own? According to me, you will no longer be suitable to work in Indian Opinion.

I cannot ask for Ba's acceptance, she will never agree. Her whole life will be filled with sadness. I don't have the courage to tell her. May God show you the correct path.

Blessings from Bapu

***

Why did Bapu do this, was it for Ba? So that her life was not blighted? Seeing how much she loved her children, it seems that this must have been mentioned to Ba at some point. Was the difference in religions the real obstacle?

***

Ba had already decided that one of the three beautiful daughters of Mashruwala Nanabhai would make for a suitable match for Manilal. Mashruwala traded in cotton. His family had been among the affluent traders. Mashruwala and his wife, Vijaylakshmi, influenced by Gandhi, had renounced physical comforts and facilities like sanyasis do. They had surrendered their lives and fortune to serve the people. Their home in Akola was open to the inhabitants of the Ashram. Ba had stayed there when she was passing through Akola. That is when she had seen the three daughters. In the normal course, she had come to be in touch with them.

One day Mrs Mashruwala said that Gandhi ji would be visiting her home. Kasturba was there already. This time Gandhi ji was coming personally. There was a celebratory atmosphere in the house. In was in 1917 that Ba and Bapu came together. The Mashruwala family found out that they wanted their son to marry one of the three daughters. Gandhi ji showed them Manilal's photo. He also said that after marriage, the girl would have to take a vow to live frugally. She would have to go to South Africa and live in Phoenix Ashram. A trip back to India would be once in three or four years. The elder daughter Susheela was standing behind the door and listening. Ba had seen her. Bapu left Manilal's photograph with them. When they left Akola, Ba had decided which girl she would like Manilal to marry.

Time went by quickly after this and just two months later Manilal's was wedded to Susheela. Under special circumstances, Bapu gave permission to the bride and groom to travel second class. For the first time, Kasturba enjoyed the pride of being the groom's mother that she had not been able to do in Harilal and Gulab's wedding. She had decided not to follow old traditions. Against custom, the bride and groom sat next to each other in front of everybody. Nobody spoke a word. Kasturba had to prompt them, 'Why are you sitting like statues? Don't you have anything to say to each other?' Susheela had come from a family where husbands and wives did not sit together in public and converse. Listening to her mother-in-law's words, Susheela shed her shyness.

***

Ba was overjoyed that Manilal and Susheela were coming to India with their one year old daughter, Sita. Ba was looking forward to spending time with her daughter-in-law. She would feed and play with her new granddaughter. Ba also wanted to know whether Susheela liked life in Phoenix Ashram. How were the people in the Ashram? But there was no time for long conversations. Just then, Bapu had declared that there would be the march to Dandi. Like all the others in the Ashram, Ba got busy with preparations.

Ba woke up at 4:00 am every day. On 12 March, 1930, she had risen even earlier. Bapu and his friends had to go walking to Dandi, two hundred and forty miles away. The law on the Salt Tax had to be broken by making salt, next to the sea. There was much opposition to this march, both within and outside the country. But this march was not just a milestone in the Non-cooperation Movement, it had shaken the English government to its core.

Ba woke up early and bathed. She wore new clothes. A lot of work remained to be done. She knew that a swarm of Indian and foreign news reporters and photographers would be gathered outside the Ashram. All of them had camped overnight in the open to cover the march. In the semi-darkness, Ba took a round of the Ashram and woke up the pupils for the prayer. She reviewed the arrangements for the food of the travellers. She was assailed repeatedly by doubts about whether a pinch of salt would make any difference to the government? Then she would think, Bapu always thinks deeply before taking such measures. To travel two hundred and forty miles to make a pinch of salt and break the Salt Law will create an impact on the minds and hearts of the people. She felt a surge of energy and hope. She trembled at the thought of three generations of the Gandhi family taking part in the march. Bapu, Manilal and Harilal's eldest son, Kanti. Kanti had been brought up by Ba and she had loved him since he was a baby. Ba's eyes filled up with tears, if only Hari would also be among the marchers ... The flag bearer of the Non-cooperation Movement in South Africa, Hari was the light in Bapu's eyes. Today father and son stood separated. Who knows how the government would treat the marchers ...

Bapu addressed his fellow travellers, 'The British government may use guns against us but we must keep calm. Those who are fearful and may surrender, should not accompany me,' Kasturba put her hand on Susheela's shoulder to give her courage. Ba was moving around encouraging all the relatives of the marching contingent. When she had first gone to South Africa with Bapu, she had seen that during a storm, Bapu had gone to each traveller to give them hope and courage. That memory was inspiring to Ba.

As the day dawned, the sun marched unwaveringly to claim its place. The prayer had ended. A day earlier, Bapu had declared in the prayer meeting that he would only return to Sabarmati after independence was achieved. Everybody had been taken aback. Now the moment was upon them. Dressed in white khadi, they were all taking leave of their families. On their foreheads shone the *gorochan tilak* put there by the women in the Ashram. Along with the others, Ba's tilak on Bapu's forehead shone bright. Reporters and photographers ran alongside Bapu. His pace was brisk.

A foreign journalist asked him, 'Do you think your country will win independence by making a pinch of salt?'

Bapu laughed, 'We are free. Freedom is a resolution that you have to make yourself.'

***

Ba's fearless declaration was echoing in the hearts of the marchers. 'Our men have set off on the path of sacrifice. They are combative and we are their wives.' Ba had stood tall, her thin frame radiated the light of determination. Her face shone with a rare light as she addressed the marchers. Bapu stood at the head of the contingent with his bamboo stick and in his sturdy walking sandals. Ba came up to him. She looked into his eyes deeply once. There was no room for words. In her hands was a brass *thali* with *sindur* soaked in ghee. She put a tilak on his forehead like a mark of remembrance, gently and intently. After that, as the line of marchers moved ahead, she continued putting the *tilak*, wishing them the best. Whoever wore a *tilak* from Ba strode ahead with pride and confidence. Her message was clear, 'Marcher, go forward and return successful and safe, we will be here to welcome you.'

All the lines of pain and hurt on her face had been erased. She had the resolute look of a braveheart. She was the image of the Mother. Bapu was the hero of the non-violent battle and Ba was the protector of the Ashram.

Slowly the marchers left. The remaining Ashram dwellers watched the long line of marchers until they could not be seen anymore. After everybody had left, Ba sat and watched the emptiness left behind by Bapu and the travellers.

***

The news of the marchers trickled in intermittently. It was difficult for the inmates of the Sabarmati Ashram to determine its veracity. But Kasturba and the others would eagerly wait for news. There was always an apprehension about when the White police would attack the marchers. It was a wonder that the police that came down heavily on minor instances of opposition was completely silent. The whole country was in the grip of excitement but the government was in a waiting mode. Perhaps the orders from Delhi were to wait and watch. The movement would slacken and end on its own. Bapu continuously sent reports about the march to newspapers through Mahadev Bhai. He was also keeping the Ashram updated.

***

After reaching Dandi, the marchers prayed almost through the night. On 16 April, 1930, Bapu took a dip in the sea at sunrise. Then he came ashore, under the touch of the golden rays, under the gaze of clicking cameras from the country and abroad, in front of 75000 people, he bent down and picked up a muddy piece of salt. The seashore resounded with slogans of victory. It was as if the waves also rose up to see who it was and slowly subsided. There was no sign of the police. Everything was self propelled. There were no arrests.

On that calm seashore, the bugle of non-cooperation resounded so that the powers in distant Delhi trembled. It was as if everybody was taking a dip in the newly bubbling waters of non-cooperation. Across the villages and towns of the country, people surged forward to make salt, in the seas, rivers and even the *pokhars.* Old people, youth, women, men, boys and girls filled their vessels with salt water. The respectable and the rich also did their symbolic bit by boiling salt water in kettles. Those Congress workers who had opposed this had also set aside their differences and were auctioning banned salt at the Congress headquarters in Bombay. Gandhi addressed the press and said, 'I want the support of the world in this struggle between power and rights.' His message spread across the world in the blink of an eye.

***

This was a non-violent non-cooperation movement that had roused the entire country. Gandhi's message rang out from Kashmir to Kanyakumari. An ordinary thing like salt, a necessity common to the poorest and the wealthy, lit up like a torch of awakening in the hands of each person. The British had no idea that an insignificant thing like salt, under Gandhi's touch, would raise the flag of freedom and transformation across the country.

***

Gandhi ji had written a letter to the Viceroy about the plans for non-violent resistance where he had mentioned taking over a salt factory in Dharsana. This was too bitter a pill for the British government to swallow. They had been trying to save themselves the trouble of widespread unrest, but now they took Gandhi prisoner and put him in Yerawada jail in Poona, ready to face the consequences. They were afraid of slapping a case on him.

When the Police van carrying Gandhi ji started, it was pitch dark. A girl ran up, cutting through the darkness and asked Bapu, 'Any message for Ba?'

Bapu laughed, 'Tell Ba, she is a braveheart.'

Ba didn't know that he had given an indication of the future by calling her a braveheart. After his arrest, Bapu had sent word that Manilal would lead the band taking over the Dharsana salt factory. Ba felt that it was South Africa repeating itself.

On 21 May, 1930, two and a half thousand satyagrahis donned white khadi dhoti*s*, shirts and Gandhi topis and reached Dharsana to lay siege to the salt factory. At a hundred yards from the factory, they held a community prayer. After this, under Manilal's leadership, a team of twenty five moved forward to surround the factory. There was a moat of water and then a circle of barbed wire. About four hundred policemen with iron tipped lathis stood at attention. They issued a warning to disperse. The satyagrahis marched ahead in pairs, silently. Manilal was leading. What took place thereafter was unimaginable. The injustice heaped on the satyagrahis and their dogged courage in the face of it, was witnessed by the entire world. Web Miller of United Press from America sent an eye witness account to the world. Iron tipped lathis struck a head, a skull cracked and a satyagrahi would crumble to the ground, bathed in blood. Then a second and then a third and one by one ... A stretcher team would arrive and take him away. The next team of twenty five would come up. A temporary hospital was set up for first aid.

Miller wrote, 'I saw that the wounded were lying on the floor in an enclosure made of palm leaves. I counted three hundred and twenty wounded, with cracked skulls who were still unconscious. Many had received no first aid. Two of them had died. In the end, he wrote a line, 'In my career of reporting from twenty countries, I had never seen such a dreadful scene.' Some other reporter wrote, 'Gandhi wins.'

***

There was no trace of Manilal. What became of him? His wife and Kasturba did not know where to look for him. Their anxiety grew apace. Had he been taken prisoner or had he suffered a serious injury ... they did not have the courage to think beyond this. If such a treacherous thought threaded its way up, they would immediately tamp it down ... no, that can't be.

Days passed and there was no news. With all their courage, a terrified hopelessness began to sink coldly into their hearts. One day there came news that he was in a jail in Surat. His skull bone had cracked but he was mending slowly. He would soon be sent to Sabarmati jail to complete his six month sentence. In spite of the news of his serious injury, the atmosphere became celebratory. When there was a real danger of losing everything and something stood redeemed, this was the only way forward.

Manilal had been brought to Sabarmati Jail. Ramdas was there too. The jail was near the Ashram. There was no permission to meet Ramdas and the other prisoners. Kasturba and Susheela went to meet Manilal. This was Susheela's first time inside a jail. She grew nauseous seeing the conditions inside. Kasturba sat calmly waiting for her two sons to be brought to the jailer's room. When Manilal and Ramdas were brought, Susheela was emotional and her voice broke. Ba chatted calmly with Manilal and Ramdas. Manilal was in a very poor shape. His head was still bandaged. She asked about the other satyagrahis. Susheela saw how much weight her husband had lost, but held her peace. Ba asked Manilal to talk to Susheela. Satyagrahis were offering themselves up for arrest. Ba felt that women should also participate actively in the Non-cooperation Movement. Meanwhile, there was a message from jail, 'All my hopes rest on the women now.' Further, 'I believe that the final victory of non-violence depends on the women.'

Kastur wondered how Bapu had divined what she felt and wanted.

***

She delegated the responsibility of the Ashram to others and she travelled from village to village and from one town to the next. Bapu's message echoed in her ears. She inspired women who were home-bound to take part in the second phase of non-cooperation. She said to them, 'Give *dharna* at liquor vends. They are the enemies of the country's independence.' Ba felt that women are better suited for *dharna*. The Indian police was chary of arresting women at that time. Shopkeepers and buyers also hesitated to walk past the women sitting on *dharna*. The women understood whatever Ba said. The sales of liquor were affected. When Bapu found out, he knew that Ba was active. He sent word to present Ba a sari woven from cotton that he had spun, as a token of appreciation. This was perhaps his biggest and deepest expression of feeling. This is corroborated in a letter, 'I believe that the capability of women is God given. Therefore they succeed in whatever task they take up.' Ba's fame spread across the nation.

Ba's work picked up pace with Bapu's approval. She was unflappable in her manner. She carried out her duties without any obvious display. Devdas was incarcerated in Gujarat town in Punjab. Ba went to meet him. When she got off the train, she saw thousands gathered at the station. Ba asked, 'Who is coming? Why are so many people gathered here?'

'We have all come here to welcome you,' came the reply.

'Me …!' Ba was astonished.

'Yes …' One young man said, 'We will take Ba in a procession into town.' Ba began to look worried. I had come to meet my child … how did I get caught up in all this? But how do I disappoint so many people, she thought to herself.

***

Lord Willingdon, the Viceroy, had invited Bapu to Shimla for a Round Table Conference. Ba had gone with him. The next day, Lady Willingdon, the Vicereine welcomed Ba, much to her surprise. She was an ordinary woman, why was she to be welcomed and that too by the Vicereine? This was a first for the Vicereine too that she had to formally invite the wife of an Indian leader. Eyebrows were raised among the British officers and their wives. It became difficult for them to decide how they should behave with a woman they had routinely ignored, but who was now the Vicereine's honoured guest.

The Vicereine said to Kasturba, 'Could you give me handspun khadi that Mr Gandhi propagates to make his country self reliant?'

'I will be very happy to do so.'

'I would like to use it connect to the people of India. Could you send me some purple khadi?'

'Certainly, I will send you lots of purple khadi. But I have a question. How will you come closer to the people of India through handspun khadi? Only if you descend from the mountains to the plains, where people live in large numbers, will you get to know them better.' Kasturba did some plain speaking. The Vicereine was silent.

***

The Indian women in South Africa had sent money in the name of Kasturba, after learning about the success of the women's movement. Ba had written an emotional letter of thanks to all those women who had been a part of the movement. It shows how Ba was viewed outside the country. Manilal had printed this letter in *Indian Opinion*:

Dear sisters,

I have received the twenty five pounds that you all collected. I am touched that you feel so close to me, even though I am so far away in India. I am very grateful. I trust that you must not be using foreign goods. Wherever you may be, remember to refrain from using foreign goods. I hope that your behaviour and lifestyle will always reflect Indian traditions and culture.

***

The London Round Table Conference of 1931 had failed. As a result, the country went up in flames of resistance. The Civil Disobedience movement had spread rapidly. The white government was bent upon crushing the Congress. Even cultural programs organised by Congress were being viewed with an inimical eye. The only objective seemed to be to diminish Gandhi's influence. In some states, even printing his picture was banned. Those books were confiscated that the government deemed objectionable. Censorship was clamped across the country. Raids were conducted in many places. People's rights were being suspended. In the month of January alone, at least fifteen thousand Indians had been imprisoned. Even women were being jailed.

Kastur was the first woman who had been jailed. In South Africa too, she had done satyagraha with her associates and offered herself to be arrested. This was the first occasion for her to be imprisoned in her own land. All the women who had been imprisoned, had been sentenced to hard labour, rather than an ordinary sentence. Because Kasturba was well known and respected, she was given a few concessions compared to younger women prisoners.

***

Ba was primarily worried about Bapu. As soon as she was released, she wanted to go to Yerawada to meet him. She was told that Bapu was not meeting any visitors. Ba wrote to Devdas, incarcerated in the same jail. Bapu replied, 'Jail means suspension of rights. Because there were many problems in sending and receiving letters, I have stopped meeting visitors.' Ba was upset by this reply. Ba had put up with many such incidents and would have to do so in the future. Bapu maintained that whoever was with him, had to pay a price. Ba and the children had to pay the biggest price. In the summer, Bapu began meeting visitors under pressure from the Congress and others, but Ba was not among them. Meanwhile Ba was arrested and again sentenced to six months. It was in Sabarmati Jail.

In September, a letter from Bapu came to the Ashram address. The envelope carried the message that this letter was to be given to Ba. It said:

'You must have heard about my fast. Do not be afraid. Stop the other women from being fearful too ... Having lived with me for forty years, I believe you will understand.'

***

The British government was planning on enacting a new law. Not only were Hindus, Muslims, Sikhs being divided for voting rights on the basis of religion, but Hindu Dalits were also getting separate voting rights. The British felt that if some power is divided amongst all the groups, the larger share of power will continue to be centred in their hands. It will be possible for them to rule India, a little longer. Bapu understood the designs of this divisive policy. To oppose the division of Hindu society by cutting off a section, he started a fast unto death. He knew that Hindus had always been unfair to Dalits. He had seen this happening in South Africa with locals and outsiders. He did not want that the British use this clause to rend this strong, but fast weakening bond and create two separate halves. He was against divisions based on caste, religion and *varna.* He had learnt much from his life's experiences and the struggles of Dr Bhimrao Ambedkar. He had personally experienced this injustice in South Africa. He wanted the house that had been shattered by centuries of discrimination and a sick mindset to be saved and rebuilt by working unitedly. *Savarna* Hindus, had for centuries divided society on the basis of caste. Whatever was left, this law would smash forever. He was fasting so that the conscience of the Hindus would awaken and he was prepared to die for it. They should be moved to acknowledge their own injustice and acknowledge the rebellion amongst the oppressed classes. They should change their own conduct forever.

When Bapu wrote this letter to Ba, he was sure that she would understand that he was fasting to save humanity from division and to bring people together. She would also understand that no matter how anybody interprets this question, this was a truth that was linked to the survival of every race and religion.

When Kasturba reached Yerawada jail to meet Bapu, he was lying immobile on a white iron cot under the shade of a mango tree in the inner courtyard. She was seeing him after nine months and that too in this sorry state. At a glance, she knew that his condition was fast deteriorating. His life was in danger. She took a hold over herself and stayed calm and balanced, as always. She expressed no anxiety or sorrow. She just murmured softly, 'The same old story.' She immediately assumed responsibility for his daily routine.

On 26 September, 1932, his health deteriorated rapidly. His blood pressure dropped from 110 to 95. His awareness levels were dropping. Ba immediately set to work without displaying any agitation. She rubbed the soles of his feet. She left it all to God's will and refused to worry. On the question of separate voting rights, commentators from both sides were negotiating to find solutions. Tensions were rising. Dr Ambedkar was resolute on his demand. On the other hand, Bapu's condition was touch and go. The government was feeling the pressure too. If something were to happen, it was hard to gauge what would transpire in the country. Just after noon, the tense and frightened negotiators somehow managed to reach an agreement.

The proposal was that instead of separate voting rights, Dalits would be given reserved constituencies. The candidates would be Dalits and everybody would vote so that one among them would emerge victorious … Instead of division of hearts, it would lead to better relations. This was called the Yerawada Pact. An unprecedented declaration was included in it which stated that nobody could be considered an 'untouchable' henceforth. When Bapu was told this, he mumbled indistinctly, 'This is my resolution. Whether I remain or not, this should remain.'

The time had come for Bapu to break his fast. Ba was standing near his bedstead with a glass of orange juice. Ba helped him to rise up on his elbow with one hand, and she put the glass of juice to his lips, with the other. With his first sip, the nation exhaled and there was a wave of relief and joy. Ba's glass was like Draupadi's never-empty vessel. Bapu looked around. Everybody's eyes were moist and relief was writ large on their faces.

***

Dr Babasaheb Bhimrao Ambedkar was an important national leader. Since the Round Table Conference, there was tension between Bapu and him. But after this decision, everybody looked relieved. The entire country had weathered a phase of uncertainty and things were moving towards normalcy. Ba walked the short distance to see off Dr Ambedkar. She said, 'It is with your support that the matter got resolved. Are you satisfied with the proposal?'

Dr Ambedkar did not speak for a moment. Then he said, 'We did not get what we wanted, but got more seats than we had expected.' He moved on and Ba came back. On the way she met Inspectòr General of Prisons, Mr Doel, who congratulated Ba, 'It is you who kept Bapu alive until the Yerawada Pact was signed.'

***

Ba thought that it was Bapu who was to be congratulated for having fasted for so many days. Although it had been such a frightening situation in itself but it also brought some boons. It had brought the whole family together. Kasturba was finishing the last week of the sentence in the female ward of the prison. Ramdas had also come there in the final days of his sentence. Devdas would be there often. Only Hari was not there. One day Manilal appeared out of the blue with apples from South Africa and oranges from Zanzirabad. Although Bapu had refused permission, he could not contain himself when he heard about the fast unto death. He came with his wife and four year old Sita. Kasturba missed Harilal. But she would not speak about it and nobody else brought it up either.

Ba would come to Bapu from her jail. She would cook on a stove. The stove had been provided so that Bapu could get proper meals after the fast. As a result, Bapu's health improved soon. Ba's weight had gone down due to eating a bare minimum but she was improving.

***

After her release from jail, Ba asked Bapu if she should resume her duties and Bapu agreed. On 3 December, 1932, in Madras, Ba represented Bapu in an anti-untouchability movement conference. She toured Harijan bastis along with other women to spread awareness among the Dalits. In the middle, she found time to dash off to Sabarmati Ashram to see if all was well there since her jail sojourn. She also went to Yerawada jail to see Bapu. He had again fasted for two days. It was for changing the policy that concerned satyagrahis not doing the jobs that were traditionally considered the jobs of untouchables.

***

Bigoted Hindus strongly opposed Ba's support for Harijans. This was the first time that Ba faced such opposition whereas Bapu was routinely confronted with such situations. In fact, Ba's coming into the forefront had fanned extreme reactions among Hindus. Their false notion stood shattered that Ba was against the uplift of untouchables that Bapu pursued so assiduously. They had heard about Ba's opposition to Dudha Bhai, Deena Ben and their daughter Lakshmi's entry into the Ashram. Ba's current position was a complete reversal. This incensed the extreme hardliners.

In 1933, Ba was incarcerated again. The government had warned her to stay away from the Civil Disobedience movement. *The New York Times* noted in this context, that Ba had been imprisoned for some secret reason. The reasons were not made public. 1933 was the year of imprisonments for Ba and Bapu. It had become part of their life's routine. In May, Bapu had sat on a fast for twenty one days on the Harijan question. Ba had been shocked and scared that he was going on a long fast so soon after his fast unto death. The government was even more frightened. What if the Mahatma died in jail? They released both Ba and Bapu.

In the beginning of 1934, Ba was arrested again. Her release was in the month of May. At the end of April, Ba got the news that she had become a grandmother thrice over within the span of a week. It was as if this was happening in the happy anticipation of her release. One foot was always in jail, far from her husband and family. The new arrivals had come to banish the pain and separation. Perhaps children-grandchildren are as big an achievement in a woman's life as is the possibility of independence for a freedom fighter. Ba was both. On 1st April a son was born in Manilal's home, Ramdas was similarly blessed with Usha on 18th April as was Devdas with Tara.

Ba had smiled and said, 'These children are the interest on the capital accumulated through prison journeys.'

***

Ba was released but life was beset with risks.

She knew that Bapu's work for the betterment of Harijans was making the bigots his staunch enemies. It was not so with Dr Ambedkar. The extremists thought that membership of the Viceroy's Council was the aim of his life ... but why was Gandhi doing this...? What sort of a Mahatma was he? All the ill feeling had fallen to his lot. When she was going with Bapu, she understood for the first time, the depth of the hatred they bore towards him. In June 1934, Ba and Bapu were going to the municipal hall in Poona in a car with many people. People were waiting eagerly to listen to his speech there. Suddenly a crude bomb was lobbed towards their car. It missed the target but seven people were injured. After prayers, Bapu thanked God that none of them had suffered grievous injuries. That night before going to bed, Ba pondered over the fact that life in jail was so secure and full of possibilities. Is it possible to give up your vow of service to save your life? Perhaps not.

Bapu wanted to close down Sabarmati Ashram. Ba knew of this. Ever since the Dandi march, the future of the Ashram was uncertain. It was almost a foregone conclusion that the government would take it over. On October 1933, to save it from a government acquisition, it was transferred in name to a Harijan Welfare Society. Most of the Ashram satyagrahis had gone to different places to work for rural uplift. There was talk of sending those remaining to other Ashrams.

Ba was about to be rendered homeless.

***

Bapu had gone to Sewagram some distance from Wardha to live in a *kutiya.* When Ba went to Sewagram, she knew he needed peace and quiet. With her life's experience, Ba had learned that uncertainty was a problem in itself and it could be handled only through work. If Bapu did not need her, she had her sons, new grandsons and granddaughters, relatives and friends who could come to her aid. For the next two and a half years, Ba lived her own life. She had become a nomad.

Ba travelled incessantly. She went with Bapu to Banaras and addressed the Harijan Mahasabha. In Ahmedabad Ramdas was unwell so she went there and got him treated. She took Ramdas's child, her granddaughter Sumitra, to Bombay for the treatment of her eyes. Devdas was in Delhi working in a high position. His daughter Tara was unwell so Ba went to Delhi. Ramdas took employment in a printing press and took his family to Bombay and Ba went to help set up their house. She went to Delhi again with Manu, Harilal's youngest daughter. She went to Shimla with Devdas. In 1936, she went to Nagpur with Bapu to attend the All India Literature Conference. There she met Harilal, her eldest, unexpectedly. He mentioned to her in passing that many people from different religions were putting pressure on him to change his faith.

Ba was shocked, 'What have you thought?' He only laughed in response.

***

Kasturba tried to forget the meeting with Hari. A strange incident took place during the next tour. The train stopped for some time at Katni station. There was a thick crowd gathered to catch a glimpse of Bapu. People were chanting slogans – '*Mahatma Gandhi ki Jai*'. In that hubbub, Ba heard a lone voice. Who was saying, '*Ba ki Jai*'? She peeped out of the windows that used to be open those days. She was shocked to see Harilal in dirty, smelly, torn clothes. He looked cold and ill. Ba's eyes were wet. How must he have come there cutting through the crowd? He raised his hand. He held an orange and came close to the window, 'A keepsake of my love, only for you.'

Ba took the orange. Harilal said to Bapu, 'You are so great, you don't need it. Ba made you great.'

Before Bapu could say anything, the train started pulling out. He walked along for some distance as if something was pulling him along. Then the train picked up speed. Ba-Bapu went far ahead and he remained standing there. The crowd was returning saying '*Jai*'. Harilal stood there for some time watching the crowd recede. Then he said *'Mata Kasturba ki Jai'* all to himself and walked away slowly. The platform was empty.

***

Ba thought about the tension that had existed between Bapu and her because of Harilal. Now it was there of its own accord. She used to give reasons to support her stand. She would quarrel with Bapu. After Nagpur, she had seen Harilal today, at the station. Alcohol and continuous indebtedness had embittered him deeply. It was harder to understand Hari than to understand Bapu. There was but one solution. He had to learn to deal with his own circumstances. What rankled was that he was making his father an object of ridicule. His letters against his father were being printed in newspapers against their own principles. Ba was deeply wounded by this behaviour of her eldest son … he was turning against himself. He was leaving everything and was being left behind like a child who has jumped and fallen into a fast flowing river. His mother was dumbstruck and unable to act.

In May 1936, news was broadcast that Mohandas Karamchand Gandhi's son Harilal had embraced Islam in the big mosque in Bombay and he was called Abdullah now. Kastur had feared this would happen when he had made a jocular reference to this in Nagpur. Hari declared at the time of changing his religion that he had done this for his own uplift and betterment. People believed that the uplift was financial. His new Muslim friends had started calling him

Maulvi. He went around giving discourses on his change of religion. After a few weeks, there was a news item about his unruly behaviour. Ba got Devdas to write a letter to Harilal:

My dear son Harilal,

I read that the police arrested you lying in a drunken state on the road in Madras. You were produced before the court and the magistrate fined you one rupee. He must have been kind-hearted to have let you off so lightly.

I don't know what to say to you. I have always told you to exercise self-control … spare a thought for your aging parents … you are giving them so much grief in their final years. Although you are born as our son, you are your own enemy.

I have found out that during your travels, you not only criticise your noble father, you also mock him. You are only pushing yourself down by doing this. He has nothing but love in his heart for you. He asked for you to stay with us. He assured you that you would be looked after. But you did not regard his wishes. He has other responsibilities in the world. What more can he do for you? He can only rue his fate. He has to bear humiliation on your account silently.

But I cannot bear the anguish that you cause me … when I get up each morning I wonder what news will I have to read today about you. Where are you, what do you eat? Where do you sleep? Are you managing on leftovers? You are my eldest son, fifty years of age. I am scared to meet you, lest you insult me.

Why did you change the religion of your ancestors? What can I say since this is your personal matter … When I read your quote that you have done this for your own uplift, I was pleased that now you will live a life of seriousness and purpose. But this hope was shattered. I have heard that you tell simple folks and strangers to follow your example. What do you know about religion? Are you in a frame of mind to take the right decisions? People can lose their way. Because you are the son of a great father, if you continue in this fashion, people will shun you. I pray that you mend your ways … your father forgives you each time, but God will never tolerate such behaviour.'

Ba kept dictating to Devdas and her eyes rained tears. She did not stop at this. She wrote another letter to the newspapers:

> *'I am writing this letter with the hope that the weak voice of a hurt mother will awaken the conscience of those Muslims brothers who were the medium of my son's conversion.*
>
> *I am incapable of understanding this act of yours. I know that thinking Muslim brethren reject this happening … instead of bringing my child back, a change of faith will only worsen the situation. You should have berated the boy instead of giving him the respect of a Maulvi. You should have tried to rid him of his bad habits. Does your faith permit you to name someone like my son a Maulvi? What pleasure do you get in puffing him up so?*
>
> *If you truly think of him as your brother, then what you are doing is not in his best interest. If your objective is to make a mockery of us, I have nothing to*

say. Do your worst. I wish to reiterate what I have said to my son that in the eyes of God, what you are doing in not right.'

Devdas stroked his own hand and looked towards his mother. Her heart was in turmoil. He wanted to ask what effect would these letters have, but he checked himself.

***

Somebody went to Harilal aka Abdullah, 'Your real mother's sermon has been published in the newspaper. The bane has fallen on us. We have puffed you up. When actually we have pulled you out of hell and shown you the true path to God. Only God knows what we have done.' Harilal was not in a condition to understand sarcasm.

***

Some miles from Wardha was a small backward village called Shegaon. It had no road, shop or post office. Bapu's friend Jamnalal Bajaj owned large tracts of land there. Bapu wanted to live somewhere quiet. In 1936, he wrote a long letter to Jamnalal Bajaj titled, 'My thoughts on living in a village.' He said, 'I'd like to live in a *kutiya.* If Ba would like to stay with me, or else alone. It should not cost more than a hundred rupees to make a *kutiya.* I will gather all that is needed to make a *kutiya* from Shegaon itself. But visitors will not come to Shegaon, I will meet them in Wardha. I will stay in Wardha on certain days.'

In July, after the *kutiya* was ready, Bapu moved there with seven associates.

***

Ba was the first member of the family to get there with her granddaughter. They had walked five dusty miles from Wardha, with the hope that they too will find a corner in Bapu's new but already full house. That village was infested with snakes. They had to return. Ba's *kutiya* could be readied by December. Until then Ba travelled amongst friends and relatives. Her *kutiya* was also made with mud plaster. It had a verandah, unlike Bapu's *kutiya.* Bapu used to call it a fashionable urban house. Ba had wandered about for three years, homeless, and finally had an abode. For her the one room and verandah were like a palace.

Slowly other bamboo and mud dwellings sprang up around these two *kutiyas.* Bapu's new followers came and stayed there. Roads were carved out of the jungle and trees planted alongside. Wells were dug. A school was opened for the children in neighbouring villages. A community kitchen was set up. Their old South African friends, Hermann Kallenbach and Henry Pollack also turned up to enjoy this hurried township and to refresh memories. In 1915, Kallenbach had come to London intending to come to India with Ba-Bapu, but the British government had stopped him on account of his being a German. He had to return disappointed. The British government had declared Germany and Germans as enemies at the time.

In 1937, Bapu felt that his solitary *kutiya* was solitary no more but was part of a settlement. He was not willing to say that it was an Ashram. But Shegaon became an Ashram. It was renamed Sevagram from Shegaon.

***

Manilal and his wife Susheela and son Arun had come to Sevagram for the first time. Arun fell ill with a high fever. Bapu put him on a six day fast. On the third day, the fever broke. As soon as the fever went down, he was extremely hungry. Susheela asked Bapu, 'Arun's fever is gone, may I give him something to eat?'

Bapu said no and ruled that they would have to wait longer. The child was beside himself with hunger. Susheela did not know what to do. Her son's demands on one side and Bapu's orders on the other. Suddenly the child felt a loving hand on his head and a glass held in the other moved towards his lips. His throat was parched. He took a sip and another. Ba was calm. She said decisively, 'I will not let my child go hungry.'

The glass had orange juice.

Bapu was watching. A questioning smile hovered on his face. He sighed and walked away. It was a struggle of two resolutions, boundless and bounded. Bapu looked helpless and this was not the first time.

***

When Subhash Chandra Bose returned from London, he came to Sevagram to meet Bapu. Most young men who had studied in London were keen to meet Bapu. Subhash was a young man just back from London and he was used to drinking tea. Tea was not allowed in the Ashram. Until he stayed in the Ashram, Ba quietly gave him tea in the kitchen. One day Bapu came when she was making tea for Subhash. Bapu grumbled, 'You are going against the rules of the Ashram.'

Ba simply pushed the glass of tea towards Subhash and said, 'Drink.'

She then turned to Bapu and said, 'This rule is for the people of the Ashram. Subhash is a guest. It is my right that I arrange for my guests the food and drink that they like.' Bapu left without a saying a word.

His face must have had the same expression as when Arun had been fed orange juice against his wishes.

***

When the inhabitants of the Ashram found it difficult to adhere to any rule, Ba was the court of appeal. Kaka Kalelkar used to say that Ba was like the universal mother, the very image of love and compassion. She would often break rules for the Ashram dwellers. Ultimately Bapu had to concede defeat in the face of Ba's practical arguments. He would take recourse in saying that the spirit of service was higher than the strictures of rules. Ba was carving out her own path. People no longer believed that Bapu's words were cast in stone for Ba. Ba had also started reading newspapers.

***

Motilal Nehru came to the Ashram unexpectedly. Bapu had a meal cooked for him personally. Ba had retired for a nap after feeding twenty five odd Ashram dwellers. Motilal Nehru came with three or four people just after that. Bapu started cooking with the help of a student. He dropped a *thali* by mistake. Even in her sleep, Ba was aware of her kitchen. May be a cat had jumped in ... She got up startled and shouted, who is it ... and she saw it was the student.

'What are you doing here?'

'We have guests. I was cooking with Bapu.'

'Why didn't call you me?'

'Bapu said not to disturb you, since you had just gone for your nap.'

After Motilal Nehru left, Ba asked Bapu, 'Why did you tell them not to wake me up?'

Bapu looked the other way, like a child, 'I am scared of you.'

Ba's face creased into a smile, 'Oh, so you are so scared of me!' Bapu had been serious but Ba made light of it.

***

A person called Nanavati used to teach music in Sevagram. One day he was teaching a lady a new *taan* and she was not getting it right. He tried several times but she would make a mistake each time. Ba was listening. She had picked up the *taans* just by ear. She helped that lady until she got it right.

***

Babla was the pet name of Mahadev Bhai's son, Narayan Desai. Babla would pass by Ba's *kutiya* on his way to learn the

Ramcharit Manas. One day he was on his way back when Ba called out to him, 'Babla, where are you coming from?'

'I had gone to study the Manas, Ba.'

'I also want to study the Manas.'

'I will tell Guruji. He will come and teach you.'

'You teach me.'

'I am still learning myself ...'

'As much as you learn, you can teach me. You can revise and I will learn. Life is to learn. Learn from every source.'

Babla had to agree. Initially, he hesitated, but then he started teaching Ba as best as he could.

***

There was an Ashram six miles from Sevagram, where women were trained to be self-reliant, according to Bapu's ideals. When Bapu shifted to their neighbourhood, the women would walk to Sevagram, on his birthday. They would spend the day there. On one of his birthdays, they wrote to him that they would come to seek his blessings. Bapu replied saying that they were welcome, but they should bring their own food. It was only possible to serve them water from the well. Bapu wanted to save on the Ashram's expenses. The women got up early and cooked hurriedly and walked the six miles to reach in time for the prayer.

The students got busy with their chores after the prayer. The women bathed at the well in the afternoon. When they were eating their food, Ba turned up. 'What are you doing? Why aren't you eating with the others in the Ashram?'

They told her about Bapu's letter. 'What rubbish!' were the words that popped out of Ba's mouth.

Ba took them with her. Whatever sweets and other things she had for the guests, she distributed among them. She had the kitchen opened. She served them whatever she could find, groundnuts, *sheera, mattha* ... Bapu passed by just then. 'What is going on?' he asked. Before answering him, Ba remonstrated, 'The Ashram is not so poverty stricken that it cannot entertain a few guests.'

'But I had written to them in advance ... what was the need for all this?'

'You write what you want,' Ba said smiling, 'Right now these girls are sitting in my verandah. They are my guests. I am their host. My guests do not leave without eating.' Bapu smiled and left.

***

Bapu began to suffer from hypertension. His blood pressure fluctuated. Shegaon was supposed to be bitterly cold. Bapu used to feel suffocated sleeping in the room so he slept in the verandah. When his blood pressure did not stabilise, the doctor had to be called. For the sake of his health, Bapu will have to sleep in the room was his advice. The problem was Bapu did not know where to go, who could he evict from their room? Seeing this situation, Mirabehn began vacating her *kutiya*. Bapu did not wish to displace anybody so he was upset. After the evening prayer, Ba declared, 'Nobody needs to be displaced. Bapu will stay with me in my *kutiya* henceforth.'

The matter was resolved in an instant. Bapu could not utter a word. Husband and wife were under one roof after a long time. That night Bapu slept comfortably. At that age, partners reassure each other with their presence.

Crowds of visitors began to turn up the next day. Bapu was troubled. He said, 'Poor Ba! I had got the *kutiya* made under my supervision so that she would get some peace and quiet. But I have come and occupied it. Wherever I go, the place turns into a public rest house. I might get upset but Ba never complains. Even if I saddle her with the biggest responsibility, ask her to do anything ...'

He would say this in her absence to visitors. One day when he was saying this, Ba heard him. She burst out laughing and so did the others. This was a time of Ba and Bapu's coming together.

***

Ba used to go with Bapu only if his health was precarious. Otherwise she was content to do her work. In the spring, she discovered that Bapu had to go to Debang in Orissa for a meeting. Ba expressed a desire to go with him. Susheela, Manilal's wife, and Durgaben, Mahadev Bhai's wife also joined her entourage. The biggest draw was Jagannath Puri, one of the four holy places in India. Neither of the three had the opportunity for *darshan* of Jagannath ji and they were keen to avail of this opportunity. They knew that the temple forbade the entry of Harijans. Bapu's orders were that self-respecting Hindus should shun such temples that forbade Harijans to enter. Ba knew this. She herself had taken part in the movement to allow entry into temples for Harijans.

Upon reaching Debang, Bapu got so caught up in political activities that he forgot all about his fellow travellers. Ba, Susheela and Durgaben left with the other women in the morning for *darshan* of Jagannath ji. Bapu did not ask them where they were going, and they did not say anything either. Bapu thought that they had gone for a walking tour. He also thought that Ba was with them, even if they stood close to the Jagannath temple, it would be like satyagraha. But Ba got caught in a dilemma, once she got there. On the one hand were her traditional Hindu *sanskars*, on the other, the new ideas that Bapu was spreading among people. Ba's religious feelings were stronger than her social duties. Her feet automatically moved towards the temple. Durgaben followed her. Everybody was astonished.

In spite of being a *bahu*, Susheela called out loudly, 'Ba, don't go inside. This temple bans the entry of Harijans. Bapu is opposed to this.' She said this with great hesitation. She knew that Ba's entry into the temple would raise a storm.

It was as if somebody was pulling Ba inside. 'I know, this is the first time I have come. Who knows if I will ever get to come again,' saying this, she went right in.

This news reached Bapu without any delay. He was stricken to his core. He was angered as he had never been before. It was as if his faith had been shattered. Ba had also realised her wrong-doing acutely on the way back. She begged for forgiveness from Bapu. Bapu's target was not Ba. In the evening, he said what he felt.

'I am responsible for this incident,' Bapu said, 'I did not pay attention to my wife's education. I also hold Mahadev Bhai guilty of not paying attention to his wife's education. If Mahadev had done so, Durgaben, instead of going with Ba, would have restrained her.'

Mahadev was shattered by this criticism. The next day, he wrote a letter seeking permission to resign. Bapu was even more hurt and said to him, 'You are like my son. Can't I say anything to you if you make a mistake?'

Time filled the fissure that had appeared between Mahadev and Mohandas. They salved their souls by fasting. But Ba could never forget this incident, in her lifetime.

***

Rajkot, where Mohandas's father Kaba Gandhi had been the Diwan, now had a Diwan who was the bane of the people's existence. This was even more so for the women of the kingdom. There were repeated reports of the molestation of young girls. Thakur would get pretty girls kidnapped. He would rape them in his summer residence near Tramba village and then release them. When one such incident was corroborated, the people began a satyagraha. The first among those to be imprisoned in the satyagraha was Maniben, the daughter of Sardar Patel. When this news reached Sevagram, Kasturba was agitated. Maniben was closest to Ba among the new lot. Ba said, 'What is happening in Rajkot? This is not just a matter of political rights but also to do with respect for women. I will not let this go. Something must be done.'

Gandhi ji wrote in *Harijan*, 'My wife is pained by the problems of the people of Rajkot. Although she has aged like me and is even less able to bear the tribulations of imprisonment, she wants to go to Rajkot. By the time this news is in print, she would have left for Rajkot ...'

Ba had actually left for Rajkot with Bapu's long time associate, Ambalal Sarabhai's daughter, Mridula Sarabhai. She had left her grandson Kanhadas under Bapu's care thinking that she would return soon. But Kanhadas's incessant crying forced Bapu to send him back to his own parents.

As soon as she reached Rajkot, Ba addressed the women saying that they had to resist unitedly for their rights and self-respect. Thakur was aware of Kasturba's activities. For him Ba's presence in Rajkot was quite shocking. On 13 February, 1939, Ba was suddenly taken prisoner and was incarcerated in the same royal bungalow where it was rumoured that the Thakur had raped the woman.

On 6 February, 1939, in *Harijan*, Bapu wrote, 'Kasturba is a daughter of Rajkot. No doubt Rajkot is insignificant on the map of India ... but for Kasturba and I, it will be foremost in the fight for independence. When we attain independence, Kasturba will have played an important role ... satyagraha is a struggle where the weakest and oldest can also participate ... all that you need is a strong heart.'

***

When Bapu found out that Ba had been put in solitary confinement, as an experienced hand, he sent a consoling message, 'Now you have the experience of staying alone. I don't remember if you have ever lived alone. Ram is always with you. If Ram is with you, it should make no difference whether anybody else is with you or not.'

When it was discovered that Maniben and Mridula Sarabhai had also been sent to Tramba, Bapu also wrote to both of them, 'It is God's grace that both of you are also there.'

Bapu was worried about Ba.

***

Bapu kept track of her in the same way as she kept track of him. Ba's being put into solitary confinement was unbearable for everybody. In Rajkot, reactions to her solitary confinement were not apparent, just like a covered vessel's contents do not get revealed, until they boil over. Bapu initially was not keen to get involved with this struggle as it might lead to complications, but now he decided to go to Rajkot and talk to the Thakur. Not just about the promises of reform that had not been kept, but also about the confinement of Kasturba and the other women. When he got there, he found out that the prisoners were on hunger strike to protest their ill treatment.

Gandhi ji had reached Rajkot in the morning. He first met the prisoners inside the jails. They all felt as if a cooling breeze had blown their way, inside hell. After talking to them, he was sure that there was no justification for the sentence they were serving. From there, he went to Tramba and met Kasturba, Maniben and Mridula Sarabhai. The Rajkumar-Thakur and his ministers were evasive. It was clear to Bapu that they would not budge without pressure. He saw only one way out – a fast unto death. He sent a notice to the Thakur to give a response until 3:00 pm the next day. Lord Linlithgow, the Viceroy in Delhi had been apprised of the situation. When there was no answer till 3:00 pm, Bapu started his fast at his own place on 3rd March. This small incident became the biggest news in the country. Bapu sent

Sushila Nayyar to give this news to Kasturba so that she would not get a shock, hearing it from other sources. Kasturba was shocked but more than that, she was sad. 'He should have told me a fast is necessary …'

'Nobody knew anything, Bapu just said this in the morning,' said Sushila. She gave Bapu's written message to Ba: *'I believe that you are calm and balanced. If not, then come to me.'*

Ba did not understand what he meant by this. Sushila explained that if she was agreeable, Bapu will ask the administration to allow her to stay with him.

Ba was dismayed. At least Bapu should have known that to ask the administration to release her is against the principles of satyagraha! Whatever were the consequences of the fast was another matter.

'In every way,' said Ba, 'I am fine here, just give me daily updates about Bapu. God had protected him earlier, and it is God who will protect him now.'

On the third day of the fast, due to pressure from above, the officers released Ba and left her at home. Seeing Ba there all of a sudden, Bapu said angrily, 'How did you come here?'

'Why, the government has released me!' Kasturba was upset by the tone of his voice. He wanted me to be released and come to him. Now he is upset that I have come.

'Where are Maniben and Mridula?'

Ba realised that in her eagerness to be with Bapu, she had forgotten her responsibility towards her fellow prisoners. But she said, 'In Tramba Jail.'

'You will abandon your associates like this?' Bapu asked as if in reminder.

'Never!'

'So what will you do?' was his direct question.

Ba thought for a moment, 'I will return to Tramba in the evening.'

Bapu was trying to divine what she was thinking but was also teasing her a bit. Ba thought it was good that she had not been trumped. If they don't let her in, she will sit outside the palace, she said.

Ba and Bapu were not tense any longer. They were content in themselves and happy with each other. Bapu's worries had dissipated with Ba's answer. He had reminded her of her responsibilities. Ba went to Tramba in the evening. Bapu said no further word. But he was thinking to himself, would he have done the same in this situation?

***

In 1956, the bungalow where Ba had been confined had been turned into '*Kasturba Arogya Dham*' a centre for women's healing.

***

After returning from Rajkot, Ba caught a cold. After some time, she contracted malaria. She became so weak and frail that Bapu was concerned. He felt that she needed better treatment but he needed her approval for that. Those days Sushila Nayyar was studying for an M.D. in Delhi. Ba trusted her but neither she nor Bapu wanted to disturb her studies.

Devdas was in Delhi and Bapu sent him a telegram about Ba's condition. Devdas was informed about Ba's arrival in Delhi. Both Devdas and Sushila were there at the station to receive her. Sushila was not pleased to see that Bapu had sent Ba alone by train to Delhi. When she spoke about this to Ba, she exclaimed, 'Oh, how does it matter? Mahadev put me on the train at Wardha. My fellow travellers took on the onus of looking after me on the way. What was the need to bring anybody along? I told them it was not necessary.'

***

Ba stayed at Devdas and Lakshmi's house. Sushila would come to check on her frequently. Her health improved rapidly. Ba liked being with her grandchildren. As soon as she got better, she wanted to go to the Ashram. Her simple life, the constant activity of the students, the morning and evening prayers … she missed all that in Devdas's house. One day, Ba asked Sushila, 'May I stay for few days in your hostel? We will do morning and evening prayers like in Sevagram.' Sushila readily agreed.

It was a hot, dry summer. In the hostel it was so hot that Ba was not able to sleep at night. To cool the room, they would splash water on the floor and run the fan at top speed. As a result of this, Ba got bronchial pneumonia. She had to go to Devdas's house again. After intense care for a few days, her condition improved somewhat. Telegrams from Bapu arrived almost every day to ask after Ba's health. Every now and again, there were letters addressed to her. Ba would listen to them and then put them under her pillow. If anybody asked about them, she would feel embarrassed. But whenever she got a chance, she would pull them out, don her spectacles and read the latest letter carefully joining the letters. It was his letters that gave her a lease of life. They say, in an illness, medicines deal with the disorder, but morale depends on the concern shown by your loved ones. As soon as she got better, Ba was raring to go to Sevagram. Devdas sent Ba with Lakshmi and the three children. Ba got busy with her daily chores as soon as she got back. In spite of weakness, her spirit and enthusiasm was astonishing.

After a few days, Bapu had to go to Northwest Frontier province with a view to strengthen Hindu-Muslim unity. Ba decided to accompany him. Bapu raised the question of her health. Ba's rejoinder was, 'Both of us can do more work for Hindu- Muslim unity. You work among the men and I will work with the women.'

Bapu smiled. 'You have become a complete politician,' he quipped.

'There is no politician who can face up to you. This is the path of love,' said Ba.

'Then Sushila must come too, only she can look after your health.'

***

Ba felt better than ever upon her return. Along with the Ashram dwellers, she also looked after her grandson and granddaughter. She felt happy to have them around her. She would make halwa and their favourite foods for them. She would get them to help her in the kitchen. When she told them stories in the evening, the verandah would get crowded with listeners. Ba was tuneful and her voice touched the heart. The children would hang on to every word she said.

The international situation seemed to be moving rapidly towards the Second World War. Bapu's engagements increased and he was available to the children only during his evening walk. He would answer all their queries. Children have many questions, but not enough knowledge to fully understand. If they went to him with their questions during the day, he would put a finger to their lips. He would continue his conversation with the others.

***

When talk of the Second World War began, Manilal's wife, Susheela and the children were in the Ashram. The atmosphere was tense, but the faces in the Ashram were relaxed. Manilal was in South Africa and seeing the impending changes because of the war, Susheela and the children had to go back. The memory that Susheela carried of Ba and Bapu, found expression in *Indian Opinion* in this way:

> '... *One day, to tease Ba, Bapu said to her, "Why don't you leave the Ashram and stay with our sons in their well appointed bungalows with their wives and your grandchildren? You will stay in comfort and you will get a chance to rule over your bahus."*
>
> *'Then he made an oblique comment, "Susheela, I see you in Ba's service all the time, has she bribed you?"*

'I also did not let this go without a retort, "Bapu, if I serve you, I will only get some hand-spun threads, but I can get a lot more from Ba." Bapu laughed uproariously and left.

'When I was packing later, Ba brought me a very soft white sari made of handspun cotton as a gift. Bapu looked at my exceptional gift but would not yield any ground. He smiled a naughty smile and said, "Do you know that half the cotton in this sari has been spun by me?"'

***

In the Working Committee in Wardha, the proposal of 'Quit India' had been passed. Gandhi had warned the British, 'Please leave. Leave India to God and its so called anarchy.' William E. Fischer was the Editor of *LIFE* magazine. He had been invited to dinner. He met Ba for the first time. He has given a touching description of an unwell Ba. He writes, 'Ba was sitting next to him (Gandhi). A wrinkled shrunken lady. Chewing on some energy enhancing food. I was told that she had been gravely ill. After her illness, and a long gap, she was dining with the others. A more beautiful, devoted and compassionate face I had not seen. Ease and patient endurance shone on each wrinkle in her face.'

***

After giving the call for 'Quit India', Bapu's caravan left for Bombay on 2 August, 1942. Ba had recovered well enough to go with them. Everybody stayed at Birla House on Napean Sea Road. Ba did not suffer any problems as she was staying in a comfortable well appointed place. The country waited eagerly for the decision of the All India Congress Committee. Those who were in support of the Congress as well as those who opposed it. Dr Sushila Nayyar, Ba's trusted physician, was worried reading the newspapers and listening to the rumours that were afloat. On 4th August, a government employee told them that Gandhi and other leaders would soon be taken prisoner. The orders had been given. Sushila was worried about Bapu and especially about Ba. She asked her Dean for leave and took the first train out to Bombay. When she reached, Bapu and her brother, Pyarelal, were in a meeting. Everybody was surprised to see her arrive without notice.

She said, 'I was told all of you will be arrested. I did not want to get left behind.'

Ba was upset, 'These battles will go on. Why are you interrupting your studies?'

Bapu was also worried. He felt quite sure about himself that the government would not rush to arrest him. Although in the Open session of Congress on 7th August, he had given a revolutionary mantra, 'I give you a small mantra ... Do or Die.' Non-violence was inherent in this. We will die but not strike first.

On 9th August, when he woke up, Mahadev Bhai said to him that he had not been able to sleep a wink.

'Why?'

'The phone rang continuously. People asked if Bapu had been arrested.'

'I don't think the government is so foolish that it will arrest the person who is helping to maintain peace.'

***

As soon as the morning prayer ended, a servant came and told Mahadev that the Police was waiting outside to meet him. Mahadev Bhai knew immediately that it was no rumour but the truth. After some time, he returned from outside and went to Bapu, 'They have come to take you.'

There was a touch of surprise in Bapu's acknowledgment, 'How much time do we have?'

'Half an hour.'

'Will they take everybody?'

No, they have a warrant in your name and Mirabehn and mine.'

'Ba?'

'No,' he said softly.

'Will you come?' Bapu asked Ba.

'As you say ...'

'No, you tell me,' Mahadev Bhai's son, Narayan was listening quietly.

'If you say so ...'

'No, what is it that you wish?'

'You tell me, I will do as you say.'

'Then do something for me tomorrow. You speak at the public meeting, instead of me.'

Ba wanted to go along to look after Bapu. She became completely still when she heard his proposal. The nation took priority. Narayan moved from near Mahadev Bhai and came and stood by Ba. Ba was finding it strange to be separated from Bapu, but she knew what she had to do. This was a greater responsibility than going to jail. Ba raised her eyes skywards and prayed silently, 'Give my partner the strength to take the struggle for the country's independence forward, and give me strength too ...'

***

The news of the Mahatma's arrest spread like wildfire across the country. Kasturba had forgotten all about the weakness caused by her illness. She was filled with enthusiasm for her new task. She was busy since the morning, talking to people, counselling them to be patient, giving instructions. She had assumed the role of her husband. There was mild tension in her mind. She did not know where the police had taken her husband and his associates. But she was strong inside.

Bapu was to have addressed a public meeting in Shivaji Park. He had already been arrested. Somebody asked, 'You can see heads for as far as the eye can see. Bapu is in jail, who will address them?'

Everybody was astonished when Ba said, 'Never mind if Bapu is not there, I will address the gathering instead.'

Some people whispered, 'Will Ba be able to take on this responsibility? Does she have the physical and mental strength to rise up to the challenge? What if she gets arrested?'

Ba's visage changed. She said, 'What an odd thing to say! The whole country has been clapped in jail. Do you think I would wish to remain outside?'

It was decided that she would go to the public meeting with Sushila. If she has to go to jail, Sushila will be there to take care of her. She got Sushila to write down whatever she had to say in the meeting. This is an excerpt:

'There is only one task before us: that we stay true to his principles. The women of India will have to prove their strength. Everybody will have to join the struggle in response to Gandhi ji's call, casting aside differences of caste and religion. Truth and non-violence is his rallying cry ...'

It was Sunday evening. Ba went down the steps of Birla House at 5:00 pm to go to Shivaji Park. On the last step, her grandson, Kanu Gandhi was standing with a paper badge. Ba asked, 'What is this?'

'Ba, this is the badge for Do or Die. Bapu had said that every volunteer should wear it on their chest. I have made this one for you.'

Ba smiled, 'This mantra is engraved on my heart. What difference will this paper badge make?'

Kasturba reached the portico and Sushila was behind her. There were many others too. A police officer was waiting there. He stepped forth, 'Mata ji, please don't go to Shivaji Park. They will take you prisoner.'

'How can a mother sit at home?' asked Ba. '... when her sons and daughters are being abused by the White government ...' Saying this she moved towards the car. A short man stood at attention, holding the car door open to take her to Shivaji Park.

The police officer followed her. His instructions may have been to arrest whoever stepped out of Birla House and he wanted to stop Ba, but he did not have the courage to take Kasturba prisoner. He stepped up and made a last request, 'Mataji, please don't go.' Kasturba looked at him and smiled and told the driver to leave. The car moved forward. Perhaps he had left the task of taking her prisoner to somebody else.

***

About eight thousand people waited patiently at Shivaji Park. When Ba's arrival was announced there was prolonged applause. Ba reached the stage and said *Jai Hind.* The public roared *Jai Hind* in return. Ba read her entire speech without hesitating and with complete confidence. The crowd went berserk. Ba's words held the charge of her feeling, there was anger about Bapu's imprisonment, and before them stood a frail woman whose husband had been sent away a day before to an unknown place by the White government. People knew him as Bapu and Mahatma. Ba was calm as she spoke and her face was radiant. As soon as her speech ended, the police spirited away Sushila and her. The police had got news that after Ba, Sushila would give a speech. People did not even realise that Ba had been arrested. Ba was taken to Arthur Jail. On the way Sushila saw that Ba was exhausted. She checked her pulse. She had a mild fever. When a tear escaped Ba's eye, Sushila queried, 'What is this Ba?'

Ba was looking out of the police car but was quiet. People were walking on the road, going about their business, as if nothing had happened. Life was moving on. It was if all the lives had become part of one stream. After some time, Ba turned to Sushila, 'Sushila, this time I have a feeling that I will not come back alive.'

Sushila felt as if an icy knife had cut through her. She said, 'Why are you saying such depressing things Ba? You inspire others.'

'No, I just felt this way. Perhaps the British government will not leave any of us alive. Their sword of violence has dulled before Bapu's non-violence. They are sharpening their swords.' Ba's voice was faint.

***

When Ba and Sushila reached Arthur Jail, Sushila saw outside that people were walking back to their homes for their evening meal or were busy with other chores. Nobody knew that Bapu had been sent as prisoner to some unknown place and Ba had been brought to Arthur Jail. Suddenly she felt like screaming and saying, what has happened to all of you? You don't even know who has come? Don't you recognise Ba? She began to sob.

***

Ba began having loose motions in jail. When Sushila asked for a doctor, he showed up the second day. Sushila asked him to get medicine. He said, 'You can have it bought.'

Who could she ask to buy medicine and the second problem was that she had no money. She asked the jailer to phone a friend. The jailer said, 'The phone cannot be used. Government orders are that prisoners are to have no contact with the world outside.'

After much argument, two apples were sent in the evening. There was no sign of any medicine. Sushila's ears rang with Ba's words. Her face looked pale. The air was fetid in the barrack where they had been sent. When she said this to the Matron, she said that they could come and sit in her room. But Ba did not stay there for long and returned to the barrack. It was even harder to go to the bathroom from there.

***

A woman prisoner had left her children behind. Ba asked after her well-being affectionately. Seeing her state, Ba forgot her own pain. She consoled her. She was worried about Bapu. Will he be able to rid India of its pain? Sushila placated her saying Bapu had left it all up to God, why do you worry? Ba's eyes mirrored the turmoil in her heart.

On the first night, the three of them were locked up from the outside, after bedtime. Inside, it was hot and suffocating. The next day they put their bedding in the verandah. The broken drain of the toilet made the place stink. However this place was more airy than the room. Because she was tired, Ba slept late. At 9:00 am, the Matron said that Ba and Sushila had been transferred to another jail. At 10:00 am, Ba was woken up and things were packed. There was no money to buy fruit for Ba. The other woman prisoner gave her purse to Sushila. It had only twenty rupees. Sushila took five rupees and gave one of her coloured saris in exchange. That woman had forgotten to bring a coloured sari.

After reaching the jail superintendent's room, Ba asked, 'Where are we being sent?'

'To Mr Gandhi,' Ba was relieved to hear this.

Both of them were made to sit in the Waiting Room at the station. As always, there was commotion at the station. Ba said, 'Sushila, the world is carrying on as if nothing has happened. How will Bapu ji attain *Swaraj* like this?'

Ba's words held so much pain that Sushila's eyes welled up with tears. She said, 'Ba, leave it all up to God, we have to do our work.'

A police officer came at the time of the train's departure. The two of them were keen to meet Bapu. They were put in the first class compartment when the train arrived and left for Poona.

***

In the morning at seven, the train stopped at a small station called Chinchwada. A police officer came in. Ba was in the bathroom. All night she had passed loose stools. Her face had turned a sickly yellow. The train was late by five minutes. There was a chair ready for her at the station. She refused to sit on it. Ba believed that you should work your body as far as possible. A car stood waiting. About half an hour later, the car reached Agha Khan Palace. Ba could only climb the stairs with Sushila's assistance. Some prisoners were sweeping the verandah. Ba asked one of them, 'Where is Bapu ji's room?'

In jail also, everybody called him Bapu ji.

He indicated that it was the last room. Both of them walked slowly till there. Bapu was correcting an article with a pencil. Mahadev Bhai stood at the back, looking at some papers. Bapu would occasionally say something or Mahadev Bhai would ask a question. When these two were quite close, Mahadev Bhai saw them. His face lit up like a child as he saw Ba as if he had found his long lost mother. Bapu's face showed tension. He thought perhaps Ba had not been able to bear his absence. He asked rudely, 'You wrote to the government to come here or have you been sent as a prisoner?'

Ba could not understand why he was speaking in this manner. Sushila replied, 'As per your orders, Ba addressed the public at Shivaji Park and as soon as she did that, the police arrested both of us and sent us to Arthur Jail. We have been transferred from there.'

She also said that since coming to Arthur Jail, Ba was suffering from diarrhoea. Mahadev ran about and arranged for a cot. They were called to identify their luggage. In spite of everybody asking her not to and in her weak state, Ba went with Sushila. When they were on the way back, they met the jail superintendent Mr Ketley. He ushered Ba in with great respect. The British officers of the government also respected Bapu. After putting Ba to bed, Sushila wrote out a prescription. It was no surprise that with the relief of meeting Bapu, her stomach had settled. Ba was active by nature. From the very next day, she began looking after Bapu and walking about. From that day itself, she began her chores of sitting with Bapu during his meal and serving him. Sushila brought Ba's food there. Ba waved a fan in one hand. The place was called a palace, but it was infested with mosquitoes. The others waved fans only when they needed to, but Ba's hands never paused.

***

Ba and Sushila had come to Agha Khan Palace jail on 11th August. On 15th August, Bapu and Mahadev Bhai went for a morning walk as always. Bapu went into the room for a massage when they came back. For some time, the sound of Mahadev Bhai's laughter could be heard from Sarojini Naidu's room. Suddenly it stopped. Somebody called out. Everybody thought that since there was an inspection tour of the Jail Inspector, Colonel Bhandari, somebody must be getting summoned to meet him. Just then Ba came running into the room. She was screaming, 'Hurry Sushila! Mahadev has fainted.'

Bapu had no idea that Mahadev's condition was grave. He stood near his bed and called out. 'Mahadev, Mahadev'. Ba yelled, 'Mahadev, Bapu ji has come, don't you hear him ... you always come running when you hear him call.' There was no answer. Sushila was weeping bitterly and massaging his chest. Slowly, Mahdev Bhai's breath became shallower.

As soon as he had stepped forward to shake Colonel Bhandari's hand, Mahadev Bhai had crumpled to the ground. Agha Khan Palace sank into silence. Everybody made their way where his body had been kept. Everybody's eyes streamed with tears. Mahadev, who had left his home and hearth to be by Bapu's side, steadfast, for twenty five years as his most trusted associate, his voice had been stilled suddenly. Ba and Bapu's calls were incapable of rousing him again.

The room where his body was kept was decorated with flowers. After being kept there for a few hours to allow everybody to pay their respects, it was taken down for the funeral rites. Ba went too. She could not stop crying. She was so weak that she could barely go down the steps. Everybody told her not to go down in this condition. She said, 'Should I not go with my Mahadev to the place where I have to go soon?'

Her chair was put close to the funeral pyre. She folded her hands and spoke, 'Mahadev, be happy wherever you go. My brother, you served Bapu ji and the country so well ... we were not able to do anything for you.' Sometimes she would ask, 'Mahadev, why did you go? Why am I left behind?'

Bapu had turned to stone. Perhaps he was thinking, a lifelong prisoner, is a prisoner at the time of death also. But there was hope for freedom ... just as Mahadev's bonds broke, the country will break its bondage. They returned at five in the evening, after the final rites. There was deathly silence. Who could they console? Time was so short that Mahadev Bhai's wife and children could not be called. This was the life of a braveheart ...

***

Ba's mind was a beehive of buzzing thoughts, turmoil, confusion and conflict. She began to say, 'Mahadev was a true Brahmin ... his going like this is most inauspicious.'

Bapu would tell her, 'Yes, for the British government, not for us ... for us it is the sacrifice of a satyagrahi.'

Ba could not rid herself of this notion. One day she said to Sushila, 'The death of a Brahmin is on our heads, right? Bapu started the war of independence, Mahadev came to jail with him and he died here. The sin is on us, isn't it?'

Sushila said, 'Ba why do you think like this? Mahadev Bhai was with Bapu for the country's independence and he sacrificed his life for that, why is there any sin in his death? And if it is, it is on the White government. He was innocent, why was he arrested? When does Bapu fight? He was doing satyagraha.'

'Yes, that is true. Bapu did not start this fight. He wanted independence with peace. It is the government who arrested people, punished them and put them in jail.'

But she could not rid herself of thoughts of Mahadev. Again and again, she would fall into a *chakravyuh.*

***

It was impossible to separate Ba from her religious beliefs. She asked for a tulsi plant in Agha Khan Palace and Sushila had brought one. She worshipped it daily. Mirabehn had an idol of Bal-Krishna in her room. Ba would make a flower offering to it each day. That was Ba's second temple. The third temple was the place of Mahadev Bhai's funeral pyre. Until there was strength in her frame, she used to circumambulate it with Bapu. She would fold her hands before it in *Namaskar.*

It was 2nd October. Bapu's birthday. Sarojini Naidu had arranged for a row of lamps.

Ba said to Sushila, 'The lamps are fine but light a lamp at Shankar's.'

Sushila was perplexed. Shankar was a policeman in the guard line up. Why would Ba ask for a lamp to be lit at Shankar's? Suddenly she knew, 'Are you asking me to put a lamp on Mahadev Bhai's *Samadhi*?'

'Yes, that is Mahadev ... Shankar's temple,' thus spoke Ba simply.

***

The atmosphere was extremely sombre after Mahadev Bhai's departure. This was even more so in jail, with the same people and the same conversation. The incident had cast a pall. Bapu found a way out, 'Let us be aware of how we spend each minute of the day. We will stay busy so that irrational thoughts don't assail us. In a violent world, non-violence has to make its place.'

He began teaching Ba Gujarati. What he had not been able to accomplish in his youth, he was determined to complete now. If he found a *bhajan* in the Gujarati tome, he would teach her by singing it. Ba would sing along. He began teaching her geography. Sometimes he would teach her history. When he straightened his back after lunch, for a while, he would read something out to her before his nap. He would discuss it as well. Ba's heart was on the mend and she was beginning to feel better. Sometimes she wondered, why didn't I learn until now?

She studied in complete earnest. But it was difficult for her to learn new things and to remember them. She would try to remember things with all her heart and soul. Bapu would ask her questions every now and then to check how much she recalled of earlier lessons. If she could not answer, Bapu would say nothing but Ba's heart would ache. She could remember so many things from her past but why couldn't she remember what was written in books? One day, Bapu gave her the task of memorising the five rivers of Punjab. When Bapu went to sleep, she hurriedly went to Sushila, 'You please write the five names on a piece of paper.' She did so and Ba looked at the paper while walking about and tried to memorise the names. But the next day when Bapu asked her, they had vanished from her memory. Using an orange, Bapu explained to her, latitudes, equator, etc. over many days. She did memorise them. Ba was as happy as a child. Many days later, Pyarelal was teaching Manu the same lesson. Pyarelal knew the terms in English and Urdu but not in Hindi. Ba listened quietly. She went to Sushila and said, 'What Pyare is calling a *rekhansh* (longitude), Bapu was calling an *akshansh* (latitude)'. When Pyarelal was told about his mistake being caught by Ba, he admitted he was wrong and made amends. Ba was pleased that she had helped Pyare correct his mistake.

Bapu was serious about teaching Ba. By listening, Ba could haltingly converse in functional English. She had no trouble talking in her mother tongue but faced trouble in writing. One day, Bapu came upon the fifth standard text in Gujarati. Bapu began reading it with Ba. It had poems and also the *ragas* in which they were to be sung. Bapu began teaching her the poems and *ragas.* For Ba this was new. Both of them sang those poems together in the evening prayer. Sarojini Naidu would laugh. She would say jokingly, 'What should we call this romance of your old age Bapu ji?' Bapu would laugh like toothless baby.

Once he wrote down a list of state capitals. Ba worked hard to memorise them. When it was time to recite them in front of Bapu, they all got mixed up. She said Lahore was the capital of Bengal. She was upset when she found out her mistake. Bapu would make her write on a slate to improve her handwriting. One day, Ba found out that the prisoners were being given note books by the prison authorities. Ba hesitantly asked Bapu, 'Will you get a note book for me?'

He put four loose sheets in her hands and said, 'First you practise writing on these sheets. When you have learnt something, I will get a note book for you too.' Ba was hurt. She put the sheets and slate on Bapu's table and said, 'I have learned the biggest lesson of my life, Thank you!' She turned and left.

Sarojini Naidu was listening. She quietly got a note book sent to Ba through Sushila. Ba turned it this way and that and said softly, 'What use is this to an illiterate?' She went and put it among Bapu's papers. That was the end of Ba's education. That note book lay among Bapu's papers for a long time.

***

One day Bapu was writing. Ba came into the room, 'What are you writing?'

'A letter to the Viceroy ...' he said, 'The government is spreading rumours about the Quit India Movement.'

'What sort of rumours?'

'They are saying that the Congress is using the Quit India movement to spread violence and wants to overthrow the government. They want to gather support for their own unjust acts here and abroad.'

'How?'

Because Ba never took an interest in such matters, Bapu was a little taken aback by her question. He explained the propaganda of the British and what effect it was likely to have on the world.

'You know that we all were taken prisoner before the movement started. We could not even begin the struggle. How can these people conclude that we are inciting violence?'

'This means that you are again thinking of going on a fast.' Ba's apprehensions were not unfounded. She said, 'You are not young any more. Repeated fasting has affected your health badly.'

Bapu laughed. 'You worry for nothing. Why did you think I would fast?'

The way Bapu laughed only cemented her doubts. She said, 'I have been with you for so many years, do you think I don't understand what goes on in your mind?'

***

When Dr Sushila Nayyar discovered Bapu's plans for fasting again, she tried to dissuade him as a doctor, but Bapu was unmoved. She went so far as to say, 'Think of Ba. In her delicate state, how will she withstand the tension that your fasting will bring?'

'None of you know Ba like I do,' said Bapu 'She has amazing strength inside and she can withstand more tension than all of you. I have learnt tolerance from her.'

He stalled the conversation regarding a fast saying that he would do so only when directed by God. For a week he meditated for half an hour every day. Everybody waited with bated breath for God's command.

One afternoon, Sarojini Naidu said to Ba, 'It is just as well that Bapu has agreed to obey God's command. Looking at his health, God will never permit him to go on a fast.'

'I know,' said Ba, 'Don't forget, Bapu will obey every command of God.'

***

It was not difficult for Bapu to get God's consent. But he also needed Ba's. This right had been earned through her sacrifice and surrender. After making his intention clear, Bapu and Ba remained closeted in a room for an hour. Ba's arguments were compelling. When they could not reach any conclusion, Bapu said, 'You have earned the place of a mother for all those who love the freedom of their country and who make sacrifices for it. On one side is my weak frame, and on the other, is the call of lakhs of people in the country who hold freedom dear. You decide if you want independence and the aspirations of the people or this weak and wasted body?'

Ba turned to stone and went out without a word. She had some papers in her hand. They contained Bapu's announcement of the fast. Ba was fully convinced that Bapu had no alternative but to fast. It was only through the fast could he refute the rumours being spread against the Quit India Movement and rebut the charge of spreading violence.

Bapu and Ba began their day together. They walked till Mahadev Bhai's *Samadhi* and circumambulated it. They prayed there. Ba murmured, 'Mahadev, for the first time, your Bapu is going to fast without you ...' Her eyes were wet. They offered flowers and returned.

***

On 10 February, 1943, Bapu's three week fast began. As always, Ba declared that she would eat only one meal a day in his support. Everybody was very concerned. Bapu took it upon himself to reason with Ba. Finally she agreed that she would consume fruit and milk twice so that she could look after Bapu.

For the first few days, Bapu was active, but by the third day, he began to feel weak. On the sixth day, his condition began deteriorating and then it worsened. Ba stayed by his bedside all day long. When Ba asked if she could give him few drops of lemon in water, he demurred. When the fast extended into the second week, the news had seeped past the gates of Agha Khan Palace. The people of the country were restless and concerned. A crowd had begun to gather at the main gate to get updates on Bapu's health. Three members from the Viceroy's Council resigned asking for Bapu's immediate release. They had been appointed initially because they opposed Bapu and were on the side of the government. World renowned playwright Bernard Shaw said, 'The King should immediately set Gandhi free unconditionally and apologise for the intellectual bankruptcy of his cabinet.' The government in Delhi remained impervious. So much so that Lord Linlithgow, the Viceroy. called Gandhi's fast political 'blackmailing'. Churchill famously said, 'If he remains obstinate, let him starve to death.'

The only benefit that accrued was that, newly released from jail, Ramdas and Devdas, were permitted by the government to go and live with Bapu for some time. The government did not want the people to agitate under the misimpression that Bapu was no more. Hundreds of people passed in front of Bapu's door to see that Bapu appeared to be sleeping. They were reassured that his breathing continued. His indomitable soul was alive. Ba would fold her hands in *Namaskar* to all the people who would pass by. She had unshakeable faith in him. On the thirteenth day, there was a sharp drop in Bapu's condition. His heartbeat became faint. His kidneys were failing. In his daily report, the doctor said that if the fast continued, his life could end by midnight.

Ba moved from near Bapu to the tulsi plant and began to pray. Her face was calm. She was unaware of the procession of people passing by Bapu. Dr Sushila and Mirabehn's eyes were welling up repeatedly at the sight of Bapu. Seeing Ba's faith and silent dialogue with the Almighty, on the basis of her medical knowledge, Dr Sushila knew it was touch and go and only a miracle could make a change. Suddenly, the doctor bent near Bapu's ear to ask if he would take a sip of water and fruit juice. His eyelids fluttered and he simply nodded. Sushila ran to the kitchen asking for two ounces fruit juice to be diluted with four ounces water and rushed back to Bapu. The juice came and Bapu sipped very slowly. Ba returned reassured and said calmly, 'Bapu will not leave us.' She did not know that he had ended his fast with the juice.

***

There were two Muslim policemen in Agha Khan Palace. Ba treated them like one of her own. She would ask them to help in the kitchen. She would share sweets with them on Eid and other festivals. There was no discrimination between

Hindus and Muslims. But she would be upset when she read history and learned about the unjust acts of the Muslim rulers. But when she saw friends such as Dr Ansari, Hakim Ajmal Khan, Khan Abdul Ghaffar Khan, his brother Dr Khan Sahib, Maulana Abul Kalam Azad, she would wonder why history recorded disturbing incidents. In Sevagram, working committee meetings were held and a large number of people would come to participate. Ba would sit on the platform and hold court. Everybody would come to greet her. She would remember who liked what. Pandit Nehru and Maulana Sahib liked tea. Mirabehn would make it. Rajagopalachari preferred coffee. Sushila used to make it. For Khan Abdul Ghaffar Khan, she would go personally and get him a lump of jagggery. Hakim Sahib used to chew paan so she would have it bought for him. For every person, she would ensure that they got their preference. With Vallabh Bhai Patel and Jamnalal Bajaj, she had a relationship of great closeness. If they had the time, Ba would share all her news about home and outside.

Ba did not like hearing anything against Hindu-Muslim unity. One day, she read in an article that Gandhi and Jinnah did not like meeting each other. Ba was angry, 'That is not true, Gandhi went to Jinnah's house to meet him. Mahadev has written this. If somebody says this in front of me, I will show it to them. I will ask them whether Gandhi had gone to Jinnah's house to meet him or not?'

Ba would say sadly after reading any criticism of Gandhi, 'People tell lies.' She was especially touchy about somebody attacking Bapu's idea of ahimsa.

***

Ba had been to jail in South Africa and had suffered. She had been jailed many times in India. Between 1931-33, she had been jailed thrice. But this time, she felt she had been unfairly arrested. She would read the newspaper and feel terrible for the injustice that the people had to suffer. Many of them must be getting jailed for no good reason. On 18 August, 1942, they were all discussing what they would do when they were released from prison. Ba suddenly said, 'Who knows whether I will even get out. It is possible that I may not be there by this evening.'

Bapu was listening. 'Why do you say these hopeless things? You are Kasturba, everybody's guide and mother. This could be true of anybody. Sushila is sitting here. She has done her M.D. just now but she could be gone by the evening. What happened with Mahadev, he went for his walk and left us. You and I were ill, but we are still around. You have to get better. Please let us care for you and stop all the worrying.'

But Ba's worries were not about to end. One day she said, 'Bapu ji is fighting with such a powerful government, they have limitless resources. How will Bapu ji win?'

Sushila countered, 'Ba, God exists. Bapu has started this struggle with trust in God and the people. The people are supporting him and so is God from up there …'

'It seems he is going against us too. Did you see how he snatched Mahadev away from us? Bapu is alone,' said Ba sorrowfully. Mahadev's sudden departure was gnawing away at her.

Bapu was quiet. Hearing this he said, 'Mahadev's going was pure sacrifice. His sacrifice will strengthen the struggle.'

Mahadev's death had sunk deep inside Ba's heart. One day she was unwell and she said irritably, 'I told you not to take on such a powerful force but you never listened to me. Now we all have to bear the consequences. The government has so much power. They are crushing the people. Until when will they bear this? What will be the final result?'

Bapu tried his best to reason with her but that day Ba was in no mood to listen. Finally he said, 'Let us seek pardon from the government, you and I.'

'Why should I seek pardon from anybody?'

'If you want, I can write a letter of apology to the Viceroy?'

Ba could never bear disrespect towards Bapu. She flinched to hear him say this. 'Young women are languishing in jail. Why will you apologise to the government when they are not? You have to bear the consequences of what you do. You and us, along with you. Mahadev lost his life in jail. He could not even set eyes on his children once. Now it is my turn.' Bapu heard her in silence. When Ba was angry, he usually took the silent route.

Ba constantly thought about the political situation in the country. Worrying about Bapu was a part of that. One day she made a suggestion to Bapu, 'Why do you ask the British to leave the country? Ours is a big country. Everybody can fit in. You tell them to stay here as our brothers.'

'That is what I do say … that you stay as our brothers, not as our rulers. If they remove their rulership, then I have no quarrel with them. I had said this in 1909 itself, in *Hind Swaraj*.'

'That is right, we cannot keep them here as our rulers. Stay as brothers and stay here happily.'

The next day during her oil massage, Ba was calm. She said to Sushila, 'Sushila, these Englishmen are rogues. They want to rule over us. They want to plunder India. That is why they have locked up Bapu ji and all the other leaders.' Sushila listened to her quietly. Ba would often doze off during her massage.

***

Bapu's fast ended on 3rd March. A day before that, the gates had been opened to the public. Bapu's retching and vomiting had stopped and his health was stable. In spite of weakness, his face looked alive. Ramdas and Devdas had permission to meet Bapu. Bapu had said that if the public cannot come, then there was no need for making a concession for his sons. The sons worked like a tonic for Ba, however. After the gates had been shut, Ba's strength had diminished. Until Bapu was fasting, she was carrying on with the strength of her conviction. Her body was also keeping up. If somebody asked her to rest during the day, she would refuse. Bapu began improving and Ba began to deteriorate. Her face was lined with sorrow.

On 16th March, Ba had trouble with her breathing and her heartbeat accelerated. It stayed like that for two hours. On 25th March, she had another such episode which continued for four hours. Agha Khan Palace had been worried about Bapu, now there was grave concern for Ba. The tables had turned. Rumours were afloat that Ba was gone. The government was uneasy. Bapu had earlier stopped her two sons from coming to meet her, but now he had to relent. The government had removed restrictions on visitors for Ba, but it was Ba who schemed to get her distant relative, fifteen year old Manu, into the palace. When she lost her mother, Manu had stayed in the Ashram with Ba for three years. Ba considered her like her own granddaughter. Upon Ba's exhortation, Sushila Nayyar and her attending physician Dr Guilder, wrote to Colonel Bhandari that Ba needed a young attendant who knew her well and understood her language. Colonel Bhandari held Ba in great respect from the first time he met her. Without any formalities, he transferred Manu from Nagpur jail to the palace. Coincidentally, Manu was transferred just when Ba had bronchial pneumonia. Manu took care of her tirelessly. Ba improved steadily and started walking around the compound. She would go to everybody and enquire about their diet. The kitchen was in the rear verandah. Ba would sit and chat with the cook. She would have Bapu's meal cooked under her supervision.

As Bapu's health improved, he began writing letters to the government. Ba began reading the Ramayana regularly or Manu would read it out to her. Gradually she finished reading the Valmiki Ramayan and the Gita.

***

Ever since she fell ill, Ba had heard the Ramayan, Gita and Bhagwat many times. She also began enjoying sports and games. It was unusual for a homemaker to take an interest in games, and that too in jail. Although it was a prison, it was different from traditional jails. The prisoners and the staff were different. They would all meet each other and also play. Sushila, Mirabehn and Dr Guilder would play badminton and Ba would watch, sitting on a chair. She would applaud a good shot. If somebody made a mistake, she would point it out. Dr Guilder and Mirabehn would play carom at night and Ba would watch. She enjoyed it so much that she began playing for half an hour herself, in the afternoons. Mirabehn was the best carom player. Ba would become her partner and enjoy her victories and be cast down at her defeats. In view of her health, it was decided that Ba should win the final match. She used to love taking the queen and like a child, she would believe that she had won, if she netted the queen. She would refuse to concede defeat. In the moment of her victory, she would forget her illness and her grief. In her last illness, when she was unable to play, the others would sit near her bed and play.

She used other ways to lessen her sadness. She liked playing with children and feeding them. She would busy herself with the few children in the Ashram but where were there any children in jail? A goat had her babies in the Palace. Manu brought one kid and Ba played with her in her lap. She forgot that it was a goat kid and talked to it, 'Don't forget your grandmother. Come and play with her every day.'

Manu would bring the kid for the next few days, daily. Ba would talk to it. One day she soiled Ba's clothes and the grandmother was upset. Manu stopped bringing it and Ba did not ask for it either.

***

In 1942, the White government grew apprehensive that without any weapons, these people would spell its end. There was a government order that the prisoners should not be given the newspaper. Restrictions were imposed on letters and visitors. Sarojini Naidu's daughter was unwell so she wrote to the government asking whether she would get news of her well being.

Ba was also concerned about all her grandchildren. After three weeks, there was a clarification from the government that prisoners could write to their relatives and give the letters to the government officials who would send them further on. Similar rules would be followed for getting cloth. Sarojini wrote a letter and handed it to the government. When Mirabehn asked for permission to write to her associates, the government maintained silence. She had come from across the seven seas and her associates were her family. Bapu conveyed his opposition to these conditions saying that he would not write to any relative.

***

Sushila's sister-in-law delivered a baby girl through surgery. A week later, her sister-in-law died. A week later, Sushila got the letter and telegram about her death at the same time. Her sister-in-law had died pining for Sushila. Sushila's mother and brother wrote requesting parole for Sushila. The request was refused because she was close to a prisoner like Gandhi. Ba told Bapu, 'It is necessary for Sushila to be with her mother in such a situation.'

Bapu made light of it and said, 'Who will look after you?'

'I know it will be difficult for me but I am not so selfish that I don't know a mother's heartache.'

Ba said to Sushila, 'You write a letter to your mother and brother,' Sushila had joined Bapu in stating that she would not write to any relative, under such conditions. Ba told Bapu that it did not matter if she had made such a declaration. This is an unprecedented emergency and could not have been anticipated. She must write a letter. Sushila wrote a letter when Bapu said so.

Her brother Mohanlal wrote back saying that their mother was not keeping well. It was hard to bring up the newborn under these circumstances.

Bapu asked Ba, 'Should we get the baby here? You will look after her?'

'I am not well myself. But if the government permits, I will do the best I can.' Bapu wrote about both possibilities to the government. Either Sushila should get parole or be permitted to get her motherless niece to jail. The government responded negatively to both proposals.

***

Ramdas and Devdas, both the brothers would come to visit. Ba's eyes would shine at the sight of them. However she would not say a word about a constant ache in her heart. She would sit and meditate before the tulsi plant. The ache would be expressed through tears sometimes. The irony was that the onlookers thought that Ba was overcome because of her devotion. One day Ba spoke about her pain to Bapu, 'You have thrown Hari out of your heart, but I am a mother. I want to hold my eldest, Harilal, once before I die. Who knows where he is and in what state?'

Bapu heard her out, 'I don't talk about it but I understand. How could you say that I have thrown Hari out of my heart? Can any parent throw out a child from their heart? Father or mother, a child lives like an ache and a joy. I know my shortcomings and your pain and his pain too. But I could never balance the two ... the pain remained unchanged in either place.'

Bapu wrote a letter to the government immediately, 'My wife is unwell. The government must be getting regular updates. My eldest son, Harilal, has not met her for a long time. Nobody knows where he is. If the police could find him, I would be grateful.'

The police found him in Poona. May be the police force was more sensitive in those days. When he found out that Ba was ill, he left without informing the police. When he reached Agha Khan Palace, he was drunk. He was chased away from the main gate. Where did he go, where he spent the night, whether he ate or stayed hungry, nobody knew. The next morning, he showed up at the gate again. This time he was in his senses. He was thin and weak. The effects of the previous day were evident. Harilal was taken to Ba. He was coughing and signs of TB were apparent.

Ba stared at him. Is this my Harilal? He asked, 'How are you Ba?'

With great difficulty she said, 'Forget about me, tell me, how are you? Since when have you not eaten?'

Ba held his hand and made him sit next to her. Her eyes rained tears. Somehow she got up and made her way to the kitchen. When she got back, Harilal had unilaterally ended the visit and left. Ba just stood there for some time and then dragged her way to Bapu, 'Hari came and went. I could not even hug him. He had no food in his stomach and no proper clothes ...' Her sentence ended in a sob. Bapu shed a tear.

He cleared his throat and said, 'Maybe, he will come tomorrow. He can hardly go without eating from Ba's hand ...' he attempted a laugh.

'I don't have much time. Perhaps he does not either. That cough of his ...'

Later it became clear that there was permission for Harilal to meet Ba once. Bapu wrote to Colonel Bhandari that Harilal should also be permitted to meet Ba like Ramdas and Devdas. Even after permission was granted, Harilal did not come. Ba nursed a hope even in her hopelessness.

There was a cable from Jal Bhai, son of Rustamji, Bapu's old friend from South Africa, 'We just found out about Ba's illness. We are arranging for Manilal Bhai and Susheelaben's travel to India so that they can be with Ba.'

Bapu sent a very formal token response, 'Ba is leaving us gradually. Manilal and Susheela should continue their work. Love, Bapu.'

***

The police was looking for Harilal. It was a Monday on 21st February. The police found him in the afternoon. Filthy clothes, an overgrown beard, the stink of liquor and he could hardly stand straight. He was brought to Agha Khan Palace in the same condition. The staff was aware of the urgency as Ba's condition was delicate. They could have taken him an hour or two later after a bath and saved Ba the pain of seeing him so. Ba had never seen her son so drunk that he had lost his senses. She was beside herself. He was removed from the room forthwith.

***

In January 1944, Ba got consecutive heart attacks. She was now completely bedridden. There was no relief from pain. Her breath was short and she could not sleep at night often. Allopathy was not making much difference to her condition so Ba asked for Ayurvedic treatment. Bapu had to engage in a long correspondence with the government for this. On 5th February, permission was granted to call an Ayurvedic doctor, Dinshaw Mehta. Verbal instructions were issued that when Dr Mehta comes to see the patient, nobody other than the two doctors should be with her. Bapu was bathing when he heard of this order. He dictated a letter to Pyarelal lying in the tub, 'It is unseemly to put these conditions on my wife as she lies on her deathbed. If she needs to use the bathroom, she will not be able to do so because Dr Dinshaw is present. If I have to enquire about her, I will have to ask somebody else how my wife is doing ... Instead of this mental torture, it is better if the government sends me somewhere else. That way my wife will have no expectations of me and I will not have to be a dumb witness to her anguish.' There came a reply by the afternoon, 'There has been a misinterpretation of the order. The nurse can be present and if you wish to make enquiries, you may do so.'

***

On 19th February, Ba slept well. She had an oxygen tube in her nose. On the 20th, she felt uneasy at 5:00 am. She kept repeating Ram-Ram. Even Celegrain could not correct the urinary problem. There was an atmosphere of despondency all around. Seeing her growing unease, Bapu sat on her bed. She felt a little better leaning against the support of his shoulder. Bapu did the morning prayers sitting there. Everybody took turns to sing bhajans. '*Shriram Bhajo, sukh me dukh me ...*' listening to these words she would forget her pain for a little while. She was given one dose of Chloral and Bromide at 9:00 am. She slept off for an hour and a half. When she woke up, she felt better. She did her daily routine by herself. She had some tea and then lay down comfortably.

She was uneasy again during the day. She kept calling out, *Hey Ram* ... *Hey Ram* ... Her painful moans were reminiscent of a goat being led to sacrifice. Bapu would spend a lot of time sitting by Ba's side, during the day. She felt the better for it. Bapu said to the people assembled there, 'Now Ba's treatment is the name of Ram. Leave aside all other forms of treatment, just give her honey and water. If she asks for something, it is another matter. I have no faith in medicines. I never used medicines in my sons' illness ... I have never heard anything other than the name of Ram. This is heartrending. It is better if I take away the medicines. If the Lord wishes to save her, He will. Or else, I will let Ba go in peace.'

That night, Dr Dinshaw had permission to spend the night there. Ba's condition was not very good. Since Sushila was not there, Dr Guilder would come and check on her. But it did not seem a good idea to trouble him again and again. There was no such formality with Dr Dinshaw. At

9:00 am, her pulse seemed erratic. Guilder had to be woken up. When Sushila came in the morning, she saw that Guilder was planted on a chair next to Ba's bed. The pulse was regular then. Ba was asking for castor oil. The doctor told her that it would cause further weakness.

'Let it be, I only have to go for my cremation now.'

'Why do you say that? Ramdas and Devdas are about to come, you have to meet both of them don't you?'

Ba smiled hearing their names. Then she became grave, 'Why do you call them, all of you are my sons. Cremate me when I die. Ramdas has to pay a hefty fare and the trains are so crowded.'

***

One day Bapu ate his afternoon meal and sat next to Ba. She was about to take a nap. Ba would lean against Bapu and fall asleep and he would not move until she got up on her own. He was quite worn out. Sushila was present and she said, 'Bapu, let me sit next to Ba. You take a nap and come back.'

Bapu did get up but when he reached his bed he said, 'If you had let me sit a little while longer, what harm would it have caused?'

These were Ba's final days. Who could possibly say that he should not sit with her so often? Never mind if she had pneumonia or any other serious illness. Even so, Guilder gathered his courage and said, 'Don't keep your mouth so close to Ba's.' Bapu did not say anything. Guilder knew.

After some time, Bapu said, 'Doctor, after living together for sixty-two years, how can I keep a distance in these moments of parting.' His eyes welled up.

Ba used to feel a burning sensation when passing stool and urine. She told Bapu, 'I want to try water treatment.' She had seen the miracle of water treatment in Manilal's illness. Bapu began giving her hot and cold baths in the tub from that day. This used to take about an hour. One day Ba said to him, 'You go. Sushila can give me the bath. You have to do so much work for the nation.'

Bapu said, 'Don't worry.' He continued with the bath.

Sushila said to him one day, 'You have such little time. I am taking care of Ba anyway. Whenever you want, I can bathe Ba. You will save an hour.'

'I know you are ready to serve Ba in every way. But in this half of my life, the opportunity to serve Ba is priceless. Until Ba will accept my care, I will gladly spare this hour.'

***

It was dusk. During an illness, many times patients are confused about the time of day. Morning may feel like evening and the other way round. Ba asked, 'Is it morning?'

'No Ba, it is evening.'

Devdas, Harilal's daughter Manu and Santokhben arrived. Ba wept when she laid eyes on them. She was upset on account of Harilal anyway. Two or three times a day, she would remember him and grieve. She said to Devdas, 'Until I could, I managed things, now it is your turn. Bapu ji is a sadhu. He has the worries of the whole world on his head. You know Harilal. Now you have to look after his family.'

Manu sang bhajans for Ba. Ba wanted Santokhben and her to sleep near her at night, but permission was not granted. Only Devdas was granted permission. By the time he got back after seeing off the others, Ba had slept off, her head in Sushila's lap. This was not a restful sleep. Because of the difficulty in urination, she was in a semi-conscious state. When Ba opened her eyes at night, she saw Prabhavati Behn sitting there. Ba coughed hard. She refused Sushila's medicine. There was an odour near Ba's bed. She had unknowingly wet the bed. She was changed and put back to rest. Sushila knew the end was near.

Devdas came and began to help. He pressed her forehead until it seemed that she had slept. Ba spoke Sushila's name and said, 'Are you also tired out?'

'No, Ba, how can I tire?' She kept pressing her forehead.

Ba's head ached and she was giddy. Symptoms of Uremia. Sushila got up to take a break at 3:00 am. Devdas was with her until 5:00 am, not knowing which moment could be her last. His heart quailed and wept.

The last night had been full of apprehension.

——***——

22 February, 1944

Sushila had stayed awake through the night. She was washing her face at 7:00 am when Ba called out, 'Sushila ...'

'Yes, Ba ...' she said coming closer.

'Take me home please, please dress me up ...' her voice had a tremor. She was shown her favourite picture of Ram, 'You are home. Look at your favourite picture.'

'Take me to Bapu ji.'

'You are in Bapu ji's room.' She felt she wanted to have him close to her. Bapu was having breakfast in the outer room. He was told to see Ba before his walk.

Bapu came smiling. Other friends and relatives stood around the bed. He said, 'You must have felt that I have left you because all these relatives have come.' He sat down.

Ba lay with her head in Sushila's lap. All of a sudden she said, 'Where will we go? Will we die?'

Earlier if she talked of death, Sushila would tell her they would all go home together. Today she said, 'Ba, all of us have to go some day, why do you worry?' Ba agreed.

After a while, Bapu said, 'May I go for a walk?'

Earlier Ba would herself suggest a walk. Today she said no. He sat down again. Ba leaned against him, eyes shut.

She said, 'We have been through *sukh* and *dukh*. Nobody should cry after me, now I am at peace.' Both their faces held a rare peace and serenity. Everybody gazed at them and then quietly left the room. Bapu sat there until ten. He would tell Ba to say *Ram nam* occasionally. It is the biggest refuge. If she coughed he would stroke her. Ba's face showed that she was at peace.

***

If the government really wished, it could have released Ba but it did not. The real reason was that If Ba's illness took a turn for the worse when she was outside, then people would demand Bapu's release. If Bapu was not released, the government would appear to be heartless. An officer of the British government had shared this with Devdas.

Ba let Bapu go at ten and Sushila sat in his place. Ba was mumbling something every now and then. She was delirious It was the first day that she had not cleaned her teeth and refused any clean up with boro glycerine. She would just mumble, will we die? Never had she shown such a fear of death. It was not Ba, it was death that was indicating its arrival. Sushila was very upset.

***

Penicillin had been procured from Calcutta by plane. The British government was providing all possible assistance. Colonel Shah and Colonel Bhandari sent this information but Bapu had stopped all medicines. Ba's desire to get better with medicines was over. Devdas was in favour of giving it.

Colonel Bhandari wanted to know Bapu's opinion. He said, 'I am not in favour of giving any more medicines. If my sons and relatives want to try, then the government should grant permission.'

Ba's pulse was irregular. Intermittently, it seemed to vanish and then it would start again. Sushila had been awake all night, so she asked Prabhavati Behn to sit there while she took a bath. When she came back, Bapu said she should take a fifteen minute walk, at least. As she walked, she prayed. 'Can't you save my Ba?' Then she answered her own question saying you know best what should happen. It is a rare person who gets a chance to sacrifice themselves in the fight to freedom. Someone as precious as Ba deserved this honour. To die by a bullet or inside this jail was the same. God was about to grant her martyrdom and it was not going to change because of the prayers of a lowly being like me. You know best.

Sushila looked at her watch. Bapu's fifteen minutes were over. She turned back.

Bapu's routine had also changed. Since many days, he was only taking liquids. The pressure of the illness was so severe that without a dietary change, he could not maintain his health. Instead of taking half an hour over a meal, he would finish off in ten minutes and sit next to Ba. He would finish off all his essential chores so that he could be by her side constantly. Sushila saw that he was there when she got back. Ba suddenly lay flat on her back. Because of her asthma, she had not been able to lie flat on her back since months. She had to lean against something or put her head on a table in front. Devdas was informed about her condition.

Devdas and Manu got there immediately. Dr Dinshaw Mehta arrived. Bapu asked if she would like to listen to *Ramdhun* but Ba shook her head. Bapu began to get the Gita chanted in the adjoining room where Devdas, Pyarelal and Kanu took turns. The idea was that Ba should hear the chanting.

She was finding it difficult to sip water at night and had no feeling of thirst. In the afternoon, Devdas brought *Gangajal* and *Tulsidal* was put in it. Ba was staring at the tulsi plant unblinking. Sushila got the plant and put it on a stool next to her. Bapu ji said, 'Devdas has brought *Gangajal* …' and Ba opened her mouth. Bapu put a spoonful in her mouth which she swallowed. After another mouthful, he decided to give it after some time. Ba would call out for Ganga ji and look at the tulsi plant. To give the others some time, Bapu went and sat on his cushion. After some time, Keshubhai came with Rami (Harilal's daughter). Surprisingly, Ba immediately sat up. The source of her strength was unknown. She said, 'Devdas has really looked after me.'

'Ba, what have I done, I just came last night. It is all these friends who have really looked after you,' he said, 'Ramdas is also coming.'

'What will he do?' Ba did not like troubling Ramdas.

She closed her eyes and lay down. She folded her hands and prayed in a faint voice, 'God, forgive me for having eaten like an animal all my life. Now I want your love and devotion.' Her face grew peaceful. As if her prayer had been answered. There was an expression of indifference now.

Kanu Gandhi took many photographs of Ba. Along with Kanu, all the family wanted a photo of Bapu with Ba.

Bapu did not like being photographed. Bapu would keep telling everybody to rest now and then. Using this, Sushila said, 'Bapu, I will rest for a while so you take over.' She hoped that as soon as Bapu would sit next to Ba, Kanu would quietly take a photo. Bapu knew so he said, 'I will take charge from here. Let all the guests keep sitting, If Ba calls, I will come there.' Sushila and Kanu's faces fell.

***

Colonel Shah and Colonel Bhandari came at 5:30 with the penicillin injection. They enquired with Bapu and he said neutrally, 'If Dr Guilder and Sushila wish, they can give it.' Devdas was already in favour of giving penicillin. There were two questions. What was the use of poking Ba with needles as she lay on her deathbed? This was Bapu's view. The other view was that there was hope until the last breath. This was the usual medical view. Penicillin had come newly in circulation at the time. It was considered a life-saving drug. Sushila began boiling a syringe at a signal from Dr Guilder. Bapu asked her, 'You all have decided and are sure that this will help?'

Sushila remained silent.

Ba had not eaten since the morning. She looked better. Everybody sat down to eat together. Guilder told Sushila that Bapu did not know that several injections of penicillin would have to be given. When he got to know, he demurred. It is not easy to take such a decision for someone close to you. Sushila was caught in the middle. She said nothing. The government had arranged for the penicillin as it did not want to be blamed for any negligence in Ba's treatment.

Bapu reasoned with Devdas, 'Why don't you trust in God? Whatever miraculous medicine you bring, you cannot make Ba well again. If you insist, I will not stand in the way. But your insistence has no basis. In the past two days, she has refused water and medicine. Now it is in God's hand. If you want to interfere, you can. But my advice is not to go down that way. Remember that poking your dying Ba every four hours with an injection is only going to cause her physical pain.' There was no room for argument after this. The doctors breathed a sigh of relief. Bapu went for a walk at 6:15 every day but today it was already 7:15. As soon as he went to the bathroom to get ready, Ba called out, 'Bapu ji!'

Prabhavati ji was sitting by her side and she asked for Bapu to come immediately. Ba's restlessness was unbearable. She sat up twice and then lay down again. Bapu asked, 'What is it, how are you feeling?'

Somewhat like a lost child in a new place, she lisped, 'I don't know where I am.' Her pulse was weak. This was happening frequently. Nobody understood why Bapu had refused to let Kanu take photos. Perhaps Ba was sacred to Bapu. He wanted to keep her image inside his heart.

Just then, Ba's brother Madhavdas came. She was seeing him after a long time. Her eyes rained tears but she could not speak. Was it the joy of seeing him or the ache of not being able to speak? Ba tried to get up again but Bapu made her lie down. He stroked her head and said, 'Don't get up. Lie down.' Ba laid her head in Bapu's lap as if that was the final place of rest.

Bapu removed the pillow from under her head. He straightened the bed. Mirabehn turned it in the north westerly direction. Bapu laughed, 'You may have been born in London but your soul is Indian.' Bapu spread out her arms and put her in the *Savasana* position. He had already sent everybody for their evening meal, by turn. In ordinary jails the evening meal is served at 6:00 and Agha Khan Palace was no exception, despite being a special jail.

Evening had descended suddenly that day. The darkness was spreading like a black sheet. Bapu looked at his watch. It was 7:30. When everybody came back, Ba's throat produced strange sounds. Devdas was standing at the foot of her bed and looking at her intently. Her youngest ... Ba's neck rolled to one side. Devdas put his head on her feet and wept like a baby calling out 'Ba ... Ba.' Two tear drops rolled down from Bapu's eyes. Who knows if it was Ba's departure or a quiet echo of his youngest son's anguish? Bapu had once asked in whose lap will Ba leave her body? Whose good fortune will it be? Sushila remembered those words. She spoke up, 'Whose lap can it be but Bapu's?' Her eyes filled up with tears.

Bapu got up from his place and went to Devdas. He put his hand on his shoulder. He signalled to everybody to vacate the room. Everybody exited wiping their eyes. A little while ago, when Ba could talk, she had said, 'I am going, if I have to go, why not today?' Those words jumped at Devdas and then settled deep inside.

***

Ba was taken down from the bed. Sushila, Santokhben and Manu gave her the final bath. As they were washing her body, they wept inconsolably. Ba had shrunk like a river that becomes a thin line in the summer. They dried her body and combed her hair. There was faint smile on her face as if to say, this is my final chore. She had carefully kept a sari with a red border made out of cotton spun by Bapu. She had said to Sushila, 'Please dress me up in this. I should have something of Bapu to remember him, as I leave.' They put sandalwood paste on her forehead. Bapu put *sindur* in her parting. Her calm face looked like a blessing.

Manu, Rami and Kanu cleaned the room where Ba had breathed her last. Mirabehn drew a square with lime powder and put an *Om* near the head and drew a swastika near the feet. Garlands were wrapped around her wedding bangle that she had always worn. Her hair was decorated with flowers. When her body was fully adorned, the radiant calm on her face shone brighter. Prayers were said and the Gita was chanted. One and a half hours had passed. Her body was placed in the *chauk* drawn with lime powder. An oil lamp was lit. It is believed that the soul needs light to enter the other world. That light goes from this world to the next.

***

All day long, throngs of people waited at the doors of the jail to get a glimpse. They wanted a minute by minute update but the government was afraid of the reaction. The people would shout *Ba-Bapu Zindabad* and then fall silent. They would pray for Ba's health. They persisted in spite of the heat, thirst and hunger. Around eight, a guard appeared near the closed gate with tears in his eyes. He murmured, 'Our Ba is no more.' There was pandemonium. Everybody kept repeating the terrible news. There was shock and sorrow. People were stunned into silence. Telegrams flew across the country. It was as if something pure had been extinguished.

***

The jail superintendent, Colonel Bhandari, came to Bapu when he got the news of Ba's death. He wanted to know what Bapu wanted to do for the last rites. Bapu gave three alternatives. The first was that her body be handed over to the sons and relatives. In that situation, there would be a public cremation. The government would not interfere in any way. The second was that she could be cremated inside the palace like Mahadev and relatives and friends be allowed to participate. If even that was not acceptable, the third alternative was that he would cremate her alone with his prison associates.

He gave an assurance that if it was a public funeral, the government need not fear any unrest or riots because his sons would take care of things. They would rather die than allow any untoward incident at such a time. The Colonel asked, 'If the cremation is outside, would you like to be present?'

Bapu looked at the Colonel and said, 'No, my relatives and sons will be there. Rest assured, I will not go.'

The government was not prepared to risk a big procession. It agreed to the second alternative and permitted a funeral inside the Palace.

***

The chanting of the Gita shlokas ended at 11:00 at night. Everybody, other than Devdas, Manu, Rami and Santokhben, was sent outside. Sushila was her closest attendant. Everybody took turns to sit next to her body. Bapu sat near the head, eyes closed as if in a *Samadhi* in the *Ardhpadmasan* pose. It was if he was watching a moving picture of Ba's journey in his heart. Or was he trying to fathom the mystery of what Ba learned through sacrifice and steadfastness? It is possible that it was a silent dialogue between two yogis. Or Ba was doing away with Bapu's worries after her departure. It was possible that Ba was sharing her concerns regarding Bapu with him. Or Bapu was telling her of his grief. He could be saying, don't take my mistakes along, leave them behind for me. I want to live with them and do penance. Mistakes crush arrogance. I have learned the lesson of non-violence from you. I have hurt you many times by word and deed. You were never violent even in word. You would surrender everything at the feet of the Lord and adorn everything with pure love in return. I have not forgotten, I remember everything. This is the only similarity between the two, neither violence nor non-violence forgets. When my friend Mir Alam in South Africa accused me before a full house, of taking £15000 from General Smuts, and betraying the entire movement, in spite of everybody's advice, I did not complain to the police. I had learnt this from you. I had also accused you of unspeakable things and sent you to your parents' home, when, during our *pheras*, I had vowed to stand by you throughout life, not very long ago. You had not complained of my cruelty to anybody. When you returned, you were as generous, loving and forgiving ...

This was non-violence of the mind that you had brought into your life before I had. Now I feel incomplete … When he rose in the morning, he was calm.

***

On February 23, her body was placed for public view. About hundred and fifty friends and relatives had come. Hindus, Muslims, Parsis, politicians and Britishers – people from all communities were arriving. Everybody folded their hands or bowed their heads in final farewell to Ba's frame. There were heaps of flowers. The Pandits who had conducted Mahadev Bhai's funeral rites had also come. Shanti Kumar, a family friend, was running about for the arrangements. He was assisting Devdas like a brother. He proposed to Bapu that they should get sandalwood. Bapu said, 'This is your generosity but a poor man's wife to be cremated using sandalwood will not be seemly. It makes no difference to the body whether it burns in sandalwood or in ordinary wood.'

A superintendent of the jail was listening. He said softly, 'I have some sandalwood, it can be put to use.'

'From where did you get so much sandalwood?'

He hesitated but thought it better to tell the truth. He said haltingly, 'During the twenty-one day fast, your condition was delicate. Then sandalwood had been arranged. The government was taking no chances.'

Bapu understood his dilemma and smiled, 'The wood arranged by the government should be used. If not for me, then for my wife … the government's money should not go to waste, isn't it?'

That Bapu could be satirical at a time such as this, was not something that brought a smile or a comment.

***

Her pyre was erected next to Mahadev Bhai's Samadhi. A mother and her son in spirit ... next to each other. Her bier was taken to the pyre. People's eyes brimmed with tears to see Bapu shouldering her bier. Bapu was making peace with his feelings as he was carrying out his final responsibilities towards Ba. He walked with firm steps. After the body was placed on the pyre, a universal prayer was recited. Bapu read excerpts from the Quran, Gita and the New Testament. Mirabehn read psalms from the Old Testament. Guilder had become very close to Ba. In a trembling voice he read from Zoroastrian scriptures. The students from the Ashram sang bhajans. Devdas gave *mukhagni* amidst the chanting of mantras. Bapu leaned on a stick and stood there until the fire had completely engulfed Ba's body. Everybody's faces appeared radiant in the light of the pyre. The flames seemed to tremble on Bapu's face and then dim on their own.

Pyarelal stood next to Bapu, instead of Mahadev Bhai. Mahadev Bhai, in the *samadhi* next to Ba's pyre, must have felt the warmth emanating from it. The afternoon sun was getting hotter. Mirabehn had unfurled an umbrella over Bapu. After bidding farewell to the guests, Bapu put a chair under a tree and sat there. He ignored the insistence of the remaining friends to go and rest in his room and sat and watched the fire turn to ash. It is only fire that turns to ash itself and turns others to ash. The sun was setting.

Among the ash, few flames glowed and the embers made their presence felt.

***

The pyre was burning when Ramdas arrived. He wished his father and sat cross-legged on the floor. He was reserved. That night, Ramdas and Devdas had permission to stay in the Palace. As the two brothers sat by Bapu, their eyes flowed with tears. Bapu placed his hands on their shoulders. 'For me it was a partnership of sixty-two years. Sometimes I would think … what if both of us went together ... but death keeps her secrets and takes everybody separately. I had prayed that if we cannot go together, take Kastur first. I will manage, but how will she live after having lived with a man like me …?'

After some time he spoke up, 'Work tires you out but parting and sorrow almost kill you with the strain … go and rest.'

'You?' These were the first words that Ramdas spoke as he had only wept until then.

'I will try and get used to living without Ba …' Both the brothers wept. Bapu signalled for them to leave.

***

Bapu was in a conversational mood all night. Who knows whether he was getting answers from Ba, recently departed. Or was it a monologue. A monologue flows faster in grief …

'If the country wins independence, you will not be with me ... I will be alone. Only you understood what freedom meant to me. Who knows how incomplete or otherwise it will be? So many people have lost their lives for freedom ...

they all must have had different notions of freedom … their ways would have been different. You chose my path and walked with me and made me walk too. That day, when my bapu went … for the first time I understood how hungry desire can be … if you begin feeding it … you could be hollowed out. You taught me to liberate myself from me … I fought the battle for my own freedom along with fighting for the country ... both of those are incomplete. But your sacrifice … something even greater than sacrifice – a ray of light that is guiding me towards the goal.

'I speak for myself. Ramdas and Devdas have just gone from here. So many Ashram dwellers had come. They are all bereft without you. Hari got no support … I could not do what he wanted, he turned away from what I wished. How I wish he could have been the Gandhi of South Africa ... he could have ... my resolution was no good to him. Parents fulfil their children's desires but we stood otherwise … why? My state was that of a sanyasi who was given to universal good but is alienated from his own. Principles liberate you from narrow ends but they also bind you leaving you no room to manoeuvre. I know you used to be unhappy, because of me and sometimes because of him. He held you in very high regard. You remember at Katni station, he got you fruit ... he said something like this to me ... Not for you … you are very great ... Ba made you great. When I said to you … you also give him some fruit … the train had started. Today I know, he was right. What he knew, I could not learn. Because of me, you let him go … a mother's greatest sorrow is her children going astray or losing them. I did not bring him and he never came. You remember, I said to you once, a person committed to service and sacrifice should adopt … *ekla chalo re* ... walk alone. You were angry. I tried, but I lost the way. You remained steady ... in the midst of everything. What is the use of saying all this now … it took quite some time to emerge from the self-created muck. Neither you nor I could do anything.' The bell at the gate struck five.

'It is morning already ... I don't know why I kept you entangled in all this, now that they don't mean much ... they are like a shadow … my delirium. It is my selfishness, I will not hold you back anymore … they must be waiting for you there ... if there is any notion of waiting in your new world … just like we wait here … even after you have left.'

***

His voice had been heard after many days. A blind singer used to sing a *nirguniya* bhajan at the gate sometimes. Ba used to stand there and listen …

Kagad likhe so kagadi, ki vyavhari jeev,
Atam drishti kaha likhe, jit dekhe tit peev …
Pritam ko patiya kya likhun, jo kahun hoy bides,
Tan me man me nain me, takau kaha sandes.
(The scribe writes on paper, he is a worldly creature
How can he write his inner vision, when he sees his beloved everywhere…
How can I write to my beloved as if she is far away
Why should I send her a message when she is in me, in my heart and in my eyes)

Bapu murmured, '*Tan me, man me, nain me ...*' and went inside.

—***—